The Spawn War

Also by Stephen Renneberg

THE MAPPED SPACE UNIVERSE

The Mothership
The Mothersea

The Antaran Codex
In Earth's Service
The Riven Stars

SF/TECHNOLOGICAL THRILLERS

The Siren Project
The Kremlin Phoenix

The Spawn War

Stephen Renneberg

This novel is a work of fiction. Names and characters are the product of the author's imagination, and any resemblance to actual persons, living or dead, is coincidental.

Copyright © Stephen Renneberg 2020

Stephen Renneberg asserts the moral right
to be identified as the author of this work

Author website
www.stephenrenneberg.com

ISBN: 978-0-9941840-7-8

All rights reserved. No part of this publication may be reproduced, stored in a retrieval system, or transmitted, in any form, or by any means, electronic, mechanical, photocopying, recording, or otherwise, without the prior written permission of the copyright owner.

Illustration © Tom Edwards
TomEdwardsDesign.com

For Elenor.

"I would not wish any companion in the world but you."
— *The Tempest, William Shakespeare*

Mapped Space Chronology

3.4 Million Years Ago to 6000 BC
Earth's Stone Age (GCC 0).

6000 BC to 1750 AD
Pre-Industrial Civilization (GCC 1).

1750 - 2130
The rise of Planetary Industrial Civilization (GCC 2).
The First Intruder War – unknown to mankind.
The Mothership (MS-First Contact 1)
Start of the Blockade.
The Mothersea (MS-First Contact 2)

2130 - 2643
The spread of Interplanetary Civilization (GCC 3) throughout the Solar System.

2629
Marineris Institute of Mars (MIM) perfects the first stable Spacetime Distortion Field (the superluminal bubble).
The MIM discovery leads to the dawn of Inceptive Interstellar Civilization (GCC 4).

2615
The Solar Constitution ratified, establishing Earth Council (15 June 2615).

2644
First human ship reaches Proxima Centauri and is met by a Tau Cetin Observer.

2645
Earth Council signs the Access Treaty with the Galactic Forum.
First Probationary Period begins.

Tau Cetins provide astrographic data out to 1,200 light years from Earth (*Mapped Space*) and 100 kilograms of novarium (Nv, Element 147) to power human starships.

2646 - 3020

Human Civilization expands rapidly throughout Mapped Space.

Continual Access Treaty infringements delay mankind's acceptance into the Galactic Forum.

3021

Dr. Anton Krenholtz discovers Spacetime Field Modulation.

Krenholtz Breakthrough enables transition to Incipient Interstellar Civilization (GCC 5).

3021 - 3154

Mass migration dramatically increases human colonial populations.

3154

Human religious fanatics, opposed to interstellar expansion, attack the Mataron Homeworld.

Tau Cetin Observers prevent the Mataron Fleet from destroying Earth.

3155

Galactic Forum suspends human interstellar access rights for 1,000 years (the Embargo).

3155 - 3158

Tau Cetin ships convert human supplies of novarium held in Earth stockpiles and within ship energy plants to inert matter (as human ships landed at habitable planets).

3155 - 4155

Human contact with other interstellar civilizations ends.

Many human outposts beyond the Solar System collapse.

4126

Earth Navy established by the Democratic Union to police mankind when Embargo is lifted.

Earth Council assumes control of Earth Navy.

4138

Earth Intelligence Service (EIS) established by the Earth Council.

4155

The Embargo ends.

The Access Treaty is reactivated, permitting human interstellar travel to resume.

The second 500 year Probationary Period begins.

4155 - 4267

Earth re-establishes contact with its surviving colonies.

4281

Earth Council issues Sanctioned Worlds Decree, protecting collapsed human societies.

4310

The Beneficial Society of Traders established to manage interstellar trade.

4498

Quantum Instability Neutralization discovered (much earlier than galactic powers expected).

Mankind becomes Emergent Civilization (GCC 6).

The golden age of human interstellar trade begins.

4605
 The Vintari Incident.
   The Antaran Codex (MS1)

4606
 The Battle of Tresik Prime.
 End of the Blockade.
   In Earth's Service (MS2)

4607
 The Nan Chen Disaster.
 The Xil Asseveration.
   The Riven Stars (MS3)
 The Siege of Serris Orn.
   The Spawn War (MS4)

Notes:
MS: Mapped Space
GCC: Galactic Civ. Classification system.
Asseveration: A solemn or emphatic declaration.

Chapter One: Hades City

Subterranean Habitat
Star HAT-P-5
Outer Lyra Region
0.91 Earth Normal Gravity
1,105 light years from Sol
1.2 million inhabitants

"Multiple surface impacts imminent," the civil defense warden's voice sounded inside my pressure suit's helmet. "Blast shelters seal in four minutes."

Hades City had been struck by system attack drones before. Its inhabitants knew every hit would send shockwaves through the moon's rocky mantle, hammering the colony's pressurized caverns five clicks below the surface. It was why everyone was fleeing to the safety of the deep shelters, desperate not to be left outside when the armored doors closed.

Everyone except me, that is.

I cranked the CivDef channel's volume down and kicked the multi-armed beetlebot in front of me.

"Enough already. Wrap it up."

Feeling nothing, it continued scanning the new k-cannon mount while the impact reverberated up my leg, triggering throbbing pain all the way to my hips. The skeletal pain was Lena's fault. She was my Earth Intelligence Service controller and had decided I needed a memory upgrade. It had required months of painful bionetic sequencing, as if I didn't already have more data crammed into my body than I could ever use.

Ignoring the dull ache in my side, I watched overworked engineers run for the airlocks, leaving me alone in the depressurized docking cavern. Hades City's subterranean spaceport was the raid's primary target, which made standing on the ship's topside hull in nothing but a thin-skinned p-suit a very bad idea.

"Complete scan. Confirm!" I ordered, demanding a response from the obstinate little machine.

"Ship commissioning ordinance eighty-three, section four, paragraph nine point two states molecular bonding must be verified to one hundred percent cohesion for service certification," it replied with its usual officious double talk.

"This is a civilian ship, beetle brain. I don't need navy certification," I declared, irritated that its simple machine intelligence was oblivious to the swarm of system attack drones about to vaporize Hades Moon's charred surface.

Surviving naval bureaucracy was the price I'd had to pay for getting dockyard priority. It had been so much easier when I'd simply gone black market, but the navy had requisitioned every nut and bolt in the city, leaving me no choice.

To get the new *Silver Lining* fitted out, Lena had done a deal with Admiral Talis, which had been a red flag to every regulation kissing brass hat in the navy. With the fleet short of ships and supplies, they hated giving me anything, especially equipment. They'd wanted the old Cabot class survey ship I'd bought with Lena's EIS credits for themselves, to use as a scout ship, but between me bribing the Astrographics Institute's sales agent and Lena whispering to Admiral Talis, I'd got my ship and my refit.

At four thousand tonnes, she was a third larger than the old *Silver Lining*, but not so big that three of us couldn't handle her. We'd stripped out two of her four decks for cargo space, and managed to hang on to all six of her small sublight engines in spite of certain navy engineers' best attempts to requisition four of them. The reduction in mass made her responsive rather than fast, although that wasn't why I'd picked her.

What made her special, what put her in navy's sights, was that she was quiet. The Cabots were science ships with huge sensor arrays and our most advanced emissions suppression technology. It made them the stealthiest ships mankind had ever built. They weren't invisible, none of our ships were, but their signatures were orders of magnitude lower than any other Earth ship and when their e-plants and engines were idling in sensor mode, they were virtually indistinguishable from background radiation. That made her survivable at a time when Intruder spawnships were ranging across a quarter of the galaxy and human Separatist raiders were everywhere in Mapped Space.

"Sirius?" Marie's voice sounded from my helmet communicator. "We're at the shelter. Where are you?"

"Still on the Lining."

"What!" she exploded. "Get down here, *now!*"

"Don't worry. The navy's new defense grid won't let anything through."

"CivDef's broadcasting impact warnings," she said, assuming I'd turned the annoying civil defense channel off again.

"They're just being cautious," I said, glancing up at the rock ceiling uncertainly. It had recently been reinforced with high tensile ribbing, strengthening the thousands of meters of volcanic rock between us and the surface. It made the docking caverns tough, but not indestructible.

Separatist raiders had bombarded Hades City with long-range system attack drones three times in the past nine weeks. Their ships had stayed long enough to assess damage, then bubbled away before the navy could engage. After the Nan Chen disaster three months ago, hit and run raids were all the Seps could muster, but their strength was recovering. Their attacks were slowly ablating the city's armored space doors and a lucky hit had even jammed them once for ten whole days.

If the Seps managed to break through, they'd cripple the city's great shipyard, the only major dock within five hundred light years. Its facilities were why Third Fleet had made Hades City its principal operating base and why the navy had invested so much in its defense. If the shipyard was destroyed, Earth Navy's ships would have to return to the Core Systems for repairs, taking them out of the fight for at least two years. That made Hades City the strategic key to all of Oh-Zero-Sixty, an immense expanse of space filled with sparsely populated human outposts and a vast array of alien worlds.

Fortunately for the navy, Hades Moon was a natural fortress, composed of hard igneous rock and tidally locked to a hot Jupiter that orbited frighteningly close to its star. When not in the shadow of its gas giant primary, the moon's surface was blasted by HAT-P-5's radiation, making attack impossible. Even when in Hades' shadow, landing a ship was risky and dropping troops was extremely hazardous.

"Sirius," Marie said anxiously, "they're going to seal the doors. You'll be locked out."

"I'm not leaving until this tinpot tyrant signs off." And from the look of it, that wouldn't be soon. "Are Jase and Izin with you?"

"They're inside, where you should be." She broke into a furious Franco tirade, cursing and pleading with me at the same time.

"That's no way to talk to your principal investor," I said lightly, hoping the taunt would take her mind off the raid. "You should show me more respect. Call me sir in front of the deckhands."

"Sir!" she snapped. "You want a mutiny before we're even out of space dock?"

I grinned silently, hearing my ploy was working.

I'd paid for her new ship with Lena's EIS money. It had required blackmail and arm twisting, but the *Mendiant* was old and cheap and even the navy didn't want her, so Lena had agreed. I'd promised Marie a free hand, providing she turned a profit and provided her boss with unlimited conjugal visits. She'd rather have owned the *Mendi* outright, but having me as a silent partner was better than becoming a ground pounder. And unbeknown to her, I had a Witari diamond ring locked away that she'd get one day, if she ever switched allegiances. Her Separatist sympathies should have made us enemies instead of lovers, but I knew how to keep a secret, even from those closest to me.

The subterranean cavern shuddered as a system attack drone struck the surface directly above the spaceport. In vacuum, there was no sound, only the sudden swaying of the *Silver Lining* as her struts absorbed the shockwave.

"That was a *big* one!" Marie said alarmed.

"Yeah, it was," I agreed, wondering how the enemy drone had gotten through the navy's new defense grid. "They've upped their warhead yield." I studied the high ceiling for cracks, but the smooth black rock showed no sign of buckling.

"Hurry Sirius."

"On my way," I said, then pointed at the navy bot.

"And if you're not done when I get back, you'll be recycling biowaste for the duration."

The beetlebot ignored me, then I ran back along the hull toward the scaffolding towers either side of the stern. The ship was unpowered for refit and the topside hatches were all sealed for pressure testing, leaving the rickety metal frameworks the only way down.

A second tremor shook the spaceport, rocking the ships alongside the taxiway and jarring the rigid frameworks leaning against their hulls. The *Lining's* portside scaffolding tower buckled and collapsed while the magclamps securing the starboard stairs slid against the triple engine housing and held.

Fearing I'd be trapped four stories up, I charged down the stairs in wild, ungainly leaps. Another quake hit and the scaffolding crumpled, forcing me to jump clear. I landed hard, sending shooting pain through my recently enhanced bone structure, then scrambled to my feet and ran clear as poles and stairs crashed down behind me.

Across the taxiway, a Rigel Blue freighter's landing struts folded, sending it lurching sideways, shattering its scaffolding like matchsticks as its hull slammed onto the rock floor.

"Sirius?" Marie asked anxiously.

"I'm fine," I replied, stumbling up the stern ramp, regretting going off the pain killers early. It wasn't the first time I'd had millions of nanobots rewrite my cell structure, but the drugs clouded my mind and I needed to be sharp to get the *Silver Lining* into space. It's what Izin and Jase expected. Neither my engineer or copilot had any idea they were part of my EIS cover and would have been suspicious if I'd slept through the refit.

Inside the cargo hold, portable lights powered by cables running up the ramp rocked as more tremors hit in quick succession. One by one, they fell over in a shower of sparks, submerging the cargo hold in darkness, then a passenger transport's struts gave way outside. When its hull hit the ground, a ripple of fiery explosions erupted from its crushed thrusters, then were instantly snuffed out by vacuum.

Knowing the Seps shouldn't be hitting us this hard, I switched comm channels. "Hades Control, what's going on up there?"

There was no response, not even an order to get off a restricted channel, then more tremors hit. Rock splinters fell from the ceiling, clattering off the *Silver Lining's* hull and showering fragments over the cargo ramp.

"Hades Control, acknowledge," I said as razor-sharp rock shards speared down across the docking cavern, any one of which could have punctured my p-suit like a balloon. Another big one hit and lights throughout the spaceport flickered as emergency power cut in.

"Ah hell," I said, my mind made up.

I charged down the ramp and across the cavern floor as black fragments rained down around me. A small boulder fell to my left, then two ships ahead slid into each other. A side-mounted engine exploded between them, then ghostly streams of air jetted from hull fractures in both ships. I skirted around them, raced through an empty berth to the airlock recess and cycled through to the elevator.

The indicator for Hades Control was blinking red from a security lockout, so I selected the maintenance level instead. The elevator climbed quickly, rocked by impact shockwaves, then the door slid open and I scrambled out into a wide corridor containing a rack filled with bulky, dirty yellow oversuits. Each suit had a metallic weave outer shell surrounding thick thermal insulation and an inner full-body cooling system. They were built to survive the short solar eclipse nights but quickly overloaded if blasted by the star's direct coronal heat.

The display panel above the airlock indicated star rise was only minutes away. That didn't leave much time to hike to the Control bunker's airlock, but there was no other way up, so I climbed into one of the armored beasts and synced my p-suit to its motion-servos. The suit came to life, sensing my movements, then I took an experimental step forward.

"Like driving a loader," I muttered, realizing the suit did most of the work.

I walked the three thousand kilogram machine to the airlock and cycled through. The airlock's immensely thick outer door was hidden from the star's direct touch inside a cave that led out to a cratered, charcoal black lunar surface.

Hades, the massive orange gas giant shielding the moon's surface from the star's searing force, filled the sky. Super cyclonic storms many times larger than Earth whirled across its surface, carrying sun-side heat to the cooler night-side hemisphere. Dividing night and day was a curved tidal wave of brilliant white light, crawling across the giant planet's surface, boiling its atmosphere. High above it, tongues of hot gas licked out into space, warning where the great planet's protective shadow ended and star rise began.

Between Hades and its cinder moon was a sliver of space streaked by minuscule points of light. They were system attack drones following the eclipse vector in from mid-system, using the gas giant to hide from the star's intense radiation. The SyADs streamed down in long curving dives toward the city gates at tremendous speed, having no atmosphere to slow them.

"No ground fire," I said, wondering why the navy's surface weapons weren't blasting away for all they were worth as a falling star raced down out of the sky. It landed beyond the black mesa between me and the city gates with a brilliant flash, then pebbles blown off the summit bounced down around me.

A timer on my head-up display began counting down to star rise, only minutes away. With no time to spare, I loped along the path at the foot of the mesa while the outside temperature indicator rose slowly and the oversuit's heavy footfalls pounded like drumbeats in my ears.

I rounded a promontory and turned onto broad shelf-like stairs that wound up through a cleft in the rock as another drone exploded beyond the mesa. The ground shook, causing me to stumble, then a female voice sounded in my ears.

"Warning! Star rise in two minutes."

I bounded up the stairs, fending off the rock walls either side as another Sep drone began its dive. It struck the mesa above me, shattering rocks and loosening boulders that fell onto the path. A small boulder struck my oversuit's shoulder, knocking me down and leaving my left arm immobilized.

"Impact damage. Upper left servo cluster disabled," the female voice declared.

"No kidding," I muttered as I got to my feet and charged up the stairs.

"Warning! Star rise in one minute. Seek thermal shelter immediately."

At the top of the stairs was a path leading to a metal archway in the cliff face. I started toward it as another system attack drone came hurtling down out of the sky, overshot the city gates and slammed into the foot of the mesa. The blast came up the path, struck the oversuit in the back and hurled me forward onto my face.

"Warning! Star rise in thirty seconds. Seek thermal shelter immediately."

"I'm trying to!"

I scrambled to my feet in the crippled suit and stumbled forward as an armored door in the archway began to close, shielding the interior passage from the star's impending heat.

"No!" I yelled and charged forward, planting a metal boot in the doorway.

Hades' brilliant day-night terminator passed overhead as harsh solar rays illuminated the moon's horizon, casting stark shadows across its surface. The black landscape took on a ghostly red hue and the oversuit's optics flickered from saturation.

"Warning! External temperature exceeds suit tolerance."

I slid my still functioning right arm through the doorway and threw the oversuit's back against the door as incinerating sunlight crawled toward me.

"Warning! Spinal servo overload!" the female voice declared as the sound of grinding metal filled my ears, then the door slid open a little and I fell through onto my back.

Sunlight streamed through the open doorway onto my boot. Its dirty yellow paint sizzled and bubbled as my good arm clawed the ground, pulling me back from the door. I twisted my hips, dragging my blackened boot clear, then the thermal door slammed shut sealing me off from the scorching sunlight. Gray smoke wafted from the oversuit, but its thick insulation and my p-suit's cooling system had saved me. With difficulty, I got to my feet and hobbled to the airlock, but it wouldn't open.

"Oversuit temperature exceeds safety parameters. Cool down required."

"Hit me," I said wearily, then cryo foam sprayed from nozzles in the airlock rim, vaporizing on contact with the oversuit and surrounding me in a cloud of steam. In moments, frost crystallized on the oversuit's metal skin, then the foaming ended and the airlock outer door swung open. I shuffled inside, dripping ice crystals as another shockwave hit.

Once through into the locker room, I blew the oversuit's emergency bolts, then climbed out and shrugged off my p-suit. The civil defense siren was wailing unchecked and the boom of drone impacts was louder here, closer to the city gates.

Outside the locker room door was the body of a traffic control officer lying in a pool of blood. He'd been shot in the back and left where he'd fallen, his lifeless eyes staring blankly ahead. I reached for my gun, then silently cursed the ban on weapons inside city limits.

Unarmed, I crept along the corridor, past offices containing a woman slumped on her desk and another man dead on the floor. They were all center mass kills, not precision headshots, indicating the killer was competent but no expert, not that it mattered. They were just as dead.

I ramped up my bionetic listener, straining for any sound of the killer and wondering where the guards were. There should have been several on this level, but none of the dead were security. Whoever the killer was, he'd made sure no one was left alive to raise the alarm.

While drone impacts continued to send tremors through the bunker, I moved toward Spaceport Control's double doors. They were ajar, revealing two controllers slumped over their consoles and a third on the floor beside a toppled over chair.

In front of the consoles was a long wall screen displaying the deep, trench-like approach to the circle of field generators known as the catcher's mitt. They caught incoming ships and dragged them down into the docking shaft, limiting the time the city doors were open and keeping heat penetration to a minimum. A field generator bunker above the two semicircular, horizontal doors was in ruins and, while the doors glowed dull red from near misses, their centerline seal remained intact.

A woman screamed and a man said, "Enter the key code, Delaina."

There was no reply, then she screamed again and panted in agony as I stole a look around the door. A man in a security uniform stood over a female traffic controller holding a gun in one hand and pressing a barbed nerve stinger into her side with the other.

"I'm waiting," he said, and sent pain blasting through her nervous system. She convulsed, then he leaned close to her face and whispered. "I will kill you."

"My children are here."

"We both know they're in the shelter," he said impatiently. "If you ever want to see them again, open the goddamned doors!"

"No," she gasped.

I reset my listener's sensitivity to base and slipped silently into the room. His back was to me as he upped the power and gave her another jolt. When she screamed, I charged forward, using her cry to mask my footsteps. The woman spasmed and slumped back in her chair, then her eyes widened in surprise as she saw me racing toward them.

The killer caught her look and spun toward me, raising his gun. I dodged sideways with ultra-reflexed speed as he fired, felt the bullet punch the air beside my face and grabbed his wrist. I pushed his gun away, blocked a punch with my free hand and kicked his legs out from under him. When his back hit the floor, I punched at his elbow, but he thrashed wildly about and I missed breaking the joint. Still on my feet, I threw my weight forward and twisted his gun down toward his face. He tried pushing it away with both hands, but I overpowered him and thumbed the firing surface, splattering his blood and brains across the floor.

He was an amateur and it was over fast, but he'd nearly got away with it. Under other circumstances, I'd have taken him alive for questioning, but with SyADs pounding the city gates, this was no time for taking risks.

I turned to the woman who was bent over in her seat, pale from shock. She was reaching for the nerve stinger in her side, about to pull it, but I grabbed her hand.

"No! Leave it in." She tried fighting me, desperate to pull the barbed electrodes out, but I overpowered her and switched it off, ending the pain.

"Thank you," she whispered.

"It'll have to be surgically removed. Hold it there until help arrives." I placed her hand on the stinger's hilt to hold it steady. "Like that. Don't move it."

She nodded weakly, then the wall screen showed a system attack drone strike the cliff tops above the city gates, triggering another earthquake. She winced in pain from the motion, then nodded toward an inactive console and mouthed the words, "Fire control."

The console was filled with grayed out indicators for sensors and weapons and had a red status marker in the top corner blinking one word: *DISARMED*. The console allowed traffic control to disable the city's defenses so they didn't destroy friendlies entering or leaving the spaceport.

I hovered my finger over the blinking indicator and looked at the traffic controller, who nodded, then I tapped it once. It turned orange and the status changed to *ARMING*. Indicator lights all across the board blinked on as the city defenses deployed, then a procession of glowing dots appeared on the traffic control screen, all following the eclipse vector toward us. If the saboteur had got the doors open and just one of those SyADs had made it down the docking shaft, it would have destroyed the spaceport and the city.

Beyond the stream of drones heading for Hades City was a green ship marker labeled ENS *Mobile Bay*. She was a heavy destroyer boosting hard toward the Separatist ships mid-system. Ahead of her, four red ship markers labeled HOSTILE 1 to HOSTILE 4 held position, watching for the city doors to open.

Several sensor and weapon indicators on the fire control console turned yellow and flashed DAMAGED or DESTROYED. Some of the drones must have targeted the defense grid, indicating Sep spies had scouted their locations before the attack.

I feared I was too late, then indicator panels across the board went green and changed to ARMED. The surviving surface batteries filled the sky with streams of tracer-like pulses that arced out toward the incoming SyADs, lacing the firmament. Exploding drones burst into fireballs in a night sky already aglow with golden tongues of coronal gas, then the tremors stopped. In their place, burning wreckage rained down over the blackened plain now boiling in the full fury of HAT-P-5's infernal dawn.

The pale-faced traffic controller nodded with relief, then we watched the *Mobile Bay's* marker approach the Sep raiders. The heavy destroyer launched a salvo of anti-ship drones at the enemy ships, but before they could reach their targets, the four hostile markers swept across the screen and vanished.

The Sep raiders had bubbled away, their attack a failure, but they'd be back and soon.

* * * *

Admiral Talis' flagship, the ENS *Solar Constitution*, dispatched a squad of Union Regular Army troopers and a medical team to the Hades Control Center. When the URA officer arrived, I took him aside while the medics stabilized the traffic controller and took her to hospital.

"Disarm the city's security force," I said in a low voice, nodding to the dead saboteur on the floor. "Do background checks on all of them and station your soldiers at critical points throughout the city."

He hesitated, wondering what a civilian was doing giving him orders. "I'm not authorized to declare martial law."

"Admiral Talis will confirm your orders within the

hour," I assured him.

The URA officer glanced uncertainly at the dead security man being scanned by a forensic bot and nodded. While he summoned reinforcements, I returned to the *Silver Lining* where the beetlebot had completed its work and a trickle of power now coursed through the ship. I took the crew elevator up to the command deck, still marveling at the Cabot's roominess. Compared to the old *Silver Lining's* cramped corridors and tiny cabins, her spacious staterooms and wide companionways made her feel like a starliner, a result of her having been built to carry soft civilian scientists on long-duration pleasure cruises.

At Lena's insistence, I'd left the top two decks virtually unchanged, ensuring we had accommodation and life support for plenty of passengers. Izin, my terrestrial amphibian engineer, hated the idea of letting crowds of strangers aboard, but tamphs disliked everyone, human or not. Now that his Intruder cousins were blasting their way across our corner of the galaxy, he knew any passengers we carried would view him with suspicion. To ease his concerns I'd bribed him with extra bot bays and a slew of custom engineering enhancements, but he wasn't convinced.

When I turned into the companionway leading to the bridge, I found soft light spilling from Jase's cabin. It came from a glowing data pane on his desk which he read with such intensity, he didn't hear me approach. The Cabot's executive officer's quarters were more polished and twice the size of my old captain's stateroom on the first *Silver Lining*, not that he cared for such things.

"Don't tell me you've drunk the bars dry already?" I asked incredulously, knowing the local watering holes did booming business after each Sep raid.

"They'd run out of air first," he replied without looking up. He was taller and younger than me, blonde and blue-eyed like most Ories, and with their hot-headedness. To see him reading with such concentration was a surprise and the troubled look on his face told me it wasn't good news. "I'm going to need some leave."

It was the first time he'd ever wanted time away from the ship. "Sure," I said, surprised. "Take as long as you want."

"No, I mean...I'll be gone for months. Maybe longer." He crossed the room to a locker, pulled out one of his fraggers and checked the load with a furrowed brow.

"Something you want to tell me?"

He put the weapon down and examined its twin. "The Hadleys have been arrested. They're in prison on Kota."

"Kota?" I glanced at the data pane on his desk. "Is that from Emma?"

"Yeah," he said grimly, explaining why he'd skipped the bars and rushed back from the raid shelter.

"And you're going to do what, exactly?"

He shrugged noncommittally, obviously intending to start a fight he couldn't win.

"Right," I said slowly, "for a girl you hardly know."

"We've been writing for a year, ever since Hardfall."

"Writing?" I said skeptically.

He touched the control panel on his desk, then a full-sized hologram of a beautiful young woman in a tantalizingly sheer negligee appeared in the center of a room. She lay smiling on a bed, her head propped up on one arm provocatively. She was speaking, although the sound was turned down.

Jase and I exchanged knowing looks, then he added meaningfully, "There's more. A lot more."

"I'm sure there is," I said, familiar with the titillating torments of interstellar love and long absences.

"I've been meaning to get back there to see her,

but…"

"…it's a Sep base and they'd kill you on sight."

He nodded. "Good thing no one knows me on Kota."

"Prison guards don't need to know you, to shoot you."

"She won't be in prison long," he said, pulling his kit bag out and opening it on the bunk.

"Hmm, so you're going to get her out, all by yourself?" This for a girl he hadn't actually slept with.

"Not alone." He held up both fraggers meaningfully. "My two friends here will do the talking for me."

"From what I hear, Kota's got more soldiers than Hardfall."

A lot more. Hardfall was a minor frontier world run by Separatist agents. Kota was a fully-fledged colony guarded by the Sep military, not that I could tell him that. As a freelance trader with one foot either side of the law, I could never explain how I had access to high-grade military intelligence, not unless I was prepared to admit being an EIS deep-cover agent.

"They're hiring mercs," he said, not needing to remind me Oresund trained the best hired guns in Mapped Space. It's why I'd recruited him.

"Suppose they DNA scan you, or someone recognizes you, or maybe they just don't like the way you smell?" We weren't exactly unknown out here and the Consortium had a price on my head, a big one, and to find me they were looking for him and Izin. That put every bounty hunter with a death wish on our tail.

"I'll take my chances."

"So you're going to sneak onto Kota, shoot anyone who gets in your way, steal a ship, outrun their cruisers and get away clean. Good plan, good," I said with mock approval.

He scowled at me. "You know what those Sep

camps are like."

I nodded somberly. "I've heard."

"I'm not leaving her there."

"I guess not," I said, deciding there was no talking him out of it.

He noticed the saboteur's blood spatters on my clothes for the first time. "You hurt?"

"Not my blood." I glanced at my stained clothes, deciding only the boots could be saved. "I'll clean up and we'll talk about this Hadley thing later."

Jase looked surprised. "I'm not asking for help, Skipper. She wrote to me. She's got no one else."

"I'm only thinking of myself." Jase gave me a confused look, then I added. "Do you have any idea how much trouble it would be training your replacement? Besides, Kota's not that far and the Seps have never seen this ship."

He gave me an appreciative smile as he realized I wouldn't let him do anything stupid, not without my help anyway. I gave him a reassuring wink and went next door to my absurdly large captain's stateroom. The comm panel on the polished simteak desk was flashing, signaling a message was waiting for me.

"We need to talk," Lena Voss said without preamble. "You know where. Sixteen hundred. Don't be late."

A glance at the desk chronometer told me she was waiting for me now, so I changed clothes and hurried off to meet her.

* * * *

A ragged gray crack now traversed the Commercial Cavern's otherwise flawless blue sky-sim. Engineers on hover platforms checked the rock strata's underlying stability while people on the streets discussed their artificial habitat's unwelcome new feature. With Sep raiders prowling every waypoint between here and the Core Systems, it could be years before replacement parts were sent out, turning the fractured sky into a city landmark.

Ignoring the damaged simulation, I headed across to Gatlin Avenue, named for one of the original wildcatters who bored beneath the surface of Hades Moon four centuries ago. A small ground car with its translucent passenger dome set to opaque flashed its lights at me. When I approached, a gull-wing door lifted and I eased myself gingerly onto the passenger seat.

Lena gave me an impatient look. She was tall, ebony-skinned with penetrating eyes that missed nothing, not even my innermost thoughts. "Still sore?"

"Only when I move." The bionetic nanobots had gone in through my throat and out the other end, ensuring there were no exterior marks detectable to tissue scanners.

"You heal fast," she said without sympathy, well aware a side effect of my EIS gene modding was accelerated regeneration.

"So why do I feel like someone jammed a molten stun stick up my butt?"

She smiled and said to the car, "Naval Residence."

We pulled away from the curb and headed toward the official home of Earth Navy's attaché in Hades City. According to Lena, it doubled as the navy's regional HQ where all military operations throughout Oh-Zero-Sixty were planned. Admiral Talis even stayed there when he wasn't aboard the *Solar Constitution*.

"Who are we meeting?"

"Talis and his senior officers," she replied. "Nice work at the spaceport by the way. Pity you killed the saboteur. I would have liked a close look at him."

By 'look', she meant use her mega-psi abilities to tear open his mind like a freeze-dried ration pack and suck out everything he knew about the Sep spy ring in

Hades City.

"He was armed. I wasn't. And they were pounding the hell out us at the time."

"Not complaining," she said, then took a white cylindrical device from her pocket and handed it to me. "He had an accomplice, but she swallowed a heart-stopper before we could get to her."

"There must be others," I said, certain the agent had killed herself to prevent giving away the rest of their group.

I wrapped my hand around the cylinder, waited for the bionetic filaments in my palm to connect, then data flowed through my threading into my newly expanded storage system.

"We're scouring the city for traitors," Lena said. "The one positive from all this is the city's finally giving us access to their internal surveillance system." She smiled with satisfaction. "Nothing like a near-death experience to focus the mind."

"How bad was it?" I asked, sampling the data filling my bionetic memory. The bio threading was all my own tissue, making it virtually impossible to detect, especially since no non-humans knew we had such technology and wouldn't be looking for it.

"A hundred and sixty drones. Thirty-four hit before you got the grid back up. We lost a docking field, some anti-orbitals and a few sensors, nothing the navy can't replace. If that Sep agent had gotten the doors open, none of us would be here now."

"The shelters would have survived."

"Until their supplies ran out."

That would take about six weeks with no hope of rescue.

"I'd rather go quick," I said as we entered the tunnel connecting Commercial to a cluster of urban caverns to the southeast. It was one lane each way, dimly lit by widely spaced ceiling lights, not that automated ground vehicles needed light to steer by. We passed a stream of ground cars going the other way at high speed then the road angled down into the moon's subterranean depths.

When my palm became sweaty, slowing the transfer rate, I switched the cylinder to my other hand, wondering why Lena was loading my storage system with alien languages. They were mostly Orion Arm friendlies and a few not so friendly.

"I always wanted to swear in a thousand different languages," I said thoughtfully, then spat out a long hissing sound. "Ishskkarssha!" I grinned, adding, "Just practicing for the next snakehead I meet."

She gave me a reproachful look. "You're getting the full xenolinguistics upgrade, virtually every language we know. And you said it wrong. It's ishskkorshi. You accused a Mataron of *marrying* your mother, not...what you intended."

"Imagine that, me with a snakehead for a father."

"Understanding major Orion languages should give you an edge," she explained. "You'll be able to read and write them all, but you'll need a vocalizer for some."

I saw the One Spawn's language load.

"Hey! I'll understand Izin. He won't need to wear his mouthpiece," I said, referring to the small triangular vocalizer he wore to convert his alien amphibian sounds to human words.

"Yes he will," she said sternly, "because he doesn't know you're threaded."

"Right," I said, adding my new found linguistics skills to the list of secrets I kept from my tamph engineer.

"Earth's linguistics experts put the Orion translations together," she said. "The Tau Cetins gave us the rest."

"Did you have to beg?"

"It was their idea. It makes us more useful to them."

Each language dataset listed the name of its

homeworld and how far it was from Earth. Some of the Tau Cetin translations were for civilizations so far outside the tiny bubble of human Mapped Space, I couldn't imagine ever meeting them. I wondered if that meant the war with the One Spawn was going so badly for our Ornithian friends that they could no longer tell potential friends from actual foes.

"Is Talis giving us an update on the Spawn War?" I asked. Most of the galaxy called it the Second Intruder War, but as the first war had occurred before humans had ever walked on Mars, we'd given it a different name.

"No, we're keeping that under wraps," she replied tensely.

"That bad, huh?"

She was Earth Intelligence Service's Oh-Zero-Sixty regional commander. It was a place doubly cursed, not just a front line in the Human Civil War, but a battlefield fought over by two galactic superpowers locked in a titanic struggle. The outcome of the Spawn War would determine the fate of every civilization from the Orion Arm to the Perseus Arc of the Outer Rim, ours included. Being the weakest of them all, we could do little more than watch from the sidelines and hope we weren't caught in the crossfire.

"The Tau Cetins are totally defensive," she said. "The One Spawn are hitting them everywhere this side of Centralis. The Fenari are hanging on by their fingertips and the Kesarn are facing extermination. There are just too many spawnships, too many places to defend."

"Better they fight out there than here."

Lena hesitated. "TC Intel believe the Spawn Fleet's going to hit Ansara, soon."

Ansara was a major Tau Cetin world in Outer Ursa Major, a smaller version of the Ornithian homeworld and the most heavily defended point in all of Oh-Zero-Sixty. It lay between the One Spawn's home cluster beyond the

Outer Rim and Tau Ceti itself. In galactic terms, Ansara was next door to Hades City. If the Intruders destroyed it, swatting the free city would be a simple matter.

"So everything we've heard is a lie," I said, realizing the public had been fed pure propaganda since the Spawn Fleet attack on Centralis three months ago.

"Not all of it. TC arbiters *are* superior to spawnships, if they meet on equal terms, but they never do. They're always outnumbered. That's why the Tau Cetins are losing."

"They told you that?"

"They don't trust us that much," she said meaningfully.

"Ah, they don't know you're mega-psi and you're reading them like data panes."

She nodded. "Every chance I get."

It was one of our few secrets the Tau Cetins hadn't penetrated, that Lena was one of four genetically engineered mind freaks who could vacuum the minds of our enemies, and our friends, without them ever knowing. If they ever discovered the truth, they'd never let her near them again, which was why so few people knew what she really was.

"Have you told Talis how badly they're doing?"

She shook her head. "He'd want to know how I knew."

"And you can't tell him you're mega-psi."

"He doesn't even know what mega-psi is, but he knows we haven't seen a Tau Cetin warship in months, only that old scout ship that carries our dispatches to and from Earth. Talis knows that means they're in trouble."

The daily Tau Cetin mail run was instituted after Centralis as a thank you for our help. It enabled us to communicate with Earth in hours instead of the usual nine months each way, long haul voyage. And it gave the TCs a chance to scan our dispatches up close. Of course, they didn't know our most secret communications were hidden in the cell structures of the threaded EIS agents who carried the dispatch cases, making it a much better deal for us than the Tau Cetins realized. Lena was certain our mighty Ornithian friends didn't know the real messages were in our people while the encrypted military and diplomatic traffic they were reading was merely a distraction.

Unofficially, Earth Council had decided we were an undeclared belligerent, mostly because the Matarons had blocked us from signing the Xil Neutrality Pact. However, thousands of other minor civilizations had signed it to save themselves. We couldn't blame them for that. Technological disparities ensured that only a handful of the most advanced civilizations could ever wage interstellar war on anything like equal terms.

"Any chance you can convince the TCs to wipe out the Matarons while they still can?" I asked as the linguistic download finished and I handed back the white cylinder.

"If they did that, they'd be no better than the One Spawn," she replied, pocketing the cylinder. "Look on the bright side, Sirius. The Spawn won't destroy us, because they promised to let Matarons do it after the Tau Cetins are defeated."

"You're a real optimist."

We emerged from the tunnel into a large circular cavern with an artificial lake at its center. Ten-story housing blocks occupied the outer reaches of the cavern, slowly giving way to up-market low rise buildings closer to the water. On the southern shore was the Naval Residence, a compact four-level structure surrounded by a nature strip of grass and trees that demonstrated Earth's wealth to the local population.

We stopped in front of a high-security barrier encircling the Residence and waited as automated sentries scanned our vehicle. When they were done, the gate opened and we drove down a ramp to vehicle drop off. We climbed out, watched a railbot scoop up the car and take it down a vertical shaft to storage, then took an elevator up to the Residence.

"Are we watching from a private room?" I asked, assuming Lena would preserve my cover.

"No, it's captains and above. They all know who you are. Don't worry, they're equipped with terminators, even Talis."

My bionetics had a terminal watch-guard function, but she was talking about an implant below the cerebrum that ensured if the wearer was ever taken prisoner, he wouldn't live long enough to give his middle name. They were inert until armed by a code known only to the wearer or they sensed intrusive interrogation technology.

"That's one implant I wouldn't want."

"If they didn't have them, the Matarons would kidnap our senior officers any time they wanted information. It's one technology we want them to know all about."

The elevator door slid open revealing a well-appointed wood-paneled hall decorated with paintings and models of warships ranging from ancient galleys to modern starships. A pair of armed troopers in dress black uniforms greeted us with granite faces, scanned our DNA codes and let us into the conference room. It had a long table in the center equipped with data panes, holoscreens and translator ports. Admiral Talis was at the head of the table flanked by his flag captain, Yuko Nishida, commander of the *Solar Constitution*, and six other four stripers. Lena and I sat at the far end leaving empty places between us and them.

Talis acknowledged Lena with a curt nod and me with a studied look that said he knew I'd killed the saboteur.

When we were settled, he said, "Captain Dietrich won't be joining us. He's staying aboard the Mobile Bay in case the enemy attempt another strike."

The captains nodded with understanding and silence.

"Firstly, some good news," Talis continued. "I received confirmation this morning via the TC mail ship that Earth Council has formally revoked its ban on orbital bombardments." The faces of the senior officers showed a mix of relief and disquiet depending on their attitude to blasting Separatist civilians from orbit. "I also received final approval for Operation Windfall."

There was a noticeable stirring around the table as they realized they would soon be going into battle.

"Finally," Captain Sokolov of the frigate *Kasimov* declared with enthusiasm.

"How soon can your ships be ready?" the admiral asked.

"The Constitution's repairs are complete," Captain Nishida said. "I'm taking her out tomorrow for live-fire testing. She'll be fully operational in forty-eight hours."

"The Nanjing's ready now," Captain Zheng reported.

Captain Quiroga pursed his lips. "The Sao Paulo is operational, but her sublight engines can't deliver more than eighty percent military power."

"That won't be a problem," Talis said. "You'll be escorting the transports."

Quiroga nodded, then Captain Azikiwe said, "Soryu's number four turret is still jammed. That hit we took at Irsalis warped its trunnion. We need a whole new mounting assembly sent out."

Talis scowled. "Put in a request via the TC courier before we leave."

"I was hoping the Tau Cetins would bring one out for us," Azikiwe said, knowing the new mount would take close to a year to reach Hades City from the Core Systems by human ship.

"Dispatches and diplomats only, that's the deal, but I'll ask. No promises." He turned to Captain Sokolov.

"Yuri?"

"The Kasimov awaits your orders, Admiral," the old Russian declared. "We are fully combat-ready."

"Did you get that case of Novy Zubrovkan vodka I sent over?"

"Yes, Admiral, thank you."

"You earned it," Talis said, then shot a questioning look at a short, plump officer with thinning dark hair.

"The Galicia can launch at one hour's notice, Admiral," Captain Sinago stated crisply.

"And Mobile Bay is combat-ready," Talis added for the absent Captain Dietrich. "The fleet will deploy at oh five hundred, a week from tomorrow. I intend to make a demonstration run through the Aleta Gap nav points. Separatist scouts will detect us and assume we're heading for Outer Draconis. Ten hours after the Orkal-IV nav point, we'll break out of the lanes and head to the rendezvous point in the Ashoka Expanse. The coordinates are in your fleet packs. We'll wait there for the assault force from Uralo IV, then proceed directly to the Chambal System."

Chambal? I gave Lena a suspicious look and whispered, "Kota?" It was where the Hadleys were being held prisoner, where Jase was so determined to go.

She smiled knowingly, confirming my suspicions. The communication Jase had received wasn't from Emma Hadley at all. It was from Lena.

"After entering the Chambal System," Talis said, "Constitution and Nanjing will approach Kota and destroy its defenses from long range while the fleet screens the transports."

On their holoscreens, a chart of the Chambal System appeared detailing the fleet's movements toward the system's second planet.

"Once Kota's defenses have been neutralized," the admiral continued, "the planetary government will be given an opportunity to surrender. If they refuse, we'll destroy the planet's infrastructure from orbit. The assault force will then land and secure its objectives. Considering the planet's inhospitable climate, once the urban areas are isolated, they should surrender, limiting civilian casualties."

Captain Sokolov caught the admiral's eye. "What if they resist?"

"I have authority to conduct unrestricted area attacks, but only as a last resort. We're going there to liberate them, Yuri, not blast them out of existence."

"And the supplies?" Captain Azikiwe added.

"That's why it's called Operation Windfall," Talis said. "Kota has the largest Separatist logistics base in the entire Oh-Zero-Sixty region. If we capture Kota Spaceport with its stockpiles intact, Separatist operations out here will be crippled and we'll be able to fully resupply Hades City. That will swing the balance of power in Oh-Zero-Sixty strongly in our favor. And if we capture Kota's energy plant intact, we'll be able to use the planet as a forward operating base."

Captain Quiroga furrowed his brow. "Admiral, Kota's ground defenses are bunkered and camouflaged by holo-concealment fields. We won't be able to target them from long range and orbital scanning will expose our ships to heavy ground fire. Even if we can destroy their defenses, by the time we land troops, they will have detonated the e-plant."

The other captains nodded, concurring with Quiroga's assessment.

"Targeting is the key," Talis agreed. "That's why Commander Voss is here." He looked at Lena, giving her the floor.

"Thank you, Admiral," she said. "The EIS will smuggle target designators and a commando team onto Kota before the fleet arrives. My people there will use the markers to designate the planet's defenses so you can destroy them in an alpha strike while the commandos capture and hold the e-plant until our troops arrive."

"How many commandos?" Captain Zheng asked.

"Six."

Zheng's eyes bulged incredulously. "Are you serious?"

"They're very special soldiers," Talis assured him.

"I'm sure they're well trained, Admiral," Zheng persisted, "but six?"

"The invasion force includes the Forty-Third Orbital Assault Battalion," Talis said. "They will transfer to the Solar Constitution in the Ashoka Expanse. When we enter orbit, they will drop onto the e-plant to reinforce the commandos."

"Admiral," Captain Quiroga said respectfully, "it'll take the Constitution at least twelve hours to reach orbit from its initial strike position. Those commandos will be surrounded by thousands of enemy soldiers."

"Militia and conscripts, not regulars," Talis said.

"The Solar Constitution will provide long-range fire support during planetary approach," Captain Nishida added.

"Yes, but the response times will be too slow," Captain Zheng insisted.

"It's a risk," Talis conceded, "but a necessary one."

"The commandos will have the latest weaponry," Lena assured them. "They'll hold out."

Captain Azikiwe of the *Soryu* scowled. "How exactly do you propose to land these six commandos before the attack begins?"

"Captain Kade has prepared a ship for the mission," she said, nodding at me.

Suddenly I understood why Admiral Talis had approved my every request, although the price was much steeper than I expected. I hid my surprise as the captains looked me over, obviously doubting the sanity of putting the success of their offensive in the hands of a civilian EIS agent.

Captain Sinaga of the *Galicia* asked, "Have you ever been to Kota, Captain Kade?"

"Once, a long time ago," I replied, "before the war."

"Before the Separatists fortified it?"

"Yes."

"Are you aware that Kota is closed to civilian shipping?" Sinaga persisted.

It was news to me, but not to Lena.

"We have a Separatist recognition signal that will allow Captain Kade's ship to land unopposed," she said.

Some of the captains relaxed, then Captain Zheng asked, "Perhaps you could get recognition codes for all of us as well, Commander Voss, then we wouldn't need to shoot anyone?"

Muted laughter rippled around the room, then Admiral Talis said, "Captain Kade is more than qualified for this mission. He was at Centralis. His role is classified, but his mission was successful in spite of what happened. That's why he was selected for this operation."

Their attitudes toward me changed from disdain to curiosity, then Captain Azikiwe asked, "Admiral, with all our ships committed to the Kota operation, aren't we leaving Hades City exposed?"

Talis nodded. "That's why we installed the new defense grid. The city will have to rely on its own defenses while we're gone. I won't risk splitting the fleet, not while Separatist naval strength is unknown."

"What about Intruder forces?" Sokolov asked.

"The One Spawn are focused on the Tau Cetins and their allies," Lena cut in. "They have no interest in our civil war. We're no threat to them and they know it."

"The Matarons don't agree," Captain Zheng said. "Their ships constantly scout our systems."

"They know more about what the Separatists are doing than we do," Captain Sinaga complained.

"The snakeheads won't do a thing," I said, "not

while the Tau Cetins are still in the fight."

All eyes switched back to me, then Captain Sokolov asked, "Are you also an expert on the Matarons, Captain Kade?"

"I've killed a snakehead or two in my time," I snapped. "Have you?"

Sokolov straightened indignantly, unaware any human had killed a Mataron in centuries. The other captains looked to Lena for confirmation who gave me one of her skin flailing looks then reluctantly nodded. Even Talis looked intrigued, but Lena didn't elaborate.

"Any questions?" the admiral asked, intent on bringing the briefing to an end. When his captains remained silent, he said, "Dismissed."

The officers snapped to attention and filed out, then Lena spoke privately with the admiral before we took the elevator down to collect her car from the stacker.

"You could have told me about Kota," I said, once we were heading back to the spaceport.

"Your reaction to Jase telling you about the Hadleys would've been different. I wanted you to be believable."

"So the fake letter was so *he'd* convince me to go to Kota?"

She nodded. "It'll be hard enough explaining your passengers."

"I take it they won't be wearing uniforms?"

"They'll look like mercenaries, just make sure no one sees their equipment. It's highly classified."

"Hmm. Jase said there were mercs on Kota."

Lena smiled slyly. "Emma may have mentioned that a merc smuggled her message out for a fee."

"To give your commandos a cover story," I said, realizing how carefully she'd crafted the lie.

"No need to thank me for making your job easier."

"Six commandos?" I said suspiciously, wondering just how special they were. "They wouldn't have a red armored fist on their shoulders by any chance?"

"They might, if they wore uniforms. And it's an Iron Fist. They came up with that symbol themselves."

"Is that their codename?" I'd met a couple of them on Centralis. They were a doomsday option, not a regular combat unit, something we hid in the shadows until we had nothing else left.

"It's just a symbol for their designation: I.F. That's all it could be, considering how many laws we broke creating them. Back then, we didn't know *IF* we'd need them, *IF* we'd get away with creating them, or even *IF* they'd be any good."

"But they are good," I said, "aren't they?"

"Better than we'd hoped. Now IF stands for many things. Instinctive Fighters. Intruder Foes. I like Invincible Force, it's the warrior maiden in me."

"You sure six can do it?"

"It's all we could spare."

"Where are the others?"

"Most are still in training, too young to deploy. The few we have are on ships like the Solar Constitution or hiding on colonies in case the Spawn come after us."

I wasn't surprised by the planning she'd put into Operation Windfall or the degree of deception. Lena had always been a master strategist and everyone, even Talis, was just a pawn to her. It was why she was the commander of Oh-Zero-Sixty, why EIS had put her between Earth and the One Spawn.

"Is Emma Hadley even on Kota?" I asked.

"Oh she's there all right, with her father, but she could never have got a message out. Kota Prison is too well guarded."

"So how's Jase going to get Emma out?"

"He isn't, but he won't know that until you're there. Once you scout the prison, he'll see breaking her out is impossible."

"He won't leave." Getting Jase to walk away from any fight was a tough ask, especially one he wanted to start.

"That's your problem."

"If the navy's going to take Kota, the prisoners will be free. All I have to do is make sure he doesn't get himself killed."

"Maybe," she said evasively.

"What else?"

She hesitated, wrestling with her razor-thin conscience. "The Sep command view those prisoners as dangerous political enemies. They're never going to let us free them."

"They're going to murder them?"

She nodded. "I've seen the order."

"If Jase knew that..." he'd start a one-man war to get her out.

"They'll wait until our troops drop. Make sure you're gone by then and under no circumstances risk yourself or *my* ship for the Hadleys."

"So I smuggle in the commandos, deliver the markers and get out of there before the shooting starts."

"Not exactly," she said, holding out her hand, always a bad sign.

Knowing she wanted to give me information too secret for anything but a bionetic transfer, I took her hand. The image of a woman in her forties with dark brown, shoulder-length hair flashed into my mind, accompanied by a DNA code and a name, Margaux Baston.

"She's on Kota," Lena said. "I don't know where."

"You want me to find her?"

"I want you to kill her."

I blinked in surprise. "I'm no assassin. You know that."

"You're whatever I say you are, Sirius. That woman must die and you're the only one who can do it," she said sharply. "When our fleet appears over Kota, the enemy will try to evacuate her. You can't let that happen." She nodded to a metal case sitting on the back seat. "That's for you."

"What is it?"

"A chameleon suit. Wherever Baston is, she'll be well guarded. You'll need the suit to get close enough to eliminate her."

"You've never asked me to assassinate anyone before. Why now?"

"She's the key to the entire Separatist strategy," Lena said. "Make sure she doesn't leave Kota alive."

I'd killed people before, but rarely in cold blood and never on Lena's say so. Now she was ordering me to do both with only the most cryptic of explanations.

"What about that recognition signal?" I asked. "Is it still current?"

"It will be, when you get it."

"From who?"

Her expression hardened. "Marie."

I didn't understand what she was talking about, then it hit me. "You've got nothing! Your whole plan depends on me convincing Marie to double cross her Sep contacts."

"She'll do it, if you ask her."

"No! She won't." Marie and I were on opposite sides of the civil war. I'd lied to her about my EIS involvement from the very beginning, but I'd never treated her like an enemy asset to be manipulated. "I won't ask her to betray her friends."

"You will, because we need Kota."

"If she ever found out…" I shuddered to imagine her fury.

"She knows people on Freehold, Sep smugglers supplying Kota. All she has to do is get you a cargo and they'll give you the landing clearance. She doesn't have to go anywhere near Kota."

"You have agents on Freehold. Get them to do it."

"We've tried. The people who have the clearances

won't talk to anyone they don't know." She gave me a bemused look. "You didn't really think I paid for her ship because you twisted my arm? It was always about the mission. She's flying my ship, Sirius, and if you want her to keep it, you'll send her to Freehold."

"Suppose she can't get me clearance?"

"Then I'm going to have some serious explaining to do to the admiral...and he's going to requisition both ships out from under us."

So even Talis didn't know how precarious Lena's plan was.

"You should have told him the truth."

"If I had, you wouldn't have two ships and you certainly wouldn't have any weapons."

Dealing with Lena was like bargaining with a Telurian dust devil, turn your back on her for a heartbeat and she'd eat you alive. Now she'd backed me into a corner leaving me no room to move.

"When do I boost?"

"In the morning. The troops will board tonight. Their equipment and several crates of targeting markers will be hidden in two container loads of shunter spares. You'll deliver the containers and the markers to your contact on Kota after you land. His name is Navin Dhar."

"Is he EIS?"

"No, but he's motivated and we pay him well."

"Hmph," I grunted, wary of paid traitors. "That doesn't give Marie much time."

"If she launches tomorrow, you can meet her on Freehold after you take care of a little side job for me. It's a passenger pick up. Nothing dangerous."

"One of ours?"

"No, he's working for the Tau Cetins."

"Why don't they pick him up?"

"He's on Niedarim. It's a neutral world, a member of the Xil Neutrality Pact. The Tau Cetins don't want to risk endangering the local population by going there themselves."

"So they send us because no one cares what humans do."

"Something like that," she said. "I don't know his name. He's Buratu."

I shrugged. "Never heard of them."

"Me neither. They're from Vela Carina, quite advanced and not members of the Neutrality Pact."

"They're Alliance?"

"Not formally, but they're pro-TC and far enough from the war zone that they're prepared to help."

"Vela Carina's pretty far," I said thoughtfully. "What's he doing here?"

"All I know is he came in from the Cygnus Rim. My guess is he's been snooping around out there for the Tau Cetins, going where they can't. The TC operative who asked me to pick him up didn't know more than that," she said with certainty, having obviously sifted through his mind for the truth.

"If it's a taxi run, why not send another ship?"

"Because the Tau Cetins requested you by name. They trust you."

"Lucky me."

"You'll find the Buratu language in your lingual update. The TCs gave us a full translation matrix so you can communicate with him."

"They've thought of everything."

"They usually do." She handed me a small golden disk embossed with a triangle inside a circle. It hung from a golden chain and was the kind of decoration worn by followers of the Unity Church. "Wear this."

"I'm not religious."

"It's Tau Cetin tech. When you land at Galisti Starport, hold your thumb against the triangle for three seconds to start it transmitting. If you're scanned, even the Spawn will think it's jewelry. All you have to do is wait until he finds you."

"What do I do once I've got him."

"He'll give you directions. There's a Tau Cetin ship waiting for him somewhere. They wouldn't tell me where, only that it's not far. You won't lose more than a day or two."

"Sounds easy enough," I said doubtfully.

"Consider it one more favor the Tau Cetins owe us." The car stopped at the spaceport entrance. "Good luck, Sirius."

The door lifted up, but instead of getting out, I turned to Lena. "I'll pick up your TC spy, take your soldiers to Kota, I'll even ice that woman you want dead, if I can find her, but this thing with Marie is a one-shot deal," I declared with barely contained anger. "Don't ever involve her again, or we're done. And when this is over that ship is hers, free and clear, or you can keep this," I said, offering her the Unity Church pendant. "Decide now."

Lena studied me in silence, peering into my mind, seeing I meant every word, discovering she'd pushed me too far. "OK Sirius, you have a deal."

I pocketed the gold disk. "I'll see you back here after Kota," I said and climbed out of the ground car with the case containing the chameleon suit.

She drove off and I headed into the spaceport wondering what I'd say to Marie, wracked with guilt at the great lie I was about to tell her.

* * * *

The spaceport's work crew had removed their cables and equipment by the time I got back to the *Silver Lining*. The interior lights were on and the wide, airtight doors dividing the lower cargo hold in half were sealed shut, allowing the forward section to be pressurized.

I cycled through the interior airlock and took the

crew elevator up to engineering where Izin sat at his command console studying a dizzying array of screens and translucent data panes. They held more information than any human engineer could handle, but his bulging amphibian eyes took them all in at a glance.

The blast door covering the energy plant's armored chamber was open, revealing the top third of a large metallic sphere partially embedded in a translucent, circular deck. It was haloed in the soft blue glow of its confinement field and surrounded by shimmering blue energy threads radiating through the transmission deck like the spokes of a wheel. Once the novarium reactor was at full power, the entire deck would become blindingly luminous, fed by millions of molecular thermocouples lining the reactor vessel's interior, converting heat directly into energy.

"Are we ready to launch?" I asked, glancing at the mass of diagnostic data filling his screens.

Izin slid a triangular vocalizer on to translate his amphibian speech into sounds I could understand. "Yes, Captain. The new confinement field stabilizer has been installed, although I have no way to test it."

"It'll work," I assured him. It was Tau Cetin designed, human built, intended to protect our e-plant's confinement field from particle attack, plugging a weakness in our technology. The new *Silver Lining* was only the third ship to receive the upgrade, although all Earth Navy ships would have them eventually.

"First-time system startup will be complete by zero two hundred hours tomorrow morning," Izin said, accepting my assurance.

"Good. We'll be taking on cargo and passengers tonight, boosting in the morning."

"Passengers?" he said uncomfortably, ever wary of humans who habitually mistrusted his kind.

"I've got to pay off this ship somehow," I replied. "Is Jase aboard?"

"He said he'd meet you at a place called Rexi's. Apparently, he was eager to talk to Captain Dulon."

"Was he?" I said thoughtfully, then went up to my stateroom where a message was waiting for me from stevedoring. They'd be loading two big VRS containers in an hour, both already cleared by port authorities. The clearances were fakes, supplied by navy to ensure nosy dock workers didn't get a look at what I was transporting to Kota.

Satisfied Lena had thought of everything, I cleaned up and headed to Rexi's Ringside for dinner. It was located in the Grotto, a subterranean crevasse eight thousand meters below the surface. Black slag walls towered above a natural amphitheater ringed by seedy bars, well-lit restaurants, and a clamoring clientele.

Floodlights beamed down through darkness onto the amphitheater stage, illuminating a pair of fighters stripped to the waist, slugging away at each other, splattering blood and teeth with every blow. Packed in around the stage was a seething mass of sweaty drunks, bleary-eyed stimheads and scantily clad women, all cheering, cursing and betting on the brutality unfolding before them.

Rexi's Ringside was an open-air restaurant high up on a spiral ledge that wound down to the stage. Five terraces lined with booths filled with people overlooked the arena while semi-naked servers squeezed through the crowd to attend the tables.

Jase waved from a booth three terraces above the cliffside railing with a drink in one hand and his vault key in the other. He saw me nod and push through the crowd toward him, then used his vault key to place a bet and order another round of drinks. Beside him, Marie and her crew watched the fight with indifference. They'd lost everything a few months ago and weren't betting, not even Gadron Ugo, her hulking first officer. He'd been a notorious prizefighter before signing on as a deckhand with Marie's father and was the nearest thing she had to family, which meant he didn't like me one bit.

When I got to their booth, I fended off a drunken bear hug from Jase and slid in beside Marie. She kissed me lightly then I nodded a greeting to Ugo across the table. He begrudgingly acknowledged me, then Omari Jang, Marie's engineer, gave me an intoxicated smile while a stocky, bald man beside her sized me up with a look.

"Eddie Nubaker," he said.

"Eddie's my new loadmaster," Marie explained over the din as we shook hands.

She cupped one hand beside her mouth and shouted to Eddie. "This is Sirius. He's the owner, so be nice to him."

"More of a silent partner," I said.

Eddie had a firm grip and made no attempt to ingratiate himself with me, which I liked right off. He was an old hand who knew loadmasters didn't have to worry about keeping owners happy. That was the Captain's job.

"He's why she named the ship Mendiant," Ugo growled through the side of his mouth.

It meant 'beggar' in Marie's ancestral language, mendicant in Unionspeak. It was her way of telling me she didn't like taking money from anyone, especially her lover. It was a sentiment the overprotective Ugo shared tenfold.

"Where's Izin?" Marie asked.

"I'd need wrist clamps and a stun gun to get him into a place like this," I replied.

"Doesn't he like prize fights?"

"It's people he can't stand."

A drink was placed in front of me by a near-naked woman twice as large as Ugo with half as many teeth. An enthusiastic grin from Jase told me he'd ordered it for me, then a roar went up as one of the combatants went down for the last time.

"Argh! Left, left!" Jase yelled in frustration, feigning a left jab, then sighed miserably as he realized he'd lost another bet. "These fights are rigged."

Marie gave me an amused look. "No wonder he's always broke," she said for my ears alone.

"It's worse when he wins," I replied, "then he dances on the table."

"Let's eat," Ugo declared, leaning forward and tapping the tabletop selector.

We all ordered, then Marie said, "Jase told me about his girlfriend." She gave me an uncertain look. "She is his girlfriend, right?"

I shrugged. "She made a good first impression."

"I bet," Marie smiled, assuming I meant much more.

"He hasn't slept with her yet."

She looked surprised. "And he wants to go to Kota for her?"

"Put it down to youthful anticipation and...holographic sharing."

"Oh," Marie said, getting my drift. "So, she's beautiful?"

"She doesn't have your accent," I said, referring to Marie's lilting Gascon inflections, "but...she does look good in...not much."

"Oh?" she said feigning jealousy. "You've been reading his mail."

"Not exactly, but I can see why he likes her."

"How long has this virtual love affair been going on?"

"Over a year. Long enough to get hot and–"

"I got it," she said, appreciating the thermal effect of a year of romantic holoporn on an enthusiastic young man trapped inside a small ship for months on end.

Two new fighters climbed into the ring. One was huge, with shoulders as wide as our table. The other was my height with a shaved head and sharply defined muscles. The giant inhaled and clenched his fists, playing to the audience, showing how much he towered over his opponent. From the roar of the fans, the giant was a crowd favorite while his smaller opponent was a complete unknown.

Jase waved his vault key at a nearby bookiebot, swiped the reader and said, "A hundred on the big guy." He turned to me with a grin. "Skipper, that's Sledge! I've seen him fight before. He's a monster. Punches like an Alkaidian rammer."

The smaller man watched Sledge the Giant impassively, making no attempt to reply to the big brute's bravado while ignoring the howling mob.

"Who's the other fighter?"

"He's nobody. Soon he'll have no teeth," Jase replied with drunken laughter.

Nobody raised his fists, eyes focused and waited. Sledge the Giant was huge and powerful, but Nobody had the ice-cool bearing of a killer.

I motioned to the floating bookiebot. "A hundred on the other guy, not Sledge."

"Yes sir, a hundred on Combatant Twenty Three," it replied, swiping my key.

Jase shook his head in dismay. "Don't say I didn't warn you, Skipper."

The announcer presented the two fighters, first running through Sledge the Giant's long list of victories, including two one-punch kills. When it was Nobody's turn, he was introduced by his number alone with a win-loss record of oh-and-oh. The crowd took it to mean this was his first fight and responded with jeers and insults while his relaxed battle stance reminded me of my EIS hand-to-hand instructor who used to beat me to a pulp once a week for laughs.

"So you're taking lover boy to Kota?" Marie asked, ignoring the fight.

"I can't let him go alone," I replied, hoping she'd offer to help, saving me from lying to her.

"You'll have to identify yourself to land."

"I haven't thought that far ahead," I said, watching the ring, pretending not to care.

"They shoot Earth-loving loyalists like you on sight at Kota," she said slowly.

"Good thing they don't know me or my ship."

She gave me a thoughtful look. "Do you want me to take him?"

"I don't want you anywhere near Kota," I declared, adding in a low voice, "in case this blows up in our faces."

"You won't reach orbit without a recognition signal."

"I'll get one. There's plenty of smuggling out of Freehold."

"Freehold? You?" She smiled skeptically. "They'll slit your throat as quick as look at you."

"They can try," I said, then gave her a sly look. "You could give me a name."

She laughed. "And have them slit my throat? No thanks."

"Guess I'll have to take my chances."

The bell sounded from the ring below and a wild roar went up as the crowd screamed for blood. Sledge the Giant and Nobody began circling each other, then Sledge charged, throwing a punch that would have caused a cave-in if he'd struck a wall. Nobody rolled under the blow, unbalancing the Giant who stumbled into the ropes. The smaller man came easily to his feet and turned calmly to Sledge without a trace of fear, then the two fighters circled each other again. A wave of uncertainty spread through the audience as they sensed Nobody was stalking their champion, picking his moment.

"Any way I can change your mind?" Marie asked.

"Sure, talk him out of it," I replied, nodding at Jase who stood on his seat, yelling encouragement to Sledge, mystified why he hadn't already put Nobody's lights out.

Marie gave me a probing look. "You never intended to go to Freehold alone, did you?"

I feigned confusion. "Not alone. I'm going with Jase and Izin."

She shook her head, not buying it. "You know I have contacts there."

"You do have a lot of friends in low places," I said, hating myself for playing her, knowing she was taking the bait.

"Spit it out, Sirius, what do you want?"

I smiled and turned to her. "An introduction, a cargo, and a landing clearance."

"I might know someone," she said thoughtfully.

"Just get my foot in the door on Freehold and leave the rest to me."

"So you three break into Kota Prison while I'm off hauling women's lingerie and powder puffs to some remote colony, where it's nice and safe?"

"Exactly." She opened her mouth to argue, but I cut her off. "Or we go to Freehold without you."

"But I can help," she insisted.

"You're not going to Kota," I said emphatically. "That's final."

"Oh?" she said indignantly. "So, you *are* giving me orders now."

It was what she dreaded, being obligated to me for buying her a new ship.

"This isn't about me and you, Marie, it's about me and him," I said, pointing at Jase. "If we can't do this alone, it won't get done." I leaned close to her, softening my tone. "And if it all goes to hell, I don't want you getting hurt."

She sighed thoughtfully. "This girl better be worth it."

Considering I knew we were never going to get Emma Hadley out of Kota Prison, I knew she wasn't. "Jase thinks she is. He'll owe you for this."

"You'll owe me."

"Well, in that case, I'll start paying off that debt tonight." I glanced at the strange concoction Jase had ordered for me. "Providing I'm still conscious after drinking whatever that is."

She smiled seductively. "You better be. This will be our last night together for a while."

"Hmm, since you put it that way…" I pushed the drink away, ensuring I'd be at my best, and turned back to the fight.

Sledge the Giant made another sweep at Nobody, who dodged easily, then anger exploded on Sledge's huge face and he charged, but this time, instead of dodging, Nobody closed his eyes. A moment later, he blocked the Giant's swing and punched Sledge so hard, he sent him flying across the ring as if he'd been shot out of a cannon. The Giant's massive body landed with a thud and lay motionless with blood smeared across his face, silencing the shocked crowd. Even Jase stood stunned, mouth open, struggling to comprehend what had just happened.

In the center of the ring, bathed in streams of light from on high, Nobody opened his eyes to survey the damage he'd wrought on Sledge the Giant.

In that moment, I knew what Nobody was.

* * * *

After dinner, Marie and I left the Grotto to spend the night together aboard the *Mendiant*. Next morning, I returned to the spaceport and boarded the *Silver Lining* through the bow airlock to find six new pressure suits in the locker room. They were all triple-ply flex-leaf, virtually bulletproof, with multiple interface points for everything from power armor to drop ship telemetry. Each suit was a made-to-measure, black market custom build, better than anything worn by elite Union Regular Army troopers.

"Nothing but the best for the serious merc," I said running my hand over one of the p-suits, then went up to engineering.

"They're here," Izin said as I stepped off the crew elevator.

"Did you speak to them?"

"Only via the intercom. A servicebot showed them to their quarters."

I headed aft past Izin's stateroom to the technician's berths. The companionway lights were out, all three cabin doors were open and the rooms were dark. Our guests had obviously hacked the power conduits to kill the lights, hiding their presence, then as I walked toward the blacked-out corridor, my DNA sniffer flashed a message into my mind:

ZYGOTE CONSTRUCT DETECTED, FOUR METERS AHEAD.

It had scanned an IF super soldier some months ago, giving it a pattern to recognize. Now it had found another. I could have ramped up my listener and gone infrared on my optics, but that would have revealed my secrets to him. Certain he wasn't going to kill me, I made like a dumb spacer and blundered blindly into the trap. When I reached the first open door, a dark shadow moved toward me with surprising speed, then white light exploded before my eyes as a particularly insidious stun blast hit me.

I don't remember hitting the deck, then system warnings appeared in my mind's eye:

BIONETICS BUNKER PROTOCOL ENABLED.
TIME UNCONSCIOUS: 124 SECONDS.

I'd been out for two whole minutes without my threading making any attempt to snap me out of it. That told me whatever he'd hit me with had disabled my bionetics, making me wonder whose tech they were using. I decided not to trigger a system revive, but regain my senses the old fashioned way. I groaned and opened my eyes, trying to focus as a bright light shone in my face.

"Who are you?" a gravel voice demanded.

"Sirius Kade."

"What are doing back here?"

"I was going to welcome you aboard," I said, holding my pounding head. "What did you hit me with?"

He switched his beam light off and the companionway lights came on. Nobody, the fighter who'd hammered Sledge the Giant into the canvas, stood before me holding a small hand weapon I'd never seen before. Three other men and two women, all armed, covered the corridor as if anticipating an attack.

"Can I get up, or are you going to take turns shooting me?" I asked, glancing meaningfully at Nobody's strange stunner. He pocketed the weapon and signaled the others to stand down, then I got to my feet blinking spots from my eyes. "I'll want those weapons stowed before we launch."

"No."

"Then get off my ship."

Nobody's granite face showed a flicker of surprise. I guess he was used to dealing with navy types who clicked heels and saluted anything that moved. "We have orders."

"I don't care." Apart from Nobody's stunner, the rest carried compact, overpowered, assault weapons that might not penetrate the e-plant's armored citadel, but could easily mess up any one of a thousand other critical systems or worse, punch a hole through the hull. When he showed no sign of complying, I added, "If you fire those things in here, no telling what damage you could do. So, it's the armory or the VRS containers on the lower cargo deck or you can hitchhike to Kota. Your choice."

"We need to get to our weapons in an emergency."

"If we run into trouble in space, your toy guns won't help you."

Nobody realized I was right and reluctantly relented. "We have a weapons locker in container two."

I nodded agreement, then looked over his companions. They all had similar, hard muscular physiques and a slightly inhuman coldness, traits engineered into them from when they were nothing more than single-cell organisms.

"The officer's mess is on the command deck," I said. "Go up anytime you're hungry, but avoid talking to my crew."

Nobody nodded. "Understood."

"You got IDs?"

"Yeah, all registered deckhands."

I almost laughed. None of them looked like spacers, not that we needed human help with a ship full of bots.

"We got two stops before Kota. None of you leave the ship before then."

"We need a place to train."

"The upper cargo deck's empty. It's all yours. Fitness and hand to hand only, no live firing. I can arrange for zero-g if you want it."

"Two-g for one hour from oh-five hundred."

"Don't break any bones," I said, wary of them doing something stupid in heavy gravity. "Do you have names?"

He pointed to each member of his team in turn. "Parekh, Riley, Ibanez, Larson, Shen," he said, then jabbed a thumb at his chest, "Dietz."

"No first names?"

"You want to be our friend?" Dietz asked coldly, signaling relationship building wasn't part of his encoding. "Read us bedtime stories?"

"Right," I said slowly, getting his measure. "My chief engineer isn't sociable, so stay out of his way."

"I don't like tamphs."

"Well you're even, because he doesn't like you." I looked over the six zygote constructs, wondering if they really were tough enough to take on a Sep army all by themselves. Whether they were or not, I didn't want to be around when the shooting started.

"I'll send a bot for your weapons," I said and went up to get a few hours sleep while we waited for the eclipse vector to open so we could boost out of Hades City.

Chapter Two: Niedarim

Lhekan Homeworld
Kappa Idris System
Trans Cepheus
0.82 Earth Normal Gravity
962 light years from Sol
1.6 billion inhabitants

During the flight to pick up the Tau Cetin agent, the six commandos drilled like machines, only coming up to the command deck to eat, not fraternize. They passed Izin several times a day without speaking, which suited him fine, while Jase spied on them occasionally while pretending to perform routine maintenance. He'd been too drunk to recognize Dietz from the prizefight in the Grotto, although if he had, he'd have understood why he'd lost his money.

"Those guys train hard," he said, impressed after one of his spying missions. "If I didn't know better, I'd swear they were trying to kill each other."

"Stay alive's more like it," I said, thinking of the

odds they'd soon be facing.

I passed Dietz a few times near the galley, receiving scarcely a nod from him. It wasn't that he resented me, just that he wasn't one for small talk and pleasantries. My first actual words to him didn't come until we were ten days out of Hades City, and it wasn't a conversation, but a ship-wide announcement as we approached Kappa Idris IV.

"We're coming up on Niedarim," I said over the intercom. "Mercenaries to remain in their quarters until further notice."

When the bubble dropped, Jase deployed our oversized sensor masts through the ship's cooling hull. They bristled with tech making us look more like a spy ship than a freighter, not that anyone was watching. Moments after our eyes opened, the collision alarm went off as the bridge screen filled with an enormous black mass tumbling toward us.

"Shield up!" I ordered, thrusting hard to port.

The *Silver Lining* rolled away as the dark silhouette slid beneath our port sensor mast, almost shearing it off, then starlight from Kappa Idris revealed it was the stern of a large alien ship. Broken decks and torn bulkheads glowed from an explosion that had torn the ship in half and scattered a thinning trail of debris and Lhekan corpses in its wake. Flotsam flashed against our shield before being pushed away, then I was forced to evade the wreck of a swept wing fighter with a blackened hole through its fuselage. It passed close enough for us to see the Lhekan pilot in his shattered dome-shaped cockpit with his frozen arms still shielding his face.

Jase ran hull geometry matches on both contacts. "The big one's a Lhekan cruiser. Got nothing on the small one."

"It's an orbital fighter," I said, judging its wing configuration made it equally at home in atmosphere and vacuum.

Jase whistled softly as yellow unidentified contact markers appeared all across the bridge's exceptionally precise spatial mapping screen. "It's crowded out there."

Our sensors revealed dozens of wrecked ships, hundreds of destroyed fighters and thousands of Lhekan corpses floating between us and the planet. It had only been a matter of luck that we hadn't plowed into a wreck as we approached Niedarim's gravity well. An orange bloom blew out into space from the side of a dead ship a few hundred kilometers away, then other explosions rippled through more distant wrecks illuminating thousands of tiny escape pods thrusting toward the planet.

"Izin, power down," I said over the intercom. "Leave me enough for maneuvering and the shield."

"Active sensors off," Jase said, reading my mind.

Our emissions' profile dropped like a stone as we glided through the graveyard of the Lhekan Fleet toward Niedarim. Many lifeboats were too far out to reach the planet or on trajectories inherited from the ships they'd abandoned that would carry them out of the system decades from now. Closer to Niedarim, small orbital craft were coming out to rescue survivors, but they were pitifully few for such a gargantuan task.

"There's a lot of chatter out there," Jase said.

"Let's hear it."

The bridge filled with thousands of voices speaking in an alien tongue, some calm and professional, others frantic and afraid. To Jase, it was meaningless babble. To me, with my xenolinguistics upgrade translating every word, it was a cacophony of shock and desperation.

"I don't understand," he said. "This is a neutral world."

"Not anymore. Shut it off."

The bridge fell silent, then tiny flashes appeared above Niedarim's eastern hemisphere. Jase zoomed an optical toward it, picking out a Lhekan warship firing at a target obscured by the planet's curvature. A single brilliant white beam from the unseen enemy cut the Lhekan ship in half, then a luminous orange explosion radiated from the stricken warship. It broke into pieces, then tiny silver lifeboats ejected in all directions.

"They're still here," I said warily, searching for the spaceport's nav beacon. There was no traffic control, no hail from the planet and no time to waste.

"They haven't seen us yet," Jase said.

There was no need to match the weapon signature. We'd both seen its like before on Centralis and knew what it meant. There was a spawnship out there and it was systematically annihilating the Lhekan homeworld's defenses.

I aimed for a point on Niedarim as far from the spawnship as possible and fed power to the engines, exceeding Lhekan approach protocols.

"What are we waiting for?" Jase asked impatiently. "Let's get out of here."

"The planet's masking our presence."

"Until it comes around for another pass."

I hesitated, calculating the odds. Somewhere down there was a Tau Cetin agent waiting to be rescued. If I didn't go down and grab him, it was only a matter of time before the Spawn captured him and that was something I couldn't allow.

"We'll be in and out before they even know we're here," I said.

Jase glanced anxiously at the shattered Niedarim warship rippling with secondary explosions. "Skipper, we could get trapped down there."

"We won't," I assured him. "That spawnship's busy fighting the Lhekans. They won't have time for us."

The Lhekans were hundreds of thousands of years ahead of mankind, in galactic terms a medium power, yet as incapable of defending themselves against the One

Spawn as we were. Even so, the spawnship would prioritize the Lhekans ahead of us, simply because they posed slightly more of a threat than a technologically primitive human ship.

"I hope you know what you're doing, Skipper," Jase said doubtfully.

"Me too," I said, angling the *Silver Lining* for a low power dive into the atmosphere. "Let's see Galisti City."

Jase matched Niedarim's topography to our nav system's surface map, then zoomed the screen image to a point halfway to the horizon. What should have been a densely populated urban sprawl, was now a charred, thirty-kilometer wide crater.

"It's gone!" he said shocked.

The Lhekan League's once-flourishing capital was a blackened wasteland surrounded by a circular firestorm ravaging the outer reaches of the city. Thick oily smoke rose from the ring of fire, feeding a funeral pyre fifty kilometers high. On the plain to the south of the crater, hundreds of tiny smoke plumes rose from the burning wrecks of ships destroyed on the ground. "There's the starport."

"Not much left," I said bleakly.

"I'm reading energy signatures outside the fires," Jase said. "Looks like street fighting."

"How close to the starport?"

He winced. "Too close to land."

If the Buratu agent had been there waiting for me, instead of in the city, he might still be alive, not that we could land on top of Intruder ground forces.

"Any other spaceports on this side of the planet?"

He panned an optical across Niedarim's surface. All the large urban regions were burning with craters at their centers. Only the smaller regional cities had survived and none of them had landing grounds.

"All destroyed," Jase said, unable to believe his eyes.

Initiate geographic search for EIS contacts on Niedarim, I thought, hoping my bionetic memory knew someone who could help me, then a response flashed into my mind.

PRIDAK TIR: INFORMANT.
LOCATION: FIREL CITY.
ASSESSMENT: POSSIBLE LHEKAN DOUBLE AGENT.

A credit hungry informer suspected of feeding us false information was not what I had in mind, but there was no one else.

"Where's Firel City?" I asked.

Jase had our planet survey place a marker over a small regional center amid an intensively farmed agricultural plain. There were a few fires burning, but no city annihilating crater at its center.

"It's rural," Jase said, shaking his head. "No spaceport."

"It's perfect."

Firel City had got off easy, which meant Pridak Tir might still be there. And like all bottom feeders, he'd be looking for a way to profit from the desperate plight of his homeworld. That was something I could give him.

"It's five thousand clicks from the starport," Jase said doubtfully.

"Yeah, but it's been hit already, so it's probably safe to land."

"You really think you can find him in this?"

"I know where he is," I said with more confidence than I felt, but Lena had promised the Tau Cetins which meant I had to try. "I just need help getting to him."

We dived through the clouds, unchallenged by Lhekan ground authorities, confirming the planet's command and control system had been wiped out. My biggest fear was an air defense unit, not realizing we were human, trying to shoot us down, but the spawnship had done its job. Not a single shot was fired from the surface, then I leveled off and skimmed irrigated farmlands dotted with enormous storage facilities and small housing clusters. There were no Lhekan farmers in sight, only automated machines working sunlit fields or standing idly by where their overseers had abandoned them. Whatever Lhekans were still down there were hiding from the menace lurking above their world.

A small city soon appeared on the horizon. Five elevated mass transit tubes led into its center from the surrounding countryside. All of them had been severed by precision strikes, isolating the city and trapping its population, although the central terminus where they met was undamaged. It was surrounded by wedge-shaped buildings that fitted together like giant jigsaw pieces and were covered by rooftop parklands and lakes. Artificial rivers fed the lakes and flowed high above the narrow streets via aqueducts, turning the entire city skyline into a patchwork garden obscuring the structures below.

Where buildings had been destroyed, rooftop wildernesses had fallen like landslides, dumping huge quantities of soil and water onto the roads. Some buildings burned out of control or had forest fires raging across their rooftop woodlands while other city blocks showed no damage at all.

Below the rooftop parks, not a single vehicle moved on the multilevel roads crisscrossing the city while floodwaters from collapsed aqueducts fed thin, muddy lakes spreading between the buildings. There were no firefighters anywhere, no engineers trying to stem the floods or rescue teams searching the rubble for survivors.

"Where is everyone?" Jase asked as we cruised low over the city, the only vehicle in the sky.

"Hiding," I replied as we passed the central terminus.

Beside it was a high walled structure with a collapsed wall. A thin veil of water cascaded from the rooftop park onto the ground, giving glimpses of a cavernous interior.

"That'll do," I said, killing the shield and easing the ship through the waterfall. Once inside, we flew slowly over a row of automated grain elevators and set down in a loading area awash with water.

"Izin, go dark," I said to the intercom.

"Shutting down now, Captain," he replied.

I climbed off my acceleration couch, satisfied we were hidden from the sky next time the spawnship passed overhead.

"Sit tight. I'll be back soon," I said, then went to my stateroom to collect the Unity Church medallion.

I held my thumb against it until it glowed, then pulled it on over my head. If we'd landed at Galisti Starport, I'd have waited for the Buratu agent to come to me, but I couldn't be sure he was even receiving the signal. That meant I had to go to him. With Spawn combat forces fighting near the starport, I loaded my MAK P-50 with Lena's shield penetrating snakehead killers, grabbed a K7 assault rifle from the armory and went down to the vehicle bay.

"Are we going somewhere, Captain?" Izin asked, eyeing my weapons.

"I'm going to pick up our guest," I replied.

"I will come with you," he said, starting to stand.

"Not this time. Someone's likely to mistake you for the Spawn and shoot you." He hesitated, realizing the Lhekans might not know what a tamph was. "Keep an eye on the mercs. Don't let them outside," I said and hurried forward to the vehicle bay.

The survey ship had come equipped with a gossamer-winged power glider and a six-wheeled all-terrain buggy. The subsonic flier was too slow for a combat zone, making it an easy kill for any anti-air weapon more sophisticated than a slingshot. The buggy wasn't much better. It had an elongated transparent dome, six oversized wheels, and no armor or weapons, but it was fast and could float across rivers on its huge tires.

I placed the K7 on the passenger seat and unlocked the magclamps holding its wheels, then Dietz's voice sounded behind me.

"This ain't Galisti Spaceport."

"Change of plan," I replied, checking the buggy's cells were fully charged and removing the umbilical.

"Our mission is Kota. This planet is under attack by the Spawn. We should not have landed here."

"You're not my only concern, Dietz."

"If you're killed, your crew won't take us to Kota," he said, revealing he knew Jase and Izin knew nothing of my mission.

"I'll get you to Kota," I snapped, pushing past him to the driver's door.

He scowled, irritated at the risk I was taking. "We'll escort you."

"The hell you will. You'll sit in your quarters until I get back." The last thing I needed was a bunch of trigger happy zygote super soldiers taking potshots at an invading Spawn army.

"We're trained for this. You're not."

"Dietz," I said going face to face with him, "you don't know what I'm trained for."

He hesitated, sensing it was no idle boast, then I climbed into the buggy and slammed the door in his face. While he watched in simmering silence, I took the freight elevator down to the lower cargo deck, entered Pridak Tir's home location into the buggy's nav system and drove down the stern door-ramp into ankle-deep water.

I drove past a row of static conveyors for unloading grain haulers, out through a large open doorway into bright sunshine, then followed the nav map through Firel City's maze of white-walled, round windowed buildings.

Smoke drifted in long plumes across the sky above deserted streets littered with abandoned vehicles and awash with shallow, muddy water. Where bombed-out buildings had collapsed, shattered masonry, uprooted trees and black soil from the rooftop parks had fallen into the narrow streets forming dams that turned the narrow roads into murky brown canals.

Eerily, there were no Lhekans on the roads or peering out through the windows. It was as if the entire population had simply vanished from existence, leaving their garden-topped city to burn and their roads to flood. If the Intruder strategy had been to terrorize the population into submission, they'd succeeded. With Niedarim's defending fleet destroyed, its surface defenses in ruins and the centers of its major cities vaporized, civilization on Niedarim had all but collapsed.

Several times, I had to back up and go around or climb onto elevated freeways that carried me past rooftop parklands, sprawling lakes, and savage forest fires. Twenty clicks from the *Silver Lining*, the buggy's nav screen indicated I'd found Pridak Tir's house. I pulled on a translator headset loaded with Cultured Lhekanese, hoisted my K7 over my head, and waded through knee deep water to stairs leading up to a low, wide door.

I tapped the touch plate, then banged my rifle butt against the door several times to rouse the inhabitants, but there was no answer. I wondered if my Lhekan informant had fled the city, then spotted three pairs of small dark eyes peering at me through a window beside the door. I waved to them, but they ducked out of sight, then the barrel of a small weapon pointed at me through the window and a deep, baritone voice sounded from the intercom.

"What do you want, human?" my threading translated.

I spoke into my cheek mike, then my translator replied in polite, diplomatic grade Lhekanese with an aristocratic accent. "I'm from Earth. I'm looking for Pridak Tir. I need his help."

"The Earth Embassy has been destroyed," the voice replied. "All the humans there are dead."

"Are you Pridak Tir?"

The voice hesitated. "How do you know my name?"

"I was told you would help me for the right price."

"Help you how?"

"Let me in and we'll discuss it."

"No. Go away."

Having no time for chit chat, I aimed my rifle at the window and waited as the three small Lhekan children squealed in terror and ran from sight. When they were clear, I shattered the window with a burst and clambered through.

A Lhekan stood in a doorway aiming a small hand weapon at me. He was a typical Lhekan male, a head shorter than me with soft brown skin, narrow shoulders, thin arms, broad hips, and a slight corpulence. His head was wider and flatter than a human's with a huge mass of thick black hair combed back on top, creating the illusion of a head three times the size of a man's. His clothes were brightly colored, mostly red and orange, with a tight waistcoat and loose pants. Even his shoes were a vivid magenta, but then the males were the peacocks of the species.

I leveled my K7 at him, but held my fire, letting him consider his next move, then I said, "Mine's bigger."

The Lhekan hesitated, clearly no fighter.

"I need to get to Galisti Starport," I said, holding up my Earth Bank vault key. "If you help me, I'll pay you well."

He studied me uncertainly. "All the ships at Galisti have been destroyed."

"I don't want a ship. I'm looking for someone. He's waiting for me at the starport."

Pridak Tir considered my request, then a female dressed in dull gray and white appeared in the corridor. Three children peeked past her legs. Two were male judging by their brightly colored clothes while the young female was dressed in light gray.

"Who are you?" Pridak Tir asked.

"Sirius Kade." I lowered my K7 showing I meant no harm. "I'll triple whatever we paid you in the past."

The Lhekan hesitated, gave his wife a reassuring look and pocketed his gun.

"This way," he said and led me into an office with ornately carved furniture, four padded chairs, and two glowing holopanels. One displayed a ground battle raging between Lhekan forces and the Spawn Army. The other was a newscast showing survivors being helped from crashed escape pods and rushed to hospital.

"How do you know this human is still alive?" he asked, barely glancing at the holopanels.

"I don't and he's not human."

"Not Lhekan either?"

"No," I replied without offering an explanation.

He stared at me, taking a long time to decide. It wasn't that Lhekans were slow-witted, but while they were older than mankind, they were somewhat less intelligent. Their technology was superior to ours simply because they'd evolved sooner and been at it longer than us. It had taken them sixty-five thousand years to pass through the Transition Phase from hunters and gatherers to interstellar civilization, a journey mankind completed in less than ten millennia. In time, if both civilizations survived, we'd leave them far behind, but that was in the distant future.

"Why'd they attack?" I asked, studying the holopanels.

"We don't know. The spawnship appeared over our

world two days ago and struck without warning. They made no demands."

It was an unexpected move. The One Spawn had carefully honored the Xil Neutrality Pact so far because it isolated the Tau Cetins. When it no longer served their interests, they'd dump it, but the Ornithians weren't beaten yet and to break it now risked offending the galaxy's other great powers, who'd so far stayed out of the fight.

"The Tau Cetins will come," I assured him.

"They cannot save us now, even if they wanted to," he replied with rank defeatism.

"Is there a way to reach Galisti Starport?"

"It is a long way from here and the Spawn are landing everywhere," he said, glancing at the news reports.

The images flashed from one battle to another, all with the same message; fast-moving robotic armies led by tamph sized soldiers in battle armor were annihilating Lhekan ground forces all across Niedarim.

"They use combat bots," I said, impressed by the speed and lethality of their machines.

"Autacs," Pridak Tir corrected. "Automated, self-aware, combat systems. There are many types. They operate alone, or under the command of spawnwarriors who fight to the death for their queens."

I watched a force of autacs outflank and destroy a defensively-minded Lhekan army unit, then an explosion killed the feed. It wasn't just a question of superior technology, the Spawn fought with a ferocity and discipline the Lhekans could not match.

"Can I get a copy of that?"

"For what purpose?"

"So we know what we're up against when it's our turn."

He was taken aback by my answer. Perhaps it was because I openly assumed the Spawn would attack us one day, or perhaps it was because I expected we'd put up a fight.

"There are some battles even a warrior race such as yours cannot win," he said slowly.

"Doesn't mean we won't try."

He gave me a long look, doubting my sanity, then took a small rectangular data strip from a cabinet and touched it to the base of the holopanel. After a moment, he handed the data strip to me. "It's encoded in simple binary. Your technology will be able to access it."

"Thanks," I said, pocketing the strip. "Now, about Galisti."

"Even if you could find this person, what purpose would it serve?"

"I promised to transport him off-world."

Pridak Tir turned to me in surprise. "You have a ship? A human ship?"

"Yeah, not far from here."

"Why have the Spawn not destroyed it?"

"They don't know we're here."

"How is that possible?"

"My ship is small and quiet."

He stared at me intently. "How many can your ship transport?"

"Not many," I said guardedly.

"I will help you, but only if you take five others with you."

The *Silver Lining* had life support for forty-six, although the refit had removed accommodation for most of them. In a pinch, extras could sleep on the cargo decks, but I had a rendezvous on Kota and a war of my own to fight. Taking his family along for the ride wasn't part of the plan.

"I can't do that."

"Then I cannot take you to Galisti Starport."

"So there is a way?"

"We have a system of subterranean vacuum tubes

the spawnship has not yet detected."

"And you can get access?"

"For the right price," he said implacably.

I wondered how I was going to explain a boatload of Lhekan refugees to Jase and Izin, certain it was the only way I was getting his help.

"OK. You just bought yourself five tickets off-world."

"Good. Wait outside."

I stepped into the hallway, then he shut the door behind me. At the end of the corridor, Pridak Tir's daughter stood watching me uncertainly.

"Hello. I'm a friend…from Earth," I said through the translator.

She tensed, as if to run away, then said, "I am Silani. Where is Earth?"

"It's very far from here."

"Are the bad Spawn there?"

"Not yet," I said slowly.

"Why do they kill us?"

I struggled for an answer. "I don't know."

Her mother appeared, gave me a sharp look, then scooped the child up and carried her away. A moment later, Pridak Tir emerged from his office.

"I have authority," he said. "We will use your vehicle to reach the vacuum station."

He told his wife he'd return soon, then we waded out to the buggy and headed back into the deserted city at high speed.

* * * *

The entrance to the vacuum station was hidden from orbital scanning below an overpass near the city center. It was a two-lane road that led deep underground to a rectangular warren crammed with vehicles. I parked the buggy in the tunnel and followed Pridak Tir into a high ceilinged hall several kilometers long filled with frightened Lhekans packed in shoulder to shoulder.

Adults and children whispered and whimpered as a small team of doctors attended to the injured. Lhekan soldiers in gray body armor with short-barreled weapons kept a narrow path open through the crowd while giant holopanels high on the walls displayed silent vision of the ground war. The civilians were arranged in orderly lines in front of tunnels guarded by the soldiers, waiting their turn to go through to the loading platforms. With Intruder ground forces landing at will, I wondered where they could escape to as clearly nowhere was safe.

Pridak Tir whispered to an army officer who led us through a tunnel to a boarding platform flanked by a wall of transparent pressure doors. The officer ushered us through one of the doors to an empty transport capsule, watched by desperate civilians.

"This is just for us?" I asked, glancing at the families outside. "What about them?"

"We're going to Galisti. No one wants to go there now," he said as the pressure doors sealed.

There was a click as we disconnected from the platform, then the transport glided silently on a repulsion field into a dark tunnel and accelerated to hypersonic velocity. Tiny lights flashed past and occasionally branching tunnels appeared out of the darkness only to vanish instantly behind us.

"You have a lot of pull," I said, wondering how a local bureaucrat got priority while his world was falling apart.

"I have connections in the government."

"Why is everyone hiding? Shouldn't they be putting out the fires?"

"It is unsafe up there," he replied, fidgeting uncomfortably. "We do not like the surface."

"But your cities are covered in forests and lakes," I said, assuming Lhekans had a taste for the outdoors.

"That is to give us a sense of being below ground. We rarely go onto the rooftops and only at night when we do not feel exposed." He removed his strangely large shoes, revealing thickly muscled feet with three long, curved toenails. "We are fossorial, evolved from burrowing herbivores."

His feet were adapted for digging, while his thin arms and narrow shoulders clearly weren't. "So when you're threatened...?"

"We retreat underground," he replied, replacing his shoes. "It took us a long time to learn to live on the surface."

I realized the rooftop parks were a psychological illusion, their way of dealing with agoraphobia. It was why the streets were narrow, limiting the sense of openness between the buildings.

"Why'd you come onto the surface?"

"One cannot build an interstellar civilization by hiding in burrows."

I guess he'd never met the Nisk, giant bugs who'd turned underground living into an industrial super culture.

"Is that where your people are going? Underground?"

"Yes. We fight where we are strongest."

"So why are your soldiers still on the surface?"

"They give our people time to escape to the under-home. We will abandon the surface soon, collapse the entrances and wait for the One Spawn to leave."

I decided not to tell him when the Spawn came, they came to stay, or maybe he just pretended not to know.

"When they figure out where you've gone, they'll go after you."

"To do that, they must dig. We are not fighters, but we know how to cause cave-ins."

So that was it. They were surrendering their surface

cities to hide in ancient caves, intending to bury the Spawn alive if they dared go after them.

"I hope your plan works," I said as we emerged into a well-lit station.

Our transport capsule mated with the platform's pressure doors, then we stepped out onto a boarding platform filled with wounded Lhekan soldiers. They lay on closely packed stretchers with horrific wounds and blood-soaked uniforms, many barely clinging to life. Medics moved among them doing what they could for the living and covering the faces of the dead with blood-red cloths. Looking across the platform, I saw many covered faces.

"Come," Pridak Tir said as guards took up position in front of our capsule's pressure doors, preventing the wounded from boarding.

"Why aren't they letting them on?" I asked as we hurried away.

"It waits for us."

With Intruder forces closing in on all sides, every moment counted, yet our transport just sat there, preventing the wounded from being evacuated.

"How long?"

"Until we return."

I wanted to protest, but Pridak Tir hurried off through a tunnel overflowing with stretcher cases to a polished marble hall filled with frightened civilians. The distant boom of explosions reverberated through the walls, shaking dust from the ceiling and summoning fearful cries from the refugees.

"Where are you meeting your passenger?" he asked as I caught up to him.

"At the starport. He was waiting for me to land."

"It's right above us," he said, and led me to an elevator.

A soldier tried to stop us using it, but Pridak Tir whispered to him and he let us take it up to the terminal.

The starport's roof had fallen in leaving a skeleton of twisted metal girders arching above us against a starry sky. All the lights were out and only the soft glow of two small moons revealed the utter devastation surrounding us. Lhekan bodies were strewn among the wreckage, partly buried by debris and covered in dust and ash.

"If he was here, he is gone now or dead," Pridak Tir said impatiently.

"If he's alive, he's still here," I replied, convinced the Buratu agent would have stayed close to the starport, hoping to pick up my signal. Now that I was here, I had to give him time to find me.

Leaving the safety of the elevator, I picked my way through the ruins to a broken wall. Two destroyed ground vehicles burned a short distance away, pushing back the darkness with flickering light. Beyond them, the starport's vast landing ground reached toward the horizon. The smoldering wrecks of burned-out ships stretched as far as the eye could see, not all of them Lhekan. If we'd arrived a little sooner, the *Silver Lining* would have been among them and we'd be dead or trapped on Niedarim. On the horizon was an orange glow from the fires raging around the Galisti City crater. Above the burning city, dark specks glided through the air firing energy blasts at the ground at the last surviving Lhekan soldiers.

"It is worse than I imagined," Pridak Tir whispered.

Record and encrypt, I thought, then my bionetic memory stored everything the threaded filaments in my eyes saw.

"The Galactic Forum will hear about this," I promised, determined they would see everything I saw, then a flying speck strafed the ground and a large orange fireball rolled up into the sky.

"That is a striker autac," he said, then a small four-legged shape sped across open ground in front of us, too fast to be an animal. We ducked down behind the wall and watched as it stopped and rolled the three short dorsal spines on its back from side to side. "And that is a spotter."

"I can hit it from here," I said, certain it was within range of my K7 rifle.

"No! They are the eyes of the Spawn. Thousands have been dropped all over Niedarim. If it sees us, it will summon others."

Two more spotters raced across the landing field and stopped two clicks apart, forming a triangle with the first spotter.

"They're coming!" Pridak Tir whispered fearfully, about to run.

I caught his arm and dragged him back against the wall. "Wait!"

His eyes searched the skies fearfully, then an inky shape swept down out of the darkness at tremendous speed, coming to an instantaneous stop a meter above the ground. It had the thick armored hull of an Intruder craft with a blunt, rakish bow and narrow, downsloping winglets. I'd seen that type of craft before in a TC briefing. It was a tactical command ship reserved for the most senior Spawn leaders.

Pridak Tir fixed his eyes upon it with rising terror. I thought he was going to run, giving away our position, but he pressed against the wall to hide as an angled ramp extended from the Intruder ship to the ground. A hatch slid open and eight diminutive bipeds wearing burnished battle suits with crimson ceremonial capes marched out. They formed a line at the bottom of the ramp and waited like statues, then from the eastern end of the wrecked starport terminal, a spawnwarrior in a mud-splattered battle suit appeared.

The state of his armor indicated he was no ceremonial soldier but had been in the thick of the fighting. He walked toward the command ship, followed by two floating spherical autacs, each with a rotating weapon on top and four long snaking arms at their sides. One was missing half an arm, showing they were not immune to Lhekan weapons. The other carried a slender child-like form with milky white skin and luminous green eyes.

"Reapers," Pridak Tir whispered, nodding toward the spherical autacs. "I don't recognize the alien."

"I do," I said bitterly, knowing he was Buratu and there was nothing I could do to help him.

A Spawn female appeared in the ship's open hatchway. She was taller than the male warriors and wore a dark red bodysuit affixed with silver decorations. A platinum headpiece swept back over the streamlined ridges of her head and the soft blue aura of a personal shield surrounded her. She carried no weapons, wore no armor, although her bearing was regal and her presence commanding.

She was a matriarch, a Spawn queen who'd chemically imprinted the warriors, making them slaves to her will. Izin had suffered such a fate at the hands of another matriarch he'd been utterly powerless to resist. Only her death had freed him. It was an evolutionary twist that made domination an integral part of their nature and why the One Spawn were so lacking in love.

The matriarch strode down the ramp, followed by a shiny, spherical reaper. I ramped up my listener's sensitivity as the mud-splattered spawnwarrior stopped before her and his reaper dropped the prisoner at her feet. The Buratu operative lay motionless in the mud, a dark bruise on his face and his clothes torn, but no sign of blood. The spawnwarrior touched the inside of his forearm and a shimmer rolled down around the prisoner, releasing him.

The Buratu sat up warily, fixing his gaze upon the female. "I am a citizen of the Buratu Sovereignty," he declared. "I demand you release me."

She ignored his plea and opened her hand. A golden

hair-like thread floated into the air and glided toward him. When it was close, it darted at his face, but he rolled away with surprising speed. One of the ceremonial guards tried to grab him, but he dodged out of reach, avoided one of the reaper's tentacled arms and leaped at the Spawn queen.

She made no attempt to evade as her personal reaper snatched the Buratu agent out of the air with a snaking arm before he could reach her. Its arm enveloped him, holding him steady in the air as the tiny golden thread speared into the side of his head and vanished. The Buratu agent screamed as the filament burrowed into his brain, then he relaxed and the reaper lowered him to the ground.

"I am Siraksha Garlen-Jor Vidah'ra of the Siraksha Clan Majestic," the Spawn Queen said. "Return to me what you have stolen."

The Buratu's face contorted and his eyes flitted wildly as he fought to resist the golden thread. "I…am…Buratu."

"Is the synapsizer functioning correctly?" Vidah'ra asked, then one of the burnished metal spawnwarriors scanned the prisoner.

"Yes, Matriarch. He is resisting."

"How?"

"Buratu have a tri-segmented cortex."

Vidah'ra turned back to the prisoner. "If you return what you have stolen, I will release you."

The Buratu's jaw clenched tightly and his luminous green eyes squinted with pain. "I have…stolen…nothing."

Vidah'ra motioned impatiently to her personal reaper. It wrapped a snaking arm around the Buratu's chest, radiating force lines into his body. The little humanoid spasmed, suppressing a scream, then the reaper released its grip, dropping him at her feet.

"Would you rather I take you to my ship?" Vidah'ra

asked, glancing up at the night sky

"You...will...fail," he said defiantly.

Vidah'ra stared at him, displeased by his resistance, then turned to the spawnwarrior who'd captured him. "You searched the area?"

"Thoroughly Matriarch."

"And you found nothing?"

"No my Queen."

"He must have disposed of it. Search again. I will send forces to assist you."

"At once." The spawnwarrior turned and launched himself into the air with a power leap that carried him out of sight beyond the terminal. His two reapers sped after him in close formation, skimming the ground, while Vidah'ra surveyed the destruction she'd wrought on the hapless Lhekan homeworld, clearly dissatisfied.

"Bring him," she ordered at last, and strode up the ramp into the ship.

Her escort reaper scooped the Buratu off the ground and followed her inside, then the ceremonial guard did the same. When they were all aboard, the hatch sealed and the command ship shot straight up into the night sky in a streak of light.

"What did she say?" Pridak Tir asked.

"I don't know," I lied, certain it was only a matter of time before the gallant little Buratu revealed all he knew to the Spawn Queen, including his intention to rendezvous with a human ship. With my TC mission a complete failure and the Buratu agent about to blow my cover, it wouldn't be long before the spawnship came looking for me. "Let's go."

I took a step toward the elevator and stopped as a small shape in the shadows rolled its dorsal spines from side to side. I raised my rifle to blast it, but Pridak Tir caught the barrel.

"Don't shoot," he whispered. "It will leave if we're no threat."

The spotter darted across the debris-strewn floor, then I wrenched my rifle free of the Lhekan's grip and fired a burst that went wide. The tiny autac leaped onto a girder hanging from the skeletal structure above the floor, pausing long enough to roll its spines toward me, then I drilled it with another burst, sending its shattered body spinning into the darkness.

"You fool!" Pridak Tir declared. "They will come now."

"It saw I was human."

The Lhekan wavered. "And humans are close to the Tau Cetins."

"Yes." As soon as the Buratu agent cracked, they'd know I was the one he was waiting for.

We started back through the wrecked terminal, then a dark mass came hurtling silently down out of the night sky. It crashed through the partially collapsed roof into the floor, burying itself deep in the ground. The impact shockwave hurled us both into the air as teetering girders collapsed and a thick dust cloud rolled over us.

"Run!" Pridak Tir spluttered, coughing as he scrambled to his feet and headed for the elevator.

With my ears ringing, I scooped up my K7 and stumbled after him. At the elevator, I peered back through the thinning dust cloud at a craterous hole in the floor, charred black and smoking from the impact.

"What was that?" I asked

"A plunger," Pridak Tir replied, repeatedly tapping the control panel with his fingertips. "It's an orbital assault vehicle."

I aimed my rifle's spectral targeter at the crater. It revealed the ghostly heat signature of a round nosed, cylindrical craft at the bottom of a vertical shaft, surprisingly intact after the hard landing. A cold spot appeared in its round stern as a hatch irised open and a skinny bipedal autac climbed out, silhouetted against the plunger's thermal glow. More followed, fanning out across its stern.

"They're massing," I said, certain we had only moments before they came swarming up out of their hole.

I aimed my K7 at the lip of the crater, about to drop a frag grenade on them when Pridak Tir snapped, "Your primitive weapon will be ineffective against them."

I hesitated as my finger hovered over the firing surface. If they had personal contour shields, a simple frag grenade wouldn't slow them down, so I shifted my aim to a cracked wall precariously holding up the remains of the ceiling and popped off three grenades from the under-barrel launcher. They landed at the foot of the wall and exploded in succession, knocking its base back, tearing it free.

The massive structure teetered and fell sideways as angular autac sensor heads peeked above the lip of the crater, scouting the terminal. In a whoosh of air and dust, the huge slab pancaked onto the plunger hole bringing an avalanche of roof girders and broken masonry with it. The autacs at the edge of the crater were crushed while those below were trapped beneath tons of rubble. When the dust cleared, only a single autac arm was visible reaching out from beneath the slab, its fingers twitching helplessly.

Pridak Tir stopped tapping the elevator panel in surprise. "You buried them."

"I gave them digging practice." It was a taste of what the Spawn could expect during their occupation of Niedarim.

The wall slab shuddered as the autacs below tried lifting it off the plunger hole, then Pridak Tir said, "That won't hold them long."

"No, it won't," I agreed, then the elevator door opened and we rode down to the underground terminal.

Pridak Tir spoke to an officer, warning him a plunger had landed, then we hurried back to the vactube platform. I stopped at our transport's pressure doors and glanced at the wounded soldiers pressed together along the platform.

"What about them?" I asked.

"Forget them," the Lhekan snapped with callous disregard for his own people. "We must go."

He stepped aboard while I backed away from the doors, refusing to get on. "No."

I turned to the rows of wounded Lhekans and set my translator's volume to maximum. "We'll take as many of you as we can. Get aboard, now!"

"What are you doing?" he demanded, stepping back onto the platform. "We don't have time for this."

"We can take hundreds," I said, then the muted thuds of multiple plunger impacts sounded from above as the Spawn arrived in force. "They're coming!" I yelled at the soldiers. "Hurry!"

Weary and wounded Lhekan fighters began limping onto the transport. Those too weak to walk were dragged or carried by their comrades while Pridak Tir glowered at me.

"We have a deal," he said.

I reset my translator volume to low. "And I'll honor it, once they're aboard," I replied, then I felt the press of a Lhekan hand weapon in my side.

"Get on the transport, Kade! We have to go now. Yours is the only ship left."

I looked down at his weapon in disgust. "That's right. And if you shoot me, who's going to fly it?"

He cursed under his breath, words neither my translator headset or my threading's linguistic upgrade understood, then he pocketed his weapon and roughly dragged the wounded aboard. When the transport was almost full, the whine of energy weapons and the thunder of explosions echoed onto the platform as the Spawn broke through into the tunnels and the Lhekan rear guard opened fire.

The growing roar of battle galvanized the wounded to move faster, then when the transport was full, Pridak Tir demanded, "Now can we leave?"

"Yeah," I said and we squeezed aboard, leaving hundreds more behind.

Explosions and the terrified screams of civilians filled the boarding platform as the Spawn reached the great hall, then our transport's doors sealed, silencing the sounds of battle. The soldiers left behind, knowing the One Spawn would soon be upon them, readied their weapons as flashes lit up the access tunnels. At the far end of the platform, Lhekan troops fired into a passageway, then our capsule disconnected from the door locks and we accelerated out of the station, leaving them to their fate.

We stood pressed by the wounded against the doors as our transport raced away at hypersonic velocity. I could barely look at Pridak Tir, knowing how ready he was to abandon his own people to save himself.

He whispered into a small communicator, keeping his hand over his mouth so my translator couldn't pick up what he was saying. I assumed he was telling his wife we were coming back and to be ready.

When he finished, he pocketed his communicator and whispered angrily, "You could have ruined everything."

I ignored him and looked over the wounded soldiers squeezed into our transport, knowing they'd all be dead now if it had been up to him. A deal was a deal and he'd get his ticket to freedom, but I'd rather have taken the lowliest soldier there than a coward like Pridak Tir.

* * * *

When we reached Firel City station, we found it even more crowded with refugees than when we'd left, all desperate to escape into the long disused, subterranean under cities. Fresh soldiers wearing spotless body armor emblazoned with a circular golden crest kept the loading platform beside our transport clear. They showed no signs of having been in battle, although the civilians and the less polished local militia treated them with deference. At the end of the loading platform was a white transport with dark windows adorned with the same circular golden crest as the newly arrived soldiers.

When we alighted, Pridak Tir yelled at a nearby officer to unload the wounded we'd brought with us, then led me along the platform toward the white transport.

"The buggy's that way?" I said, pointing in the opposite direction.

"Come." He pulled me roughly by the arm to a gold crested soldier with five golden triangles on his collar. "This is Kade, captain of the human ship," he said and turned to me. "This is Marshal Narl, commander of the Lhekan Royal Guard."

The Marshal looked me up and down uncertainly. "Can he be trusted?"

"He is reckless and aggressive, but…" he looked back at the soldiers being unloaded from our transport, "he insisted on rescuing our wounded."

Marshal Narl glanced at the injured soldiers, then at me. "How close is your ship?"

"It's in the grain loader near the center of the city."

He considered my answer carefully. "How certain are you the One Spawn have not detected your ship?"

"Not at all."

"Can you launch without being seen?"

"Not if the spawnship's overhead."

Marshall Narl hesitated as if the weight of Niedarim was on his narrow shoulders, then he touched a silver disk in his ear. "Bring them."

The white transport's pressure door slid open and a Lhekan male in a dazzling gold, red and yellow suit emerged. He had a web of platinum threads sewn through his massive edifice of hair and he carried a jeweled baton inlaid with gold and silver. Every Lhekan soldier in the terminal snapped to attention as one while the wounded sat up respectfully or struggled to their feet.

He was followed by a female in a plain white suit, wearing no jewelry, and their three children dressed in flamboyantly bright colors. Behind them came a tall, slender humanoid with soft blue skin and piercing dark blue eyes. She was an Uvo, a race which Earth knew almost nothing of. She had a large, gently ridged and hairless head, refined facial features and supple arms that ended in long, delicate fingers. She wore a willowy light green silken robe that flowed around her as she glided serenely after the Lhekans.

Marshal Narl saluted the Lhekan peacock with crossed palms up. "Suzerain. This is the captain of the Earth ship I told you about."

The golden peacock studied me uncertainly. "Are you sure his vessel will suffice?"

"There is no other, Highness."

"Is it fast?"

"No Highness, it is not."

"Is it a combat vessel?

"No my Liege, but it did evade detection by the One Spawn."

"So far," I added warily.

The Suzerain's reluctance was obvious, but he had no other choices. "Very well."

Pridak Tir made the crossed palms salutation to his sovereign, then turned to me. "Captain Kade, this is his Highness Alif Kinar Osil the One Hundred and Third, Esteemed of the Ascended and Suzerain of the Lhekan League. He and his family are the passengers you agreed to take off-world."

"*His* family?" I said. "What about your family?"

"We will remain here in the undercity."

"It is imperative Intruder forces do not capture the Suzerain," Marshal Narl explained. "They would make a puppet of him and our people would lose hope."

I suddenly realized Pridak Tir had been in a hurry to leave Galisti, not to save himself, but to ensure his civilization's leader escaped Niedarim.

The Suzerain motioned for his wife and three sons to come closer. "You agree to transport my family and I off-world?"

"Yes, but I can't guarantee your safety," I said, certain both Lena and the Tau Cetins would have ordered me to take them if they were here.

"No one can," he replied.

"If the Spawn cannot capture the Suzerain," Marshal Narl explained, "they will try to kill him, leaving our people without a leader."

I nodded, glancing uncertainly at the graceful Uvo hanging back behind his wife and children. "Am I taking five or six?"

Pridak Tir saw my confusion. "Highness, Captain Kade agreed to transport five passengers. That was the number your equerry requested."

"Arleen Torel has decided to come with us," the Suzerain said.

"Is she an ambassador?" I asked.

"She is a valued member of my royal retinue," he replied, "and under my personal protection."

The Uvo stepped forward, adding in perfect Unionspeak. "I am the children's tutor and governess."

"She would be in grave danger if captured by the One Spawn," the Suzerain added.

"Why? What do they want with a governess?" I asked.

"They have long desired to take one of my kind a prisoner, to study," Arleen replied.

"Hmm…I can take six, but you've got to understand, I can't outrun a spawnship."

"You won't have to," the Marshal said. "Our remaining fighters will make one last attack when you launch. They will disrupt the spawnship's sensors long enough for you to escape."

He was sending them on a suicide mission, one I hoped would not be in vain.

I turned to the Suzerain. "Where do you want to go?"

He said nothing but looked to the Marshal as if tongue-tied.

"We have a command cruiser in deep space," Marshal Narl said. "It will transport the royal family to one of our distant colonies to establish a government in exile." He turned to the Suzerain. "If you are ready, Highness, we will escort you to the human ship."

Alif Kinar Osil the One Hundred and Third motioned with a flick of his fingers to proceed, then the Marshal led us through the station to the buggy. Two large, armored vehicles waited beside it. They were equipped with heavy weapons on swivel turrets and were manned by royal guardsmen.

"Take them to the Firel Grain Handling Center," Marshal Narl ordered, then the escort commander gave a Lhekan salute and climbed aboard the lead vehicle.

I opened the buggy's side door. "Lhekans in the back, Uvos in front," I said, allocating seats by legroom, not rank.

The Suzerain hesitated, giving Arleen a silent look.

"His Majesty would prefer to ride in the armored vehicles," she said on his behalf.

The black vehicles were thickly armored hovertanks with the Suzerain's circular golden crest painted on their sides, designating them as targets. If we got cornered, they'd be lumbering death traps.

"Your choice, Highness, but this is faster," I said, jabbing my thumb at the buggy. "If we get attacked, I won't be waiting for you."

He stiffened, unused to being addressed with such informality. "I accept your suggestion, Captain Kade," he said, then he and his family climbed aboard the buggy.

I turned to Pridak Tir waiting to one side, having changed my mind about him. "I can take your family."

"No. Once my wife and children are safe in the undercity, I will join my cohort."

"You're military?"

"I was once commander Third Contingent, Lhekan Royal Guard," he said simply. "Now, I serve in the citizen militia."

I should have known. He was no corrupt bureaucrat, but a plant designed to feed the EIS whatever the Lhekans wanted us to know. I looked at him with newfound respect, realizing he was about to fight an underground tunnel war he had little chance of winning and that made him something else entirely. It made him a patriot.

"Good luck," I said wanting to shake his hand, but aware it was a custom unknown to his people.

"Thank you, Kade. I regret we could not save your Buratu friend."

"Me too," I replied and climbed into the buggy beside the Uvo.

We followed the first guard vehicle up to ground level while the second fell in behind us a little too close for comfort. It led us through narrow streets awash with shallow water, staying under aqueducts and elevated freeways as much as possible to hide our movements from prying eyes orbiting the planet. Several times abandoned ground vehicles blocked our way, but rather than go around, the lead tank simply drove into them without stopping, tossing them aside like toys.

"Can't they go faster?" I demanded impatiently, glancing apprehensively through the buggy's transparent canopy at the sky.

"Not in these narrow streets," the Suzerain said.

The grain loader appeared in the distance, barely four clicks away, then the lead tank fired a stream of energy tracer at the road ahead. A tiny autac leaped into the air and landed on a window sill three levels up, then the tank behind us fired a burst that shredded the spotter before it could jump away.

"They've found us," Arleen Torel said calmly.

The lead tank stopped while its cannon swiveled left and right. Two guardsmen jumped out with long-barreled weapons and ran forward along either side of the street.

"No, don't stop!" I shouted in frustration.

"They must clear the way," the Suzerain explained.

"Too slow," I complained, jamming my hand on the claxon, trying to get the hovering pillbox ahead of us to move, but it just sat there scanning for targets. "They're going to get us killed."

"The Lhekans do not lack courage, Captain Kade, but they are methodical and cautious," Arleen said as the two guardsmen took forever to check the cross street.

When the guardsmen decided it was safe, one waved for us to advance. The lead tank moved forward to pick up the soldiers. They backed toward it, covering the street with their guns, then a brilliant white blast flashed down out of the sky and the tank exploded, hurling the guardsmen against the nearby buildings. The hovertank was instantly engulfed in flames as a sleek Intruder ground attack craft flew above us at high speed. The tank behind us opened fire, but the attack craft banked sharply away over the rooftops, out of sight.

The rear tank reversed toward a side street expecting us to follow, but driving that slow was my idea of stupid. I fed power to the wheels, sending the buggy lurching toward the gap between the wrecked hovertank and a building.

"What are you doing?" the Suzerain demanded,

glancing back at the second tank.

"Getting out of here," I said, narrowly avoiding the flames from the burning tank as we squeezed passed it.

"You're leaving the escort behind," he declared.

"I don't like standing still when I'm getting shot at."

We cleared the burning wreck as the Intruder strike craft dived into the narrow canyon between the buildings and raked where we'd been only moments before. The rear hovertank returned fired, but the Intruder craft was too fast. It climbed, rolling away as the second tank started after us, firing over our heads, anticipating the strike craft's next run.

I pushed the throttles fully forward, sending the big-wheeled buggy slicing through the shallow water, hurling spray at the buildings on either side. Behind us, the second armored vehicle crashed through the gap between the burning tank and the building, slamming the wreck into the far wall.

Directly ahead of us, an energy blast shattered an elevated freeway three stories up, sending huge masonry slabs splashing onto the road. The Intruder craft dived through the smoke, firing continuously, forcing me to swerve into the cross street under the freeway. Energy blasts struck the road behind us as the second hovertank charged after us, filling the sky with glowing tracer. The Intruder craft evaded the Lhekan blasts with a spiraling roll and banked away with a burst of speed.

"Wait for the escort!" the Suzerain ordered.

"They know where we're headed," I said, fighting to keep control of the buggy as we aquaplaned through axle-deep water beneath the elevated freeway.

The hovertank slewed around the corner behind us, smashed into a wall and plowed on through deepening water, trying to keep up. Behind it, the Intruder craft performed a tight vertical loop and dived at the elevated freeway above us, firing continuously. Giant slabs rained down ahead of us, forcing me to swerve as spray broke over the buggy's dome while the hovertank crashed through fallen freeway slabs, shattering them to pieces.

Above us, the Intruder craft nosed down and fired through a collapsed section of freeway, blasting the hovertank apart. Flaming debris flew in all directions, then the strike craft flew low over us and turned away to position for another run.

"That's why I don't wait," I said grimly as the Suzerain and his wife looked back in silence at the burning hovertank, then a blast hit a building ahead, collapsing it onto the road. I swerved sharply to avoid being crushed, turning into another side street that suddenly angled up and carried us onto the freeway.

"Oh ho," I said as the strike craft circled for another attack.

"They can see us," Arleen said calmly, craning her neck to watch the attack craft.

"No kidding," I said, looking for a way down.

An aqueduct crossed the freeway ahead, and beyond it, an off-ramp came into view. I accelerated hard for the exit as the attack craft dived down between the white-walled buildings, strafing the road ahead of us. Suddenly, a long section of freeway collapsed before us, cutting us off from the exit.

"Hold on!" I yelled, steering for the precipice as the strike craft raced up behind us.

"Stop you fool!" the Suzerain ordered, then we hurtled off the elevated freeway's ragged edge.

His wife and children screamed in terror while Arleen Torel grabbed her seat with both hands, but said nothing. The strike craft fired as we fell through the air, but its energy blasts flashed above the buggy's transparent dome, then our big wheels splashed down into a deep pool. Muddy water washed over the buggy's dome as the Intruder craft raced above us and crashed into the aqueduct above the freeway, unable to pull up in time. Through the brown water, we saw a fiery orange flash, then as we bobbed to the surface, flaming wreckage rained down into the lake.

"You are insane," the Suzerain declared angrily. "Take us back, immediately!"

"Your guards are dead," I said, throttling down until the buggy's big wheels were moving slowly enough to swim us across the lake toward a rubble weir. A bombed-out building had collapsed onto the road, forming a dam that had filled with water. "If you want to join them, go ahead. There's the door."

Alif Kinar Osil the One Hundred and Third bristled. "Do you know whom you address, human?"

"I do, that's why I'm giving you a choice," I replied as we paddled past the burning tail of the Intruder craft protruding from the lake.

"My liege," Arleen said as the buggy's wheels touched solid ground and we climbed out of the water. "I suggest you trust him."

He gave her a surprised look. "Why should I? He nearly killed us all."

"Yes, but he is correct. If you go back now, you will die or they will use you to enslave your people." She glanced meaningfully at the wrecked strike craft in the lake. "And he did save our lives."

"You're damn right I did," I said, glad there was at least one person on this planet with some sense.

The Suzerain exchanged a long look with his wife, then sat back in his chair. "Very well. Take us to your ship," he said like he was doing me a favor.

I gave Arleen Torel an approving nod and drove onto the road. We stayed under the aqueduct for several blocks, using it to hide from the sky, then I turned into a side street and headed toward the large white grain handling structure now visible in the distance.

"My ship's in there," I said nodding toward it, then a small four-legged shape darted out of a side street in front of us. I slammed the throttles forward, running the spotter down and crushing it beneath the buggy's big wheels.

"It had time to call for assistance," Arleen said.

I swerved under an elevated road that ran past the grain loader to get out of sight, then set the buggy's communication's range to minimum. "Silver Lining, do not acknowledge. Prep for immediate launch."

A section of the elevated road exploded as a dark mass smashed through it and buried itself in the ground. I slammed on the brakes, skidding through shallow water into a shockwave of dust and dirt blasting out from the impact point. We came to a stop, blinded by a roiling brown cloud, then one of the Suzerain's children pointed at the water outside.

"Look, papa," he said as the water flowed forward, draining into the plunger hole.

"How do they survive that?" I wondered aloud, peering ahead.

"Ultra-adaptive cellular acceleration fields," Arleen Torel explained.

"I wouldn't want to land that way," I said, then slammed the buggy into reverse and raced back out of the dust into clear air.

"The grain center is that way," the Suzerain said, pointing forward.

"We won't make it," I said, certain an army of autacs were about to come storming up out of the plunger hole. I reversed into the first side street, hoping we could go around, but it was a dead end. I backed up, then grabbed my K7.

"Wait here," I ordered and opened the door.

"You cannot fight them alone," the Suzerain said.

I glanced at Arleen who, considering our narrow escape, was surprisingly unruffled. "Don't let them leave."

I jumped out and ran to the corner of the building for a look. Spotters were leaping out of the plunger hole and scampering through shallow water to higher ground, then a spherical reaper, dripping with water, floated up from below, its cannon rotating slowly searching for targets as its four long snaking metal arms writhed through the air.

I pulled back behind the wall as it fired an energy blast across the street into the building opposite, attracted by the movement of a bird on a windowsill. The front wall collapsed in an avalanche of broken masonry, rooftop trees, and dark soil. Not daring to show my face again, I ran back to the buggy and took up a firing position behind its front wheel.

"We're trapped," I said through the open driver's side door.

The Suzerain leaned toward me and whispered. "Do not let them take me alive, Captain Kade."

I glanced uncertainly at his wife and children, knowing they would see. "I can't do that."

His wife extended her hand. "Give me your small gun. I will do it to protect the children," she said, exchanging a look of agreement with her husband.

"I am only Suzerain while I live," he explained.

"But they'll capture your children," I said.

Arleen seeing my mistake, said, "The Suzerain of the Lhekan League is not a hereditary monarch. He is the head of state for a collection of autonomous worlds, randomly selected from citizens outside of government and the military. His children are not his heirs."

"So if dies…?"

"Another will be chosen," Arleen explained. "Only citizens who do not seek power are eligible to rule, while those who desire power are forever prevented from holding it."

"You see, Captain Kade," the Suzerain added, "if I am dead, my children are of no value to the Spawn."

Having no desire to kill an overdressed alien with bad hair while his children watched, I handed my P-50 to his wife, hoping she wouldn't have to use it.

I returned to my firing position behind the wheel, then a spotter scurried past the end of the street. I took aim as it turned toward us, but before I could fire, a heavy projectile struck the tiny autac side on, hurling its crumpled metal body across the road in a shower of short-circuiting sparks. It looked like the work of a heavy sniper round, the kind Izin specialized in, but I'd told him not to leave the ship and he never disobeyed a direct order–unless he chose to.

I jumped into the buggy and yelled into my communicator. "Izin, get out of here, now!"

"What is it?" the Suzerain asked.

"Mutiny," I replied, then the spherical reaper floated into view at the end of the street and turned its cannon toward us. "Oh ho."

The reaper was surrounded by the soft blue aura of a shield that neither my K7 nor Izin's sniper rifle could penetrate. I slammed the buggy into a tight reverse turn as the reaper fired. A burst of energy blasts flashed in front of the buggy's transparent dome, shattering a nearby building as we lurched backward. The reaper's cannon swiveled after us, then as we ran out of road, three streams of kinetic tracer coming from beyond the plunger hole punched through the reaper's shield, shredding its spherical hull. It exploded and fell onto the road in flames.

"Those weren't energy weapons," the Uvo said surprised.

"No, they weren't," I agreed with annoyance.

She turned to me curiously. "They were static force projectiles."

Tau Cetin designed snakehead killers to be precise, fired from multiple automatic weapons.

"Looks like it," I agreed as I realized what Lena had meant when she'd said her super soldiers had the latest weaponry.

"We'd heard the Tau Cetins had been accused of giving you restricted technology," Arleen said, "although we did not believe it."

"They gave us nothing."

She studied my face as if it revealed all. "That is not true. The Tau Cetins broke Forum transfer protocols…for humans?" she said slowly, scarcely able to believe the once-revered custodians of galactic law would do such a thing for the lowliest interstellar civilization in the galaxy.

"Prove it," I said, then all hell broke loose.

The chatter of automatic weapons and the shriek of Intruder energy blasts assaulted our ears, then a thunderous explosion sent gale-force winds roaring over us. The shockwave blew out the windows of every building, sent freeway masonry blocks bouncing past our dead end street like toys and hurled dust and black smoke high into the air above the plunger hole. When the wind faded, a metallic leg fell from the sky and landed close to the buggy, startling the children. Wide eyed, they watched autac limbs and smoking metal rain down all around us while a billowing black cloud rolled down street.

The metal hailstorm ended in an eerie silence, then we heard the splash of footsteps through shallow water approaching. A man emerged from the dark cloud wearing full body armor and casually balancing an assault rifle larger than my K7 on his shoulder.

"Who's that?" the Suzerain asked.

"Nobody," I replied cryptically.

Dietz pushed his combat helmet's visor up and yelled, "What are you waiting for, Kade?" He jabbed his thumb over his shoulder toward the grain loader. "Haul ass." Not waiting for my response, he turned and walked back into the cloud.

"Where are the Spawn?" the Suzerain asked, shocked at Dietz's casual disregard for their presence.

"Dead," I replied. "All dead."

"That's impossible," he declared, surveying the autac remains littering the road, falling into a shocked silence as he realized it was true.

I drove forward into the thinning cloud, past a scorched black crater that had been the plunger hole. Its sides were fused like black glass and shimmered with heat, and thick black smoke and steam boiled up from the burning assault lander at the bottom. Scattered around the crater were pieces of melted and burning metal, some from the lander, some from dismembered autacs.

"What kind of weapon does that?" the Suzerain asked aghast.

"I don't know," I replied, and this time Arleen knew I was telling the truth.

Beyond the plunger hole was a dead spawnwarrior lying face down in shallow water, his battle armor riddled with bloodied holes. The five Lhekans studied the grizzly scene with hatred, while Arleen looked on with pity and pain.

Ahead of us, six super soldiers and a tamph jogged across the parking area toward the grain loader. Izin carried his long-barreled sniper rifle in one hand while Dietz's team kept their eyes peeled and their weapons level, ready for more Spawn to appear.

The Suzerain studied their discipline and speed as they vanished into the grain facility. He didn't know they were zygote constructs engineered to fight Intruders with a militarized version of Lena's psionic abilities, but he'd seen what they could do.

"Do the Tau Cetins know what your soldiers are capable of?" he asked.

"Hell no," I replied, "and if I get you out of here in one piece, you won't tell them. You won't tell anyone. Understood?" I turned to him, waiting for his answer, wondering what I'd do if he refused.

"You have my word, Captain Kade, and that of my family." He turned to his wife and children with a look that ensured they understood it was a royal decree.

"That includes you," I said to Arleen.

"The Uvo do no harm," she replied. "We share no secrets. We will not reveal the new-found violence of your species."

Hoping that meant Izin and Dietz hadn't thrown away years of secrecy for nothing, I followed them into the loader facility. The Suzerain leaned forward as I drove toward the ship.

"Captain Kade," he said somberly, "do not think badly of us because of the ease of our defeat. We are not warriors. Not like the One Spawn." He looked at the K7 rifle beside me thoughtfully, then took my P-50 pistol from his wife and handed it to me. "Not like you."

"What happened here isn't your fault," I said, sliding the P-50 into its holster.

He placed his hand on my shoulder. "Will you help us? Will you help my people?"

I turned to him in surprise. He wasn't asking for my help, but for a human army to liberate his conquered homeworld. I was dumbstruck. Mankind was the youngest and weakest interstellar civilization in the galaxy, considered by many to be primitive barbarians. We didn't figure in galactic affairs, had no power to influence events, yet he thought we could free his people. It was madness.

"I wish we could," I said, fearing we couldn't even save ourselves.

When we reached the *Silver Lining*, I drove up the ramp and parked on the lower cargo deck, certain it wouldn't be long before the Spawn came to investigate the fate of the plunger. The Suzerain and his party climbed out of the buggy while Dietz and his team stowed their weapons in the VRS containers holding the shunter spares for Kota.

I motioned the Suzerain and his retinue toward the crew elevator, then pulled Dietz aside.

"That was stupid," I said in a low tone so his team wouldn't hear. "If you'd been killed, Windfall would've been scrubbed."

He peeled off his body armor off unconcerned. "You endangered the mission, Kade, not me."

"While you're on this ship, you obey my orders."

"Your pet tamph overruled your orders. He unlocked the container, told me to bring you back. You can thank me later."

I'd have to have a word with Izin, but that didn't excuse Dietz's recklessness. "Suppose your weapons were ineffective against Intruder shields?"

Dietz snatched a black rifle off the rack beside him. It was similar to my K7, only bigger.

"K8 Multi Environment Combat rifle." He ejected the magazine and showed me the load. Instead of the standard six-millimeter round my K7 used, his weapon fired eight-millimeter rounds with a thin purple band at the base. "Special ammo, like nothing you've ever seen before. Punches through any shield."

I drew my P-50 and ejected the clip, showing Dietz it was loaded with the same purple banded, eight-mil ammo he was so proud of. Snakehead killers had been secretly designed for us by the Tau Cetins to give us a weapon that could pierce Mataron contour shields. They were incredibly expensive and difficult to produce, yet Dietz and his trigger happy grunts had fired them off like training rounds.

"I was killing snakeheads with these things while you were still in boot camp."

He grunted, more impressed by the idea of shooting Matarons than the ammo itself, then he slammed the mag back into the rifle and opened the under-barrel launcher, revealing a short projectile, thicker than a standard frag grenade.

"You got these?" he asked.

"What is it?"

"One-milligram novarium warhead in a whoop-ass, shield penetrating durillium jacket."

"Novarium!" I exclaimed.

It was the rarest element in the universe, couldn't be synthesized, could only be created by a supernova explosion and it powered all our energy plants. Without it, there'd be no interstellar travel. For more than two thousand years, mankind had survived on a trickle of the stuff gifted to us by the Tau Cetins, although one look at Dietz's N-grenade convinced me we'd broken that deal and put our provisional status with the Galactic Forum at risk.

"I noved the Spawn lander with this bad boy."

I assumed 'nove' was grunt slang for blasting a target with a novarium weapon.

"How many you got?" I asked.

"Enough to win a small war. Apparently, we've got a whole lot more of this N-stuff than anyone knows."

That was my doing. A couple of years ago I'd discovered the location of a novarium asteroid in the interstellar void, way beyond the limits of human Mapped Space, along with the astrographics to get there. I thought we'd use it to power our ships, not make weapons, but I saw now that was naive.

"Good job, Dietz, now the Spawn know we've got novarium weapons," I said sarcastically, certain they'd scan the area and have it figured out by sunset.

"They were going to find out sooner or later. Now they'll think twice before hitting us."

"Or they'll exterminate us from orbit before we become a nuisance," I snapped. "I suppose Izin saw it all?"

"He was on overwatch," Dietz said, confirming Izin now knew his guns for hire had weapons no merc had any right to. He placed his rifle back in the rack and peeled off his body armor. It was lighter than I expected, top quality in its class, but we had better.

"Why aren't you wearing the heavy stuff?" I asked.

"We need to move fast."

"Right, because you know when to duck." It was what another super soldier had told me once before.

"Something like that," he said slowly as he realized I knew he was engineered with a sixth sense that gave him a psionic survival instinct. It was why he'd been able to flatten Sledge the Giant with his eyes closed, why his kind were so hard to kill.

"Stay away from our guests and don't answer Izin's questions. He's the curious type."

Dietz nodded indifferently, then I joined the Lhekan royals and Arleen on the crew elevator. I wanted to give Izin both barrels for disobeying my orders, but there wasn't time. When we passed engineering, the Suzerain spotted Izin at his chief engineer's console.

"You *do* have Spawn aboard," he said with alarm. "I thought I saw one outside but assumed I was mistaken."

"He's not Spawn, he's a tamph, a terrestrial amphibian from Earth. Same species, but different."

"No matter how loyal you think he is," Arleen said softly, "he can be imprinted by their matriarchs and turned against you."

"Only if they get close to him," I replied, well aware of the danger, certain Izin would never let that happen again. When we reached the command deck, I pointed to the empty officer's quarters astern. "You can bunk down there."

"I have the coordinates for the rendezvous," Arleen said.

"You come with me," I said, leaving the Lhekans to find their own way to their quarters astern while Arleen and I went forward. "Is the rendezvous point far?"

"Only a few light years."

"Good. The sooner you're all off my ship, the better," I said, uncomfortably aware they made us a target. When we entered the bridge, I motioned her to the acceleration couch beside mine and made the introductions. "Arleen Torel, Jase Logan, the second-best pilot on this ship."

Jase greeted her with a curious look. "Prelaunch is complete."

"Any sign of that spawnship?" I asked, sliding onto my couch and activating my console.

"Nothing on passives."

"The Lhekans are going to run interference for us, but they don't have much left and our trigger happy friends in the cargo hold just made us a bunch of enemies."

I powered the thrusters, got the *Silver Lining* into the air and heading for the open side of the facility. The waterfall had dried up and late afternoon sunshine was now beaming in.

"Captain," Izin's voice sounded over the intercom, "I have an access port malfunction at frame fifty-one."

"Is the hull sealed?" I asked, hoping it wasn't going to stop us getting clear of Niedarim.

"Yes, Captain. Internal pressure is steady."

"OK, send a hull crawler to fix it."

Jase smiled and shook his head. "Next he'll be polishing the sensor masts."

"I heard that," Izin's voice declared.

The *Silver Lining* neared daylight, then the giant building's ceiling exploded behind us as a plunger smashed through the roof and buried itself in the floor.

"We got company," Jase declared, throwing an image of the dust shrouded plunger hole onto the bridge screen.

I fed power to the main engines, blasting the grain loaders with our backwash and launching the ship out into sunshine. The moment we cleared the building, I stood her on her tail and headed for space. Plungers were hurtling down out of the sky all around us for twenty clicks. Their spread indicated the Spawn didn't know where we were while their numbers showed a determination to avenge their defeat at the hands of our psionic gunslingers.

"That didn't take long," I said, surprised how quickly the Spawn counter-attack had come.

"The One Spawn do not accept defeat lightly," Arleen said.

Internal acceleration fields kept us oriented to the deck at one gravity while our six engines pushed us toward space at twenty times that, producing a long glowing comet tail pointing down to Firel City. We climbed vertically as plungers crash-landed around the city center hurling dust plumes into the air, then all across Niedarim's surface, Lhekan fighters launched from their hiding places and climbed much faster than us toward a battle they knew they couldn't win.

When the air thinned and the darkness of space appeared, five Intruder craft began firing down at the tiny points of light streaking toward them. Tiny explosions twinkled above the atmosphere as the fighters exploded, doing little damage, but buying us time.

"What are those things?" Jase asked. "They're tearing the fighters apart."

"Autac interdictors," Arleen explained, "launched by the spawnship."

"Will they follow us?" I asked.

"They are capable of interstellar travel, although they usually remain linked to the Command Nexus, the artificial intelligence that operates the spawnship and coordinates its operations."

"So where is it?" Jase wondered aloud, looking for the spawnship.

"Can you detect antiprotons?" Arleen asked.

"Sure," he replied. "Why would we want to?"

"Intruder shields emit them after high energy interactions. If the spawnship is under attack, antiprotons from its shields will spiral along Niedarim's magnetic field lines to us, revealing its location."

Jase looked impressed and reset the sensors.

"You know a lot about spawnships for a governess," I said, angling the bow ninety degrees to the ecliptic, aiming for a clean bubble straight up out of the system as soon as we cleared Niedarim's gravity well.

"The Uvo have studied the One Spawn for millennia," she said simply.

"I'm detecting antiprotons," Jase said, "coming across the equator."

"It's a ghost image from the other side of the planet," Arleen explained. "When it vanishes, the spawnship will have destroyed the Lhekan forces attacking it."

"Then it'll come for us," I said.

I entered a random point beyond the system's heliopause into the autonav, intending to hide our true intentions from the Spawn. Once clear of the system, we'd jump again for the rendezvous point, offload the Lhekan royals and be on our way.

The spacetime distorters charged as we raced to the edge of Niedarim's gravity well while the spawnship's ghostly blur oscillated above the equator. All around us, Lhekan fighters sacrificed themselves to save their sovereign, drawing the attention of the interdictors and filling the space above Niedarim's outer atmosphere with hundreds of tiny explosions. One of the five autac interdictors broke away from the battle and headed toward us at tremendous speed.

"We got company," Jase declared, then a blunt-nosed isosceles trapezoid with sloping sides and a flat stern appeared alongside, instantly matching our course and speed.

Arleen studied it carefully. "It's a Type I, far

superior to the most powerful Lhekan ships."

"We need to buy time," I said, seeing we were still more than a minute from flat space.

"Hit it with a drone," Jase suggested belligerently.

"If you attack, it will destroy us," Arleen said, glancing at the console in front of her. "Can I communicate with it from here? Audio only."

"Sure." I leaned across to her console and selected comms, then she spoke in a deep guttural dialect which my linguistic upgrade translated for me.

"I am Ambassador Aksirana Galitorious of the D'kol Empire. Your unprovoked attack on Niedarim has forced me to use this ship to transport myself and my staff off-world. I order you to withdraw immediately," Arleen declared, then the bridge screen and our consoles flickered with interference. "Cease your scanning immediately. I have bio suppressors enabled. You will not detect me."

The autonav, sensing Niedarim's gravity had fallen away retracted our sensor masts, then the interdictor replied in the same dialect.

"Deactivate your suppression field."

"Or what! I am third cousin to the Emperor himself. An attack on this ship will be considered an act of war by the Empire of D'kol."

She motioned for me to hurry, then the autonav released our spacetime distorters, letting them form our superluminal bubble.

"Do not engage your star drive," the interdictor ordered.

"I want to speak directly with your matriarch," Arleen barked.

The interdictor fired as our bubble formed. Isolated from the universe, the *Silver Lining* accelerated to over fourteen hundred times the speed of light and was gone before the energy pulse reached us. On the bridge screen, the autonav course simulation appeared, calculating our journey out of Kappa Idris. With no way to see through the bubble's quantum distortions, we were completely blind, navigating by Tau Cetin astrographics alone.

Jase breathed a sigh of relief. "That was close."

I turned to Arleen, pretending I didn't understand Kolug. "Whatever you said, worked."

She gave me a long look, giving me the uncomfortable feeling she knew I was deceiving her. "Yes," she said slowly, "whatever I said."

"They should have blasted us," Jase said.

"Is that what you would have done?" she asked.

"Hell yeah! Always shoot first."

"Autacs possess great tactical intelligence, but they are only machines. They lack your aggressive instincts."

"It did fire on us, eventually," I said.

"Yes, but only after it was sure I was lying."

"Will they come after us?"

"Most definitely. At this moment, the matriarch is reviewing the interdictor's report. When she sees there were Lhekans aboard, she will have our course vector searched."

"That's why I did a blind jump, to throw them off."

"Evading a spawnship is more difficult than you realize," Arleen warned.

"They missed their chance," Jase said, confident there was no way to track us now.

"The One Spawn are resourceful," Arleen said, unconvinced. "Underestimate them at your peril."

"I don't," I assured her, summoning the autonav screen to my console. "Now give me the rendezvous coordinates."

If the One Spawn did pick up our trail, I wanted them chasing the Lhekan command cruiser, not us.

Chapter Three: Slide Space

Interstellar Void
3.2 light years from Pre-SN-30259
Trans Cepheus
Black Hole gravitational anomalies
959 light years from Sol
Lhekan Celestial Mechanics Team

Fifteen hours out of Kappa Idris, I introduced Arleen to Izin. She was curious about him, although he was more concerned with one of his broken toys than her.

"I've lost contact with the hullbot I sent to repair the access port malfunction," Izin said, ignoring her stare.

"The bubble must have fried it," I said.

"It ceased responding nine seconds before we jumped."

"Interdictor field emissions could have disabled it," she suggested.

"Perhaps," Izin said uncertainly, then Arleen and I took the crew elevator up to the command deck.

"It is remarkable two such aggressive species as

yours and his can coexist," she said after the elevator doors closed. "Earth is the only world inhabited by his kind that they do not rule."

"We didn't give them a whole lot of choice."

"No, you didn't," she agreed, obviously aware of how Izin's ancestors had been marooned on Earth during the First Intruder War. "Would you really have exterminated them if they hadn't accepted peace on your terms?"

"I guess we'll never know."

"They must have believed it possible, or they would never have agreed to your terms."

"That was a long time ago," I said evasively, sensing she was testing me, studying my every response.

We returned to the bridge and Jase went off to get some sleep, then when we were alone, she said, "The Suzerain would like to watch your soldiers train."

"Absolutely not, and they're mercenaries, not soldiers."

She gave me a knowing look. "Captain Kade, do you know why I was selected to tutor the Suzerain's children?"

"You're good with kids?"

"I am what the Uvo call a Sublime Empath. I sense your emotions as easily as you see the clothes I wear."

"Hmm…So what am I feeling now?"

"Discomfort. You fear I know when you are lying."

"And do you?"

She leaned toward me confidentially and whispered, "Every time."

A chill ran down my spine, filling me with an urgent desire to get her off the ship.

"Did you mean what you said, that the Uvo don't share secrets?"

"Yes. It is why we are trusted."

"I'll hold you to that," I said, assuming she wouldn't blow my cover.

"The Suzerain wonders why your soldiers are so much more effective than even his elite royal guard."

"A natural killer with a knife is more deadly than a pacifist with a blaster."

"The Lhekans are not pacifists."

"They're not warriors either."

She accepted my assessment without argument. "Mankind's inability to produce a miniaturized power source for handheld energy weapons should be a significant handicap, yet you have turned your inferior kinetic technology into formidable weapons."

"Magnetic acceleration isn't so bad." It propelled projectiles at far higher velocities than explosive propellants ever could, although atmospheric friction constrained their range.

"It is your static force projectiles that make your kinetic weapons effective," she said, wondering why the Tau Cetins had gifted us such a useful technology. "The Suzerain is in desperate need of natural killers with formidable weapons."

I shook my head. "Earth Council will never send a human army to Niedarim, no matter how much they'd like to. They can't."

"The Suzerain will be disappointed to hear that."

I had sympathy for an exiled leader of a conquered world, but there really was nothing we could do to help him, at least not formally. "There are alternatives."

"Such as?"

"Human mercenaries. They wouldn't be as good as the mercs I have on board, but they'd make good use of Lhekan energy weapons."

"They would fight for the Suzerain?"

"They'd fight for the devil himself if he paid on time and offered a victory bonus."

"And your Earth government would permit such an arrangement?"

"They might turn a blind eye, if the mercs wore

Lhekan uniforms so their allegiance wasn't in doubt."

"That could be arranged. How many of these mercenaries are there?"

I smiled. "How much money you got?"

"I see," she said with understanding. "I'm sure the Suzerain's emissaries will wish to discuss terms with your government."

"Not the government, but I know someone they should talk to."

Earth Council would want deniability, but Lena's EIS contacts might gladly supply the Lhekans with all the mercenaries they could afford. They might even secretly subsidize the deal, to build trust with the Lhekans and keep the Spawn busy.

Arleen did her sublime empath thing on me, instantly grasping the subtleties of my offer. "That would be acceptable, Captain Kade."

She might read me like an unlocked holopane, but her manner eased my wariness. She'd demonstrated a mastery of physics, spoke Kolug like a native and could talk the One Spawn's artificial intelligence in circles, which made her the most overqualified governess in the galaxy. She was from a race Earth had no contact with, whose only image we'd ever seen was a poor quality two-dee snapped secretly by a diplomat three centuries ago. The Uvo weren't traders or members of any alliance, yet I'd once overheard a Xil agent refer to them as if they were held in the highest regard by the rest of the galaxy. Wondering why, I invited her to dinner, leaving the ship to fly itself.

"I've had the galleybot prepare a selection of dishes from Earth's four major civilizations," I said as we sat down in front of a smorgasbord of meals. I indicated each civilization's delicacies in turn. "These are from the Democratic Union, where I come from. And these are from the People's Federation of Asia, the Indian Republic, and even a few Cali specialties."

"Thank you, Captain Kade," she said politely. "I am honored you have gone to so much trouble."

Jase shoveled food onto his plate from every dish while Arleen carefully selected from the vegetable dishes only.

"Are the Uvo vegetarians?" Izin asked as he opted for south Asian rehydrated fish.

"We are herbivores."

"We're not," Jase said with a mouth full of meat.

She tried fried rice from east Asia, chewing slowly. "Your world produces food with an amazing variety of tastes."

"I'll pass your compliments on to the galleybot."

She gave me a puzzled look. "My impression was it lacked self-awareness."

"It does," I replied, realizing the Uvo had little understanding of human levity.

"The Captain dislikes machines smarter than himself," Izin said dryly, "which doesn't leave much room for simulated intelligence."

"Fearing a superior intellect is an irrational anxiety," she said simply.

"Hear that Izin?" Jase taunted. "Don't be afraid of my humongous brain."

"It's not you I'm afraid of, it's her."

Jase and I stopped chewing, stared at him in astonishment then turned to each other.

"Did he just say what I think he said?" I asked incredulously.

"It sounded like he said she's smarter than he is?" Jase said. "But that couldn't be right, because…no one is."

I gave Izin a searching look. "Are you feeling alright?"

"I'm perfectly well, Captain."

Modesty was not one of Izin's flaws, especially where his superior amphibian intellect was concerned.

"What makes you think Arleen is smarter than you?"

"Her brain mass is four percent smaller than mine, but the electrical field she generates is a hundred and twenty percent greater."

"Wait," I said surprised. "You scanned her *brain*?"

"Someone had to," he said simply, implying I'd let her aboard too easily.

"You should have asked me first," I said stiffly.

"I do many things on this ship without first asking your permission, Captain."

"Like sending Dietz to rescue me after I specifically ordered you not to let him leave the ship."

"I made a rational decision, Captain, based on the fact that the ship is safer when you're in command, and I do not wish to take orders from him," he said, indicating Jase with a look.

Jase stopped chewing. "Hey! I give good orders."

"Nevertheless–"

Arleen touched my arm gently, restraining me. "It's all right, Captain Kade. He was protecting you and your ship and I am not offended."

"She is an alien of unknown origin and capability," Izin said flatly. "Letting her and the Lhekans aboard in a time of war puts us all at risk."

Wishing he'd told me in private, I turned to Arleen curiously. "Is he right?"

"His calculations are correct, although we do not regard intellect as highly as you do," she replied. "We see the mind merely as a stepping stone to something greater."

"But you're a teacher," I said, "even if you're overqualified to be tutoring children."

"Having the Suzerain's children receive the best possible education is part of the reward for his sacrifice."

"Sacrifice?" Jase said. "For being king of an entire planet?"

"He is the Suzerain of the Lhekan League, not just

one planet," she explained. "His life is not his own, although none of his descendants for ten generations can ever take his place, ensuring no possibility of hereditary power. It is a carefully crafted system designed to prevent the rise of dictators. And it has served the Lhekan people well for millennia."

"Why do the Lhekans regard education by the Uvo so highly?" Izin asked.

"We do not simply educate the mind, we teach the transmutation of knowledge into wisdom. It is why my sisters instruct many of the galaxy's future leaders, but only in societies inclined toward true inclusiveness, as we define it."

"So no Matarons?" I said.

"They have not asked for our guidance and we would refuse if they did. Others, such as the Nisk, we would gladly serve, but they do not require our assistance."

"What about the D'kol?" I asked.

"We have trained every D'kol Emperor for over two million years," she replied.

"Is that why you speak their language?"

"The Uvo speak many languages because communication is the key to achieving our goal."

"Which is?"

"Galactic peace, both politically and in a deeper sense." She sampled a thinly sliced vegetable from North America.

"Potato fries," Jase said. "My favorite."

Unable to swallow, she spat partially masticated potato into her hand, then lowered it below the table so the small cleanerbot gliding around the floor could vacuum it off her palm.

Mildly embarrassed, she said, "It would have been more to my liking if it had not been boiled in triglyceride and covered in sodium chloride."

"But that's how we like them, deep-fried and extra

salty," Jase said enthusiastically, loading more onto his plate now that Arleen had surrendered her share.

"So is Alif a good king?" I asked.

"His people think so. It is not easy holding power one does not desire so others who do are prevented from taking it. He would rather have been a farmer." She took a sip of a non-intoxicating drink. "One does not always get what one wants in life, but if one is fortunate, one receives what one needs."

"Where will he go now?" Izin asked.

"To a Lhekan colony world. He will decide which one after he boards the command cruiser. It is best none of you know where in case you are captured by the One Spawn."

"Thanks for thinking of us," Jase said sourly.

"Why'd they do it?" I asked. "Why'd the Spawn break the Neutrality Pact?"

"Only they can answer that," she replied, lowering her eyes momentarily. She might have been able to spot a lie from orbit, but she was no master at hiding the truth herself. There was something she wasn't telling us.

"We know very little about the Uvo," I said.

"What would you like to know, Captain Kade?" she asked with disarming directness.

"Where are you from? Why have we had no contact with your people?"

"What do you do for fun?" Jase asked.

"What is the strength of your military?" Izin added.

"Are you thinking of invading us?" she asked amused.

"No," he replied, "but the galaxy is at war and no one is safe."

She studied him the way Lena did when she was vacuuming my brain, then answered. "We have no military at all. We are contemplatives, philosophers, students of all knowledge." She turned to me. "Our homeworld is beyond what you call the Whirling

Dervish Nebula over twenty thousand light years from Earth."

That put it in the Sagittarius Arm, far from the war zone, although not out of reach considering the Spawn Fleet's capacity to strike deep into the heart of the galaxy.

"How is it you know human astronomy?" Izin asked, aware that the nebula's name was a purely human construct.

"I looked through your star charts in my cabin. I do not understand the correlation between a religious zealot sworn to poverty, spinning in circles, and a star-forming region, but the Uvo do find allegorical meanings most interesting. They reveal much about how a species thinks."

"Allegorical," Jase said proudly, "that's us." He turned to me with a puzzled look. "What's allegorical?"

"You like hidden meanings," she explained. "And you think poetically, something the One Spawn are incapable of doing."

"Hear that Izin," Jase said with a smirk, "you're not poetic, not like us."

"Your understanding of poetry," Izin replied, "is limited to drinking songs and rhyming four-letter expletives."

"Hey!" Jase said with mock indignation. "You try singing all twenty-six verses of 'There was a young man from Mars' while drinking a four hundred kilogram Syrman under the table. That takes talent."

"I would like to hear that song," Arleen said intrigued.

"A few more of these," Jase said, holding up his drink, "and I'll be happy to sing it for you."

"Don't get him started," I warned, receiving a disappointed look from Jase.

"As for why you've had no contact with us," Arleen continued, "there has been no reason to meet. Even if your application for full Forum membership is granted this century, it will be thousands of years before humanity will be given the astrographic increments necessary to reach Uvona. There is no hurry."

"A pity," I said.

"What about fun?" Jase prompted.

"Fun produces only temporary happiness. For us, every living moment is filled with a far richer quality," she replied without elaboration.

"Which we don't understand?" I asked.

"Some of your people do, but very few. Nevertheless, everything we have is within your reach, Captain Kade, if you so choose."

"Why only a few?" Izin asked.

"All intelligent life in the universe is created equal, but it does not remain equal," she explained. "Consciousness evolves over immense spans of time to great heights. Each individual progresses at his own speed, some faster, some slower, some barely at all. It is why you have serial killers and saints and everything in between."

"And the Spawn?" I asked.

"They progress rapidly in some ways and not at all in others."

We talked some more, mostly about human likes and dislikes, then Arleen went to prepare the royal family to leave while Jase and I went up to the bridge for the rendezvous with the Lhekan command cruiser, hoping there were no spawnships waiting for us. And in the back of mind, I had an uncomfortable feeling Arleen had learned more from us than we had from her.

* * * *

The autonav flashed a hazard warning as we neared the rendezvous point, then a tunnel-shaped zone of steeply curved space appeared on the bridge screen simulator.

The curvature was so extreme it could easily have collapsed the bubble, yet it wasn't listed in the catalog. It was one of those obscure phenomenon hidden in the Tau Cetin astrographics module that only appeared when we got too close. The TCs didn't want to tell us of its existence, but they also made sure we didn't kill ourselves by flying into it.

Their infallible mapping system allowed us to grope our way between the stars, blind inside our superluminal bubbles. Without it, we wouldn't have been able to avoid the near infinite, undetectable dark matter hazards littering space. Their gift defined human Mapped Space. It gave us access to a spatial sphere several thousand light years across, but no further, and was annoyingly strict at ensuring we saw nothing mankind's probationary status with the Galactic Forum didn't entitle us to.

"Want to drop the bubble for a look?" Jase asked.

"Not with a spawnship on our tail," I replied. Our course plot ended at the edge of the anomaly, a few seconds short of instantaneous destruction, but I wanted to know more than the cryptic Tau Cetin warning was giving us. "Arleen to the bridge," I announced over the intercom.

When she arrived, I motioned her to the acceleration couch beside me and pointed at the tunnel through space crossing the T of our plot line. "What is that?"

She glanced at it with instant recognition. "It relates to technology mankind does not possess."

"The rendezvous point is right on top of it."

"Providing you go no further than the coordinates I gave you, your ship will be in no danger."

Seeing she wasn't going to say more, I said, "Is the Suzerain ready to transfer?"

"He and his family are waiting at the bow airlock. I'll join him after giving instructions to the Lhekan ship."

"You give orders to their ships?" Jase asked.

"The Suzerain never issues orders himself. Only his retainers do that."

"He told me to take him back to the station on Niedarim," I said.

"Yes, because he thought you were going to get him and his family killed, although tradition has it that his retainers anticipate his every need. They offer and he either accepts or refuses. As I am his only retainer on this ship, I have the honor of speaking on his behalf."

"Not very efficient."

"Governing by royal assent is far less oppressive than ruling by decree. It ensures absolute power is exercised only in the negative."

I plugged a random destination away from the anomaly into the autonav in case Intruder ships were waiting for us on arrival, then when the bubble dropped, Jase deployed the sensor masts through our cooling hull. The bridge screen course simulation was replaced by three Lhekan ships floating in front of a wispy circle of light surrounding an impenetrable blackness.

"No spawnships," Jase said with relief as the first scans came in. "Lots of microgravity waves though."

I studied the telltale halo of light beyond the Lhekan ships. "That looks like gravitational lensing," I said. Lensing was caused by extreme gravity bending light from distant stars, but there was nothing in the Tau Cetin astrographics system to indicate a cause.

"You think the TCs missed something?" Jase asked.

"They don't miss anything," I replied as I realized what the tunnel-shaped hazard was. "There's a black hole out there and it's moving."

Jase whistled softly as he got a velocity reading. "And how. Nine percent."

"That's too fast to be natural," I said, glancing suspiciously at Arleen. When she said nothing, I nodded to Jase. "Let's have a closer look at those Lhekan ships."

Jase focused our opticals on an enormous vessel made of six circular segments. Each segment was larger than our biggest super transport, making it more a mobile space station than a starship. Docked alongside it was a cargo vessel with oversized sublight engines while holding position eight hundred kilometers astern was a Lhekan command cruiser.

I used the autonav to extrapolate the black hole's trajectory. It was heading for an old star seventy-two light years away, a star with a spectral reading warning it was in bad shape.

"Hmm." I put the pieces together, then turned to Arleen. "Why are the Lhekans moving a black hole toward a star that's about to go supernova?"

She gave me an approving look, impressed I'd worked it out. "It will not explode for another seven thousand years. When it does, it will destroy Niedarim and every other inhabited world within hundreds of light years."

"Unless they lower its mass."

"Yes. Twelve hundred years from now, the Lhekans will place that black hole in close orbit around the star, close enough for its gravity to pull gas from the star's surface, lowering its mass and preventing it exploding."

"Turning a supernova into a white dwarf is quite a feat."

"More likely a neutron star," she corrected.

"How are they moving it?" Jase asked.

Arleen hesitated, unwilling to risk compromising Forum transfer protocols.

"Artificial gravity?" I guessed.

She relaxed. "The Lhekans have been sliding that black hole for over five thousand years. Two thousand years ago, they repositioned their gravity well generator behind the black hole to decelerate it into orbit."

"That's why the Tau Cetins didn't put it in their

catalog. They don't want humans learning how to move black holes around the galaxy."

"The celestial mechanics for such a maneuver are advanced and your species does have a propensity for turning peaceful technology into weapons."

"Who? Us?" I said innocently, imagining how one mighty curveball pitched at the Matar System would end our snakehead problems once and for all.

"The freighter accelerates out to the slide fleet with supplies every few months while the base ship relocates along the flight path for the next pass," she explained, then a hail sounded in the bridge.

"Attention unidentified human ship. This is Lhekan League restricted space by authority of Galactic Forum Emergency Decree Ursal-One-Five. You are ordered to withdraw immediately."

"They don't know what happened to their homeworld, do they?" I said.

"No, nor do they know who we have on board. Allow me." She selected comms on her console then spoke in perfect Lhekanese, which my linguistic upgrade automatically translated. "The One Spawn have attacked Niedarim. The Suzerain and his family are aboard this ship. They require immediate evacuation."

"Understood. Prepare for transfer," the Lhekan officer replied, then the command cruiser's engines glowed and it turned toward us.

Arleen stood and clasped her hands together, palms up in the formal Lhekan gesture. "Thank you for your hospitality, Captain Kade. The Suzerain wishes to express his gratitude for your assistance...and your suggestion." It was her way of telling me–without Jase knowing–I'd soon be hearing from his emissaries regarding the mass hiring of human mercenaries.

"He's welcome. Now get off my ship."

"Oh ho," Jase said as she started toward the companionway. "Something just went past us real fast, following our course plot. Damn thing almost hit us."

I turned to Arleen. "How are they tracking us?"

"Your superluminal drive produces ripples in spacetime which their sentry probes can detect and use to estimate your course. The faster you move, the larger the ripple."

"Like a bow wave?"

"More like a wake. They cannot scan through their own superluminal fields, so they will stop frequently to confirm you are still ahead of them. They can follow you, providing they do not fall too far behind."

"Now you tell me."

"When they discover we are not ahead of them, they will retrace their course, searching for your spatial wake."

I glanced at the black hole's ring of light on the bridge screen, realizing the Intruder ship should have flown straight into the black hole's gravity well by now. Instead of a point of light in the center of the lensing ring marking an explosion, it was still black as night.

"They didn't hit the gravity well," I said.

"They would have detected the change in spatial curvature and stopped in time," Arleen agreed. "Now they will be determining if your ship was destroyed."

"Which means they'll be coming back," I said, glancing at the Lhekan command cruiser racing toward us. "That's why they're in such a hurry." I studied the escape course I'd plotted into the autonav, realizing it wouldn't work. "Is there any way to throw them off our tail?"

"Spatial wakes can be disrupted by other ripples in spacetime," Arleen replied.

"Ripples...from another wake?"

"Another ship could cause an interference effect, but it would depend on the size and velocity of the ship, and the wakes would have to intersect," she said, then hurried off to join the Suzerain at the forward airlock.

The Lhekan cruiser rolled bow over stern and decelerated toward us. She was eight times our mass with far more powerful engines, yet the rollover told me she was closer to us in technology than to the Intruders, who could stop a spawnship on a pinhead without a rollover.

When the Lhekan ship was only three hundred clicks from our bow, Jase suddenly declared, "They've found us!"

Before I could see what he was looking at, streams of orange energy pulses leaped from the cruiser toward a point in space twenty thousand kilometers away.

"It's tiny," Jase said, focusing an optical on an arrowhead ringed by raked silver spikes protruding from its stern. We glimpsed the sentry probe for only a moment, then it streaked away before the Lhekan energy blasts reached it. "It's heading back to Niedarim."

"To get help," I said and opened a channel. "Lhekan cruiser, the Suzerain is waiting at our bow airlock. You are cleared to connect."

"Confirmed."

The cruiser matched our velocity, lightly kissed our bow, then an adaptable housing extended over our airlock mating the two hulls.

The Suzerain's voice sounded over the intercom. "Captain Kade."

"Ah, yeah?"

"It is unlikely we will meet again, but...you made a friend today. Thank you."

"You're welcome."

An indicator flashed on my console, signaling the airlock inner door had opened. It seemed to take an eternity for the Lhekans to cycle through, then at last, the outer door sealed and the cruiser moved off.

"Three contacts!" Jase announced. "Heading straight for us."

The Lhekan command cruiser immediately bubbled

out while I plugged a new course into the autonav. The *Silver Lining's* bow started to come around onto the new heading, then the Lhekan base ship and the supply freighter jumped away leaving us alone in space with the Intruder ships.

"They're interdictors," Jase said, "coming in fast."

"Almost there."

I overrode a flashing autonav safety warning, hoping I wasn't about to get us all killed, then two interdictors raced up either side of us while the third appeared directly overhead. The two beside us locked green beams on us, holding the *Silver Lining* in place, while the third glided down, intending to attach itself to our topside hull.

"They're going to board us," Jase declared anxiously.

"Not today," I said, activating our bubble.

Spacetime curved sharply around us, slicing through the interdictor above us and severing the green beams holding us in place. There was no explosion inside our bubble, but a blast of intense heat momentarily washed over the outside of the superluminal field as we streaked away. The severed underside of the interdictor bounced gently off our hull, floated back out to the bubble wall and was sucked away in a flash of white light.

The course simulator reappeared on the bridge screen showing we were following a straight line toward the tunnel-shaped hazard zone. Where the course plot crossed into steeply curved space, it flashed bright red.

Jase's eyes widened in surprise. "You didn't."

"It's the only way to throw them off."

"It'll tear us apart."

"Yeah, they'd be crazy to follow."

"The One Spawn are not insane," a female voice sounded behind us, "but they will take risks when it is to their advantage."

I spun around to discover Arleen standing in the hatchway. "You stayed?"

"For now." Her eyes lifted to the main screen, taking in our course plot to disaster. "It appears I have made an unwise decision."

"Captain," Izin's voice sounded from the intercom, "I'm detecting spatial curvature inside the bubble."

"Nothing to worry about, Izin," I assured him, "It's just a black hole."

Arleen returned to her acceleration couch as the collision alert sounded throughout the ship.

"Curvature's spiking," Jase warned.

"Not yet," I said, watching our field stability drop like a stone in high-g, knowing every second put us deeper into the hazard zone.

"Skipper!" Jase pleaded, wincing.

"Now," I said, tapping the kill switch on my console.

The superluminal bubble surrounding the *Silver Lining* dissipated, dropping us onto the edge of a spatial chasm that fell steeply toward the black hole. With a sigh of relief, Jase ran the sensors out as the black hole raced toward us at nine percent the speed of light. Spacetime curved sharply around us, eliminating any hope of raising the bubble again, then Jase got his first close up look at the monster hurtling toward us.

"It's four solar masses. Diameter, twenty-four thousand meters." He relaxed. "We're a hundred million kilometers off its trajectory."

"Plenty of room," I said.

"There will be no lethal side effects," Arleen said.

The autonav plotted the black hole's trajectory, how its gravity would pull us in and slingshot us away into space on a new heading. "It'll be here in an hour, we'll bubble in two," I said, then spoke to the intercom. "Izin, shut down everything we don't need."

"Spinning down now," he replied. "And Captain,

the confinement field stabilizer installed in Hades City works."

"Glad to hear it." I smiled, never doubting the infallibility of Tau Cetin technology, then the bridge screen flashed white from an object exploding uncomfortably close to the *Silver Lining*.

"They're shooting at us!" Jase declared.

"No," I said, seeing damage control hadn't reported a hit.

Jase studied his console. "It was a bubble collapse, eight hundred clicks away."

"It was a sentry probe," Arleen said. "If it had been an interdictor, the blast would have destroyed us."

"That's one for us!" Jase declared triumphantly.

"Spawnships carry millions of sentry probes," Arleen said.

"Oh," Jase said deflated.

"If they can identify our position, a blast like that could destroy us," she added.

"They've got to find us first," I said as we slid down steeply curved space into the black hole's grip, gaining velocity.

Six million kilometers away, another sphere of light bloomed out of the darkness as a second sentry probe threw itself against the black hole's gravitational barrier.

It was only the beginning.

* * * *

The wall-mounted screen in my stateroom was filled with a circular blackness that blotted out the stars. It was unlike any black hole I'd ever seen, devoid of a glowing accretion disk of captured matter spiraling toward oblivion. Facing the inky hole in space, brilliant explosions bloomed with monotonous regularity as Intruder sentry probes hurled themselves against the black hole's gravity well.

"They're persistent," I said to Arleen as we watched the suicidal spheres of light wax and wane every few seconds.

"It is one of their strengths," she replied.

"Seems kind of stupid to me."

"They're letting you know they're out there and they haven't given up."

I watched another detonating sentry probe flare in the distance, then turned to a more pressing matter. "So, why did you stay?"

"I wish to return home."

"That's twenty thousand light years away. Too far for us."

It would be a fourteen-year voyage if we had the astrographics to get there, which we didn't. Traveling so far through an ocean of uncharted dark matter, blind inside the bubble, had an incredibly high collision risk. It was why Mapped Space was mankind's home and its prison. In less than fifty years we might be granted galactic citizenship, gaining access to more Tau Cetin star charts, but even then, they wouldn't reach to the Whirling Dervish Nebula.

"The Suzerain is heading to a world far from Uvona," Arleen explained. "If I'd gone with him, I might never have seen my home again."

"The Uvo are well connected. You could have found a ship."

"We have many friends, but few ships visit our homeworld. And I did not expect the One Spawn to assume the Suzerain was still aboard your ship."

I sensed there was more to it than that. "Why are you so afraid of them?"

She hesitated. "The One Spawn want to study us, to learn how to construct technology to replicate our natural abilities. They would fail, but they do not know that."

"I've heard you're telepathic."

"Only one in seven of our females are natural

telepaths. They belong to the Sibylline Sisterhood, the leaders of our society. I am not one of the seven. I am merely an empath, although the One Spawn do not understand the difference."

"It sounds like you people should arm yourselves."

She gave me an amused look. "A warrior race would think that."

"Even pacifists have to defend themselves sometimes."

"We are spiritual aesthetics, Captain Kade, peaceful, not pacifist. There is a difference. We identify with the One Life. When there is only One, there is no other to be in conflict with. That is why we are truly at peace."

"Maybe, but if I were you, I'd start sleeping with a spawnship killing weapon under my pillow."

"That would mean fighting against ourselves."

I furrowed my brow. "How's that?"

"For us to take a life, any life, is to attack ourselves because we identify with the livingness in all beings, even the One Spawn."

"I'm sure they don't see it that way."

"Their world is the illusion of form, the diversity of outward appearance. Ours is the essential Unity of spirit. They seek to divide what we know is indivisibly One. That is the essence of separativeness, to us, the greatest of all evils."

"We agree on one thing, they are evil."

"Less evolved," she said simply. "Separativeness is the force that permits them to treat others the way they do. It is the same dark force tearing human civilization apart."

The Consortium and its allies were certainly the 'dark force' driving our civil war. Not many could see it because they kept their real motives hidden. It was why I couldn't convince Marie she was on the wrong side.

"So, what am I to do with you?"

"There is a Syrman outpost on Jel Kara. I could get a ship there."

Jel Kara was too small to be on any human trade route, but Syrman ships were faster than ours. They could get her someplace where she could pick up a ride home.

"I have to go to Freehold first."

She thought for a moment. "Orbiting Holbrook's Star?"

I nodded. "How'd you know?"

"When I decided to come aboard your ship with the Suzerain, I used the Galisti Starport catalog to see what human colonies were in this region."

"You were at the starport?" I asked surprised.

"We went there looking for a ship to take the Suzerain off-world, but we were too late. They'd all been destroyed. Then Pridak Tir told the Suzerain's attendants about your ship and we took the vactube to Firel City."

"That's why you were waiting for me," I said. "Are you sure about Jel Kara? The Syrmans are TC allies."

"So are humans."

"Technically, we're neutral."

"No one believes that, certainly not the One Spawn."

I nodded. "OK, I'll drop you at Jel Kara after Freehold," I said, then the ship shuddered as a weak shockwave hit us and the bloom of an exploding Intruder sentry probe filled the wall screen.

"That was…close," Arleen said surprised.

"Skipper," Jase's voice sounded from the intercom. "They can see us. We're radiating polarons."

"Shut it down."

"I don't even know what's causing it."

Izin's voice cut in. "Captain, the polaron emissions are coming from life support."

"What?" Our life support system was large and

complex enough to produce everything we needed to survive in space for years, but one thing it didn't produce was quasiparticles. "How?"

"Captain," Arleen said slowly, "are there ionic crystals in your life support system?"

I shrugged. "I don't know, maybe."

"Life support is one of your few systems still operational," she said. "If ionic crystals were energized, they would produce polarons."

"But someone would have to reroute power to–" I froze. "Izin, where in life support?"

"Fluid reprocessing."

"The tank farm?" I said thoughtfully. Crawlways ran past there from frame fifty-one, where the access port malfunction had occurred and Izin's hullbot had disappeared. It was one of the few places where the ship could be entered from the outside. "Izin, we've got a stowaway on board. I'll be right down."

I grabbed my P-50, loaded it with shield penetrating snakehead killers under Arleen's knowing gaze, then we went down to engineering. Izin was waiting with a shrapgun, a short-barreled hand cannon that could clear a companionway with a single conical blast.

"Fluid processing's internal sensors have been disabled," he warned, then led us through dark companionways and a series of reprocessing compartments to a circular hatch in the overhead with the number fifty-one stenciled beside it.

"Should we summon the soldiers?" Arleen asked.

"The last thing I want is them blasting holes in the hull," I replied.

I aimed at the small hatch above us and nodded to Izin who opened it with an engineering remote. The hatch door swung down and a metallic bipedal suit fell through and crashed onto the deck. It was spawnwarrior battle armor, open from the shoulder to the waist, and it was empty. There was an eight-mil hole in the shoulder and a bloody smear down the outside of the suit, indicating at least one spawnwarrior had survived the encounter with Dietz's team outside the grain loader.

I pulled the back fully open, revealing blood streaks on the spongy metal interior. Unlike human battle suits, the Spawn suit had no screens, controls or movement sensors inside.

"How do they steer this thing?" I asked.

"Sensors and suit systems interface their implants directly while response fields control its movement," Arleen explained.

"Just your size," I said to Izin, then ran my finger over a cylindrical gap no bigger than my palm at chest height. "It took something with it."

"A weapon perhaps," Izin said, shining the beam light attached to his shrapgun into the overhead crawlway.

"It must have jumped on the hull before we left the loader," I said, recalling the leap I'd seen a spawnwarrior make at Galisti Starport.

"The suit would have jammed your sensors," Arleen said as Izin played his light over small, bloodied handprints inside the crawlway, near the airlock hull crawlers used to get topside.

I climbed up the narrow ladder below the hatch and looked inside. A dark blood smear led off through the crawlway aft.

"I'll go after him," I whispered down to Izin. "You cover the tank farm door in case he tries to escape."

"You'll need this," Izin said, handing me his beam light. "And Captain, be careful what you shoot at. Starships do not react well to hypersonic projectiles."

"Yeah," I agreed grimly and pulled myself up into the crawlway.

Arleen climbed up behind me. She was taller than me, but her slender form left her with more room to move. I gave her a dubious look, thinking an unarmed pacifist alien governess would be no help in flushing out a wounded spawnwarrior.

"It'll be dark in there and you'll need help finding him," she said, reading my mood.

"You can sense him?"

"I'm starting to. He's weak but dangerous."

"Don't get in the way."

I clipped Izin's beam light to my gun and crawled forward, following the blood smear. It led past bio organics and gas processing to the large fluid processing compartment astern. I switched the beam light off and pulled myself quietly up toward the sounds of bubbling liquids and humming machines. A circular pressure hatch had been pushed open and several small bloodied handprints left behind were just visible in the feeble light.

I waited for Arleen to come up behind me, then she pointed toward the stern, sensing that's where the wounded spawnwarrior was hiding. I nodded and lowered myself quietly down into the compartment. The air was humid and even though the lights were out, the glow of status displays silhouetted rows of transparent tanks and the pipes linking them. Some tanks were mixed by paddle-shaped stirrers while others steamed as their contents evaporated or were broken down by electrolysis. With the ship all but shut down, the air was hotter and more humid than usual and condensation was building on every surface.

Bionetic enhancers, boost audio, boost infrared, I thought.

The bubbling and humming of the tank farm roared in my ears and the heat saturated my vision, drowning out any possibility of using bionetics to detect him. I reset my enhancers to base as Arleen climbed down and again pointed to the stern, confirming he wasn't dead. I was uncomfortably aware he had Izin's sonic vision and might well be watching me now, waiting for a clear shot.

I left her crouching in the darkness and crept between the tanks, peering through their translucent sides for any sign of the wounded spawnwarrior. Somewhere to my left was a hissing sound that shouldn't have been there. The tanks were sealed against leaks to keep moisture out of sensitive electronics, but he must have released steam into the atmosphere to blind the tank farm's thermal sensors.

The curved sides of the tanks distorted shadows and warped the ghostly lights of the displays, ensuring I could have been staring straight at him and not known it. A rustle sounded behind me and I spun around, raising my P-50 to fire. Arleen recoiled with raised hands, then I gave her a sharp look, thinking how close I'd come to shooting her.

"He's moving," she whispered and pointed to the right.

I signaled for her to stay there and crept toward him, moving from one tank to the next, straining to hear alien footsteps. Shadows stretched around the translucent curves of the tanks as I inched forward, creating a sense of motion all around me.

"He's behind you!" Arleen yelled.

I dived sideways as a flash lit up the compartment and the tank beside me exploded, releasing a tidal wave of dark, pungent liquid. It washed me into another tank, slamming my head into a pipe, dazing me momentarily. Struggling to keep my head above the murky liquid, I dropped my gun as another white blast flashed past my face and shattered a clear water tank. I spat sour waste from my mouth as purified water washed over me, mixing with the effluent, then a small form with an oversized, streamlined head darted between the tanks and vanished into the shadows. He had a small weapon in one hand while his other arm hung limply by his side.

I looked for my gun, but it had been swept away in the flood, so I slipped into the shadows and hid. The spawnwarrior would follow his natural instinct as an ambush predator and try to sneak up behind me rather than take me head-on, unaware I was now unarmed. Resisting the urge to go after him, I crouched low and used the bubbling tanks for cover, letting him make the next move.

The ship shuddered as another sentry probe exploded nearby. The black hole's extreme spatial curvature was bending the polaron emissions' path, disguising our exact location, but the Spawn attacks were getting closer and all they needed was one lucky shot.

There was no sign of Arleen, although she'd know empathically I was in trouble. As the ship stabilized and the sloshing tanks calmed, I heard the faint rhythmic stirring of liquid as the spawnwarrior came toward me, then my DNA sniffer got a hint of him.

TERRESTRIAL AMPHIBIAN DETECTED.
SIX METERS AND CLOSING.

My sniffer read him as a tamph, not a Spawn, not knowing the difference. Scarcely daring to breathe, I spotted a small, distorted shadow on the other side of the tank I hid behind. It was circling around, unaware of my position, so I waited until he was close, then leaped out at him–and froze!

It was a maintenance bot, inspecting the wrecked tanks and groping the shallows with its robotic arms, collecting broken fragments off the deck. Out in the open and exposed, I dived sideways as a brilliant white energy blast flashed past me, fired from close range. I slid into a tank and turned as the wounded spawnwarrior appeared out of the darkness and aimed his weapon at me.

A high pitched, amphibian command sounded to his right. My linguistics upgrade translated the Spawn word instantly. "Stop!"

He turned toward Arleen who held my P-50 by its body, not its hilt.

"Shoot!" I yelled.

Arleen ignored me and spoke in the Spawn language. "Lay down your weapon. We will not harm you."

The spawnwarrior realized she wasn't going to use the gun, saw that I was unarmed, and snapped his gun up, aiming at her head. As his arm reached full extension, a thunderous boom echoed through the tank farm and he was hurled sideways through a transparent tank, his torso shredded and bloody. The bubbling tank exploded, flooding the deck and pinning his body against the shattered inner wall, then Izin emerged from the darkness holding his shrapgun level. He waded through the receding torrent to the spawnwarrior, saw his distant cousin was barely moving, clinging to life, then he fired again at point-blank range making sure the job was done.

I got to my feet and snatched my gun from Arleen's hand, "You should have killed him."

"I cannot," she said simply.

"He would have killed us both," I snapped, holstering the P-50 and turning to Izin who was wading across to a reprocessing tank. A small cylindrical device was wedged between the tank wall and the filtration system's control unit.

"It's energizing the semiconductive material in the control unit," he said as Arleen and I approached.

"It's the Spawn suit's power unit," Arleen said.

I gave her a puzzled look. "It's not using our power?"

"Only to mask its presence. It knew, even though we powered down, we had to keep life support running."

"The quantum effects are generating the polaron emissions," Izin said, raising his weapon to blast it, but I put a restraining hand on his arm.

"I have a better idea. Remove the control unit without breaking the connection and follow me."

Three Intruder probe detonations later, the

maintenance bot that had lured me out of hiding carried the Spawn power module and the filtration control unit to the airlock. A thrusterbot, waiting there to meet us, took both pieces and climbed into the airlock. We watched on the small screen beside the inner door as it clambered out onto the hull and leaped clear, then its low power thruster activated, carrying it and the polaron generating assembly away into space. Slowly, the glow of its thruster shrank to a distant point of light, then a sentry probe exploded against the gravity well, closer to it than us.

"They bought it," I said with relief.

"Simple, but effective," Arleen said.

"That is another precision engineering bot you owe me, Captain," Izin declared ungratefully.

"Add it to the list," I said, then went back to my stateroom to change, shower and have my stinking, putrid clothes ejected into space.

* * * *

"There they are," I said as a cluster of tiny lights appeared at the edge of the circular blackness.

Jase zoomed an optical, resolving the lights into seven support vessels and a large cylindrical base ship. The images were misshapen and stretched from supergravity distortions which decreased as the ships hurtled toward us.

The Lhekan flotilla had their sterns angled toward the black hole. Their oversized sublight engines glowed like luminous stars, resisting the pull of the black hole's gravity, precisely holding position beyond the threshold that would have torn them apart. A luminous orange energy beam from the base ship cut through the blanketing darkness to a funnel-shaped structure closer to the event horizon. Radiant blue rings ran up the funnel's neck while a brilliant white light radiated from its conical mouth toward the black hole before fading away.

"I thought they'd be behind it," Jase said, noting the Lhekan fleet was to one side of the black hole.

"They are behind it," Arleen said. "That is an optical distortion caused by spatial curvature. To them, we appear to be further out than we actually are. The funnel-shaped structure is a singularity field generator. It constricts spacetime, slowing the black hole, while the black hole's gravity tows their fleet behind it. The Lhekan ships are far enough out to avoid the horizontal compression and vertical stretching effects of extreme gravity, with the help of very powerful acceleration fields that also reduce the effects of time dilation."

"That's quite a balancing act," I said.

No wonder they didn't want us scanning it. That kind of technology could be used to move planets and shape entire solar systems, which was why all our masts were out gathering enough data to keep Earth's reverse engineering boffins busy for centuries.

Forty million clicks behind us, an Intruder sentry probe burst against the edge of the onrushing gravity well in pursuit of Izin's decoy bot. The explosion unfolded in slow motion, gradually expanding then slowly fading away as time dilation did its thing.

"Why don't they send a ship in after us?" I wondered aloud.

"Sentry probes are not designed for relativistic travel," Arleen explained. "An Interdictor could catch us if it knew where we were. One may even be intercepting your hull maintenance machine as we speak."

I checked we were still on course for a slingshot out behind the black hole, for once, not entirely trusting the autonav. Calculating a hyperbolic trajectory through steeply curved spacetime, while dodging a black hole four times the mass of Earth's sun, that happened to be charging toward us at nine percent the speed of light, required some serious number crunching. When I finally satisfied myself that the ship's mighty machine brain was up to the task, I let the autonav take the helm. A long sweeping curve appeared on the bridge screen, then our thrusters fired, putting us on course for the black hole's choppy wake.

Footsteps sounded from the companionway, then Dietz and his five team members appeared at the threshold of the open hatchway. Military discipline prevented them from stepping onto the bridge–even of civilian ship–without permission.

"We've never seen a black hole before," Dietz said stiffly.

"Come in," I said, motioning for them to enter.

They filed in quietly, taking up positions behind our couches, and watched the black hole's halo of lensed star light grow rapidly in size. Slowly, the Lhekan fleet slid around behind the black hole as we fell deeper into the gravity well until eventually they were dead astern of it, where they'd been all along.

"They're hailing us," Jase said.

"Ignore them," I said, hoping our silence would convince the Spawn we hadn't survived the encounter.

Izin stepped onto the bridge, squeezed between Dietz's super soldiers, noted with irritation that Arleen was in his seat and took the couch beside Jase.

"Didn't want to miss the fun?" Jase asked.

"Playing chicken with a black hole is not my idea of fun," he replied.

"Amen to that," Corporal Larson muttered.

"Here it comes," I said as the halo grew rapidly in size and the inky blackness expanded against a carpet of stars.

It took several minutes to approach, passing within a few million kilometers of us, dragging the Lhekan Fleet behind it, then we slid out into the black hole's wake on an entirely new course while it raced away. We watched it shrink in size until all that remained was a halo of flashes from exploding sentry probes as the black hole led the Spawn away from us.

"They have no idea where we are," Jase said.

"The Spawn are detonating on both sides of the spatial tunnel," Izin said suspiciously.

"Yeah, because we outsmarted them," Jase said.

"No, *we* didn't." Izin watched sentry probes bloom and fade, then turned to Arleen. "It was the Tau Cetins, wasn't it? They made sure the One Spawn have no astrographics for this phenomenon."

She gave him a long, uncomfortable look, but said nothing, reminding me that the Uvo never reveal the secrets of others.

"I'll be damned," I said slowly. "He's right! The Spawn don't know anything about it, which means the Matarons don't either." I studied her face, saw that it was true and smiled incredulously. "Huh! The Tau Cetins have been fudging the maps for millennia! They hid the location of this black hole from the snakeheads, so they couldn't give it to the Spawn."

"It is the only possible explanation," Izin agreed.

"The Tau Cetins know their enemies," Arleen said meaningfully.

Jase grinned. "Oh, that's sneaky."

Trade routes and star systems were one thing, but obscure locations requiring specialized knowledge was something else entirely. The Tau Cetins had been responsible for mapping the Orion Arm since long before *Homo Sapiens* had come into existence. That gave them ample time to modify the region's star charts in ways their ancient enemy might never suspect, in ways that someday might play into the hands of the exceedingly devious Ornithian Consociation.

"So, the Spawn don't know where the wake is," I said, thinking ahead.

"They could find out if they conducted a proper

survey," Arleen said.

"They don't have the time, not with the Tau Cetins breathing down their necks," I said, checking the autonav again, finding we were drifting obliquely through the black hole's wake. "Why didn't you tell me the Spawn had a blind spot?"

"It wasn't my secret to share."

"Is there anything you *can* tell me?" I asked.

"We should go now while the gravity wake is at its strongest."

I turned to Izin. "Light her up."

He hurried down to engineering to power the e-plant while Dietz and his grunts resumed their training. Not wanting to give the Spawn a chance to catch us again, I plotted a series of random jumps through the black hole's wake, doubling back once just in case they got lucky.

"The Spawn will be unable to track a ship this small through a spatial wake this big," Arleen said.

"Just being cautious," I replied. "How'd you know the Tau Cetins were tinkering with the charts?"

"The Ornithians are effective at keeping secrets, except where the Sibylline Sisterhood are concerned."

"Right," I said, realizing they were like Lena, only with better access and there were more of them.

"Do the Tau Cetins know you read their minds?"

"Of course. The entire Forum Membership know our capabilities."

"You told them?"

"We have no desire to deceive."

I wondered what her sisterhood would make of Lena, who would deceive her own mother for an edge.

"Why'd the Tau Cetins include the black hole in our maps?"

"The data is secure and they wish you no harm."

"What if a snakehead ship came this way?"

"That would be…unfortunate."

"We have it and they don't," I said, realizing any Mataron ship that crossed this anomaly would never return home.

"As I said, Captain Kade, the Tau Cetins know their enemies."

"They sure do," I replied, releasing the autonav for a series of evasive jumps that would end at Freehold where I hoped Marie would be waiting with a fat cargo and a ticket to Kota.

Chapter Four: Freehold

Non-aligned Commonwealth
Holbrook's Star
Lacerta In Extremis
0.86 Earth Normal Gravity
930 light years from Sol
140,000 inhabitants, mostly human

"Follow glide slope eight niner four," the Raw Deal controller drawled as we dropped into Freehold's atmosphere. "Upper troposphere winds are easterly, gusting to three thousand K's. Surface visibility is under two hundred meters. Be advised, unmarked peaks intersect your vector. Terrain mapping is required on approach.."

"Understood," I replied. "You want to see our transponder?"

"Hell no! You want some asshole turning you into salvage?" he snapped and closed the channel.

"That's a first," Jase said.

Ground controllers normally chewed my butt off for

not having the transponder on, but here, where even UniPol didn't have a station, broadcasting your identity made you look soft and ripe for the picking.

"Would your own people really shoot us down for money?" Arleen asked.

"Only if they could reach the crash site first and had the guns to defend it."

"Such casual violence," she said. "I'm beginning to understand why your species were barred from interstellar space for so long."

The Embargo had ended four and a half centuries ago, but many humans still hadn't learned their lesson. It was why Earth Navy, Unipol, and the EIS existed, and why we couldn't let the Seps break human civilization apart.

"They should have beacons on those mountains," Jase muttered, scanning the surface for high peaks in our way.

"There were, but the winds tore them apart," I said, dropping the *Silver Lining* into the glide slope.

The planet's surface was mostly alpine and prone to tremors from a hundred and forty tectonic plates grinding against each other. Fifteen degrees above the equator, a forest of nav beams rose across a ninety kilometer wide stretch of jagged, windswept mountains. They marked the extent of the spaceport which, due to the terrain, was a collection of isolated landing pads carved into cliffs, most out of sight of each other. Freeholders had tried shaving mountaintops, but the high winds and ice made exposed landings treacherous and left ships vulnerable to trigger happy salvage hunters.

The planet was infamous for the assorted pirates, bounty hunters, and smugglers who called it home, most of whom would shoot you in the back for a pair of ill-fitting space boots. That's why Raw Deal, its only large settlement, allowed surface jamming. It gave those on the ground anonymity, even if it screwed up the very terrain scanning needed to avoid clipping a mountain on the way in.

"This is nuts," Jase said, glancing anxiously from his static-filled scanner display to a bridge screen showing nothing but a blur of dark gray, supersonic cloud.

"Would you like me to do your job for you?" Izin asked from the couch beside him.

"You could do better?"

"A myopic Minkaran mist-walker could do better."

"Nice," Jase said indignantly. "There's at least seventeen ships down there jamming us."

"Refract your scan arc."

"What do you think I've been doing," Jase snapped, then surreptitiously made the adjustment, noticeably sharpening the surface topography.

Raw Deal had originally been called Lucky Strike based on Captain Holbrook's scans of a world rich in rhodium, rhenium, and palladium, although it was nothing of the sort. Holbrook had doctored the readings to boost his discovery bonus, thinking no one would get out this far until long after he was dead.

Unfortunately, greed has its way and promises of riches triggered a rhodi rush that turned into a miserable struggle for survival once the mother lode ran out. By then, Freehold's icy winds, earthquakes and lack of spares ensured the miner's ships were in no shape for the long haul back to the Core Systems, so they changed the name and went after credits another way. All except one particularly vengeful rhodi rat who made it all the way back to New Liberty where he permanently ended Lewis Holbrook's days of falsifying geoscans. That was over three hundred years ago and not much had changed since.

"The masts are acting like lightning rods," Jase said as the clouds flashed around us and increasingly strong winds buffeted the ship, pushing us out of the glide slope. A lightning bolt ten times longer than the *Silver Lining* struck our dorsal mast, triggering an alarm. "We just lost the gamma wave receptor."

"We don't need it," I said with both hands on my console, fighting the ferocious crosswinds.

At four thousand meters, in air slightly thicker than Earth's sea-level atmosphere, we dropped below the electrical storm into misty cloud. Shadowy silhouettes of ragged peaks hemmed us in on all sides, sometimes shielding us from the winds, sometimes channeling them toward us.

I banked and weaved around snow-capped mountains, following the beacon down, then without seeing the pad, I throttled back and descended vertically into a narrow gorge. The steady winds weakened, replaced by powerful gusts that hit us unpredictably.

"We're not alone," Jase said as a trio of neutrino markers appeared on the bridge screen where e-plants were ticking over in the murky grayness below. "There are three ships down there tracking us, all weapons hot."

"They're playing it safe," I assured him. If Raw Deal had been a controlled port, docked ships would have had their e-plant's idling and their weapons stowed, but out here, they were telling us not to mess with them. "When we're down, we'll do the same."

A wind gust thinned the clouds, giving us a glimpse of a dark hulled ship twice our size perched on a ledge on the far side of the gorge. She showed no transponder signal and had us target locked with weapons tracking, but held her fire.

"See," I said, "they're just saying hello."

"Yeah, real friendly," Jase said sourly.

The clouds closed in again, hiding our neighbor as a proximity warning sounded and a vertical rock wall loomed out of the grayness ahead. Below it, a rectangle of flashing landing lights perched against the cliff appeared out of the mist. The landing lights enclosed a narrow shelf with a single yellow centerline and no docking beam atop a twelve hundred meter high cliff.

"That can't be it," Jase said. "We won't have gear clearance."

"I gave them our dimensions," I said, hoping they knew their business, then a gust of wind pushed us toward the cliff face. I feathered the thrusters, fighting for control. "Pull masts," I said quickly, "eyes only."

Jase retracted the sensor masts, leaving only the opticals exposed, then I eased the *Silver Lining's* stern around toward the cliff. Another gust pushed us across the pad, scraping the bow on rock before I could ease back.

"There goes the paintwork," I muttered as Arleen gripped her couch with both hands. When we were side on and lined up, I lowered the gear and slammed the ship down hard.

"Oops," I said as we rocked on our shock absorbers.

"We've got two meters between the struts and the edge," Jase said, angling an optical to show the starboard side of our hull extended out over the precipice while the port side almost touched the rock wall.

"Tight," I said through gritted teeth.

"The struts are icing up," Jase said.

Our thrusters had melted the surface ice as we came down. Now the melt refroze to our struts, locking us to the pad.

"We could still slide off," Izin declared pessimistically.

"Not as good as maglocks, but better than nothing," I said, checking the outside airspeed indicator. The winds weren't strong enough to blow us off the pad, so I crossed my fingers and cut the engines.

Izin slid off his couch, avoiding looking at the gorge on the bridge screen. "I'll be in engineering until we leave."

"Stay and enjoy the view," Jase taunted, adjusting

an optical to look down into the racing winds, playing on tamph's inherent fear of heights. "Oh man, no way we'd survive that fall. What do you think, Izin? Certain death?"

Izin hurried out without responding as a wicked grin spread across Jase's face.

"The first humans must have had a strong desire to land here," Arleen said, visibly relaxing.

"More a sickness," I replied. "We call it rhodi fever. Pays eighty thousand credits a kilo."

It wasn't good judgment or a heroic pioneering spirit that had determined the landing spot, but Holbrook's grossly exaggerated mother load. It had cost lives and wrecked ships, but at that price, greed knows no fear.

Arleen gave me a bewildered look. "I'm unfamiliar with that disease."

"It's highly contagious, among humans."

"There's a recorded message waiting for us," Jase said and put it through.

Marie's face appeared on the bridge screen. She didn't look happy. "Hi, Sirius. I couldn't get what you wanted. I tried, but there's nothing. Come see me when you get in. We're on Pad Two One Four."

"We'll go now," I said, sliding off my couch.

"I take it there's no law against weapons here?" Jase asked.

"You'd be naked without them."

"I'd like to accompany you," Arleen said. "I've never been to a human world before."

"This isn't a good example," I said, hoping to talk her out of it.

"Considering your anxiety levels, Captain Kade, you may find my presence helpful."

Having an alien empath along whispering in my ear was a tempting offer, but she'd draw too much attention. "Two smugglers looking for work is one thing, but you, I couldn't explain."

"Say I'm a member of your crew."

"No one would believe I had an Uvo deckhand."

"How many humans even know what an Uvo is?" she asked. "Besides, I sense there are non-humans here too."

"Hmm." A strange alien on the run from her own kind might improve my cover, although she'd have to look the part. Silky robes and soft blue skin screamed wealth, which in this place could get us all killed. "You'll need to look less...conspicuous."

"Your pressure suits are extensible." She glanced at Jase, who was almost as tall as she was, although his shoulders were broader. "I'll borrow one of his over garments."

"Something with a hood," I said to Jase. "And remember what we're here for. No bars, no fights, no trouble."

Jase raised his hands innocently. "I won't shoot anyone, who doesn't deserve it."

Considering Raw Deal's reputation as a low life magnet, that didn't reassure me.

* * * *

Sub-zero winds blasted across the landing pad as we walked down the stern ramp. We caught fleeting glimpses through the racing clouds of two ships perched precariously on the far side of the gorge, then a small tremor shook the ground. The pad's surface ice cracked and tiny rocks showered down from above. When the shaking ended, a ground-level panel slid open in the cliff face and a small scooperbot scuttled out and vacuumed up the rock fragments.

"At least they keep the pad clean," Jase said uneasily, then we hurried across to a corroded pressure hatch inset into the cliff.

Beside the hatch was a large cargo door that had been stripped back to bare metal by the winds, although the seals on both entries looked tight enough to keep the cold out and the heat in. Both doors had been cannibalized from old ships and were operated by simple binary touchpads rather than security locks.

When I tapped the door control, the pressure hatch swung in releasing a cloud of warm air that frosted on contact with the cold. Eager to escape the wind, we stepped inside and followed a narrow cave slung with overhead cables and feeble lights into the mountain. It emptied into a large tunnel running parallel to the gorge that was haphazardly laid with a path of dirty metal gratings. Nearby, two unwashed stimheads cast suspicious looks our way as they whispered to each other and blew purple smoke from their nostrils.

Arleen winced at the smell. "The atmosphere here is chemically contaminated."

"Wait until you smell the good stuff," Jase said, inhaling appreciatively.

She gave him a perplexed look. "You are a strangely self-destructive species."

A burly spacer with dark stubble on his chin, an old-style single shot exploder on his hip and a get-out-my-way swagger strode down the corridor toward us. He was accompanied by a vaguely humanoid Meropan with dark brown skin and eyes, a broad mouth and thin black body hair. Battered, gray plate armor covered his chest and a long-barreled weapon hung from his shoulder.

"Which way to Pad Two One Four?" I asked.

"Screw you," the spacer growled as his hand moved to his exploder in case I objected to his tone. Beside him, the Meropan emitted a guttural laugh as my DNA sniffer read them both and flashed their tracking sheets into my mind.

The human was Zahir Deeb, a small-time Cali brigand occasionally employed by the Rashidun black market syndicate. He was wanted by UniPol for violence and misdemeanors although the EIS considered him little more than a third rate thug. His companion was Urkis Nogal, a bigger catch, wanted by his own people for piracy, outpost raiding and a string of Access Treaty infractions. The Meropan Patrol had even authorized his ship's destruction if it couldn't be impounded, although no Earth ship would risk fighting superior alien technology.

"Their speech was aggressive, but they were wary of you," Arleen whispered as they moved off down the passageway.

"They should be," Jase said belligerently, never one to let a slight pass him by.

"Everyone here is afraid," she added, empathically sensing an undercurrent of fear all around us. "They hide it, but it's there."

"It's a survival instinct," I said, making a mental note to send a sighting report to the MerPatrol, although their wayward citizen would be long gone by the time they got here. The two spacers disappeared into a side cave, then I glanced at her elegant face. "Cover up."

Arleen pulled the hood on Jase's knee-length coat over her head, concealing her fine features. She was unarmed, but the ill-fitting coat and her height would make any potential attacker think twice before challenging her.

Deciding not to risk a confrontation with the twitchy human and his Meropan companion, we headed in the opposite direction trying to look as if we belonged. The cave passages were filled with unsavory humans and a smattering of aliens, all outwardly ready for a fight, yet careful not to provoke one.

The passage led deeper into the mountain where boisterous voices punctuated by drunken shouts and the occasional boom of a discharging weapon echoed to us. Soon we emerged into a low ceilinged cavern lined with ramshackle bars, grimy workshops, and cramped housing blocks. Wretched stimheads eyed us suspiciously from the shadows while scantily clad women sought prolonged eye contact, ensuring we knew what they were selling.

Two drunks burst out of a bar, fists flying clumsily at each other. The smaller one landed a lucky haymaker, sending his opponent's teeth and blood splattering in front of us. When the bigger man fell down, his opponent kicked him repeatedly in the stomach and face until he was unconscious.

"What are you looking at?" The short man growled at me as if one fight wasn't enough.

Jase tensed, but I caught his arm.

"Nothing," I said and guided Jase and Arleen past him, then my bionetic listener heard the click of a charge activator.

I spun around as the drunk raised a rusty staple gun, the kind used in prefab assembly. It wasn't a real weapon, but at that range, it could have cut my spine in half. I darted forward with super reflexed speed and punched his wrist before he could fire, knocking the makeshift weapon out of his hand. It fell barrel first onto his boot and went off, shooting a titanium staple into his foot. He yelped in pain and hopped back on one leg, then fell to the ground reaching for his boot as drunken laughter rippled through the onlookers.

Not giving his friends a chance to intervene, I took Jase and Arleen by the arms and whispered, "Let's go."

Arleen glanced back as I led her away. The big man was coming to, holding his blood-smeared face while the other winced as he levered the staple out of his boot with a homemade shiv.

"So much hatred," she whispered.

"They're mad at the universe for being stuck here," I said, then a skinny man missing two front teeth with bulging, bloodshot eyes stepped in front of us.

"Want tasty tasty?" he asked, offering me his open hand. It contained four stim cylinders, each a different color.

"I want directions, to Pad Two One Four."

He scowled and turned away, but I grabbed his shoulder with one hand and held up my vault key with the other. "A hundred credits."

The stim pusher gave me a scheming look and a toothless smile. "Hundred and fifty."

"A hundred or I'll clean my boots with your face."

His smile faded, then he raised his reader. I entered the amount and swiped his scanner, then he nodded toward a dark passage. "Down there to the end, turn right. Five or six down."

"If you're lying, I'll decorate the bow of my ship with your head."

He scowled resentfully. "Old Skandi's no liar."

I let him scurry off into the crowd to warn his friends how dangerous we were, then we started toward the passage he'd indicated.

"You're a skilled deceiver, Captain Kade," Arleen whispered. "You had no intention of harming that pathetic creature."

"He didn't know that."

We followed Old Skandi's directions for two clicks, climbing slowly through the mountain to a wider and brighter passage than the one near the *Silver Lining*. After trying several side passages, we found the *Mendiant* on a partially leveled plateau shielded on two sides by low cliffs. The pad was the other side of the mountain from where we'd docked, and out of the wind with a much easier approach.

The *Mendiant* was five times the size of the *Silver Lining*, kind of boxy with a bulge above the bow containing her bridge. She had a pair of underpowered sublights astern, three large cargo doors along her port side, all sealed up, and fore and aft mounted popguns that were actively scanning, more for show than effect.

"Marie knows the drill," Jase said, watching the *Mendi's* mini cannons slowly rotate.

"She's been here before," I said.

When we reached the forward airlock, it swung open, confirming they were keeping a constant watch in port. Eddie Nubaker met us at the airlock and led us up to the galley where Marie greeted me with a quick kiss and a rebuff.

"You're late," she said, glancing curiously at Arleen behind me.

"I had a few errands to run. Rescued the king of a star empire, escaped the Spawn Fleet, even dodged a black hole. Nothing special," She gave me a puzzled look, then I made the introductions. "This is Arleen. She's an Uvo empath. No hiding your feelings from her."

"Oh? You must hate that."

Arleen pulled her hood back. "Hello, Marie Dulon."

"Welcome aboard," Marie said.

"So," I said relaxing, "all this way for nothing?"

"I'm sorry, Sirius, I tried every one. There's just nothing going to Kota, not anymore. Earth Navy has shut down all their suppliers. Freehold is dead."

"We saw ships docked on the way in," Jase said as he poured himself a coffee.

"They've been waiting for months for cargoes," Marie said. "Most have laid off their crews and are sitting the war out."

"Is there anyone we can bribe for a landing clearance?"

"Only if you want your throat slit. One of my contacts had something urgent, but I missed it by a day."

"Who's your contact?"

She eyed me warily. "Ruslan Glebb. He owns the local casino. I don't normally do business with him, but I was desperate. He'd been looking for a ship for months.

Was offering a big completion bonus too."

"For months? What kind of cargo?" I asked suspiciously, wondering why, with so many ships looking for work, it had been stranded.

"Volatile. That's why no one would touch it. It's loading tomorrow."

"It's still here?" I said thoughtfully. "Do they need help moving it?"

"No, their ship's bigger than both of ours combined. Even if it wasn't, they'd steal the Silver Lining the first chance they got."

"Where's their ship?"

"Don't know. Freehold is very particular about sharing that kind of information, but you can find them at Zhulov's most days. It's a blood house. Lots of fights, hard-drinking, gambling." She glanced at Jase. "You'd like it."

Jase grinned, already certain he was going to get a chance to try it out for himself.

"Who are we looking for?" I asked.

"The captain's Meropan. Don't know his name, but his first officer's a human called Zahir Deeb."

I pretended to hear the name for the first time. "The Mero doesn't wear plate armor and carry a long barreled beamer by any chance?"

"Yeah, that's him. They're notorious bullies and very dangerous."

"Not as dangerous as us," Jase said.

Marie looked dubious. "You're not going to do anything stupid are you?"

"I just want to make friends and go to Kota," I said innocently, then turned to Arleen. "But not you, not this time."

Her Uvo empathic abilities told her there was no point arguing. "As you wish. I will remain on your ship while you…make friends," she replied in a tone indicating she knew friendship was the last thing on my mind.

As usual, she was right.

* * * *

I saw Arleen back to the *Silver Lining* and retrieved a piece of EIS equipment from my stateroom, then Jase and I took a creaky elevator down to the bottom of a narrow ravine. The elevator shaft opened into an enclosed walkway made of salvaged bulkheads that whistled and banged from the freezing winds outside. It ran alongside a wild ice melt river to the remains of an old passenger ship that wreckers had lured to disaster with a false landing signal. They'd killed the survivors and looted the ship without ever being brought to justice.

Her name was the *Moyale*. She lay upside down between bleak cliffs and the white-capped river on almost level ground. Her bow had been torn off and her engines stripped for parts while her midsection had been hull patched against the cold. She was part boarding house, part bar and was powered by the ship's old emergency generator which had been in constant use for over three hundred years.

It was almost midday and the bar was only half full. There was no music, no stimheads, only a few quiet drunks and a couple of tables of intensely serious gamblers. It was an upside-down room, with the ship's overhead now the floor and a ceiling stripped of deck plates.

Urkis Nogal and Zahir Deeb sat at a table with three men and two women. They were playing a Sino-tech game that had been popular in the People's Federation of Asia back when the rhodi rush was at its height. The players sat in front of long thin screens filled with image tiles of ancient warlords, beautiful princesses and mythical dragons, each accompanied by small Hanzi characters. Shimmering above each player's tile screen were three vertical bars–red, blue and green–while in the center of the table was a holographic pile of gold with a number floating above it indicating the prize pool. Surrounding the gold was a slowly rotating ring of image tiles each player studied intently, searching for a high scoring placement.

"Ever played that before?" I whispered to Jase.

"Have I!" he said, wincing. "Peking poker. It's mahjong, Russian roulette, and eight-card Betty all rolled into one. The green bar is how much money you got left, red is the bet, and blue's your score."

"Any way to cheat?"

"Sure, if you know how to hack the randomizer. A couple of guys did it once on Ardenus. Almost got away with it too."

I scanned my bionetic memory base for Peking poker, then my mind filled with several thousand beginner strategies, none of which looked easy. The name of the game was placing your tiles where they earned the most points based on the tiles beside them. Tile affinities, fortunate colors and lucky numbers determined bonuses and penalties that could radically alter the value of a placement. Some tiles could not be split once together while others required particular tiles to be in play before they could be used. When a player couldn't place a tile, he discarded one, missing a chance to earn points even though his green money column clicked down. It was crazy and complicated, but it kind of made sense.

"Guess I'll have to wing it," I said, reaching for my Earth Bank vault key.

"Don't do it, Skipper. They'll end up owning the ship."

"Not if I start a fight first," I said with a smile. "Just don't let them kill me."

Jase took a seat and ordered a drink while I wandered across to the table to watch. Zahir Deeb, the

Cali cutthroat, glanced at me with a flicker of recognition, but said nothing while his Meropan companion paid me no attention at all.

The players took turns declaring bets, selecting images on their thin horizontal screens and picking their spot on the tile ring. When a tile was played, it appeared above the pile of gold, increasing the prize pool and decreasing the player's money bar, then it slid down into the rotating tile ring to the player's chosen placement, increasing his blue score bar. Played and discarded tiles were replaced by the randomizer, ensuring the player's screen was always full. After multiple rounds, the circular ring was crowded with tiles, then a tall slick-looking man in a fancy suit played a fire dragon and declared, "Tiaozhan."

My bionetic game memory, not my linguistics base, translated the word: *Challenge*.

There were groans around the table, then a bearded man muttered, "Chengren." *Concede*.

With less grace, the others studied the circle of tiles looking for a way to counter his dragon call, then they rolled their displays face down in surrender. When the last display had been turned over, the gold number vanished and Slick's green column grew a little higher.

"Got room for one more?" I asked.

"No," Zahir Deeb grunted without looking up.

"I got forty thousand credits here that says you do," I said, holding up my vault key, instantly getting their attention.

"It's a fake," the shaven head woman declared scornfully.

"Easy to prove," I said.

The bearded man looked me up and down, then nodded to the barman who brought an ancient reader over to the table. He checked my balance and raised his eyebrows in surprise. "It's real."

"Fine by me," Slick said, eager to get his hands on

my credits.

The bartender swiped my key and gave me a tile screen, then I sat down without offering my name. A green column appeared above my screen, showing the credits I was about to lose, then a small golden crown appeared in front of Slick, indicating he had first draw.

"Fire dragons are wild, earth dragons are free and princesses are double," he said. "Buy-in for a hundred."

It took me a moment to figure out the jargon, then a row of image tiles appeared on my display and the betting began. Bearded Man opened with a white tiger and bet conservative. Skinhead Sally matched him with a lesser air dragon. Her muscular girlfriend discarded three tiles, then I opened with a Khan and matched the bet. A fat, Pudding Faced man consorted my Khan with a princess and bet high, then Urkis Nogal, the only non-human in the game, tried to impress by dropping a golden dragon, revealing he had no idea what he was doing. Even I knew to save major dragons for point blitzes and declarations. Zahir Deeb gave Nogal an exasperated look and played a lowly shield bearer.

After three rounds of bets, discards, and placements, my head was spinning and the strategy I'd followed was in tatters. After four rounds, mild-mannered Pudding Face was on top, Slick was doing well and the rest of us were way behind on points.

When Pudding Face won the hand, he showed too much excitement to be the real tile shark. That had to be Slick, who was careful not to win too much, not that I cared. Each time either of them won, Deeb's irritation increased. Pudding Face didn't notice the Cali's deteriorating demeanor and couldn't hide his amateurish delight at his mounting column of credits. Slick, on the other hand, watched Deeb with complete understanding and no fear, telling me he was not only armed but had accomplices ready to step in if the suckers got twitchy.

After a while, I realized each time Deeb bet big,

Pudding Face won. It happened too often to be luck. Someone was funneling Deeb's money to the fat little shopkeeper, making him a target.

Across the bar, Jase sat quietly in a dark corner nursing a drink he never touched, keeping his twin fraggers where he could get to them in a hurry. I made a show of downing too many drinks, outpacing the others, while my bionetics neutralized the intoxicants before they affected me. I began slurring my words, making mistakes and cursing my bad luck each time I lost.

After two hours, I was down fifteen thousand and swaying in my chair. Deeb was too, only for him it was real and he'd lost twice what I had. As for Nogal, the only thing he'd learned was how to lose his plate metal shirt without realizing why. In their eyes, Pudding Face was soaking up their credits, while Slick made steady, unspectacular gains.

"You are one fine player," I said to Pudding Face, eyeing his big green credit column, knowing Slick had made him the fall guy.

"Thank you, sir," he said modestly. "I'm not normally this lucky."

I turned to Slick. "You done good too."

Slick shrugged indifferently and glanced at his patsy. "Not as well as Michal, but I can't complain."

"What's your name?" I asked.

"Alexi Zhulov."

"Ah, this is your place," I said drunkenly, realizing all it took to fix the game was to own the randomizer.

We played a few more hands, then Pudding Face won big again and Miss Muscles sighed in despair. "That's it for me boys. I'm out."

"Same here," Skinhead Sally said. "I'm busted."

"It's his fault," Deeb spat, glaring at Pudding Face. "He's got our money!"

"Not all your money, just most of it," I said, laughing at the sliver of green floating above his tile screen.

"I don't see no big green in front of you," he declared angrily, then pointed at Pudding Face's towering column. "I never seen anyone win like that."

Pudding Face tensed. "The tiles favored me tonight, friend."

"The hell they did!" He lunged across the table with a short-bladed knife in one hand.

I caught his wrist before he could slash open Pudding Face's throat and drunkenly dragged Deeb across the table onto the floor. I punched him clumsily in the face, hard enough to slow him down and drawing his anger away from Slick's fall guy.

Deeb twisted his knife hand away and stabbed at me, but I drove his knuckles into the floor, knocking the blade free. He telegraphed a big left hook with his other hand, which I could easily have blocked, but I slipped my free hand into his pocket instead and let his fist fly. He landed a jarring punch that sent me sliding back. Before I could get to my feet, my DNA sniffer warned the Meropan was behind me. I spun around, deflecting the butt of his long-barreled beamer away from my head, then twin fraggers blasted the skeletal ceiling. The bar fell instantly silent as all eyes turned across the room to Jase.

"I hate sore losers," he said menacingly, leveling both weapons at Deeb and Nogal with a look begging for an excuse to use them.

I stumbled to my feet, saw Pudding Face was unhurt and Slick had moved well away, then Jase and I backed up to the door.

"I wouldn't come after us if I were you," Jase said.

We stepped outside and hurried back through the metal passage to the elevator. When it began rattling its way up to Raw Deal, Jase holstered his weapons.

"How much you lose?" he asked.

"I think the boots are still mine," I replied lightly,

certain Lena would understand why I'd thrown her money away.

"I hope that was worth it."

"It was, if you want to go to Kota." I showed him the personal tracker I'd collected from my stateroom. On its screen, the homing beacon I'd slipped into Deeb's pocket indicated the Cali thug was still in Zhulov's waiting until it was safe to leave.

"You tagged him."

"Got to find his ship somehow," I said, then we returned to the *Silver Lining* to wait for Deeb and Nogal to find their way home.

* * * *

"I'm not authorized to loan equipment to civilians," Dietz declared outside the giant VRS container where his super soldier arsenal was stored.

"It's not a loan," I said. "You won't be getting them back, and it's the only way you're going to Kota."

His jaw tightened with irritation. "How many you want?"

"One should do it. No, make it three. And a remote detonator, clamps and climbing equipment."

"I want the detonator back."

"No promises."

"Hmm. This could start a war."

"Nah. I'm doing MerPatrol a favor."

Dietz considered my intentions. "Want me to go with you?"

"No, I want you to stay out of sight," I replied, unlocking the container.

When the big door swung open, Dietz went inside and rummaged around for a while, then returned with a military-style backpack. He pulled out a cylindrical detonator.

"Power on," he said, pointing to an on-off slide

selector, then to a touchpad. "Detonate." He returned it to the backpack and produced one of the three N-grenades I'd asked for. He flipped open a tiny plate on its side revealing a sliding switch. "Fire mode selector: safety, contact, proximity, remote. You want remote." He then took a three-clawed clamp from the backpack. "Grenade goes in here," he said, pressing the grenade in with a snap as the claws grabbed it. "You want to hear that click. Right?"

I nodded. "Got it."

"It's contact sensitive." He turned the clamp bottom-up and made a light hammering motion. "If it hits metal, a mag clamp activates. Any other surface, it fires a barbed anchor spike." He put the grenade and clamp back in the pack and pushed it into my chest. "Don't kill yourself."

"I'll try not to."

"And Kade, if you're going to be captured, detonate a grenade. Do not, I repeat, do not let anyone get their hands on those things. And don't throw them into a ravine thinking no one will find them."

"Understood," I said soberly, then resealed the VRS container and returned to the bridge where Jase had a terrain map up on the bridge screen. The tracker was sitting on his console feeding in the homing beacon's position.

"Deeb's stopped moving," Jase said. "He's on a peak southwest of here. Nav beam identifier Zero Eight Five."

"That's it."

"When do we go?" Jase asked.

I glanced at the bridge screen giving us a panoramic view of the *Silver Lining's* surroundings. Two of Freehold's stars had set, while the third, visible above the planet's axis, wouldn't set for another seven months. Raw Deal operated a standard twenty-four-hour clock, even though the kind of nights known on Earth were rare astronomical events.

"It won't get any darker," I said and tapped the intercom. "Izin, it's time."

"I'll meet you at the ramp, Captain," he said, then Jase and I headed for the crew elevator as another tremor set the *Silver Lining* rocking on her struts.

* * * *

Pad Zero Eight Five stood atop a rocky outcrop shaved level during the first years of colonization. A bridge across a narrow chasm to the east led to a cargo door inset into a mountain whose peak was lost in the clouds and which shielded the pad from the prevailing winds. On the other three sides, sheer cliffs dropped into a narrow, mist-shrouded canyon. It was a precarious position, but the sheltered pad was far enough from the mountain that large ships could land in relative safety.

"They'll be watching the bridge," Jase said as we observed the pad from across the gorge.

"Bound to be," I agreed.

We hid behind a rusting cargobot on an empty landing pad, peering through racing clouds at the Meropan ship. She was a rounded hexagon of dark, unpainted metal with sloping sides that curved into a shallow dome on top. Spaced evenly around her base were six tilting engines on stubby arms, giving her maneuverability belying her size. Between the engine mounts were six cargo doors. Only the door facing the bridge was open, with a ribbed ramp extending down to the pad. Above the cargo doors was a ring of circular hatches for weapons and sensors, marking her as more privateer than freighter.

It was no surprise she had a human as first mate, especially one with a penchant for violence. The Meropan Meld was a minor power in the Orion Arm, barely sixteen thousand years ahead of mankind, which almost made us peers. It was why Meropans weren't above recruiting human spacers to make up their crew numbers when shorthanded or even serving on human ships themselves when they couldn't return home.

"They've scrubbed her Meropan registry," Izin observed, noting the absence of MerPatrol hieroglyphics on her hull.

"They don't want anyone knowing who they are," I agreed.

Nogal, Deeb and a furry-faced Gienan walked down the ramp.

"They got a whole menagerie in there," Jase muttered as he watched them head toward the freight bridge.

When they were halfway across the bridge, a small, four-engined hopper came flying around the mountain, hugging the cliff to keep out of the wind. The three spacers barely glanced at it as it flew low over their heads and headed for a metal platform two clicks south. When it landed, the pilot leaped out and attached cables to its hull so it wouldn't get blown off, then a man in a white thermal suit climbed out, followed by a stretcherbot with a transparent bubble to shield its occupant from the elements. On the hopper's fuselage were stenciled the words: *Raw Deal Medevac*.

"It's an air ambulance," Izin said, observing it through his telescoping eyes.

"They barely looked at it," I said thoughtfully as Nogal, Deeb, and Catface disappeared through a pressure door into the mountain. "It must fly over them all the time."

"I don't fancy doing vertical lifts in these winds," Jase said, eyeing the fuselage winch for hauling injured people off the ground.

"You won't have to hover," I said, "just fly slow."

"What?" He gave me a puzzled look, realized I'd found our way onto the Meropan ship's landing pad and focused his scope on the hopper. "That thing's got to be two hundred years old."

"Maybe three," I said and turned to Izin. "Can you cover us from here?"

Izin studied the clouds racing through the gorge. "No Captain. The winds are too strong, even for me."

"Then you just bought yourself a ride," I said, sliding my monoscope into my pocket.

Izin glanced apprehensively at the precipice below, realizing what I was asking. "On second thought–"

"Too late. You're with us. If all goes according to plan, you can keep your eyes closed the whole time."

"We have a plan?" Jase asked surprised, then we went back inside the ridge to find our way through Raw Deal's tunnel network to the other side of the canyon.

* * * *

The air ambulance office was located in a quiet part of Raw Deal. The passage outside was poorly lit and deserted and the door gave way easily as I levered it open. We slipped inside and hurried past two desks and stacks of boxes full of spare parts to an unlocked pressure hatch. It opened onto the windswept landing platform the four-engined medevac hopper was tied to. The old air freighter was flanked by rusting storage containers and a small refueling station that was one random spark away from catching fire.

Izin and I released the anchor cables while Jase climbed into the pilot's seat and checked the controls.

"There's no flight controller," Jase yelled, staring at an empty receptacle where the aircraft's flight management module should have been. The contact points were rusted with age, indicating the air ambulance hadn't had auto-guidance for years.

"You'll have to fly manually," I said.

"In these winds?" Jase said uneasily, familiarizing

himself with the normally automated thrust-vector controls. He scowled and rubbed grime from the fuel indicator. "Two thirds full. At least we won't run out of fuel."

Izin climbed into the sparsely equipped medical compartment with his rifle bag and assembled his long-barreled sniper rifle. I followed him in and pulled a bolt gun from Dietz's backpack.

"This ain't going to work," Jase called over his shoulder as he practiced adjusting four pairs of vector sticks and throttle sliders.

"Sure it will. Just set thruster levels and focus on vectoring," I said, sliding an anchor spike into the bolt gun. "All you have to do is fly low and slow past the cliff. And don't stop, no matter what."

The magnetically accelerated bolt gun had a short harpoon on top, exposed so the line attached to its tailfin wouldn't snag. I clipped one end of my elasticized climbing rope to the tailfin and the other to my harness. The anchor spike could support twenty men, if it was imbedded in rock that could take their weight.

"Suppose you miss, Captain?" Izin asked.

"That's what these are for," I replied, holding up a pair of six legged cambots, each the size of my fist. Their bodies were high tensile durillium with a spring-loaded camalot for anchoring in crevices at one end and a safety line secured to my harness at the other. They had enough AI to work with me, taking turns running between crevices, ensuring I always had an emergency anchor point.

I snapped safety lines onto both cambots, activated the position indicator on my belt and checked they were reading my relative position and velocity. The data would tell them when to move, when to hold and when to catch me if I fell.

"Have you ever done this before, Captain?" Izin asked dubiously.

Upload rock climber skill set, I thought, then the skills and experience of an expert mountaineer flowed from my bionetic base into my mind. In a flash, I knew how to scale the tallest mountains in Mapped Space, knew every technique, had used every piece of equipment. It didn't look so hard and what I lacked in hands-on experience, my gene modded ultra reflexes would make up for. Or so I hoped.

"Sure," I said, "plenty of times."

"You never mentioned it before," he said suspiciously.

"Come with me. I'll show you how."

"I'd rather eat one of your anchor spikes than go out there."

"When you pick me up," I yelled to Jase, "hover in close."

He glanced at the big Meropan ship uncertainly. "They'll see us."

"It'll be too late by then." I checked my three lines and readied the bolt gun. "Let's go."

"Hang on," Jase warned and pushed the four throttle sticks forward with both hands.

The hopper lifted up off the platform and slewed sideways as the wind hit. Izin grabbed a handrail and turned his bulging eyes away from the open fuselage door as we slid above the landing platform and out over the misty void.

"You OK?" I asked.

"If tamphs were meant to fly, Captain, we'd have feathers, not sonar," he grumbled, battling his species' innate fear of heights.

"You going to be able to shoot?"

"I don't know," he said, holding on so tight his knuckles were turning white.

Jase juggled the four vector-sticks, banking clumsily, almost flipping us over, then we lurched sideways. He cursed under his breath, brought our nose around and started a shallow dive toward the cliffs below the Meropan ship. Shifting winds buffeted us, constantly pushing us off course while Jase learned in seconds what local pilots took months to master.

"Like driving a bus," he called out, then we rolled steeply, "–with no syncro!"

I pulled my climbing helmet on, then the visor's head-up display illuminated telling me ambient temperature was seven below, oxygen was at nineteen percent and both cambots were FREE.

"I need four hands," Jase complained as we wobbled and slid tail-first toward the cliff.

"Izin will help you fly."

"No! Izin won't!" the tamph declared as we banked steeply into a power dive.

"I got it," Jase reassured us as we leveled off, racing for the cliffs.

I disabled helmet comms so there'd be no chatter for the Mero ship to detect and readied the bolt gun. "Too fast!"

Jase pitched the nose up, bleeding speed as we slid in under the Meropan's hull. Two of her engines and part of her hexagonal hull hung out over the edge, giving her optics a clear line of sight–if they were looking this way.

"Bring the tail around!" I yelled. Jase's hands flew across the vector sticks, then the hopper side slipped toward the cliff face. "That's it…a little more."

The rock face was cracked and slick with ice. The closer we got, the more the winds died down, then as we raced up to the wall of gray rock, I aimed the bolt gun ahead of the hopper and fired. The finned harpoon shot across to the cliff, trailing the climbing rope uncoiling at my feet. It slammed into the rock so deep, only its tailfin was visible, then I hooked the bolt gun to my belt and took a cambot in each hand.

"Don't leave me hanging," I yelled with a grin, then

as the hopper passed the anchor spike, I leaped out into the freezing air.

Halfway across, I threw the cambots up at the cliff face and reached for bare rock with my gloved hands. I landed with a thud, couldn't get a grip, and slid down the icy surface. The lightning-fast cambots darted across the rock wall, searching for a fissure to clamp into, then the safety lines connecting us tore them off the rock. All three of us fell together until the elasticized line to the anchor-bolt snapped tight, stretching as it slowed our fall. It recoiled at the bottom, bouncing me back up as the cambots dropped past me. I snatched the ice pick off my belt and crashed it into the rocks as I slowed, then the cambots scampered up the cliff either side of me, searching for anchor points.

I looked over my shoulder, saw the hopper flying away as Izin's small hand slid the fuselage door shut. High above me, the Meropan raider showed no sign of having seen me yet. I hoped they were all drunk or gambling or doing whatever Meropan brigands did for laughs.

On my HUD, Cambot Two's status indicator changed to ANCHORED as its camalot locked into a crack in the wall. The other cambot scurried up the rock to a point higher than the first and embedded itself in place.

Safe for the moment, I dug my spiked boots into the cliff, activated my harness-winch and walked up the rock face as it wound in the line. When I reached the anchor spike, the nearest cambot retracted its camalot and scampered up the cliff face to a new crack. Once it was ANCHORED, its twin did the same.

With both cambots taking my weight, I let off the reel and climbed past the anchor-bolt, using the ice pick and my spiked boots for traction. Every few meters, I dug in and waited while one or other of the cambots climbed a little higher. I didn't need to tell them anything. They knew from sensors in my boots and the pick when I was secure and wouldn't move unless all three had contact.

When I was well above the first bolt and my HUD showed both cambots were ANCHORED, I used the bolt gun to set a second safety point. There was no response from the Meropans to the crack of the anchor-bolt hammering into the rock, so I clipped my main line to its tailfin and clambered to within fifty meters of their ship.

The cambots repositioned themselves as I retrieved a grenade clamp from my backpack and slammed its base against the cliff face. Its harpoon speared into the rock with a loud crack, then I set the first N-grenade's mode selector to remote and snapped it in, locking the clamp's claws around it. With the first charge set, I worked my way across to a point below the middle of the Meropan privateer and set the second N-grenade.

Faint voices sounded from the landing pad, but no one appeared as I started crab-walking across the cliff again and the cambots took turns scurrying above me. When I reached a point below the side of the Meropan ship, I slid a spike into the bolt gun preparing to set another safety, then heard humming behind me. I twisted around to see a small spherical sensorbot with a large optical in its center, staring straight at me. I immediately fired the anchor-bolt into its eye, sending it tumbling away in a burst of sparks into the clouds below.

Knowing I didn't have long, I quickly set my next safety and planted my last N-grenade, then angry voices shouted down at me from the cliff's edge. Three Meropans stood there, gesticulating furiously. One aimed a two-handed weapon down at me, but his chest exploded before he could fire and he toppled over the edge. His body fell past me as his companions turned and looked back along the cliffs, searching for the shooter. They spotted the mcdevac hopper, hovering in the shadow of the mountain, and Izin lying flat on the medical compartment's deck, aiming his long-barreled SN6 through the open fuselage door.

A large door in the Meropan ship slid up and a ramp extended out into open air, then a round cargo-lifter carrying three armed Meropans and a human floated out. The lifter dropped quickly toward me, buffeted by the wind as three of the four spacers opened fire. Energy blasts shattered rock and melted ice all around me, then Izin fired at the pilot, missing and striking the control console. The lifter immediately corkscrewed into the cliff and exploded as two more Meroes came down the cargo ramp and began shooting down at me.

Tied to the anchor spike, I was an easy target, so I released my belt reel, disengaging from the main climbing line. The two cambot safety lines snapped taut, taking my weight and preventing me from swinging.

"Avalanche!" I yelled, triggering the cambot's rescue mode. "Go right!"

Cambot Two's HUD indicator switched to FREE, then it raced above me, past its twin, and clamped itself into a fissure. It ANCHORED, giving me a swing point, then Cambot One went FREE and ran past Two.

"Good boys!" I muttered and kicked away from the cliff, running across the face like a pendulum swinging beneath Cambot Two. Their simple machine intelligences didn't know there was no avalanche, could see no falling snow, but they believed I knew better and were trying to save me.

Cambot One ANCHORED, then Two scurried to a new swing point as the spacers on the cargo ramp and at the edge of the cliff shot down at me. Energy blasts flashed around me, searing rock and ice as I ran, then I ducked under a narrow overhang and crashed my ice pick into the cliff, coming to a bone-jarring halt.

I reached for the detonator as energy blasts struck the ledge above me, shattering the rock and peppering me with fragments, knocking the detonator out of my hand. I grabbed for it, but it clattered against the cliff face and fell.

"Release!" I ordered and both cambots let go of their anchor points. The three of us dropped beside the cliff as the remote bounced off a minuscule ledge, then I snatched it out of the air with one hand.

"Anchor! Anchor!" I yelled desperately, then Cambot One caught a crevice and locked itself in place.

The line snapped tight, slamming me hard into the cliff face. I drove my ice pick into the rock with one hand as Cambot Two fell past me, then I activated the remote with the other. Three tremendous explosions shook the massif simultaneously, blasting out horizontally from the cliff, hurling millions of tons of rock into the misty canyon. The top of the shaved peak collapsed and slid into the gorge, carrying the Meropan ship with it.

The raider rolled onto its side as it rode a waterfall of rock into the void. One engine passed close to my face, forcing me to press my visor into the cliff, then the Meropan ship dropped away. Its engines glowed, coming to life one by one as giant boulders hammered its hull, pushing it further over onto its side.

Above me, the rock Cambot One clung to shattered. Its status changed to FREE and we both fell after the Meropan ship. The whole mountain seemed to be collapsing as we dropped toward the mist, then Cambot Two's line snapped tight and pulled me away from the rockslide. I swung blindly through swirling dust out into clear air, then I caught the rock face with the pick and Cambot One scrambled below me to a fissure and locked itself in place.

Far below, the Meropan ship fell into the chasm, its six engines glowing as its bridge crew tried to save her. She started to right herself as giant boulders pounded her hull, then one of her engines was crushed and exploded. In a panic, the crew pushed her remaining engines to full power, sending her spiraling uncontrollably across the gorge into the cliffs. She exploded, filling the chasm with brilliant white light and sending a shockwave rolling through the canyon.

A ferocious wind crushed me into the rock wall, tearing at my clothes. My hand slid down the pick handle, but the straining cambots hung on as the shockwave faded and the burning wreck fell into the clouds. Above me, less than half the bridge remained, its ragged end jutting out from the mountain, now high above what was left of the decapitated peak.

I clung to the rock face watching the cloud below flicker from the fires at the bottom of the gorge, then a four-engined dumper and a small air taxi with a turret gun came racing up the gorge at high speed. I tensed, thinking they were coming for me, but the dumper released a beacon that hovered above the cloud while the taxi took up a guard position above the marker.

They were wreckers, staking their claim.

The dumper glided into the mist to scout the find, then the medevac hopper emerged above the torn peak and dropped toward me. Jase brought her in dangerously close, then Izin slid the fuselage door open, but couldn't bring himself to stand in the open and offer me his hand. I caught the safety rail, put one foot on the cabin deck and released the cambot lines, then pulled myself in. I barely got my hand inside before Izin slammed the door shut and locked it with obvious relief.

"You made the shot," I said, impressed he'd been able to overcome his chronic acrophobia.

"I made two."

"The second missed," I said.

"You're alive, aren't you."

I smiled and slapped his shoulder. "You made two."

Jase looked over his shoulder. "I thought you were going to blow it *after* we left?"

"Change of plan."

He grunted and turned the hopper toward the medevac platform, leaving the two little cambots clinging to the frozen cliffs beneath what had once been Pad Zero Eight Five. Dietz wouldn't be pleased to lose them, but at least he'd get his detonator back.

* * * *

I spent the night with Marie aboard the *Mendi*. She'd arranged an intimate dinner for two in the ship's cavernous cargo hold beside a live holofeed of the snow and wind blasted mountains outside. A storm had rolled in, dropping the temperature to thirty below, although we were dressed for summer, drank chilled champagne and imagined we were anywhere but Freehold. Outside our little island of light, hidden in the cargo hold's darkness, Marie had even rigged a hullbot to add to the ambience with soft, romantic music.

"If I didn't know better," I said as we waited for dessert, "I'd swear you were trying to have your way with me."

She smiled. "I wouldn't need to go to this much trouble for that. We both know you're a sure thing."

I nodded, letting my eyes descend to her ample cleavage. "Yep," I replied with exaggerated helplessness.

"I'm not skipping my soufflé," she warned, knowing the look in my eyes.

"You have your dessert now, I'll have mine later."

"Hmm," she said, glancing at the bare cargo hold with a hint of anxiety. "So, what are we going to do?"

"Your cabin's closer and it's too cold to go back to the Lining tonight."

"That's not what I meant," she said soberly. "We can't go to Kota and we can't keep flying around empty. We'll go broke in a month."

We'd never be broke, not with Lena bankrolling us,

but I couldn't tell Marie that.

"Did you do what I asked?"

"Yes, I spoke to him," she replied. "I told him we were leaving tomorrow if we couldn't find a cargo."

"He'll call." Considering no one else would touch Ruslan Glebb's contract, we were now his only option.

She shook her head, unaware of my rock climbing exploits. "Sirius, he's got nothing for us."

I leaned across the table and kissed her. "Trust me. He'll call."

A small galleybot with a ridiculous red ribbon around its primary optical arrived with a soufflé baked the way Marie's mother used to make it. She ate it with unusual slowness, exaggerating how much she enjoyed each spoonful, taunting me with her eyes and a knowing smile, making me wait.

When she finished, she sighed. "That was so good, I could have another. It'll only take an hour to bake." She gave me an innocent look. "You don't mind waiting, do you?"

I gave her a long look, saying nothing, knowing it was a game.

Eventually she relented and stood up, holding out her hand. "Let's go."

We went up to her cabin where she made the wait worthwhile. In the darkness, she didn't notice the bruises on my chest and legs from slamming into the cliff below Pad Zero Eight Five. Later, after the passion subsided and we were starting to fall asleep in each other's arms, her comm system beeped.

Sleepily, Marie rolled over and saw the caller name on the console. "It's him," she said surprised.

"I told you he'd call."

She turned to the intercom. "Audio only. Accept."

"Marie, my darling, I'm so glad I caught you," a Slavic accented voice sounded from the speaker.

"Ruslan," she said, feigning confusion. "Do you

know what time it is?"

"Apologies for the late hour, my dear, but I have something for you after all."

"Couldn't it wait until morning?"

"I didn't want to risk you launching before we spoke. It seems my previous carrier has suffered a regrettable accident."

"Oh really?" she said, giving me a suspicious look. "What kind of accident?"

"There was a tremor. They happen all the time. Unfortunately, it caused a landslide that ah…finds me in need of a new partner. Are your two ships still available?"

Two ships? I grabbed her hand, getting her attention and held up my forefinger emphatically: one ship only!

Marie shook her head, putting a finger to her lips. "Yes, Ruslan, we'll see you tomorrow morning."

"I'll be in the casino at eight."

"We'll be there at eleven. I have a long morning planned," she said, running her hand down my chest, all the way down, indicating we'd be taking breakfast in bed.

"As you wish, my dear. I'll be waiting."

The intercom link terminated, then I exploded, "You're not going to Kota!"

"His cargo's too big for your ship alone. We have to go together, otherwise, it's no deal."

"That's not what we agreed."

"It's not up to me." She nodded to the intercom. "It's up to him." She studied my face, seeing my anxiety, not understanding why. "We'll land together, unload the Mendi and I'll be gone before you and Jase go anywhere near the prison. I promise."

It was a terrible idea, not least because Kota would be bombarded from orbit and invaded, two more details I couldn't share with her. It worried me enough that I considered calling the whole thing off.

"Are we doing this or not?" she asked.

I gritted my teeth and nodded. "We're doing it."

She smiled. "I knew you'd see it my way."

I grunted unhappily.

"And by the way, Ruslan thinks you work for me."

"What?"

"He knows me. He doesn't know you. I had to tell him something."

"This just gets better and better."

"Don't worry, you won't have to call me Boss," she said mischievously. "Captain Dulon will do…although considering it is two ships, maybe it should be…Commodore Dulon. That has a nice ring to it, don't you think?"

"Don't push it."

She laughed, delighted at having got one over on me, then tried unsuccessfully to kiss my concerns away.

* * * *

Lassider's View Casino dominated one of the peaks above Raw Deal. When we stepped out of the elevator, a pungent mix of stale drinks, human vomit and stim fumes assaulted our senses. Arleen coughed but said nothing. She'd invited herself to the meeting to put more humans under her microscope and I'd agreed, figuring having an empath at my side might prove useful. Izin, on the other hand, had opted out while Jase would have investigated the local pleasure palace whether I'd agreed or not. To keep up appearances, Marie had invited Gadron Ugo along, sensing Glebb, like all petty thugs, had an innate respect for physically imposing presences.

Even though it was early, the gambling tables were full, the music loud, the lights flashing, and gold paint and glitter were everywhere in a panoply of tackiness. Triumphant shouts and groans of despair rang out as semi-naked dancers gyrated on elevated platforms and servobots carried drinks, fume sticks and variously colored stim tubes to the clientele. Beyond the tables was a long curving window with a panoramic view of snow-covered mountains that reached all the way to the horizon. Many of the nearby peaks had ramshackle structures with hand-painted signs in front like *South Peak Supplies*, *Guns & Beer* and *Girls by the Dozen*.

Jase sniffed appreciatively. "Ah…" He fixed his gaze upon a large round table with three small balls bouncing randomly on pressure fields, then the fields vanished and the balls bounced several times before settling into numbered red and white slots. "They've got tri-ball!"

"Not today," I said.

"One bounce, Skipper, that's all," he promised.

"They're cheating," Arleen warned, sensing the croupier's deception.

"Of course they are," Marie agreed, amazed Jase didn't expect it.

An old Chardrey class freighter passed in front of the casino's long window, making heavy work of maneuvering against the strong winds and pelting snow. It pitched to port, then its thrusters glowed, pushing it back onto its approach vector.

"Weather's clearing," Gadron Ugo said, anticipating a favorable launch tomorrow.

We watched the freighter drop below the ridgeline, then a dark-skinned man with gold plated knuckle stunners on each hand and a comm piece in his ear came toward us.

"You Captain Dulon?" he asked.

"Yes," Marie replied.

"Mr. Glebb's expecting you, ma'am. This way."

He led us between the gambling tables to ornate double doors decorated in mid-twenty-fourth century gold opulence that fooled no one. Beneath the glitter were armored, auto-locking blast doors that could have taken a direct hit from a slammer gun with barely a scratch. There was no proximity sensor, yet they slid apart as we approached, indicating our every step was being watched.

Inside was a large, luxuriously appointed room with a continuation of the long curving window enclosing the gaming floor. A deeply padded chair behind an impressive simwood table sat opposite the door. It was flanked by walls decorated with paintings of heroic, first wave pioneers overcoming the elements and taming a wild, tectonically unstable, alpine world. They weren't half bad, proving even a place as wretched as Freehold couldn't resist mythologizing its past.

In the center of the floor was a circular window overlooking the snow whipped precipice beneath the casino. Two support girders reached up from the mountain below at forty-five degrees, supporting the jutting outer edge of the casino and giving Lassider's clientele the impression they were floating among the clouds.

Two men stood in front of the curved window. My DNA sniffer read them both and flashed their UniPol tracking sheets before my eyes. One was Ruslan Glebb, a gaunt, ghostly pale man in a black suit with white trim. He was adorned by garish, platinum jewelry and had a darkness under his eyes that revealed he shared his customer's taste for exotic chemicals. According to the Unified Police Force, he was an enterprising local racketeer with links to both the Rashidun and Shiva syndicates, without being a sworn member of either.

The other man was a low rent, gun for hire by the name of Yudi Varno. He was heavyset with shoulder-length, unkempt hair and a square jaw bristling with stubble. Circular metallic prosthetics surrounded by grizzly scars on both sides of his head hid where his ears had been burnt off in punishment for a past error of judgment. Unlike Glebb's perfectly tailored suit, Varno's was ill-fitting and bulged with hard edges from poorly concealed weapons. If Glebb was the brains, Varno was the muscle. He specialized in stand-over work, moonlighted as a bounty hunter, and judging by his current employer and general lack of ears, wasn't particularly good at either.

Both were small fish in a remote, stagnant pond that even UniPol had little interest fishing in. But it was their pond and we needed their help, so I'd decided to be suitably accommodating.

"My dear," Ruslan Glebb said with exaggerated civility, taking Marie's hand. For a moment, I thought he was going to slime her fingers with a kiss, but he merely held on too long.

"Ruslan," Marie said with an ingratiating smile as is if they were old friends, even though I knew she thought he was a Simulian snake on two legs and would have her hand decontaminated when she got back to the *Mendi*. "This is Kade, the captain of my other ship. He'll be helping me with the cargo."

"If he checks out," Varno growled, holding out a contact scanner for me to touch.

I eyed it suspiciously. It was a crude device, only as good as the library it referenced, but one bad entry would send us all scrambling for weapons.

"I have no secrets from Ruslan," Marie said, enjoying her role as Boss Lady.

I placed my palm on the reader, letting Varno scan my DNA, then he did the same for Jase. The retired bounty hunter ignored Marie and Ugo, whom he'd already cleared, and turned to Arleen. She placed her hand on the sensor plate curiously, then the DNA scanner beeped three times in protest.

Varno studied her delicate face in surprise. "What are you?"

"I am Uvo."

Varno turned to Ruslan Glebb uncertainly. "No

read."

"She's with me," I said.

Glebb eyed her curiously, gave me a searching look, ensuring I knew he'd hold me accountable for her every action, then nodded to Varno who activated the DNA scanner's data link. Jase and I prepared for bad news and bloodshed, but Varno's DNA library wasn't a good one, because we both came up clean.

Varno fixed his eyes on me, not satisfied. "Kade?...I know that name."

"We've never met."

"Didn't say we had."

There was an awkward silence, then Arleen broke the tension. "Why is there a human suspended below this structure?"

Glebb eyed her curiously. "How'd you know that?"

"He is very cold and...afraid," she replied thoughtfully.

I walked to the floor window and paced around it until I spotted a cable reaching down from the casino's outer edge. A man hung by his feet, swaying in the freezing wind. He was shivering and covered in ice crystals and his arms were wrapped around his chest in a vain attempt to stay warm.

"Who is he?" I asked.

Glebb followed me to the edge of the window and looked down. "Someone who disappointed me."

"Mr. Glebb doesn't like to be disappointed," Varno said as the others came up beside us.

"Obviously not," I said, certain I was going to disappoint him.

Glebb removed a communicator from his pocket and spoke into it. "Are you still alive down there, Soly?"

"I'm...I'm here...Mr. Glebb," a stuttering, frozen voice replied.

"Have you learned your lesson yet?"

"Ye–...sir."

Glebb returned the communicator to his pocket. "He's not sorry enough, not yet." He turned to me, forgetting the helpless wretch dangling below. "I'm surprised we haven't met before, Captain Kade."

"I don't normally get out this way."

"That's a survey ship you're flying, isn't it?" he asked, revealing he'd already looked us over.

"Converted. She's quiet, hard for Earth Navy to see."

He arched his brow thoughtfully. "Hmm, so you're a smuggler."

"If the pay's good enough."

"This is not a smuggling job, but I'd advise against being boarded."

"I hear the cargo's volatile."

"Ninety tanks of hydrazine. Nothing to worry about."

No wonder no one wanted the contract. One spark would be enough to incinerate an entire ship.

"We won't take any leaking tanks," Marie said, making it a clause in our contract.

"Yudi's scanned them all. The seals are good."

"We'll check them anyway," I said.

Glebb shrugged. "As you wish. I like people who are careful with my property. Just avoid any loyalist worlds and you won't have any trouble."

"We can do it in one jump," Marie said.

"Good. This shipment's already three months late."

"We getting a dangerous goods bonus?" I asked.

"Of course, on delivery," he replied, then his eyes narrowed. "How quiet is your ship?"

"Quiet enough that I'm not on his scanner," I said, nodding at Varno.

Glebb looked pleased. "Hmm. You do this right, Kade, and I'll have more work for you. Well paid work."

I feigned interest, then he motioned at a tiny optical high on the wall. A casino guard came in carrying two titanium lockboxes which Glebb opened with his own DNA code.

"These are for you," he said, handing them to me and Marie. "Reseal them now." We reset the locks with a touch, then he added, "They're rigged with thoron detonators, so be careful who opens them."

"What's in them?" I asked, suspecting I already knew the answer.

"Landing clearances and contact details for my associate on Kota. He polymerizes the hydrazine into lightweight insulation for a local construction business. Since the civil war began, prices have gone up considerably."

It sounded legitimate, then Arleen asked, "What's in the hydrazine?"

Glebb fixed a cold stare on her. "Why do ask?"

"Arleen's an empath," I explained, guessing she'd sensed deception. "That's why she's part of my crew."

"An empath? That's how you knew about Soly," he said intrigued, then turned to Marie. "It's nothing dangerous, I assure you."

"I'll scan my tanks anyway," I said.

Glebb gave me an irritated look, then came clean. "There are over five thousand soldiers on Kota, all eager for the kind of distraction my associate and I are only too happy to provide."

"Ruslan," Marie said uncomfortably, "you know I don't carry stims."

"Yes, my dear, but you're desperate and my customers are waiting. And I'll pay you ten times what you'd normally make."

Marie fell silent, on the verge of walking away, but I couldn't allow that.

"We'll do it," I said. Once I had the landing clearance, I'd dump his narco tanks in space, use his clearance to land on Kota and be gone before his partner even knew he'd been double-crossed.

Marie glanced at me, guessing my intentions, and nodded. "We have a deal."

Ruslan Glebb smiled. "Thank you, my dear, I won't forget this. And you have nothing to worry about. My associate runs Kota Spaceport security. He'll be waiting for you when you land. No one will search your ships."

It was a veiled threat, ensuring we understood that if we landed without the narco tanks, we'd be as good as dead. Not only could I not jettison them, but Marie was now going to Kota, whether I liked it or not.

"Good to know," I said.

"You see? No risk," he assured us.

"Unless your hydrazine blows up in our faces," Jase said sourly.

"See that doesn't happen," he said, placing full responsibility on our shoulders, then Lassider's View shuddered from a small tremor. Through the circular floor window, we saw ice crystals shake from the poor wretch below.

"He don't look so good," I said.

"On Freehold, Captain Kade, if you show weakness, you will be taken advantage of, in the worst possible way."

I nodded appreciatively. "When does the cargo load?"

"Today. Yudi will see to it."

I pocketed my exploding lockbox, wondering what Lena would make of being the silent partner in a drug-running syndicate. Considering the stakes, I guessed she'd have grabbed it with both hands.

Glebb produced his communicator again. "Soly, did you spill blood on my mountain?" When there was no reply, he added, "Soly?"

"He's dead," Arleen said, no longer able to sense the tortured man's presence.

"Hmph," Glebb grunted, more impressed by her abilities than the death of his minion. He switched channels and said, "Release him," then Soly's frozen corpse fell into the misty abyss and the cable retracted. "He always was a weakling."

"We need to get back to our ships before the tanks arrive," Marie said, hiding her revulsion.

"Of course, my dear," Glebb said, then we took the elevator down to Raw Deal in silence in case he had it bugged.

"I'll meet you on the Mendi in an hour," Marie said after we stepped clear, then she and Ugo went back to Pad Two One Four while we returned to the *Silver Lining*.

On the way back, Arleen was silent, disturbed by Glebb's casual cruelty.

"I told you not to come," I said.

"There is much hatred for that man," she said. "His own people are plotting to kill him."

Even I knew that, and I was no empath. Men like Glebb hid in every shadow in places like Raw Deal and whether he lived or died would make no difference. Nothing would change.

* * * *

While we waited for the hydrazine to arrive, I visited Marie for our final farewell ahead of weeks apart in space. It was a steamy goodbye, then as we lay in each other's arms, I prodded the lioness.

"So...do I salute you now, Commodore?" I asked.

"That won't be necessary, Lieutenant Kade."

"Lieutenant?"

"Ensign Kade. I don't want you getting any fancy ideas."

"How'd you like to *walk* back to Hades City?"

"Relieving me of command already?"

"At least you wouldn't have to worry about hydrazine blowing your ship apart."

"We can still cancel," she said soberly.

If Lena and Earth Navy weren't expecting me to land Dietz and his team on Kota, I'd have killed the stim deal in a heartbeat, but I had an invasion to meet.

"I promised Jase he'd get a chance to bust Emma Hadley out of Kota Prison. I need to let him see it's impossible."

"You're not going to get her out?" she said surprised, propping herself up on an elbow.

"You heard Glebb. There are thousands of Sep soldiers on Kota." More even than he realized.

"So pull out of the deal."

"I can't. Jase would go to Kota alone and get himself killed."

"He is a hothead," she conceded.

"Put sniffers on every tank. Dump any that leak. We'll show Glebb's man on Kota the sniffer logs to prove we had no choice."

"Ruslan will be furious. We'd never be able to land here again."

The ship rocked slightly as a tremor shook the landing pad.

"I can live with that," I said watching our drinks slosh in their glasses.

"Your alien friend is quite…stunning. Should I be jealous?" she asked, only half-joking, ignoring the biological obstacles to interspecies relationships.

"She's just a passenger I picked up for extra credits."

"Passengers don't come to drug deals with Ruslan Glebb."

"I didn't know what you'd got me into."

"She's sharp," Marie said thoughtfully, "picking up on that poor man outside."

"And Glebb's lies about the stims."

She nodded. "We could use her."

"She's not looking for a job and…she thinks we're

barbarians."

"She said that?"

"No, but Glebb shocked her."

"Does she know about us?"

I chuckled. "She's an empath. She knows."

"Hmm, I'm going to have a long talk with her, find out what dark little secrets you're hiding from me."

"Secrets?" I said innocently. "Me?"

"Yes, you." She gave me a searching look. "Sometimes, Sirius, I think there's more going on in that pretty little head of yours than you let on."

"I'm an open book," I declared. "Ask me anything."

"I'll ask Arleen instead. Where'd you find her?"

"Niedarim. I stopped there looking for some exotics to trade."

"I've heard the Lhekan homeworld is quite beautiful."

"It was, before the Intruders hit it. We got out just in time."

Marie's eyes widened in surprise. "The Spawn attacked Niedarim? But the Lhekans are neutral."

"Now they're occupied. That's why Arleen needed a ride."

"Lucky you came along," Marie said, resting her head on my naked chest. "The Tau Cetins will take care of the Lhekans. They've probably already driven the Intruders off by now."

"Yeah," I said, knowing the Ornithians couldn't even protect themselves, let alone all the weaker Orion Arm civilizations. I pretended everything would be all right, that the Lhekans would be liberated, that the mighty Tau Cetins were invincible and that fairy tales always came true.

I didn't tell her that sometimes, nightmares also came true.

* * * *

By the time I returned to the ship a line of eight-wheeled flatbed haulerbots, each carrying a capsule-shaped hydrazine tank, stretched from the cliff face cargo door to the *Silver Lining's* stern ramp. I stopped below the port engine cluster to watch a hauler turn on its length and roll slowly up the ramp. The dirty white tanks were all stamped with red hazardous material symbols and showed signs of corrosion, but Izin's mark was also on them signaling he'd personally checked each one.

I waited as an empty haulerbot, having unloaded its cargo, drove down the ramp. When it turned to head back into New Deal, my DNA sniffer flashed a warning into my mind.

PROXIMITY ALERT: YUDI VARNO.

I turned in time to glimpse the blue electromagnetic flash of his weapon firing. Instinctively, I dived away, but even my ultra-reflexed speed wasn't fast enough. Varno's slug grazed my right shoulder, spinning me around with surprising force. I slipped on the icy pad, my shoulder burning, then my threading's nerve blockers kicked in, killing the pain.

Varno fired again as I scrambled to my feet, running for cover. He went for a head kill, but I was already moving too fast and the shot whizzed behind me. In his hands was a short-barreled mini-mace, a brutal close-range weapon that roared like a thunderclap each time it fired one of its oversized twelve-mil slugs. If not for my sniffer's warning, it would have punched a fist-sized hole through my chest.

I ran under the hull cradling my right arm, desperate to put distance between me and the explosive hydrazine. Halfway across the pad, Varno strode toward me, tracking my run with his gun, firing again, barely missing me.

"Sirius Kade," he yelled over the howling wind, confident I had nowhere to go. "I knew I'd heard that name before."

I took cover behind a landing strut, then stole a look around the side. Varno fired immediately, sending a big slug ricocheting off the strut into the hull's underside as I pulled back. In no hurry, he circled around looking for a clear shot.

"The Consortium must want you bad for what they're paying. What'd you do, Kade, pork some big shot's missus?"

I reached my good arm across my chest and awkwardly drew my P-50. I was trained to shoot with either hand, although I'd always made an awkward southpaw. Good thing Varno was overconfident, wasting his advantage by coming in close.

"With what I'm going to collect on you, Kade, I won't ever have to set foot on another of these stinking backwater shitholes."

I edged around the strut–keeping it between him and me–letting him think of all the money he was about to make. When he was itching to collect, I showed myself briefly, then darted back behind cover as he fired and stepped out the other side. While he was still fighting recoil, I played it safe with a chest shot, got my angles wrong and put the slug into his throat instead. It was a mistake I'd never have made with my good hand, but he hit the ice just as hard.

Yudi Varno, permanently retired bounty hunter, lay beside his oversized mini-mace, his lifeless eyes open and blood trickling from both sides of his mouth. I holstered my gun, gave his corpse a quick pat-down and found a small comm pane with my picture on it.

"Hmph," I grunted impressed when I saw the Consortium had increased the bounty on my head to ten million credits. "That's more like it," I said, certain the Consortium's Chairman, Manning Thurlow Ransford, didn't want me paying him another visit.

Varno had pulled the contract off a Consortium black net repeater in Raw Deal. Not wanting to tip off the competition, he'd issued no formal acceptance, intending to ice me first and claim his reward after I was dead. That was good. It meant the Consortium didn't know where I was. What wasn't so good was the encrypted message he'd sent to Davit Varno who, according to his UniPol tracking sheet, was Yudi's younger brother. Davit was on Corsal, over three hundred light years away, and wouldn't receive the message for months. When he did, it wouldn't take him long to figure out why his big brother was no longer answering his calls.

Certain Yudi Varno's greed had stopped him sharing his little secret with Ruslan Glebb, I pocketed the comm pane and dragged his lifeless body across the landing pad. It left a dark smear trailing beneath the *Silver Lining* that froze almost immediately, painting a picture for any investigator who came looking for him.

I rolled his body to the edge of the pad and looked over, confirming the bottom was hidden from sight by the thick gray cloud below.

"This is one backwater shithole you're never leaving," I said and kicked his corpse over the side.

It bounced like a rag doll against the cliff and vanished into the swirling grayness, then I retrieved his weapon and tossed it after him. Feeling faint from blood loss, I went aboard hoping the medbot could get me in shape for Kota. I'd been lucky. Varno's tankosaur gun had only grazed me–gauging flesh, not breaking bone–but my shoulder was already freezing up and my hand was so weak, it couldn't even hold a gun.

It couldn't have come at a worse time.

* * * *

Izin entered medbay as the medbot sprayed instaderm over my freshly sanitized shoulder. Within moments, adaptive cells clone matched my DNA, forming a bioseal over the wound that would eventually be indistinguishable from natural skin.

Izin looked at it curiously. "Should we expect company, Captain?"

"No, but keep an eye out just in case."

He glanced at the scans on the diagnostic screens, estimated the size of the projectile that had carved a trench-like groove through my shoulder, and gave me his expert opinion.

"You were lucky to survive."

"Bounty hunter," I explained. "Should have expected it in a place like this."

"Will they find the body?"

"Not before we launch."

With luck, enough snow would cover Yudi Varno's body that it wouldn't be found until the planetary winter ended forty thousand years from now.

"The last of the hydrazine tanks have loaded and the cargo door is sealed," Izin said. "I've set the atmosphere filters to scan for N_2H_4. If there are any leaks, the lower deck will automatically decompress after a ten-second warning."

That might be enough time for a tamph, but humans required a little longer to get to safety. "Make it thirty seconds."

"As you wish, Captain," he replied. "I detected slight damage to the ship's underside thermal coating. I assume that was caused by the bounty hunter?"

I nodded. "Patch it before we boost."

"It's being fixed as we speak."

"It could have been worse. He could have hit the N_2."

"Do you want the hullbot to remove the frozen blood from the landing pad?"

"Ah, you saw that, did you?"

"I could hardly miss it, Captain. Perhaps I should permanently assign a hullbot to follow you around, in case you kill someone else before we leave?"

It was tamph black humor, although Izin never laughed, never admitted he was making a joke. I liked to imagine he was smiling under the triangular vocalizer he wore over his mouth, even though tamphs lacked the musculature for such a human expression.

"It wasn't my fault."

"It never is," he replied as the medbot finished patching me up.

I eased myself off the medbed, feeling light-headed from blood loss. My right shoulder was now encased in a spray-on immobilizer that gave the synthetic cells time to integrate into my shoulder.

"Let me know when your bots are stowed. I want to get off this rock before his friends coming looking for him," I said, not that I expected Varno had friends.

"Yes Captain," he said and left for engineering.

I returned to my stateroom for clean clothes, then went to the bridge. Arleen and Jase watched me tentatively slide onto my couch, glimpsing the white immobilizer under my shirt.

"You having fun without me, Skipper?" Jase asked.

I winced, deciding not to risk piloting the ship out of New Deal with only one arm. "You take her up."

"Incoming signal," Jase said. "It's the Mendi."

I pulled my shirt up a little higher, hiding the bandage from Marie, then her face appeared on the bridge screen.

"We're boosting now," she said. "I'll see you on Kota."

"We'll be a little late," I said. "I'm dropping Arleen off on the way."

"You didn't tell me that." She furrowed her brow. "You're doing this just to stop me talking to her, aren't you?"

"You got me. I'm going to maroon her on the first asteroid I see, just to stop you two swapping stories."

"If you want, Arleen, you can come with us," Marie offered. "And you can tell me all his dirty little secrets."

"Thank you for the offer, Captain Dulon," Arleen replied, "but I am in a hurry to get home."

I smiled at Marie's annoyance. "Don't wait for us on Kota. Dump your cargo and get out of there. We'll meet you in Hades City in two months."

"Safe flight," she said, then her face vanished from the screen.

Arleen leaned toward me and whispered, "Is Marie an empath? Is that why she suspects you have secrets from her?"

"She's a woman," I said meaningfully, "and you and her are never going to talk."

Izin's voice sounded over the intercom. "All hullbots are stowed, Captain, and the incriminating remains of your handiwork has been removed from the landing pad."

"Thank you, Izin," I said dryly, convinced he was enjoying cleaning up after me a little too much.

Jase gave me a curious look, then expertly lifted us off the narrow landing pad and climbed through Freehold's fierce winds as I set the autonav for Jel Kara, our last stop before Kota.

Chapter Five: Jel Kara

Syrman Restricted Mandate
Inyati System
Outer Andromeda
1.14 Earth Normal Gravity
898 light years from Sol
695 Syrmans

A hot brown world devoid of oceans appeared on the bridge screen moments after the bubble dropped. Its surface was a patchwork of desolate highlands and vast arid plains dissected by feeble rivers that snaked their way to isolated endorheic lakes. Jel Kara's albedo was high, making it bright enough for dark Syrman eyes, although its mass and gravity were on the small side for their tastes.

"Doesn't look like a Syrman world," I said.

"It's not," Arleen said. "It's a Wabiniok territory."

Jel Kara's astrographics entry had it listed as claimed, but not by whom. That was a dead giveaway for a world controlled by an advanced civilization that had chosen to limit communication with primitives like us.

"I didn't know the Wabiniok had colonies in Orion."

"It's not a colony. One of their survey ships found it about one point six million Earth years ago, at the end of their third expansion phase. They claimed settlement rights under the Compatible Biosphere Rule, but never got around to colonizing it."

According to our astrographics system, Jel Kara's indigenous life consisted of spiny plants that sifted moisture from the planet's dry air and nocturnal, rodent sized creatures that lived off crawling insects. Their genetic markers must indicate no possibility of intelligent life ever evolving there, making the planet an evolutionary dead end and, therefore, eligible for colonization. Priority for such rights always went to species most suited to the planet's habitat, while marginals and terraformers got increasingly lower priorities.

"The Wabiniok granted the Syrman's extraction rights," she added, "providing they didn't damage the biosphere."

"That must have cost the Syrmies a fortune," Jase declared.

"Why would it?" she asked. "The Wabiniok are masters of supergravity mining. They have access to far more concentrated resources than are found on any planet."

"Such as?" I asked.

"Collapsars. Their molecular resource densities are far higher than anything found on terrestrial worlds." She was talking about stars that had come to the end of their lives, had ceased all nuclear reactions and collapsed under the pull of their own gravity to extreme densities. "One collapsar contains enough heavy elements to supply a major civilization for hundreds of thousands of years."

"So why keep the planet at all?"

"The Wabiniok Civilization has been dormant for over half a million years, nevertheless, they wish to preserve Jel Kara for future generations, in case they enter another expansion phase."

"I wish someone would give us a planet," Jase said.

Arleen gave him a perplexed look "They have. Many of your worlds had prior claims on them, all of which were waived in your favor."

"I didn't realize the galaxy was so charitable," I said.

"Most human worlds are marginally habitable, which is why the existing claims had not been utilized, and it would be irrational to deny you what others have no use for."

"The unwritten law of the galaxy, use it, or lose it."

"It is not galactic law, Captain Kade, but it is customary to be generous to younger species. Most civilizations initially claim more than they can use, although humans tend to settle everywhere they can."

"We do like real estate," I said, searching for the Syrman base. "So where are they?"

There was no beacon, which was surprising for a Syrman outpost, and out of respect for the Wabiniok's dislike of uninvited guests, our Tau Cetin astrographics contained no surface scans. The only signs of intelligent life were a few dead straight, graded roads that circled the planet and converged on a point closer to the north pole than the equator.

"No ships in orbit," Jase said, "just three comm sats in geostat. We could try all channels."

"That might not be prudent," Arleen said.

Without a position fix, we couldn't hail the outpost with a tight beam while an omnidirectional signal would drift through space for years, making it easy for Intruder sentry probes to pick up our trail. Considering the Syrmans were Tau Cetin allies and a legitimate target, they might not even answer a general hail for fear of alerting the One Spawn to their presence.

"We'll sneak up on them," I said, nosing the *Silver Lining* down into Jel Kara's clear skies. We dropped toward the equator, picking up a north bound dirt road which I hoped would lead us to their base.

"Something's down there," Jase said as an optical detected a glint of sunlight on metal.

"I see it," I said, bleeding velocity and going down for a closer look.

The glint came from a procession of long white vehicles stopped in the middle of a salt pan. It was a road train comprising several dozen high sided ore carriages towed by an enormous thirty-six-wheel engine. They all rode on unusually wide black tires designed to prevent them sinking into the dust and ensuring they compacted the ground with each passing. The train had run off the dirt track, taking four kilometers to stop and leaving dark ruts in the pristine salt pan's crusty white crystals.

"Could be a breakdown," Jase suggested as we circled at low altitude.

"It's too far off the road," I said uneasily, taking us in closer, discovering black blast marks on one side of the engine. The control cab door was open and lying face down near a huge front wheel was a Syrman with a dark stain on his back.

I glanced at Arleen. "You sense anything?"

"There is no life down there."

Assuming whoever had killed the driver was long gone, I set down near the engine. Izin and Dietz met us on the lower cargo deck, Izin with dark sun goggles for everyone and Dietz with a weapon from the armory. With our eyes properly shielded, we walked down the cargo ramp into baking heat.

Dietz took one look at the road train, trusted his psionic instincts that there was no immediate danger, and examined the Syrman's wound with an expert eye.

"Energy weapon. Can't tell what type." He touched the body's dark bloodstain, finding it bone dry. "Been dead a while."

Jase crushed a small, twelve legged crawling insect under his boot. "No bugs on him. I guess they don't like the taste."

"On the contrary," Izin said, studying tiny marks on the ground around the body. He lifted the dead Syrman's shoulder revealing a mass of insects sheltering in the shade of his body as they fed on him. "They don't like the sun."

Arleen's eyes were on the engine, seeing something we didn't see.

"What is it?" I asked.

"That engine housing is reinforced calinium," she replied slowly, studying the blast marks. "It's been sub-atomically disrupted."

I'd never heard of calinium, but it didn't sound good. "Spawn weapons?"

"Possibly," she replied apprehensively.

Intruder ships could easily have beaten us to Jel Kara, or maybe they were simply eliminating TC allies wherever they found them. Either way, Arleen's chances of picking up a ride home were looking increasingly slim.

"You still want to go to the base?"

"If it's still there."

"We'll land out of sight and take the flier in," I said, deciding not to risk the ship.

We returned to the *Silver Lining* and followed the dirt road for two thousand clicks before coming upon a second road train. It was parked beside an automated drilling rig flanked by a small power plant, a comms tower, and an ore loader. The vehicle's engine was a blackened, burnt-out wreck while the undamaged loader sprayed ruddy colored ore onto an overflowing and partially buried carriage.

We circled the ore extractor in silence, finding no sign of life, then continued north at very low altitude. When an immense plume of industrial smoke and steam appeared on the horizon, I knew we were close and put the *Silver Lining* down in the shadow of a sun-bleached mesa.

"Dietz," I said over the intercom, unlocking the two big VRS containers storing his gear. "You and your team gear up. Meet us in the vehicle bay."

"Understood," he replied.

"You too, Izin."

"Yes, Captain."

Jase gave me a curious look. "Who's staying with the Lining?"

"You are."

"Now wait a minute–"

"I need you to pilot the flier, and be ready in case we have to get out fast."

He scowled, reluctantly accepting his fate, then we went down to the vehicle bay. Dietz's team was waiting, dressed in full battle kit: combat helmets with optical visors, compression plate body armor custom made for each soldier, encrypted field comms, tactical sensors, and K8s loaded with enough snakehead killers and N-grenades to fight a small war.

Arleen and I climbed into the front seats with Jase. Dietz and his two largest grunts took the back seats while Izin squeezed into the rear cargo compartment with the three remaining commandos. It was all elbows, knees and assault rifles, but he didn't complain, even though he hated being jammed in amongst them.

We took the cargo elevator down to the lower deck, squeezed between the hydrazine tanks and rolled down the stern ramp into blistering heat. I cranked the folding gossamer wings out to full extension, then Jase got us airborne with some neat vectoring and followed the foot of the mesa around to an arid plain leading to the

Syrman base.

In minutes, a fortress-like structure twenty clicks wide rose above the horizon. Columns of black oily smoke and thick white steam belched from rooftop vents, rising high into the still desert air. Landing platforms dotted the walls high above the ground and locked double doors large enough for a Syrman road train faced the dirt road we'd followed up from the south.

"Not very inviting," Jase said.

I glanced at Arleen. "You sure about this?"

"No, but I need a fast ship."

And it would take weeks for me to get her someplace else in the *Silver Lining*, so I nodded to Jase to take us in. When we were close, he followed the towering metal walls to the west. All of the landing platform doors were sealed, although the structure showed no sign of having been attacked. At the western end of the base, a chain of mountainous slag piles stretched away toward a distant blue lake, fed by long, slender waste conveyors that were running even though empty. We flew over them, continuing around the structure to another pair of giant doors facing a straight dirt road leading off to the north.

"Nobody's home," Riley said, peering through the flier's transparent fuselage.

Arleen stared at the ancient metal walls, transfixed in thought.

"What is it?" I asked.

"Something," she replied uncertainly. "It doesn't feel...right."

At the eastern end of the structure was a landing ground scorched black from millennia of use. The burnt-out wreck of a small, slender ship lay on one side of the empty field, strangely far from the structure. While most of its hull was blackened by fire, there were glimpses of mirrored surfaces that had escaped destruction.

"It's Tau Cetin," I said. It was the smallest TC ship I'd ever seen, and even though it had been gutted by fire, there was no doubting its origin.

"They hit it on the ground," Dietz said.

Facing the landing field was another set of giant doors, only these had been blown open. One lay flat on the ground, the other hung precariously at an odd angle. In front of them were the scattered remains of two wrecked transports and a handful of dead Syrmans, killed as they ran toward the base.

"They didn't put up much of a fight," Riley muttered.

"They're civilians, dumb ass," Ibanez snapped.

I turned to Dietz. "You want to go in low or high?"

He showed a flicker of surprise as he realized I was giving him the choice, recognizing he was the ranking military commander.

"Always high," he said.

We circled back around to the southern side, then I spotted a landing platform with a small wingless aircraft parked on it. The aircraft appeared to be undamaged and the platform door was half-open.

"There," I said pointing, then Jase put the flier into a long slow turn.

"There's a dead Syrman in the pilot's seat," Izin said, studying the aircraft with his telescoping eyes.

Jase brought us in over the platform and hovered just above the Syrman aircraft. The pilot was slumped over the controls, the upper part of his head had been blown off and a large hole had been punched through the aircraft's dome-shaped canopy.

"No infantry weapon did that," Larson said.

"Strafed him," Dietz agreed, pointing to a line of holes across the landing platform the same size as in the canopy.

Jase touched down behind the Syrman aircraft, keeping it between us and the pad door. He left the flier's engines powered, waiting to see if their whine drew attention, but no one appeared.

"Not very curious, are they?" I said.

"Corpses ain't curious," Riley declared, eyeing the dead Syrman.

Arleen leaned toward me. "If there are survivors, they're not close."

I nodded to Dietz, giving him the green light, and popped the flier's hatches.

"Everybody out!" he yelled. The commandos jumped clear and formed a skirmish line covering the pad door. "Larson and Parekh, you're on point. This is a tactical advance to battle. Watch for civilians and trust your instincts–you know what I mean."

The team moved toward the landing platform door with their weapons at eye height while Izin, Arleen and I stayed back with the flier. With only one usable arm, I'd dispensed with the sling and reverse holstered my P-50 to suit my left hand. I couldn't convince Arleen to carry a weapon, but she'd at least agreed to wear a chest plate over her p-suit borrowed from Dietz's stockpile. Izin, of course, was armed to the teeth.

Larson and Parekh went through the door first, followed by Dietz and the rest of the team. I waited and listened, but there was no sound of combat, so I signaled Jase to go. He lifted off and raced away at high speed, then I led Izin and Arleen into a narrow hangar where two aircraft similar to the one outside were parked.

Dietz's team covered a door at the end of the hangar as Larson and Parekh stepped in front of a proximity sensor. The door slid open, letting a wave of hot air and the din of hammering and hissing flood the hangar, then they stepped through and peeled left and right. The others followed, then Dietz's voice sounded over the industrial cacophony.

"Clear!"

We stepped through onto a metal walkway high

above a sprawling industrial facility. On the floor below, a row of steaming cauldrons poured molten metal into narrow channels that carried bubbling orange lava throughout the complex. Automated sluice gates controlled the flow, directing molten streams and measuring precise quantities into ingot molds and smaller cauldrons where alloys were mixed. White cryo gases blasted the ingots, cooling them before they were flipped onto conveyors and carried to giant presses where they were hammered into plate-like slabs. Steam and smoke and the deafening beat of the presses filled the chamber while conical ceiling intakes sucked polluted air out and floor vents pumped clean air in.

There were no Syrman supervisors anywhere, not even in the observation room suspended from the ceiling. Dark flash burns scarred some machinery and a waterfall of molten metal poured from one cauldron where it had been holed halfway up by an energy blast.

Dietz's troops were spread out either side of us on the walkway, covering the floor. "It was over quick," he said with a grim look. "Not much damage. The Syrmies must have surrendered as soon as the Spawn got inside."

I turned to Arleen. "Which way?"

Her eyes stared absently at a bubbling cauldron, sensing our surroundings, then she pointed to the left. "That way."

"Hostiles?" Dietz asked.

"Fear and...confusion," she replied.

Dietz nodded to Larson and Parekh who lead us across a walkway above a molten lake fed by the damaged cauldron. We clambered down eight flights of metal stairs, through oppressive heat and steam, to a door half a click from our entry point. The two point men went through first, then we followed them into a control room whose walls were lined with screens hissing with white noise.

Izin examined the consoles, testing various controls.

"The exterior sensors have been destroyed, however, interior sensors are functioning, but disabled."

"Can you activate them?" I asked.

"The lockouts have been encrypted, Captain. It appears the Syrmans did it."

"The Spawn must have been trying to get control," Dietz said.

"There's something through there," Arleen said, indicating the next door.

After a nod from Dietz, Larson and Parekh led us through a corridor to a cafeteria filled with bench tables and wide Syrman sized chairs. Plates of partially eaten food and half-empty drinking mugs sat on the tables while dispensers along the walls held uncollected meals and poured dark liquid into mugs that overflowed onto the floor.

"They didn't get much warning," Larson said.

"Finish the sweep," Dietz ordered, then we moved through the cafeteria, past a washroom area with showers still running, to another door.

Larson activated the proximity sensor, then winced as the door slid open and the pungent stench of decaying flesh flooded the corridor. I suppressed the urge to gag as Larson and Parekh stepped through, then there was a long silence.

"Dietz, you got to see this," Larson called, then we filed into an auditorium large enough for the processing plant's entire workforce.

There was a raised stage opposite our entry point flanked by chairs stacked high against the walls. They surrounded hundreds of decomposing Syrman corpses laid out in tightly packed rows. Most had been shot in the head once, although those few who'd resisted had multiple wounds.

"Asesinado demonios," Ibanez muttered in his own language. *Murdering devils.*

"They've done worse," Arleen said, holding her

hand over her nose and mouth against the smell of death.

"Doors!" Dietz barked, aware the gigantic facility was far from secure.

Parekh and Ibanez jogged between the bodies to an exit on the far side of the auditorium while Shen and Larson took up opposing positions at the side entrances.

"Record it all," I said to Dietz. "The Forum has to see this."

He pointed at his tiny helmet cam. "Been going the whole time."

Izin knelt and examined one of the bodies. Syrmans were shorter than humans with a much heavier build. The high gravity and bright sun of their homeworld accounted for their massive musculature, darkly tanned skin and small dark eyes inset below a protruding brow. Izin turned the Syrman's head and studied a tiny hole in the back of his skull. It was surrounded by a burn mark indicating an energy weapon had fused the wound on contact.

"He was lying face down when they killed him," Izin said. "They all were."

"Syrmans are tough," I said. "I never figured them for lying down and waiting to have their brains blown out."

Dietz furrowed his brow in confusion. "Why'd the Spawn risk a ground assault? They could've smoked this place from orbit."

Izin pointed to a small circular mark at the back of the Syrman's head. "Something was attached here."

"The One Spawn have an interrogation device that leaves such a mark," Arleen said. "The Syrmans would have been powerless to resist."

"That's why they landed. They wanted information, about us," I said.

"Movement!" Shen yelled and dashed through the door.

The sound of her boots pursuing heavy, pounding

footsteps echoed into the auditorium as she raced away down a dark corridor. Dietz and Riley charged after her, then Izin and I followed them through a series of dark passages. When we lost sight of them, Arleen caught up, sensing their presence.

"This way," she said, leading us down a side passage.

"In here!" Shen called out of the darkness, then the thud of a heavy object striking a wall reached us.

We turned a corner, saw Dietz in a dimly lit room ahead, and ran toward him. They were in a geology lab lit only by white noise from the wall screens. A crazed Syrman, with wild blinking eyes, hurled mineral analyzers and ore sample boxes at Shen. She evaded each frenzied attack while Dietz and Riley aimed their K8s at the Syrman, looking for a shot.

"Don't kill him!" I yelled.

"If he charges, he dies," Dietz said coldly.

The Syrman tore a blue-white analyzer from a benchtop and hurled it at Shen who ducked under it. The machine smashed through a wall, then the enraged Syrman tried to wrench a heavy storage locker free, taking his eyes off her. She immediately leaped at the four hundred kilogram brute and slammed the butt of her K8 into his massive head with enough force to kill three men. The mighty Syrman fell face-first against a bench, toppling it over as he slid to the floor. Shen dropped her rifle and jumped on him, grabbing his huge left wrist and slapping a silver band over it. It formed a self-sealing loop, then she locked his right hand behind his back with the other end of the band.

"Will that hold?" I asked.

"It better, for his sake," Dietz replied, aiming at the Syrman's head.

Riley tied the Syrman's thick ankles together with another locking band and stepped back. "Barely fits," he said doubtfully.

The mountain of muscle regained consciousness, roared angrily and tried to break free. Shen and Riley grabbed their guns and backed away as he thrashed violently on the floor. I thought the locking bands were going to cut through his thick hide, but he soon tired and stopped struggling. He turned his face away, exhausted, and whimpered like a confused child.

"He has the same mark as the others," Izin observed, "only his is bloodied."

"He tore it off," I said, suspecting that's what had driven him crazy.

"Anyone know their lingo?" Dietz asked.

It was one of the languages in my linguistic update, but my pronunciations would be poor and I couldn't explain how I knew their language. Even so, I had to know what happened. I was about to volunteer when Arleen stepped forward.

"I speak Syrmat."

"Ask him what happened," I said.

Arleen approached the whimpering goliath cautiously, kneeling beside him and placing her hands either side of his head. The Syrman shuddered in fear, his eyes wide with terror. He became transfixed by her gaze, unable to look away, then slowly relaxed and fell silent.

"Nice trick," Riley muttered. "Does she read palms?"

"Zip it," Dietz whispered, not wanting to alarm the Syrman.

Arleen made a soothing sound, bringing the Syrman hypnotically under her control. His body went limp, then she spoke in his native tongue. To human ears, it was a guttural babble, but my threading translated her words into my mind.

"Why did the One Spawn attack?" she asked.

"Lhekans...Lhekans..." he mumbled, showing no surprise that she knew his language. "They got..." His eyes glazed over into silent confusion.

"What did the One Spawn want?" she persisted gently. "From you."

He blinked, trying to focus. "They thought…we had it."

"Had what?"

The demented brute opened his mouth, fighting for sanity and whispered, "Memories…stolen…memories."

She stiffened as if the answer meant something to her.

"What's he saying?" Dietz asked in a low voice.

"It's meaningless gibberish," Arleen replied, removing her hands, letting the Syrman slide back into madness.

"It sounded like he was telling you something," I said, hiding my surprise at her lie.

She stepped back from him. "His mind is shattered. He doesn't know anything."

"Too bad," I said suspiciously, immediately regretting my words.

She turned sharply toward me with a penetrating look, sensing I didn't believe her. With visible annoyance, she looked away.

Behind us all, a deep, growling voice demanded, "What are you doing here?"

Dietz's soldiers spun toward the voice, raising their weapons. I turned, surprised my sniffer hadn't detected an approach, then saw a dirty-faced Syrman on one of the screens. He wore the same grubby yellow jacket as many of the corpses in the auditorium and had a pressure bandage over the bridge of his broken nose.

"We're traders," I replied.

"You don't look like traders," he said, inspecting Dietz's body armor and weapons.

"We saw a vehicle on the road south of here. It had been attacked, so we came in armed."

He took the news grimly. "You look like soldiers."

"They're mercenaries. I have a passenger here that wants to buy transport on one of your ships." I motioned to Arleen who faced the screen so he could see she wasn't human. "Who are you?"

"Tido Rivas," he replied. "My shift was doing deep shaft maintenance when the Spawn came."

"We should meet."

He considered the risk. "Wait there. We'll come to you."

* * * *

Three stocky Syrmans stepped into the geolab carrying laser welders and meter long magnetic wrenches for weapons. They looked and smelled as if they hadn't washed in a week and acted as if they expected to be ambushed at any moment.

"I'm Kade," I said while Dietz and Riley kept their distance in case the Syrmans became unfriendly.

Tido Rivas motioned to his two companions. "Lodi. Trema." He looked us over, taking particular interest in our weapons, then regarded Izin with visible hatred. "What's he doing here?"

I stepped between them ensuring he didn't club Izin to death. "He's part of my crew."

"I heard there was tame Spawn on your world."

"My people have not been part of the One Spawn for over two thousand years," Izin said.

"You are what they are," Tido Rivas said, unconvinced.

"If you were his enemy, you'd already be dead," I assured him.

The Syrman contained his desire for revenge, mostly because we had real weapons and all he had were rusty old tools, then he turned to Arleen. "You're Uvo?"

"Yes, I am."

He grunted. "There are no ships coming. Intruders

destroyed our last supply vessel three weeks ago."

"Why is there a wrecked Tau Cetin ship outside?" I asked.

"It landed a couple of weeks ago. They didn't say why. They just sat there. A spawnship destroyed it from space before we knew it was there. They never had a chance."

"The Tau Cetins will come looking for it," I said.

"Hrrh!" Tido said with a contemptuous Syrman cough. "They don't even know it's gone."

"They have eyes everywhere."

"Not anymore," Arleen said. "The Suzerain told me the Spawn Fleet destroyed the Ornithian surveillance system months ago. They won't know that ship is missing until it's overdue." She turned to Tido. "I heard the Ornithians are arming your ships. Won't one of them come to investigate?"

"No. They're guarding Sarlo and Ansara."

Sarlo was the Syrman homeworld, barely sixty-nine light years from Earth. Like Sol, the Syrma System was within the Tau Cetin inner defense zone, which was why the TCs were arming its inhabitants. Human ships couldn't power TC weapons, but even if they could, we wouldn't qualify for that kind of help until we became citizens almost half a century from now.

"Why are you sending ships to Ansara?" I asked, recalling Lena had discovered the TCs expected the Spawn Fleet to attack Ansara soon. It was the most heavily defended world between here and Tau Ceti and was the jumping-off point for TC operations into the conquered Perseus Arm. If it fell, it would be a disaster from which the Ornithians might not recover.

"They give us weapons, we give them a few ships," Tido replied. "That was the deal."

"And you know this how?" Izin asked.

Tido glared at Izin but didn't reach for his laser welder. "Heard it from the last supply ship we saw."

"A bunch of Syrman ships with TC weapons won't stop the Spawn Fleet," Dietz said.

"They're not alone," Arleen said. "The Ornithian Fleet is there."

"Since when did the Tau Cetins start sharing military secrets with spiritual aesthetics?" I asked sharply, still smarting from her lies about the crazed Syrman.

"The Ornithians made the same offer to the Lhekans they made to the Syrmans," she replied stiffly. "Weapons to defend themselves in exchange for a few ships going to Ansara. They didn't say their fleet was there, but the Tau Cetins are obviously concentrating their forces and gathering their allies to defend Ansara. The Lhekans refused because they did not want to break the Xil Neutrality Pact."

"If that is true," Izin said, "what do the One Spawn want with this world?"

"We have nothing." Tido glanced at an instrument pad on his forearm, checking the time. "We can't stay here. They'll be coming soon."

"Who will?" Dietz snapped.

"Autacs," Tido Rivas replied. "The Intruders left a small force here. They patrol every few hours." He motioned for his two companions to help the crazed Syrman to his feet. They grabbed his arms, then Shen removed his ankle restraint while leaving his wrists bound.

"Can we make it to a landing platform?" I asked.

"No, there isn't time."

I lifted my communicator to call Jase, but Tido caught my hand. "They monitor all channels."

"They must have seen us land. I have to warn my ship."

"Did you try to contact us from orbit?"

"No. There was no beacon, no hail from the planet. We came straight in."

Tido grunted approvingly. "Their landing vehicle is buried between two particle furnaces which generate high energy fields powerful enough to conceal their presence from orbital scans, and blind their own sensors."

"Is that why you disabled your internal sensors?" Izin asked.

"Yes. We can move without being detected. There wasn't time to lock our communications system. They're using it to monitor incoming signals and transmit messages into space. If you'd tried to contact us, they'd know you were here." Tido glanced at his instrument pad. "We must go. If you stay here, they will find you."

"Get the others. We're moving," Dietz said to Riley, who hurried off to the auditorium

"Did you move the bodies?" the Syrman asked anxiously.

"I examined one," Izin replied, "but left it in place."

"Let us hope the autacs do not notice the body was disturbed or they will search for us."

Riley returned with the rest of Dietz's team, then the three Syrmans led us through a series of back passages, carefully skirting the complex's main industrial areas. We came to a vertical shaft with an old elevator and rusting spiral stairs.

"They're monitoring the gang lifts," Tido said, leading us down into the dimly lit stairwell, past vertical pipes radiating heat. He motioned to the pipes that vanished into the darkness far below. "Jel Kara has a rapidly spinning, iron core. We tap its geomagnetic field for power. There are twenty-nine shafts like this one, all interlinked by tunnels. They allow us to move freely when the Intruders are not patrolling."

After a long climb down, we entered an ancient substation controlling the flow of geomagnetic energy to the surface. A dusty control panel with a single wall screen faced double bunks set against the opposite wall.

Syrmans in filthy coveralls sat on the bunks or at a table laid with drinking mugs and an assortment of makeshift weapons. Another Syrman stood watching a screen cycle through different views of the industrial complex.

"Did they detect us?" Tido asked as his companions dragged the crazed Syrman to an empty bunk and tied him down with electrical cable.

"No," the Syrman at the screen replied, "but the autacs are beginning their patrol."

The screen displayed a dark hole between a pair of grimy industrial machines four stories high. Three spotters leaped up out of the hole and darted off into the shadows, then three skinny bipedal autacs a meter and a half tall appeared with a weapon for one hand and a gripping claw for the other. Shiny black, rhombus-shaped sensors rotated on top of their rigid torsos and the soft auric light of contour shields glowed around their bodies.

"They're flankers, light attack units," Tido Rivas said. "Fast and dangerous."

"We know," Dietz replied, revealing he'd been well briefed on the Intruder order of battle.

"They ain't so tough," Larson said.

"Their energy weapons will cut right through your body armor," Tido said, "and their shields render your projectile weapons useless."

"That's what you think," Riley declared boastfully. "We turned a bunch of those things into scrap metal on Niedarim."

"Riley!" Dietz snapped, annoyed at the grunt's reference to their static force ammo.

Dietz's eyes narrowed as a taller, thickly armored tripod leaped out of the plunger hole. It had no arms and a twin barreled turret where the head and shoulders should have been. "They've got gunners."

"Yes, only two that I've seen," Tido Rivas said, "that twin cannon unit and a single heavy."

Dietz glanced at me. "They're assault variants."

"They blew out our eastern doors," Tido added.

"Will they see my ship?" I asked.

"They patrol outside sometimes, but don't go far from the processing plant."

"If everyone's dead," Dietz said, "why are they still here?"

"The Spawn leave reconnaissance units on outpost worlds like Jel Kara," Arleen explained. "If they encounter enemy forces, they transmit a contact report into space for sentry probes that periodically pass through such systems. If the sentry probe detects a report, it immediately takes it to the nearest spawnship."

The Syrman at the console watched the flankers move off, then said in Syrmat. "They're taking route two."

Tido started a timer on his arm pad. "They will return in forty-six minutes."

"So we sit tight," Riley said confidently, "wait for them to go back down their hole, then we bug out."

"How?" Izin asked. "If we call Jase to pick us up, they will detect our signal."

All eyes turned to Izin, then Dietz nodded gravely. "Yeah, he's right."

"We could go to him," Arleen suggested.

"All our vehicles were destroyed during the attack," Tido said. "You would have to go on foot."

"In this heat?" Riley said, making a face.

"It's too far," Shen agreed, sizing up Arleen, Izin and me with a look. "And they'd slow us down. We'd dehydrate before we got there."

"Jase will try to contact us before we're halfway," I said.

"And the autacs will pick up his signal and report our presence," Arleen added.

"Can't let that happen," Dietz said.

The troops read his intention. Most nodded grimly.

Several checked their weapons. No one questioned his decision, including me.

"When do you want to do it?" I asked.

Dietz studied the plunger hole on the screen. "After the patrol. We'll hit them when they're all down there together."

Tido's dark, beady little eyes saw our mood had changed, then realized what we'd decided. "You can't be serious. You'll be slaughtered, and us with you."

"We don't have a choice," I said.

Dietz turned his attention to the screen. "How many are down there?"

"At least forty," Tido said, "but one is enough to kill us all."

"One's all I need," Dietz said, tapping his N-grenade launcher meaningfully.

The Syrman leader scowled. "They are autacs. Their purpose is to destroy lesser races like us. You can't attack them with your primitive projectile weapons."

"Watch us," Larson said.

I turned to Arleen. "If there's no message in space, what happens?"

"The sentry probe will assume there is nothing to report and will move to the next monitored system."

"No news is good news," Riley declared lightly.

"A spawnship will come, eventually," Arleen said. "When they assess the damage, they will recognize your weapons. They'll know we were here."

"Then we must make sure there is no damage to assess," Izin said.

Dietz turned to Izin with a growing appreciation for his brutal directness. "How do we do that?"

"The geomagnetic energy required to operate such a large facility must be substantial," Izin said. "All we need do is overload the power system."

"But that would destroy...everything," Tido protested.

"That's the idea," I said.

"You ask the impossible."

"They killed your people," Dietz said. "You want to even the score?"

The other Syrmans started whispering among themselves as those who knew our language translated for those who did not. Quietly, they picked up their makeshift weapons and gathered around us.

I thought they were going to club us to death, then one said, "We do."

There were growls of agreement from the dirty, desperate Syrmans, then Tido relented. "If we cut the energy flow to the furnaces, the explosion will appear to be an industrial accident."

"How big?" Dietz asked.

"Big enough," the Syrman leader assured him.

"Do we need to attack the plunger?" Larson asked. "Won't the blast take care of them?"

"We could not get clear in time. You'll have to call your ship to evacuate us all."

"I will, after the spawn are destroyed," I promised. "I'll take all your people out."

"There's an auxiliary site on the north polar plain," the Syrman said. "We can survive there until the war ends."

I just hoped Jase didn't call while we waited for the autac patrol to return to its rat hole, giving Dietz and his psionic soldiers time to clean them out.

* * * *

"That's all of them," Tido Rivas said as the last flanker leaped into the plunger hole.

Two miners untied the crazed Syrman, then we went back up the metal stairs to ground level. The other Syrmans went off to sabotage the geomagnetic control center while Tido guided us through a labyrinth of dark passages and industrial facilities to a ten-story high chamber.

Steam hissed from rusting machines, clouding the air, as the deafening hammer and roar of heavy machinery assaulted our ears. In the noise and heat, my bionetic sense boosters were useless, limiting what I could see and hear to a few meters. As we neared the center of the chamber, two enormous cylindrical particle furnaces wrapped in tangled pipes and coated in centuries of grime loomed before us, reaching almost to the ceiling. They poured molten metal into narrow channels that run beneath grates in the floor to nearby casting and milling facilities.

We worked our way around the base of one of the giant furnaces until we saw sunlight beaming down through a ragged hole in the ceiling created by the plunger assault craft. It had struck the ground like an orbital blast, tossing floor plates and machines aside like toys. Dietz's team crept forward carefully, stalking their enemy, searching every shadow, while Tido became increasingly agitated.

"We must hurry," he declared impatiently. "Once my people start the overload, they won't be able to control it."

"I understand," I said, "but we don't want to run into an ambush. Let them do their job."

We moved up beside Dietz who pushed up his visor. "Can't see nothing in this soup. IR is saturated."

Izin stepped in front of him and peered into the steamy shadows. "There is no movement ahead."

"You can see through that?"

Izin touched the bulging lobe on his forehead. "Sonic vision."

Understanding flashed across Dietz's face. "Right. Same thing the Spawn have."

"You should train against tamphs on Earth," I suggested, "learn how it works first hand."

"The brass won't let us near them," he replied, not hiding the distrust Earth's military had for tamphs.

"A pity," Izin said. "We could help you."

"I reckon you could," Dietz said, no longer considering Izin an enemy. "You're on point."

"Thank you," Izin said and started forward, pinging the path past the furnace.

"Stay behind us," I said to Tido, then Dietz and I followed Izin until a wall of twisted floor plates and overturned machines, thrown up by the plunger impact, appeared ahead of us.

"There are sonic obstructions ahead I cannot see through," Izin said.

We waited for the others to catch up, then I turned to Arleen, no longer sure I could trust her. "You sense anything?"

"Autacs are machines, Captain Kade, not living entities. They could be all around us and I wouldn't know."

It seemed like the truth, so I turned to Dietz and said, "We'll have to do this the old fashioned way."

He nodded and used hand signals to direct his team to covering positions around the plunger hole. They disappeared into the shadows, then he pumped an N-grenade into the launcher.

"What is that?" Tido asked.

"Retribution," he replied and crept forward, followed by Izin and me, then he glanced back at us. "I've got this."

"We know you have," I said, unwilling to let him approach the plunger hole alone.

Dietz grunted indifferently. "Your funeral."

We crept up to the impact debris and peered through to the exposed rock surrounding the plunger hole. A spherical device with long vertical spines top and bottom and four short horizontal spines around its middle floated above the hole, rotating slowly. Tiny red lights blinked from the ends of its spines although it showed no weapons.

"It's a lookout," Dietz said, turning to Izin. "Can you take it with one shot?"

"I don't see a shield," he replied, "so yes, but it will trigger an alert."

"I only need them blind for a few seconds."

Izin replaced his fin-stabilized pinpoint sniper rounds with less accurate exploding detonators then slid his sniper rifle's long barrel through the tangled metal and took aim. "Ready?"

Before Dietz could answer, the soft clatter of rapid footsteps sounded behind us. I spun around as a four-legged spotter stopped and waved its sensor spines at us. I fired my P-50, but with my left hand, I was too slow and it darted away. I followed it with my gun, anticipating its movement and fired again, drilling its unshielded torso and sending its body sparking across the floor plates.

"Look out!" Dietz yelled as a snaking arm flew up out the plunger hole and whipped toward us. He and Izin dived apart as the arm crashed down between them.

The sensor hovering above the plunger hole shot high into the air, giving the autacs in their underground bunker an overview of our positions. Dietz scrambled onto the debris wall, then the robotic arm flashed toward him. He leaped into the air as it smashed the twisted metal beneath him, landed on his feet and charged across hard-packed soil toward the plunger hole.

The robotic arm swept after him, aiming for his back, but Dietz's psionic senses warned him and he dived flat as it cut the air above him. He came up on one knee and fired a burst of snakehead killers at the silver tentacle, flashing through its contour shield and cutting it in half. The severed arm slumped onto the ground, then he jumped to his feet and ran forward as three more snaking arms whipped up out of the plunger hole toward him.

"Izin, the sensor!" I yelled, realizing the reaper was keeping its body hidden in the hole.

Izin fired from a standing position, blowing the lookout apart and blinding the autacs below ground, then he scrambled onto a large overturned machine, searching for a better firing position. I ran after Dietz, who was diving and dodging all four robotic arms at once, using his psionic survival instincts to evade every attack with split-second luck.

Four-legged spotters followed by bipedal flankers suddenly sprang out of the plunger hole, leaping high into the air and landing on the furnaces and walkways above. The soldiers covering Dietz immediately opened fire, hunting them with streams of tracer, forcing them to keep moving. The autacs were fast and agile, jumping between platforms and walkways, shooting energy pulses from their weapon arms.

Dietz's team never let the flankers settle, firing a few bursts and moving moments before they would have been killed. They knew with psionic timing when to lay down covering fire, when to shoot, to evade, as energy blasts exploded all around them. The autacs fought with fearless, robotic precision while their intuitive adversary anticipated their every move, confounding them time and again.

To my left, Larson fired from the shadows, destroyed a flanker as it landed on a walkway, then he darted away as an autac he never saw fired from his flank. On the other side of the battleground, Riley, for no reason, spun on his heels and blasted a flanker as it landed behind him, a moment before it would have shot him in the back.

"They know when to duck," I muttered, running after Dietz, shooting at the silver tentacles flailing around him. He jumped over one, then another wrapped around his legs as he landed and lifted him into the air.

"Dietz!" I yelled, holstering my P-50 and holding out my arms.

Hanging upside down, he threw his K8 to me. I caught it with both hands, sending shooting pain through my injured shoulder as the robotic arm slammed his body into the ground with a sickening thud. He lay motionless, then the arm lifted him up and smashed his helpless body down again. Dietz's face was smeared with blood, but his eyes were open and his arms pushed weakly against the silver tentacle, still trying to free his legs.

Izin jumped down and raced across open ground with a burst of tamph speed. He dodged a silver tentacle and fired an exploding round into the arm holding Dietz's legs, blowing it apart. The end of the arm collapsed, then Izin grabbed Dietz's body armor and dragged him roughly away as a silver tentacle swung toward me. A stream of gunfire erupted from the darkness, severing the snaking arm, signaling the soldiers were now covering me.

With tracer crisscrossing the air, I charged toward the plunger hole. A silver tentacle crashed down in front of me, forcing me to hurdle over it, then I rolled under another arm as it whipped at my chest. I came to my feet at the edge of the plunger hole, then the spherical reaper controlling the snaking silver arms floated up in front of me. It was surrounded by the soft glow of a contour shield, illuminating the rounded stern of the plunger assault vehicle below. Three small field propulsion domes bulged around an open airlock that was rapidly filling with flankers massing for an attack.

The energy cannon crowning the reaper's body swiveled toward me, then four streams of tracer hit the cannon simultaneously, flashing through the autac's shield and tearing the weapon apart. I had a clear shot and aimed at the open airlock, but the reaper dropped below ground level, blocking my line of sight.

"You know what this is, don't you?" I said, certain it knew how the plunger on Niedarim had been destroyed.

I swung the K8 sideways and fired at the hole's inner wall. There was a pop as the novarium grenade shot from the launcher, then tentacled stumps speared after it. The grenade flew past the reaper, ricocheted off the rock below a silver arm and fell through the plunger's open hatch into the massing autacs. Flankers inside the crowded stern chamber grabbed vainly for the N-grenade as it bounced between their legs, out of reach.

I turned and raced away, silently counting the seconds, then threw myself down as the N-grenade detonated. A scream filled the air as a black volcanic eruption blasted up out of the plunger hole. A great force pressed down on my chest so hard I couldn't breathe, then it faded as debris from the collapsing roof rained down around me. The steep sides of the plunger hole began to subside, forcing me to scramble forward as the ground gave way beneath my boots. I thought I was about to slide into the lava pool at the bottom when the ground stabilized and I got clear. I relaxed, breathing a sigh of relief, then the smoking, armless wreck of the reaper crashed down beside me.

There was a shocked silence as humans and autacs stared at the collapsed plunger hole, then the shooting began again. At first, I thought it was a counterattack, but the autacs were leaping away, scrambling up stanchions, running along walkways and gantries, heading for the ceiling. The soldiers fired after them, downing several, then with my ears ringing, I got to my feet and ran to where Izin was sheltering with Arleen and Tido Rivas. Dietz sat beside them, grimacing in pain, propped against an upturned machine. His face was smeared with dirt and blood and one arm was pressed across his chest.

"Can you walk?" I asked.

He nodded. "Got a few broken ribs. Nothing your medbot can't fix."

"They're climbing toward the roof, Captain," Izin said, staring up into the darkness with his telescoping tamph eyes. A spotter leaped from a heavy lift hoist to a walkway, then scuttled toward an intact part of the roof.

"Can they send a signal from up there?" I asked Tido.

"Yes, if the transmitter is still working."

"It's working," I said, certain that's why the surviving autacs were retreating to the roof.

"Spotters could interface it directly," Arleen said.

I turned to Tido. "How do we get up there?"

"There's a service elevator behind number two furnace," he replied.

"Too easy…to get trapped," Dietz wheezed as I handed him his rifle.

"Is there another way?" I asked.

"There are stairs that way," Tido said pointing across the chamber.

Dietz activated his communicator, no longer caring who heard him. "Fall back on me," he ordered, then Tido lifted him to his feet like he was a feather.

The soldiers came in firing sporadically at flankers who'd taken up defensive positions high above us, covering other autacs heading for the comms tower. When we were all together, Tido led us through narrow, steam filled passages between greasy machines to metal stairs rising alongside a wall.

Izin and I jogged up the stairs, eager to get to the roof, immediately drawing the attention of the autac rear guard. They came leaping toward us, springing from stanchions to walkways as Dietz's team fired up at them with uncanny timing, throwing off their aim. Autac energy pulses flashed around us, then one flanker was caught mid air by a stream of tracer and fell into a cauldron of boiling metal. Another was hit as it hung beneath a walkway and become entangled in suspension cables and a third fell into a giant industrial press and was crushed.

Izin and I clambered up the stairs, firing sporadically as the soldiers fought a running battle behind us, calling to each other over their communicators.

"There's two behind us!"

"One at nine o'clock."

"Shen, above you."

"Damn, they're fast!"

"Got one!"

"I got three already," Riley boasted.

At a landing halfway up, Izin and I paused to give them a chance to catch up. He fired two carefully aimed shots, both ricocheting harmlessly off autac contour shields.

"We're wasting time, Captain," he said as Tido bounded up after us holding Dietz's arm across his shoulder, barely letting the soldier's feet touch the stairs.

I turned to Dietz. "We're going on ahead."

He nodded as another of Izin's expertly aimed shots deflected off an autac contour shield, then he fixed a hard look on Izin. "I hate tamphs," he growled through gritted teeth. "Never thought one would save my life. Here." He offered his K8 to Izin. "Kill something with this."

Izin handed his sniper rifle to Tido, took the K8 and inspected the magazine, seeing it was loaded with snakehead killers. He gave me a knowing look, recognizing it was the same kind of ammo I used. He replaced the mag and tested the weight. "I will put it to good use."

Dietz spoke into his communicator. "Kade and the tamph are going for the roof. Cover them."

Izin and I sprinted up the stairs as the whine of magnetic accelerators filled the air behind us. The autacs tried to cut us off, but Dietz's soldiers put up a wall of tracer, destroying several flankers and driving the others back.

Ibanez ran past Tido and Dietz, taking the stairs two at a time, pausing only long enough to shoot into the darkness when an autac got too close. He was trying to stay with us as we climbed. When we were high above the decaying industrial complex, a flanker leaped out of the darkness, caught an exposed girder and launched itself through the open ceiling onto the roof.

"They're waiting for you Kade," Dietz's gravel voice sounded in my ear.

I glanced at Izin who was breathing heavily. "That's good. Izin's tired of chasing."

"If I'd known you'd have me climbing stairs," Izin growled breathlessly through his vocalizer, "I'd have brought a jump-pack."

A flanker dropped out of the darkness several steps above us and lifted its weapon arm to fire. Before I could raise my P-50, a stream of tracer cut the air between me and Izin, flashed through the autac's shield and knocked it back over the railing. I glanced back to see Ibanez lower his K8 and speak into his communicator.

"Low on ammo," he announced as he continued climbing after us.

"Same here," Shen said.

"I'm out," Larson declared.

"I got one reload," Riley said.

Izin glanced at the mag indicator on Dietz's assault rifle. "This weapon is almost empty, Captain."

"Make it count," I said, and took the stairs three at a time. Izin tried to keep up, but he was built for bursts of speed, not endurance. With my EIS gene mods boosting the rate I metabolized oxygen, I was always going to outrun him no matter how hard he tried.

He paused at a landing, leaning on the railing, breathing hard. "Don't wait for me, Captain," he panted, then I bounded up the stairs to a rusting metal door.

I eased it open for a look. The flat metal roof was strewn with square ribbed vents belching steam and black smoke that obscured my vision. From out of the murky cloud, an energy pulse flashed toward me. I stepped back as it struck the door, blasting a hole through it and almost tearing it out of its frame.

I boosted my optics for infrared and my listener to high frequency then stole another look outside. The hot gases pouring from the vents blurred the air crimson. It was a false image, compensating for infrared being beyond human visual perception. It was the same for my listener, giving me false signals for frequencies beyond my audible range. Even so, there were no autac hotspots, no percussive rap of metallic feet on the plated roof. They were hidden and waiting, knowing time was on their side.

I pushed the door wide open, stepped into view as if to step out, then jumped back as energy blasts shredded the door, knocking it down. Before it hit the floor, I charged out into the swirling mist and smoke, and raced around the stairwell housing. Energy blasts flashed past me, then I ducked behind the housing and stopped.

I switched my P-50 to my preferred right hand, then supported by my left, raised it to eye height ignoring the pain in my shoulder. The clatter of robotic feet rang through the air as one flanker moved left of the stair housing and two others went right. The solo flanker was closest, so I swiveled toward its approaching footsteps and waited. When its ghostly silhouette emerged from the mist, I put three into its chest, turning it into scrap metal, and spun the other way.

The two on the right separated. One hugged the stairwell housing while the other circled, trying to get me in a crossfire. When the first peered around the edge of the housing, I grazed it with a headshot, sending it stumbling out into the open, and finished it with a double to the chest.

Somewhere out in the swirling steam, the third flanker froze, silencing the chatter of its metal feet. It waited for me to reveal myself, showing the kind of cunning I never expected from a machine. Knowing time was its ally, not mine, I crept forward, one cautious step at a time, fearing the merest creak of the metal roof under my boots would give away my position. My head was on a swivel, going left and right, peering through the red mist, then a pair of glowing metal legs disguised within a shimmering crimson plume appeared ahead. It was standing above a thermal vent, hiding in its heat, unaware its boiling metal skin betrayed its presence.

I fired and dived away as it sent a glowing energy pulse flashing past me. My heavy slug hit the flanker low in the abdomen and it exploded, hurling thin arms and legs across the roof, revealing I'd found its weak spot.

I got silently to my feet, listened for metallic footsteps, then inched forward in search of the Syrman transmitter. Soon, Izin's panting voice sounded from my communicator.

"I'm on the roof, Captain."

"Go left," I whispered, edging to the right.

I couldn't see him as we crept through the wafting cloud, but Izin's natural stealthiness and his sonic vision made this sneaking game more his kind of fight than mine. We inched forward, then a burst from his K8 shattered the hissing of the vents and a wrecked autac collapsed onto the metal roof ahead.

I slipped between a pair of vents belching black smoke, then the mist ahead thinned, revealing a short tower with a dome at its peak. A flanker and a spotter climbed to the dome, then the flanker used its claw hand to tear at the dome's base while the spotter clung to a cross beam a few meters below.

I aimed at the flanker and fired, but the shot

ricocheted off a cross beam, alerting it to my presence. It made no attempt to hide, but peeled the dome's metal skin back making a hole large enough for the spotter.

Ignoring the pain in my shoulder, I fired again, clipping the flanker's torso. The impact knocked the precariously balanced autac off its perch, but its claw arm hung tenaciously to the dome's metal base, peeling a metal strip off as it fell. The bipedal autac bounced off a cross beam, crashed through the roof and vanished below, then the little spotter scuttled up the stanchion toward the dome. I fired repeatedly, but my bad shoulder threw off my aim, then my P-50 beeped empty and the spotter crawled inside the dome.

I lowered my gun and spoke into my communicator. "Izin. Take out the transmitter. Use the launcher."

"It's too high, Captain," he replied.

"Shoot the stanchion."

There was a popping sound to my left, then a black N-grenade arced through the mist toward the tower on a low trajectory. The grenade ricocheted off a stanchion leg, bounced across the roof and disappeared into the billowing steam and smoke. A moment later, the gray cloud flashed white as the N-grenade detonated, vaporizing the far side of the complex.

"Sorry, Captain."

"Your shot was perfect, Izin. The grenade was on a timer, not contact."

A stream of tracer from his K8 peppered the heavy metal base of the dome, doing no damage, then the clang of metal feet landing on the roof suddenly rang out behind me. I spun around, saw two flankers standing ten meters away, and pressed my P-50's firing surface, but it beeped, reminding me it was empty, then the chatter of Izin's K8 fell silent.

"I'm out of ammunition, Captain," he declared.

"Yeah, me too," I said, eyeballing the flankers as they raised their weapon arms together in robotic precision.

The black clouds above the two flankers billowed toward me as an enormous shadow glided out of the mist like a monster from the deep, then twin streams of light flashed down from the cloud as two kinetic cannons fired together. They blasted the autacs with heavy naval rounds, overloading the flanker's light contour shields and shredding them instantly. I blinked in surprise, then the *Silver Lining* glided out of the misty blackness and passed overhead.

"You didn't think I'd let you have all the fun, did you?" Jase's voice sounded in my earpiece.

"Destroy the tower! *Now!*" I yelled at my communicator.

Both k-cannons swiveled and fired, shattering the communications dome in a fiery explosion, then the *Silver Lining* performed a slow banking loop around the burning tower.

"I came as soon as I heard the grunts chattering," Jase said as he brought the ship in low and hovered above the roof, lowering the stern ramp.

Ibanez emerged from the stairwell door with his gun level, saw the *Silver Lining* and relaxed. "Roof is secure," he announced over comms, then took up a covering position on the ramp, out of reach of the thruster down blast.

Tido Rivas and Dietz arrived with the rest of the team and quickly climbed the ramp. Tido lowered Dietz to the deck and looked back at the burning comms tower.

"You humans are as warlike as they say," he said.

"You better believe it," Riley declared belligerently.

"When the Spawn realize what you are, they will exterminate you."

"Only if they find out it was us," I said.

"They'll detect your comms," Tido said.

"The hell they will," Dietz wheezed.

I held up my communicator. "Low power, short-range. If they're not here soon, the signals will dissipate into background interference."

"Hrrh," the Syrman grunted thoughtfully. "You turn weakness into an advantage."

"We improvise," I said as the other Syrmans came running onto the roof. They clambered up the ramp, then I sealed it shut and called Jase over the intercom. "Head north, fast. This whole place is about to go up."

Izin activated an emergency stretcherbot for Dietz, but he refused to get on.

"Your blood is messing up my deck," I said, then he scowled indignantly and lowered himself onto the stretcher. We were all dirty from smoke and ash, but his troops seemed as sharp and fresh as ever. Even Dietz, with his broken ribs, looked like he still had plenty of fight left in him.

"I am surprised none of them are dead," Izin said in a low voice as the stretcherbot jammed a pain killer in Dietz's arm and stabilized his torso in a stasis field.

"They were lucky," I replied, psionically lucky.

I left Izin to supervise Dietz's transfer to medbay and took Tido Rivas up to the bridge. Jase was on his couch piloting the *Silver Lining* north at mach twenty. The bridge screen was split fore and aft, showing the dry arctic plain ahead and the receding Syrman base astern. The high-walled industrial complex was prickling with electricity and lightning clawed the air, then it exploded in a brilliant blue-white flash that filled half the screen.

"You do that on purpose?" Jase asked.

"Just covering our tracks," I replied, sliding onto my couch. "Anything out there?"

"Just us. You expecting company?"

"I hope not," I said, turning to Tido Rivas. "Show him where you want to go."

Jase summoned a map of Jel Kara's northern hemisphere, then Tido identified a spot two thousand clicks from the pole.

"It's a biomass processing plant," he said. "You'll see its tanks as we approach."

Jase adjusted his course, then I turned to Tido.

"You need food?"

"No. The arctic station produces food and water for our entire workforce. We can survive there for years."

In minutes, four large white tanks beside a small rectangular structure appeared. There was no sign of damage or Intruder forces, so Jase put us down close to the building.

Tido pushed both his fists together and bowed slightly in a Syrman salute. "Thank you for avenging my brothers."

"Remember, we were never here."

"What humans?" he grunted wryly and went below.

Jase lowered the ramp, then the Syrmans appeared outside with their crazed companion and hurried across to the station. The others went inside while Tido paused long enough to watch us begin our climb.

"She didn't get off," I said, certain I'd not seen Arleen stay behind with the Syrmans.

"You want to go back?" Jase asked.

I shook my head. "There's a sentry probe due any time."

Jase scowled. "Don't the Spawn have something better to do than chase us–like conquer the galaxy?"

"You'd think so," I said thoughtfully.

We cleared the atmosphere and had an anxious run to the edge of the planet's gravity well, watching our screens all the way. When we passed minimum safe distance, Jase pulled our sensor masts and we bubbled out to the heliopause, then began a series of random jumps to confuse any sentry probes trying to pick up our trail.

I slid off my couch and headed for the companionway. "You've got the first watch," I said and went in search of our increasingly unwelcome Uvo, intent on discovering why she'd lied.

* * * *

Arleen answered the door to her cabin, surprising me with her nakedness. She was thinner than a human woman, flat chested with delicate arms and legs, no body hair and an ethereal, yet unmistakably alien beauty. The pressure suit she'd worn into the Syrman industrial complex was discarded on the floor and her robes from Niedarim were flung carelessly over the back of a chair.

"I'm surprised to see you're still aboard," I said, turning my back politely.

"Averting your eyes, Captain? Does my appearance offend you?"

"Just giving you some privacy."

"If I cared for privacy, I would have locked the door," she said amused. "Personal modesty is unknown to my kind." She stepped into the shower, set the thermal indicator to cold, then a fine icy mist sprayed her body.

"We have locks for a reason," I said, walking into the room, but keeping my distance.

"Nudity neither arouses nor offends us," she called from the shower. "For us, the form is merely an instrument of expression in this dimension."

"We're not that enlightened," I said, wondering if Marie would be so open-minded about me watching a female shower, even if she was a shapeless alien.

"Is there something you want?" Arleen asked as she scrubbed grimy smoke residue from her skin.

"I was wondering why you didn't stay on Jel Kara?"

"The Syrmans said there were no ships coming," she replied, turning to let the water run down her back. "I had no choice but to stay aboard. Is that inconvenient for you?"

"I don't have time for more detours. I have to go to Kota next."

"I understand. Perhaps after Kota, we can work something out. I will arrange for you to be well paid. That is the human custom, is it not?"

"It's not the payment that worries me, it's that mad Syrman. What was he jabbering about?"

She gave me a reproachful look. "You know exactly what he said."

Her empathic ability saw straight through me, so I came clean. "So why'd you lie?"

"Hmm...I did, didn't I." She conceded. "You are a surprise to me, Captain Kade. Your engineer is a Spawn–"

"–He's a tamph.

"...you have a gun-slinging drunk for a copilot–"

"–What Jase does in his spare time is his business."

"...you understand Syrmat perfectly well, an uncommon skill for a human trader–"

"How many human traders do you know?"

"You're the first," she said, not admitting she was wrong. "And even though you have close personal ties to your crew, you constantly deceive them." She gave me a searching look. "But we won't discuss that, will we?"

"You're very observant for a governess."

"Most intriguing of all, Captain Kade, are the mercenaries you're transporting, who fight like...they're not quite human, and whose weapons are surprisingly effective against the One Spawn."

"How they fight and the weapons they use is their business."

"If you say so," she said, rebuffing my lies. "It's almost as if the Tau Cetins designed your ammunition so you could defend yourselves against the Spawn."

It was like a thunderbolt from the heavens. It had never occurred to me the Tau Cetins had an ulterior motive for giving us static force technology. I'd always assumed it was just to help us deal with the Matarons, even though the Matarons were no threat to us while the Tau Cetins were around to keep them in their box. To give us one small technology that made our primitive kinetic weapons deadly against the Spawn required an astonishing level of scheming, a level worthy of the Ornithian genius for subterfuge.

They'd told us nothing of their real motives, made us promise to use static force projectiles in tiny quantities, in secret and only against the Matarons, yet all along, they *knew* we'd mass-produce them and use them against anyone who threatened us. It was a staggering deception that had fooled the entire galaxy and the One Spawn. And us! The Tau Cetins had been monitoring life on Earth for millions of years, seen mankind rise from primitive hominids to signatories of the Access Treaty, had studied every war we'd ever fought and got inside our heads like no one else ever had.

No wonder they knew us so well.

She tapped the shower control and the water stopped flowing, then the drier blew warm air over her lithe body as she studied me intently.

"You really didn't know?" she asked, genuinely surprised. "I suspected it when I saw what your soldiers did on Niedarim. Today confirmed it. Your static force ammunition is far more sophisticated than you realize, far beyond what is required to defeat a handful of Mataron assassins."

"But just what we need to fight the Spawn."

"Ground combat is where the Tau Cetins are weakest. Their ships are magnificent technological achievements, but they lack the savagery of true warriors."

"Something we have in abundance," I said, completing her thought.

She stepped out of the shower and came toward me.

I ignored her nakedness and faced her down, still waiting for my answer.

"Yes, I lied to you," she admitted, "but only because the others were listening."

"They're not listening now."

She studied me with her large dark blue eyes as if searching for something. "The One Spawn *are* hunting us," she said at last, pulling on her silken robe.

"But not because they think the Suzerain is aboard."

"No. The Matriarch hunting us has no interest in him. She never did."

"She wants you."

"Not even me, although in a way, I am why she went to Jel Kara."

"But she couldn't have known we were going there. Even I didn't know that."

"Vidah'ra knew." She looked into my eyes, waiting for me to figure it out.

"The Buratu agent?…The Tau Cetin ship they destroyed on Jel Kara was waiting for him."

"Yes."

"You met him at the starport. He told you the Tau Cetins were waiting on Jel Kara, that's why you got me to take you there. That's how the Spawn knew. They broke him."

"He would have told them everything before he died."

"Why'd you risk it?"

"I hoped he'd hold out long enough for us to reach Jel Kara first. I was wrong."

"So they know about me, my ship."

"They know the Tau Cetins sent a human to meet the Buratu agent, and that he met me instead."

"So, you are an operative?"

"No. I am a child's tutor, a sublime empath, just as I told you."

"I find that hard to believe."

"Nevertheless, it is true. Uvo empaths like myself are scattered across the galaxy teaching the future leaders and thinkers of many civilizations. We have no political allegiances."

"So why did the Buratu involve you?"

"When the One Spawn invaded Niedarim, he was desperate. He knew he was going to die and I was his only hope."

"He told you he was waiting for me?"

"He didn't know your name, only that you were human. I realized who you were when the Suzerain told me he was to be taken off-world by a human ship, the only one on Niedarim. It had to be you."

"Why didn't he ask the Lhekans for help?"

"How could he? They wanted to remain neutral, had repeatedly refused to help the Tau Cetins. They would have handed him over to the One Spawn if they'd known who he was."

"If that's true, why didn't the Spawn issue an ultimatum before attacking Niedarim?"

"That would have given the Lhekans time to request help from the Ornithians. The Matriarch Vidah'ra, with just one spawnship under her command, could not take that risk. She attacked the moment she arrived. We were at the summer palace when the bombardment began. I accompanied the children and the Suzerain to the starport, but it was already too late. All of their ships had been destroyed. That is when I met the Buratu agent."

"If the Uvo are neutral, why'd you help him?"

"We have signed no pact, have no military power, but we are not blind to what is happening," she said with a trace of sadness. "At the starport, amid the terror and panic of the Lhekan people, I sensed a singularly courageous presence. He was calm, resigned to his fate, unafraid, yet searching for someone. For you."

"I was late."

"At first, he was suspicious. He said he was waiting

for a human, then I told him there was a human ship on Niedarim, but it was far away. He couldn't trust the Lhekans and he knew the Spawn were coming, so he asked me to find the human ship. That is when he gave me this, to give to the Tau Cetins." She reached into her robe and produced a diamond-like cylinder two centimeters long. "This is what Vidah'ra is after. It is why she invaded Niedarim and captured the Syrman base on Jel Kara. It is a memory crystal."

"Memory! That's what the Syrman was babbling about."

"Yes. The Spawn interrogated them, but the Syrmans knew nothing."

"What's on it?"

"The memories of a great mind structure."

"That must be some mind, considering all the people they killed for it."

"Do you know what a Command Nexus is, Captain Kade?"

"It's a Spawn artificial intelligence. It commands fleets, armies, formulates strategies, thinks faster than any biological entity ever could. Is that a Command Nexus?"

"Not its cognitive power, just some of its memories. The memories of Siraksha Three."

"Siraksha?" I said recalling where I'd heard that name before. "That's the Matriarch's family."

"Her Clan Majestic. They were responsible for planning the Intruder assault on the galaxy, including the campaign against the Ornithians. Siraksha Three was the coordinating intelligence. Its memory structure was obtained by Kesarn infiltrators and passed to the Buratu agent." She held the memory crystal up like it was the greatest treasure in the universe. "Now I have it."

"Let me guess, it's everything the galaxy ever wanted to know about the Spawn but were afraid to ask."

"It reveals the locations of their secret bases, supply

routes, listening posts and, most important of all, their grand strategic plan."

I furrowed my brow. "So why don't they just change their plans?"

"The Spawn Fleet could, if they knew."

I blinked. "How could they not know? You said it yourself, the Buratu told them everything."

"He told the Siraksha Clan Majestic," Arleen said, wiping beads of sweat from her face.

"So, it's useless," I said disappointed.

"For the Spawn Fleet to know what we have, the Siraksha Clan Majestic must admit their failure to the other great clans. That is something they are loathe to do, because it would mean utter disgrace."

"They'd risk defeat rather than disgrace?"

"You do not understand the machinations of the One Spawn." She took a deep breath, steadying herself.

Her skin was flushed and pale. I'd assumed it was from her cold shower, but now I wasn't so sure.

"Their power structure," she continued, "is built upon an alliance of clans led by matriarchs who despise each other. They constantly compete for personal power. For the Siraksha to reveal a failure of this magnitude would cause the other great clans to censure them, perhaps even unite against them. That is why they keep it hidden."

"That's insane."

"The clans are aligned out of necessity, by a common language and a desire to rule, yet they are torn by mutual distrust and petty jealousies. The One Spawn is one in name only. They demonstrate group selfishness on a scale unknown to the rest of the galaxy."

"You don't know our history," I said dryly.

"Your species has had many selfish groups plunge your people into catastrophic wars, but they were always defeated by selfless groups. Your present civil war is such a contest, led by criminals with a common hunger for wealth and power."

"Our history does tend to repeat itself."

"If you survive your civil war and the Spawn invasion, you will have come too far to repeat that pattern again, or to follow in the footsteps of the One Spawn."

"I'm not that optimistic," I said, fixing my eyes upon the tiny crystal in her hand. "So what now?"

"The Siraksha Clan Majestic will do everything in their power to find us and recover this memory crystal. They will search anywhere there are fast ships that could take these memories to the Tau Cetins."

"It would take us months to reach Ansara," I said, certain the *Silver Lining* wasn't the answer.

"The war may well be over by then," she said, swaying faintly.

"Are you OK?" I asked, stepping toward her.

"I need to…" Her eyes closed and her knees gave way.

I caught her as she fell, surprised at how hot she was to the touch. "Arleen?" I said, lowering her gently to the deck.

She was burning up. Her breathing was shallow, her skin clammy to the touch. She tried to speak but produced no sound, then she pressed her hand into mine, clasping it before lapsing into unconsciousness. Cradling her with one arm, shocked by how fragile she seemed, I looked down at my open hand as she let go.

It held the diamantine memory crystal.

* * * *

"What's wrong with her?" I asked as the medbay bioscanner finished passing over Arleen's body. She lay in a deep coma with a high fever and a racing pulse.

"I'm a combat medic, sir, not a xenobiologist," Shen replied.

Maybe so, but she had more medical training than anyone else aboard and the ship's diagnostic system couldn't make any sense of Arleen's alien life signs.

"Her metabolic rate is very high, Captain," Izin said uncertainly.

"I don't even know what her body temperature should be," Shen said helplessly. "I can't risk using our biochems. They could poison her."

"There's no data on the Uvo in our medical system," Izin said. "We have nothing to baseline her readings against, except my original scan. That shows her electrical field has increased thirty percent while her brain activity is negligible."

"Could it be an organism from Jel Kara?" I asked.

"The biofilters would have detected it, Captain," Shen replied doubtfully.

"Her body is being attacked at a cellular level," Izin said. "If the cause is an alien organism, we must all be immune to it."

"I could take a blood sample, try to find a way to synthesize plasma for her," Shen suggested, touching Arleen's sweat-soaked skin. "She's dehydrating fast. She's going to need fluids to stay alive."

"Do it," I said, glancing at Dietz lying unconscious on the nearby bed, surrounded by a sterile field. The medbot had opened his chest in five places and was force-knitting his broken ribs together. With luck, he'd be walking in a few days and could start light training in a week.

"We could go to a non-human world," Izin suggested. "They might have medical knowledge of the Uvo we do not."

And fast ships, which was why they'd all be watched by the One Spawn.

"No, Marie's waiting for us on Kota," I said, certain any further delay would be a disaster for Operation Windfall. I took Arleen's hot, sweaty, lifeless hand, searching for any response.

"She's unaware of your presence, Captain," Izin said.

I nodded sadly, certain I could do nothing for her, then went up to the bridge and set course for the Chambal System.

Chapter Six: Kota

Separatist stronghold
Chambal System
Outer Cassiopeia
1.02 Earth Normal Gravity
854 light years from Sol
210,000 inhabitants

"They're jamming us," Jase announced moments after we unbubbled. We were sixty-five million kilometers from Kota, close enough to eyeball the planet, yet far enough out to run if they didn't like the look of us. "They're ranging us."

"Reverse vector their targeting beam," I said.

Jase pushed our sensor masts out to full extension and triangulated the signal.

"It's not coming from the planet," he said, focusing an optical on a cylindrical object in geostationary orbit.

It was an armored defense platform, the kind used by civilian contractors in places where the navy was rarely seen. Its axial turrets had been replaced by a sophisticated suite of dishes, aerials, and emitters that were dumping narrow band static on our sensors while tracking our position.

The bridge speaker crackled to life with a terse command from traffic control. "CSS Morgan's Reach, transmit your recognition code now."

Our transponder signal was genuine, matching a commercial star ship of similar mass to us, although by no means our twin. The real *Morgan's Reach* was fourteen hundred light years away and had never been to Oh-Zero-Sixty, so Kota Control had no reason to suspect we were anything but a genuine Separatist blockade runner.

"The hail's coming from the platform too," Jase added.

"It's an unmanned relay station," I said, certain whoever was calling the shots wanted to keep their location hidden, making it a good bet they weren't at the spaceport.

I activated Ruslan Glebb's code and held my breath, hoping they weren't going to start shooting, then Kota Control declared, "CSS Morgan's Reach, you are cleared to land. Transmitting your approach vectors now. For your own safety, do not deviate from this course."

A three dimensional, zigzagging flight path appeared on the bridge screen. The surprisingly sharp angles would force us to keep our velocity down, so inertial drift didn't carry us out of our lane.

"That'll take hours!" Jase exclaimed.

"Yeah, it will," I said suspiciously.

"They've stopped jamming us," he said as the weapons lock indicator winked out, then a cloud of tiny contact points appeared on the bridge screen between us and Kota. They enveloped the planet four to ten million kilometers out. Other armored orbitals appeared, scattered throughout the cloud, all equipped with a full complement of weapons to defend the planet rather than act as communications relays.

"Oh ho," Jase said as he got a read on the cloud. "It's a minefield."

"Let's see one."

A four-meter long spherocylinder powered by a single high acceleration engine appeared in an image box on the bridge screen. My threading quickly identified it as an old anti-ship drone of a type Earth Navy had decommissioned more than twenty years ago. The Consortium must have picked them up for scrap, refurbished their systems and shipped them out here in secret. Now, floating in high orbit, hiding under a blanket of static, their purpose was obvious.

"It's a seeker mine," I said.

"There are thousands of them," Jase said uneasily.

There'd been no mention of mines at the Hades City briefing, which meant Admiral Talis was about to come charging in with his entire fleet, unaware of what was waiting for him. Knowing hesitation would look suspicious, I set the autonav's drift tolerance to zero and gave it the helm.

"Getting out's going to be harder than getting in," I said as we crept into the minefield.

Kota's cold, dark brown surface slowly grew in size as hugged our approach vector. Frozen tundra plains covered the poles instead of white ice caps and a thin smear of green banded a third of the equator where humans lived. Between the settled zone and the northern permafrost was a vast conifer forest spanning thirty degrees of longitude. It had been transplanted in seed form from Earth and now formed a dark green island amid a world of dry brown plains. A thin band of small blue lakes–none of which had existed before man's arrival–dotted the equator, stretching no more than a few degrees north and south.

When humans first reached Kota, it had been the driest habitable world mankind had ever discovered, perfect in every way except for its lack of water. With human help, that was slowly changing. A flotilla of ice miners scoured the outer reaches of the Chambal System, sifting through billions of icy objects for rare comets with low deuterium to hydrogen ratios, rendering them suitable for planetary watering. Once found, ice miners towed then in to Kota's orbit where they were broken up prior to being dropped into the atmosphere.

"There's a berg coming in," Jase said, focusing an optical on a dirty white mountain of ice drifting toward low orbit.

It looked like a comet, except its long wispy vapor tail–created by the solar wind–pointed toward the star rather than away from it. The leading tail was caused by thrusters on the comet's planet-facing side decelerating it while tail particles caught by the star's gravity raced ahead. Flying beside the comet was an aging space tug, nursing it into orbit, while seeker mines in its path moved aside to avoid being run down. When the comet and tug had passed, the mines returned to their assigned positions, confirming someone on the ground had remote control over them, even if they chose not to exercise it for us.

The comet jockey expertly maneuvered his frozen mountain to one of four converted supply ships. The other three floated alongside comets of varying sizes, acting as base ships for demolition teams that broke the comets apart. The pieces were then fed into mass accelerators on the supply ships' hulls and launched in a continuous stream at Kota. The atmosphere vaporized the ice on entry, killing any frozen organisms along for the ride, and allowing the hydrogen to mix into the oxygen-rich atmosphere, forming water molecules.

The increasing water vapor in the atmosphere was slowly warming the planet, forcing the permafrost to retreat and increasing the surface water at the equator. It was an attempt to copy the primeval watering of Earth, a process that had increased the planet's precious supply of greenhouse gases and turned man's homeworld from an uninhabitable snowball into a garden world.

"That's a mass extinction waiting to happen," Jase prophesied as he watched the comet's thrusters fire with carefully calculated precision.

I shook my head. "It'd skip off the atmosphere if they messed up the approach."

"Unless they get that wrong too."

The autonav pulled a series of hard sliding turns and we passed out of the minefield, then I took the helm and inserted for Kota's only spaceport. It was a graded dirt field outside Khandwa City, the planet's capital, located half a degree above the equator. Our dive was long and slow, giving their anti-orbital weapons a chance to practice painting us while Jase fixed an optical on the sprawling, square grid prison complex at the northern edge of the forest.

East of the compound was a small landing ground where a handful of ships were parked close together while to the west, standing off by itself, was a large, domed e-plant. A veritable flood of neutrinos poured from the energy plant, indicating its output far exceeded the needs of the planet's tiny population. A high capacity transmission beam linked the e-plant to the prison and another ran south through a series of conduit towers alongside the road to Khandwa City. Smaller feeder beams led off from the capital to the planet's three other cities, marking the colony's dependence on its single, remote energy source.

Jase studied the prison as best he could from that range. "Doesn't look so tough."

"That's a big e-plant," I said apprehensively. "It could power a lot of pulse cannons."

If that was its purpose, it was a long way from the spaceport and the cities. The open beam feeders would bleed energy everywhere, suggesting they were added as an afterthought to keep the local population happy.

Jase sobered and ran a thermal scan, looking for heat blooms. "Don't see any heavies."

"Doesn't mean they're not there," I replied, certain they were.

Kota Prison slipped from sight as we lost altitude and passed over rows of kilometer square sunhouses. The transparent structures produced most of the colony's food supply, using the feeble equatorial sun to grow crops that would normally have been impossible on such a cold, unusually dry world. The sunhouses ended in sight of the spaceport's aging comms tower. The rusting structure was flanked by a row of tumbledown warehouses and a spartan barracks with several military vehicles parked in front. The only ships on the landing ground were old space tugs of the sort we'd seen guiding icebergs into orbit and at least two of them didn't look spaceworthy.

"Where's the Mendi?" I wondered, certain Marie had beaten us to Kota by days.

"You did tell her to dump her cargo and go. And you are the boss," he said with a wry smile, implying she gave the orders.

"Marie following instructions? That would be a first," I mused, turning my attention to the dilapidated warehouses at the edge of the landing ground.

Their roofs were holed, several were missing doors and one was no more than a shed storing unused earth moving equipment. They were nothing like the war-winning logistics center I'd been told to expect. Either naval intelligence, the EIS, the navy, the army, and Lena had all got Operation Windfall horribly wrong or Kota wasn't what it was supposed to be.

"I'm picking up ranging beams, one south, one northeast," Jase warned. "I still don't see any weapons."

"Let's give them a show," I said and made a clumsy effort at landing, going down fifteen degrees to port. We hit hard and rocked on our struts, looking every bit like greedy amateurs crazy enough to run Earth Navy's blockade for big credits.

"Ah! There it is," Jase said, feeding an image of an armored turret onto the bridge screen.

It was hidden in a natural rock formation and covered by a camouflage net sewn with radiation absorbent strips to soak up sensor pulses from space. The outline of a heavy pulse cannon was barely visible in the shadows and, unlike the warehouses, it was in mint condition. Between the camouflage, the absorption net and the orbital jammers, Earth Navy would never hit it without a marker.

"Where's the other one?" I asked.

"Can't see it, but I'm picking up underground neutrinos southeast of here."

"An underground e-plant?"

"A small one, with lots of signal suppression."

It was positioned to power both spaceport batteries, so even if Talis took out the transmission beam from the north, it wouldn't silence the big guns down here. I wondered if there were other emplacements we hadn't detected, then two ground vehicles started toward us from the barracks. One was a long black skimmer with dark windows and polished silver trim, the kind of chauffeur driven craft usually found on wealthy Core System worlds. It was a sign of money that came too easily, in quantities that never ran out, and it had no place on a remote colony like Kota.

Its ground effector kicked up clouds of dust partly obscuring the brown and gray camouflaged armored vehicle following behind it. A soldier in helmet and goggles sat in an open turret on the army vehicle, aiming a swivel-mounted suppressor at us.

"Not very welcoming, are they," Jase observed.

"No, but they sure are eager."

Certain our guests knew exactly what we were

carrying, we strapped on our guns, pulled on some cold-weather gear and went down to wait for them to arrive.

* * * *

The black skimmer pulled up in a cloud of dust beside the ship while the armored vehicle stopped under the stern in front of the ramp. The gunner aimed his suppressor into the cargo hold as two muscle modders in cheap suits got out of the limo. They eyeballed Jase and me as we waited at the top of the ramp, then one slapped the limo cab roof twice, indicating it was safe.

A swarthy little man wearing a knee-length, synth-fur hooded jacket climbed out and shivered at the cold. He ambled onto the ramp, shook dust from his shiny black shoes, then took his time lighting a short, fat fumer.

"Which one of you is Kade?" he asked, sucking on his fumer and exhaling orange smoke.

"I am."

"Basu Manjhi," he said, looking me up and down and introducing himself as if his name meant something.

He walked to the top of the ramp and made us wait as he silently counted the hydrazine tanks behind us, being overly obvious about not blocking the gunner's line of sight. It was a hollow threat, as one burst from the suppressor would have detonated the hydrazine, killing us all.

"The transports will be here tomorrow," he said at last. "The tanks will be scanned after delivery. If it's all there, you'll get your money. If not...you'll get something else."

"Those tanks aren't going anywhere until we get paid," I said.

"That's not how things work around here." He glanced over his shoulder at the suppressor, emphasizing the point.

The soft whine of magnetic accelerators powering up sounded from inside the cargo hold then Dietz and Riley stepped out from behind the white gas tanks and aimed their heavy assault rifles at Basu Manjhi. The two muscle junkies at the foot of the ramp tensed and drew their pop guns for show.

Manjhi studied Dietz and Riley, took the fumer from his mouth and slowly blew orange smoke into the cargo hold. "One word from me and those tanks go up in flames, along with you and your ship."

"And your chems," I said, making it obvious I knew he was bluffing.

He gave me a long look and smiled. "That's ballsy, Kade. Stupid, but ballsy." He nodded. "All right, we'll do the scan here."

I nodded to Dietz and Riley, who backed out of sight, then Manjhi motioned to his bodyguards to put away their noisemakers.

"Not everyone on Kota is as understanding as I am," he said. "You should tell your crew not to be so eager to start a fight.

"We're crew," I said, motioning to Jase and myself. "They're mercs, getting off here."

Understanding flashed across his face. "Who've they signed on with?"

"Qintero's Free Company."

"Hmph. Qintero! He's a pig," he said contemptuously.

I'd never heard of Qintero's Free Company, but if they were typical Sep mercs, they'd be a collection of criminals, drunks, and deserters whose courage lasted only until the credits ran out. Their kind wouldn't be missed when the Union Regular Army put them down.

"Our other ship has the rest of it," I added.

"They had nothing."

"They left already?" I was surprised Marie had, for once, done as I asked.

Basu Manjhi shook his head. "They ain't never leaving. "

I stiffened. "What'd you do to them?"

"Me? Nothing." He nodded at the army transport. "My associate thought they'd double-crossed us when he found out all they were carrying was hydrazine." He winced. "He's not a forgiving man."

For a terrible moment, I thought they'd murdered Marie and her crew, but Manjhi's indifference told me they weren't dead. "Where are they?"

"In the camp up north. My associate confiscated their ship to cover his losses."

"He's lost nothing. We've got it all."

I'd scanned the tanks before we left Freehold. Eighteen of them contained pressure vessels full of stims. If Marie had been carrying only hydrazine, Ruslan Glebb had played favorites, protecting her by giving me all the contraband and all the risk. Only it had backfired because she couldn't explain why her tanks had no stims.

"I want to talk to your associate."

"No you don't," Basu Manjhi said meaningfully.

"Where is he?" I demanded icily.

Manjhi hesitated, sensing the change in my demeanor. "At the camp."

"He works at the prison?"

"He runs it. General Trask is in charge of planetary defense. That gives him certain privileges."

"Domar Trask?" I said warily.

"Yeah. He commands the Sixth Brigade up there. You know him?"

"Heard of him." I'd had a run-in with him in Outer Draco, killed one of his favorite lieutenants back when he was a top Sep military commander. He must have fallen out of favor since then to be cooling his heels on a dead-end prison planet like Kota. "He's not the kind of man I'd expect someone in your line of work to partner with."

"Not my choice, but it works. He gets the hydrazine, I get the product. Everybody wins."

"He wants the hydrazine?" I said surprised.

"Don't know why." He sucked thoughtfully on his fat fumer. "Not my business, but he sure uses a lot of it."

I realized Manjhi wasn't Trask's partner, just his errand boy. And if Trask wanted the hydrazine, it wasn't a cover for the stim trade, it was the trade.

"Will he release the other crew once he gets this delivery?"

"The only way out of Kota Prison is feet first," he replied fatalistically.

"When Glebb hears you hijacked the other ship, imprisoned its captain–who happens to be a close personal friend of his–he'll cut off your supply."

He grinned cynically. "Glebb has no friends."

"Why do you think she wasn't carrying your product? Because she's his contact, not me. I'm the one who takes all the risk because I'm expendable, not her."

Basu Manjhi's demeanor wavered. "I don't know why Trask impounded her ship, but she wasn't the first." The diminutive drug lord took a long pull on his pungent fumer, dropped it on the deck and stubbed it out with his shiny shoe. "If I were you, Kade, I'd forget the other crew, take your money and get out of here before Trask takes your ship as well."

To press the point would have drawn suspicion, so I backed off. "All I care about is the money."

"Keep it that way. You'll live longer.

He walked back down the ramp to his skimmer and drove off amid a whirl of dust toward the city while the armored vehicle returned to the barracks near the old warehouses.

"Trask!" Jase said bitterly. "Could this get any worse?"

I didn't tell him Earth Navy was about to make the sky fall in. All I could think about was busting Marie out of Kota Prison, which was good news for Emma Hadley and very bad news for General Domar Trask.

Dietz came up beside us and watched the black skimmer vanish into the distance. "We could have taken them."

"They'd have blasted the hydrazine," I said.

"They'd have never got a shot away."

He was probably right, but that would have drawn Trask's attention, something I couldn't afford to do while Marie was under arrest.

"Why'd you get involved?" I asked. I hadn't told him to cover us.

"Just showing some initiative," Dietz replied, hinting his psionic sense had warned him of trouble. He'd decided to show Basu Manjhi that trying to strong-arm us would cost a lot of lives, including his. It was his way of making sure no one interfered with his mission or mine.

"Captain," Shen's voice sounded from the intercom.

I stepped over to the comm panel. "Yeah?"

"Arleen's awake."

"I'll be right up."

* * * *

Arleen lay on a sensor bed barely long enough for her lithe form. A drip fed fluid into her arm and metabolic sensors attached to her temples and chest sent readings to a bank of screens beside her bed. After weeks of fever with no food and only the drip for sustenance, her normally soft blue complexion was so pale, she looked like a ghost. When I arrived, Izin and Shen were trying to make sense of her life signs.

"Her body chemistry has stabilized, sir," Shen whispered.

"Whatever it was, Captain," Izin said, "it appears to have rewritten her cell structure. Her body mass has increased twenty percent, her bone density has more than doubled and her muscle tissue is thickening at an incredible rate."

Shen nodded to the tubes feeding both her arms. "She's consumed over thirty units of the Uvo plasma I synthesized for her, enough to replace her blood supply five times over. It's all that's keeping her alive."

I approached her bunk, seeing her breathing was shallow, but even. "Arleen?"

"Yes...Captain," she whispered hoarsely, half opening her eyes.

"Is there anything we can get for you?"

"Maltose," she rasped.

I turned to Shen. "Do we have that?" If it was a stim, I'd never heard of.

The combat medic leaned toward Arleen uncertainly. "You want...malt sugar?"

"C twelve...H twenty-two...O eleven," she replied.

"The recycling system can synthesize it," Izin said.

"How do we administer it?" Shen asked.

"Drink," Arleen replied.

"If it was an aqueous solution," Izin said, "her body could convert it directly to energy."

"Get on it," I said.

He hurried off to life support and I turned back to Arleen. Her eyes shifted meaningfully to and from Shen several times, then she fixed her gaze to me and waited.

I turned to Shen. "Could we have a moment in private?"

"Yes, sir," she said and left medbay.

"You have...the crystal?" Arleen whispered weakly.

"It's hidden." If I'd been able to read its contents, I'd have stored its data in my threading where it would have been invisible to all but the most intrusive biomolecular scan, but as that was impossible, I'd had to find a more creative solution.

"If they catch us…they will search the ship."

"I know."

"You can't hide it…not from them."

"I can try." Intruder tech was millions of years ahead of our own, but even they could look in the wrong place.

"Say I have it…It's what the Buratu would have told them."

"They'll torture you."

"I am…almost ready."

"You don't look ready." With her pallid skin and gaunt features, she looked like death.

Izin returned with a container full of golden brown liquid. He placed a tube in her mouth and she took a sip, then without another word, she emptied the entire container. When the tube dropped from her lips, she sighed with relief.

"More," she whispered.

"I'll bring a larger container," Izin said and hurried back to life support.

"Where are we?" Arleen asked.

"Kota."

She closed her eyes, relaxing. "They will come…soon," she whispered and fell fast asleep.

* * * *

"I'm delivering the shunter spares tonight," I said to Jase as he arrived in the galley. He opened a freshly heated ration pack and sat opposite me as I quickly finished my dinner.

"What time are we leaving?"

"I'm going alone. I want to pump our customer for information on Kota Prison. He'll be more inclined to speak if I'm by myself. As soon as I get back, we'll fly up to the prison for a look."

Before he could argue, I threw my empty ration

pack in the recycler and went down to the vehicle bay where I found Dietz looking over the flier. His broken ribs had made an astonishing recovery, showing that his zygote engineered healing rate was far superior to my gene modding.

"What's the range on this thing?" he asked.

"With a full charge and sunny skies, she can stay up for days," I replied, indicating the solar collectors on top of the wings which continually recharged the power cells in-flight.

He nodded appreciatively, running his hand over one of the thrusters. "How long to cover a thousand clicks?"

"A few hours. Longer if you power glide," I said, sensing he was not making idle conversation.

"Qintero's Free Company is south of Kavali, five hundred kilometers east of here. The e-plant is north." He gave me a meaningful look. "Can't go commercial."

"And this occurred to you…when?"

"I logged twenty hours in a simulator before we came aboard."

"Of course you did." He'd known from the beginning he needed my flier. He just hadn't bothered to share that information with me until now. Neither had Lena, making me wonder what else she hadn't told me. "I'll do the flying."

"We go in tonight, the whole team."

"You've still got thirty hours," I said, wondering what the rush was.

"We've got to take the objective before the fleet arrives so the Seps can't destroy it. To do that, we have to be in position before the attack."

"They wouldn't blow up an e-plant so close to their own troops."

"Maybe not, but they could mess it up bad. Put it out of action for years."

"Suppose Talis is late?"

"That's what the N-grenades are for."

"Six against six thousand," I said lightly. "Nothing you can't handle."

Dietz scowled, not appreciating my levity. "You get us up there tonight. We'll hike in before dawn, hunker down during the day, hit it after dark tomorrow night."

"They'll be patrolling the forest."

"They won't see us. Once we're inside, they won't risk using their heavies for fear of hitting the reactor. We won't have that problem. When the fleet makes orbit, we'll light up whoever's left and watch them burn."

It sounded simple enough, but he was assuming Lena's contact on Kota would be able to place target designators on every surface battery in the next twenty-four hours and that the navy could knock them all out from long range. Neither was guaranteed, especially with the minefield and orbital jammers to contend with. If it turned into a slugging match, the fleet could be held at bay for days or even forced to withdraw. That would leave Dietz and his psionic super soldiers trapped with no hope of relief.

"I'm scouting the prison tonight," I said, climbing into the buggy. "We leave after midnight."

"We'll be ready."

"Tell Jase you're working for me now," I said, then drove onto the freight elevator for the ride down to the lower cargo deck.

Dietz had cleared his gear out of the two VRS containers filled with shunter spares before dark and our cargobots had loaded the containers onto a pair of over-worked four-wheeled flatbed transporters I'd hired from a local transshipment company. I slaved their guidance systems to the buggy, switched on the floodlights and led them in convoy onto Khandwa Road for the drive into the city.

Considering the size of the enormous e-plant to the north, the capital was surprisingly dark. There were no streetlights, no luminous signs and the windows were all shuttered against the cold. Kota's two small moons were visible, but they did little more than turn inky blackness into shades of gray.

The dusty city streets had no signs, although the EIS supplied navmap was passably accurate. It led me to a dilapidated, two-story structure with a large vehicle door, no ground-level windows and metal shutters on the second floor. It was all locked up and gave the impression no one was home. Above the vehicle door was an old flaking sign written in large Hindrasi characters with small Unionscript letters below that read:

NAVIN DHAR SYSTEM HAULAGE

I stopped in front of the vehicle door, illuminating it with the buggy's floodlights. The old thermobond coating was bubbled and peeling, revealing patches of solid dark gray metal. It wasn't armor plate but looked tough enough to withstand anything civilian weapons could throw at it.

I kept the motor running as the two robotic flatbeds pulled up behind me waiting for instructions. A short distance away, dark silhouettes of men standing around a wood fire turned toward me, eyeing my convoy and its unknown treasures with interest. Expecting unwelcome company, I honked the horn, shattering the stillness with a piercing claxon that drew no response from the building. Fearing Navin Dhar was off hunting comets at the edge of the Chambal System, I watched three men come toward me from the street gang. Two held heavy metal bars while the third approached my driver's side door.

I quietly unholstered my P-50 and held it in my lap, aimed at the door. My right arm was still weak, but usable, and more than ready to teach local hoodlums not to bring clubs to a gunfight, even if it risked attracting the local authorities.

The leader pulled the buggy's door open and ran his eyes over the interior, assessing its worth. "What you got in the boxes, mister?"

I lifted my P-50 and aimed at the center of his mono-brow. "Headstones. Want one?"

The hoodlum's eyes focused on my gun, momentarily unsettled, then he grinned and glanced meaningfully at a dozen men emerging from the shadows on the other side of the buggy.

"I'll take them all," he said grinning with confidence, triggering muted laughter from his gang.

I silently cursed myself for not bringing a few stun grenades along for the ride, then a burst of heavy weapons' fire flashed above the buggy. All eyes lifted to the top floor of the building where a shuttered window was open and a leather-faced man stood with an antique Vel Penetrator in his hands. The weapon was in mint condition and its owner carried it like he knew how to use it.

"I won't tell you again, Bharat," the man growled. "Stay out of my business." He spat a black liquid onto the ground in front of the buggy, splashing its fat tires.

"Didn't know this goat herder was yours," Bharat sneered, taking his grubby paws off my sparkling clean door and stepping back from the buggy. He held his arms wide, showing more respect for the old Vel than he did for my P-50.

"Everything on my property is mine." He aimed at Bharat's head. "You're on my property."

Bharat broke and ran into the shadows, then in a heartbeat, the street was empty. The man above looked over the two containers behind me, chewing absently.

"Them my spares?"

My DNA sniffer confirmed he was Navin Dhar. He was a contractor, not a professional agent, but he'd been on the EIS payroll a long time and had just saved me from a messy misunderstanding with the local arm twisters, so I gave him the benefit of the doubt.

"Yeah," I said through the buggy's open door.

He touched a control on his belt and the big ground floor doors rumbled apart. While he kept watch, I drove inside, followed by the two flatbed transporters, then the doors rattled shut sealing off his private bunker. In front of the buggy were shelves crammed with black and dusty parts, everything from engine spares to ice harpoons. If I hadn't known better, I'd have thought Navin Dhar was a junk dealer, not a comet hauler.

I climbed out of the buggy as he came down creaking stairs. He walked with a limp, had dark tattoos around his neck and a bulging pot belly that stretched his jacket tight. At the bottom of the stairs, he spat an oily liquid into a spittoon as he chewed something that stained his lips and teeth black. I holstered my P-50, making sure he saw my hands were empty, then he set the Vel down and grabbed a beam light off a filthy benchtop.

"I'm Sirius Kade," I said, offering my hand.

He grunted, ignored my offer of friendship and ambled to the first container. "Code?"

"Double one, double two."

He entered the number, then when the container door opened, he shone his light inside and inspected the contents with an expert eye.

"You got T8 microthrusters in there?"

"Ah?" I summoned the manifest from my bionetic memory and skimmed through the list.

"I told them, I needed two T8s."

I read the manifest aloud. "Universal Dynamics T8 Mark III micro thrusters with workshop spares. Quantity two."

He grunted with satisfaction. "About time. Can't steer class ones with T5s." He spat again into another strategically positioned spittoon and turned toward me.

He coughed up a lung, then asked, "What'd you say your name was?"

"Kade."

"It was stupid coming here at night."

"I'm known for my looks, not my brains."

He sized me up carefully. "They must breed them ugly where you come from."

I nodded. "Even you'd find a warm bed on a cold night."

He nodded thoughtfully. "I like ugly women. Low expectations."

"Then you won't disappoint."

He shook his head sadly. "Always do." He spat an impressive two meters into a metal bucket under the workbench and grinned.

I decided in spite of his disgusting habits, I liked him. "Everything you asked for is there, except the mass converters. Can't get those."

"Would've been surprised if you had."

I stepped past him into the VRS container, squeezed between tightly packed storage units straight out of the factory, and retrieved a metal box hidden at the back. I climbed out and set it down in front of him.

"There's another case of these back there," I said as I opened it, revealing five rows of flat cylinders as wide as my hand, each with a magclamp on one end and a particle beamer inside a domed housing at the other. "Mark seven naval target designator. Effective range, ninety light minutes." I pointed to the domed housing. "It automatically orients itself to the planet's gravitational field and beams straight into space. Undetectable to ground-based sensors."

Navin Dhar picked one up and turned it over curiously. "What about satellites?"

"Only if they cross its beam."

He nodded approvingly. "How long have I got?"

"Twenty four hours."

"Not much time," he said, calculating the effort required.

"Can you do it?"

"I got three brothers, nine cousins, two uncles, and a niece. None of them like Seps. They'll help."

"Can you trust them?" I asked, guessing on Kota, spying for Earth was a family business.

He looked at a colorful painting of a beautiful young woman on the wall. Unlike most everything else in Navin Dhar's bunker, there wasn't a speck of dirt on it.

"She was my wife until a bunch of drunken Sep soldiers killed her while I was away prospecting," he said with hatred in his eyes. "It ain't a question of trust."

Any doubts I had about Navin Dhar's commitment to the mission vanished. We were paying him in spare parts and cold credits, but he'd have done it for free.

"The navy will be in-system tomorrow night. The troops drop the next day," I said, assuming Talis could knock out the surface batteries and get through the minefield.

"There'll be payback. Not just from us."

"Earth Navy won't allow reprisals, so…don't wait too long."

His expression hardened. "They'll disappear fast, die slow, out where no one will hear them scream."

"Your business," I said, then pocketed four target designators.

"What do you want them for?" he asked.

"I have some people to bust out of prison."

He gave me a surprised look. "Why not wait for the navy to take over?"

"Would you?" I asked, well aware Kota Prison was full of political prisoners from Separatist controlled worlds. If they fell into our hands they'd help us retake their home planets, something Domar Trask would never permit.

"Can't say I would," he replied ominously. "You after the scientists? Is that what this is about?"

"What scientists?" I asked surprised.

"They work in the big white building up there, beside the camp. Real secretive. A couple of sun-farmer boys tried sneaking in one time to see what they were up to. Never saw them again."

"You think they're hiding something up there?"

He nodded, walked back to his shelves and rummaged through a bunch of rusty boxes. "Here it is," he muttered to himself, then limped back with a piece of shiny, jet black rock. "If I had to guess, I'd say it's got something to do with this."

He tossed the fist-sized rock to me. It was surprisingly heavy and cold to the touch.

"What is it?"

"We call it black rock."

"Catchy name."

"Geologists call it hydro something..." he said, straining his memory. "Hydro-seques-tium."

I'd never heard of it and my threaded encyclopedia had no record of it. I held it up, watching its polished surface reflect the light. "It's shiny, but...it's not metal...or crystal."

"It's an inert compound. Forms in interstellar space. Don't know how, but it's rare. An asteroid full of the stuff hit Kota three billion years ago. Killed every living thing on the planet."

"Let me guess, it landed a thousand clicks north of here."

He nodded. "The prison's sitting on top of a mountain of it, not that anyone would know. They wiped the old geoscans, even on Earth. I heard a bunch of Sep eggheads talking about it one night in a bar in town, laughing like they'd fooled everyone."

Deleting geoscans from every data center on every human world would require massive reach and lots of credits. It was the kind of thing Chairman Ransford's Consortium could do, if they had a good enough reason.

I stared at the shiny black rock flickering in the light wondering if Lena knew about it, suspecting she did. "Why do the Seps want it?"

He shrugged. "It's worthless."

"Mind if I keep this?"

"Sure, just don't tell them where you got it."

I pocketed the inky black rock from interstellar space and asked, "When will you plant the markers?"

"We'll start tonight." Navin Dhar looked at the painting of the beautiful young woman in the colorful dress hanging on his wall, then spat into a spittoon and wiped his black-stained lips. "We'll get it done," he promised, eager for revenge.

* * * *

I placed Navin Dhar's geo sample on the engineering console in front of Izin. "I want to know what's special about this rock."

Izin turned from his bank of screens and picked it up, feeling its weight. "What is it?"

"Hydro…sequestium," I said carefully.

"There's an analyzer in storage, part of the science equipment we saved during refit."

"I want to know by morning. How's Arleen?"

"Her fever has broken. She's sleeping now."

"Good," I said, then went forward to the vehicle bay.

Dietz and his team had loaded the flier with their gear and were performing final weapon checks. They wore full body armor beneath loose-fitting adaptive camo oversuits that changed color and pattern as they moved. It wasn't the invisibility of a chameleon suit, but in the shadows of an arboreal forest, they'd be almost impossible to see when stationary.

Jase was there too, checking the flier. "Are they coming with us?" he whispered.

"Change of plan and employer," I replied. "They'll be running interference for us tomorrow night."

Jase's eyes widened in surprise. "I thought you were going to try to talk me out of it."

"I was, but circumstances have changed."

He gave me a knowing look. "Marie's up there."

"Not for long," I said and nodded to Dietz.

"Mount up," he ordered, then the troops squeezed aboard with their weapons between their knees while Jase and I took the piloting positions.

"We're over max weight," Jase warned, nodding at the landing gear load indicator.

The gossamer-winged power glider was a science research craft, not an assault transport. It wasn't designed to carry six soldiers with body armor, heavy weapons and packs crammed full of ammo, rations and medical supplies. I glanced at the bulky packs on the cargo tray, wondering what we could throw out.

Dietz shook his head. "We need it all."

Considering the fight he was about to start, I wasn't about to argue.

"We'll do a rolling start and vector off the ground," I said to Jase, who gave me a dubious look.

Once we were outside the ship, I cranked the wings out to full extension, kept our nav lights off so the barracks wouldn't see us and angled the twin tilt thrusters for straight-line speed.

"This is going to be bumpy," I warned and started the flier forward.

She rattled her way across the rough landing ground, then at take-off velocity, I angled the thrusters down and nosed up.

The flier lurched into the air briefly, bounced once, then lifted enough for me to angle the thrusters back to horizontal flight, gaining speed. I gave the barracks a wide berth, crossed Khandwa Road and skimmed sunhouses glowing with crop lights all the way to the forest. After climbing to treetop height, I stayed on manual but gave the autopilot collision avoidance authority.

Off to the west was a laser-like line of light running through the forest. It was the transmission beam from the e-plant, marking the location of the road and making navigation easy. Either side of the light was a vast arboreal darkness, filled with conifers from Earth's Siberian plain.

They'd been selected because the small surface area of their spiny leaves reduced the tree's need for water. The slowly increasing greenhouse gases now prevented the ground in the southern latitudes from freezing, giving the trees a tolerable environment and allowing the formation of a simple ecosystem. Small Siberian animals released into the forest fed on pine seeds dropped by the trees while larger predators hunted the smaller creatures. The forest was on the verge of providing the colony with meat and hides, reducing its reliance on energy dependant sunhouses, although it would be at least a century before terrestrial crops could be grown in the open.

The dark Siberian forest stretched north for more than an hour before we glimpsed a human habitation. It was a square island of light close to the road comprising a cluster of rectangular buildings and several ground vehicles. The flier's nav map indicated it was a biome engineering depot responsible for monitoring the health of the forest, and for cloning and releasing animals into it. Occasionally, we spotted slow-moving lights twinkling through the trees from ground vehicles on the north-south road, but we kept our distance so they wouldn't see us.

Eventually, lights bloomed on the horizon just short of the permafrost zone. One was off to the west where the e-plant dome– bathed in light– rose starkly above the trees. The other was a cleared field containing Kota Prison and beyond it, rows of lights where the Separatist soldiers were camped. They'd constructed some timber buildings from cut trees, although most soldiers were billeted in portable prefabs.

"There are eight surface emplacements around the prison," Dietz said. "Six more guarding the power station."

"How many around Khandwa city?" I asked.

"Only the two covering the spaceport."

"The prison's more important than the capital?" Jase said, puzzled.

Dietz shrugged. "The e-plant's here."

Navin Dhar's shiny black asteroid was also here, buried below the ground, although I made no mention of it. Instead, I folded the wings and put the overburdened flier down hard in a small clearing behind a hill. We climbed out into freezing air, exhaling mist with every breath as our skin prickled from the subarctic cold. Larson scanned the forest with a motion tracker and nodded it was clear, then the troops unloaded the flier while Jase, Dietz and I headed up the hill.

Pine cones and needles crunched beneath our boots in the still night air, then as we reached the hilltop, the prison came into view in the distance. It was a large rectangle, surrounded by inner and outer laser fences. Searchlights crisscrossed each other, sweeping over rows of prisoner huts and roving across the open ground outside the prison all the way to the forest.

Dietz produced a military biscope to survey the area while I focused my monoscope on the camp. It took only moments to discover sensor towers and autoturrets guarded the prison on all sides.

"Sensors are full-spectrum," Dietz noted with a professional eye. "The turrets are pop and shoot. Looks like twenty mil, rapid-fire cannons. Must have sensor guided targeting."

"I don't see any blind spots," I said.

"Nope," he agreed. "They got overlapping fields of fire south, east…all sides. It's a killing zone."

"No sensor bots near the trees."

"Don't need them," Dietz said.

"The fences are excimer lasers," I said, focusing on the thin purple beams projecting between the emitter posts surrounding the camp. They couldn't cut butter, but they'd summon the wrath of the autoturrets if their beams were interrupted.

"Yeah," Dietz agreed. "The fence posts will be sensitized. No way to touch them without triggering an alarm."

My chameleon suit was infra-red shielded to prevent thermal sensors picking it up, so crossing no man's land between the forest and the fences wouldn't be a problem. Getting through the fences would be.

On the east side of the prison was a single level administration block and a vehicle park beside an enormous circular gas tank. A large pipe ran from the tank, above a laser fenced path, to a long white building north of the camp. The white structure stretched almost the full length of the prison and had two levels of windows along its side. To the north were smaller buildings for civilian workers while to the east was a landing ground with five ships parked with their bows to the white building.

"There's the Mendi," I said, realizing I'd missed seeing her on the way in.

She was the largest of the five, bathed in light and surrounded by a flurry of activity as cargobots squeezed huge gray cubes into her open cargo holds. I held my hand out for Dietz's powerful, military-grade optical in an unspoken request. Without a word, he placed it in my hand and I gave Jase my monoscope.

I zoomed in on the *Mendi* for a closer look. The

gray cubes were much larger than standard vacuum-radiation-sealed containers and were constantly monitored by civilians with handheld sensors.

"They look nervous," Jase said.

I'd been distracted by the gray containers, but he was right. The civilians watched their every move, scanned every step and frequently spoke into their communicators.

Two Sep army officers emerged from the white building. One was a heavy-set, square-jawed man I recognized immediately. His companion was taller and female with a horizontal scar across her cheek, close-cropped white hair and a stim enhanced muscular build. The soldiers snapped to attention as they passed, receiving curt salutes in reply.

"There's Trask and Stina Kron," I said.

"He's shorter than I remember," Jase said, "or she's taller."

"What are they loading?" Dietz asked.

"No idea," I said slowly, certain whatever they were, Trask hadn't fallen out of favor with the Sep high command. He'd been given a mission of the highest importance.

Trask and Kron inspected the cubes, looking at the wheel clearance apprehensively. The cargobot suspensions were riding on their axles, indicating the cubes were almost too heavy to carry. The civilians monitoring the loading spoke briefly to Trask, who didn't seem happy, then he and Stina Kron returned to the building.

"I'm going to have a closer look at that e-plant," Dietz said, taking his biscope out of my hands.

"Back soon," I said to Jase and followed Dietz along the hill to a gap in the trees.

The energy plant's brightly lit, off white dome rose into the dark night sky, dwarfing the surrounding forest. I waited while Dietz surveyed the terrain, the Sep army camp, the glowing transmission beams, and the dome.

"It'll have better security than the prison," I said.

He nodded. "I'll nove the perimeter, wipe the defenses and be inside before they know what hit them."

"You could destroy the dome," I said, recalling the power of the N-grenade blast I'd seen on Jel Kara.

"If I drop one eighty meters out, it'll hold."

"You simmed it?"

"Someone did. Inside fifty, the dome cracks. Inside twenty, the core breaches." He gave me a sideways look. "Pray there's no wind."

I hoped whoever was running his numbers knew what they were doing, or two days from now, we'd all be dead. With growing unease, I estimated the distance from the e-plant to the lights of the Sep army base. The closest prefabs were barely five clicks away, although the encampment itself stretched off far to the east.

"Their troops are close," I said. "If they catch you in the open…"

"We'll nove them at the start. Have to split the team, but got no choice."

"Can you take them all out?"

"Not with grenades. Those troops are spread out so they can't be smoked from orbit. Probably sleeping below ground." He studied the army structures, looking for a weakness. "Sure is a lot of them."

"That's no second rate militia garrison," I said, certain that whatever was happening on Kota, it wasn't what either of us had been told. And if Trask was here and still in favor, his Sixth Brigade was a front line assault force, not a bunch of conscripts and farm boys.

Dietz studied the pattern of lights and fires carefully. "Neat rows. Straight lines. Have to be regulars. The mercs must be guarding the cities."

"They'll recover fast," I said, thinking his mission was suicide.

Dietz jaw hardened. "I've got my orders."

I wondered if his blind determination to follow those orders was part of his zygote engineering. Had we sunk so low that human free will meant so little? Or maybe it was just Dietz's way of finding out if he was hard enough to succeed no matter what cards he was dealt.

"How close are you going in tonight?"

"Close enough to see what they got." He looked off to the west. "We'll cross the road before dawn, set up an observation post in the morning and camo down for the day. Hit them late tomorrow night. Have to go in fast, make sure they don't detonate the core."

Crunching footsteps sounded as Jase came up beside us and handed my monoscope back with a worried look. "I've seen casino vaults easier to crack than that place."

"Maybe we don't have to break in," I said thoughtfully.

"You want to knock on the front gate and ask for an invitation?"

"It might be just that easy."

We headed back down the hill to the flier. The troops were waiting with packs on their backs and sensor goggles over their faces. Dietz strapped his bulky pack on, untroubled by the weight in spite of his recent injuries.

"I don't suppose I'll be seeing you again," I said.

"No, but you'll hear us."

We shook hands, then he led his squad into the dark forest.

"Whatever you're paying them," Jase said, "it's not enough."

"I'm not paying them. You are," I said with a grin, then we boarded the flier, climbed on thrusters up through the trees and headed back to Kota Spaceport.

* * * *

We returned to the *Silver Lining* before dawn. There were no lights on at the spaceport or the barracks and no one challenged us as we landed. We stowed the flier without anyone noticing, then I went up to see Izin about Navin Dhar's shiny black rock.

"This substance is a mystery, Captain," Izin said uncertainly as he sifted through screens of data. "It has some strange endothermic qualities that might render it chemically unstable, but without the proper equipment, I cannot say more."

"So it's only *chemically* reactive?" I asked, thinking if Trask was interested in it, there had to be more.

"Dietz's grenades are far more explosive than this inert rock, Captain, if that is what you're asking."

"Thanks. Bag it for me," I said, deciding to put the sample in storage for now and let Lena's boffins figure it out later.

I left Izin and went up to the galley for breakfast. Arleen was there shoveling food into her mouth from five steaming ration packs simultaneously.

"If you keep eating like that, you'll be back in medbay in no time," I said, sitting opposite her with a breakfast pack.

"I'm starving," she mumbled through a mouth full of food. Her voice was deeper than before, although the hoarseness of thirst had gone. The loose-fitting, white medical gown she wore revealed glimpses of sharply defined muscle as if she'd been training with Dietz for weeks, not lying in a coma.

"What happened to you?"

"Biology. It's a survival mechanism. It happens when our lives are in danger."

"Because you expect the Spawn to catch us."

"They will catch us, it's only a matter of time."

I tapped the comm panel beside the table. "Jase, anything on the sensor log?"

There was a brief silence as he checked the night's

readings. "Nothing scanned us from orbit."

I gave Arleen a reassuring look. "Maybe they gave up."

"They never give up." She picked up a half-full container of water and gulped it down, spilling liquid down the sides of her mouth and neck, then handed it to the galleybot for a refill. "The only safe place is in space, inside your superluminal field."

Even if she was right, hiding inside the bubble for months was no way to win a war. "We can't leave. Not yet."

"Izin told me about Marie. You're going to risk everything to free her? She means that much to you?"

"She does."

Arleen leaned forward and whispered, "Then tell her the truth." The galleybot returned with her drink, which she drained by a third before putting it on the table.

"Is that the sublime empath speaking?"

"I'm no longer an empath," she said regretfully, "but I know this: if she finds out you've been lying to her all this time, she'll never forgive you."

Arleen's fixed gaze told me there was no point denying it. "What do you know?"

"You surround yourself with deception, torn between love and duty. That is your inner conflict. Your heart wants one thing, your head another."

There was an uncomfortable silence as I realized how easily this Uvo had seen through me. "What about Marie? What did you sense from her?"

"She loves you, and fears you."

"Fears me?" I said surprised.

"She fears she cannot trust you." Arleen started eating again, this time more slowly. "We both know…she can't."

"There are things I can't tell her."

"One day, Captain Kade, you may have to choose

between your secrets and your heart." She sat back, studying me with her beautiful alien eyes. "Choose wisely, or you will lose her."

Arleen might no longer be an empath, but she was right about Marie, about the tightrope I'd been walking with her for years.

"That's a choice I hope I never have to make," I said and went to get some sleep before the long day ahead.

* * * *

"Are you sure about this?" Jase asked as I attached a flexi-pipe to one of the hydrazine tanks.

"You got a better idea?" I replied, watching the universal connector seal around the tank's outlet valve, then I spoke into my communicator. "OK, Izin, start pumping."

A hiss filled the air as hydrazine was sucked from the tank and fed into the ship's recycling system where it would be broken down into nitrogen and water.

"You know how toxic that stuff is?" he said, trying to talk me out of it. "If it gets on your skin…"

"I'll be wearing a pressure suit and my gear will be sealed in a container."

"Including your gun. If they find you in that tank, you won't be able to get to it."

"They won't find me," I assured him as the pressure indicator hit zero, then I spoke into the communicator again. "It's empty."

Izin pumped nitrogen into the tank to prevent a flash explosion. When the pressure went above ambient, preventing oxygen seeping in, a small scrubberbot opened a maintenance hatch at the bottom of the tank. The stench of ammonia wafted out as the bot climbed inside and sealed the hatch, then it began cleaning hydrazine residue from the tank's interior.

"It's a thousand clicks to the camp."

"It'll give me a chance to get some sleep…and it's the only way in. Just be ready to pick us up when we come out."

"I should go with you."

I shook my head. "I need you to handle the exchange with Basu Manjhi. Don't let him take the tanks until he hands over the delivery bonus. If it's too easy, he'll get suspicious. Just make sure he scans the stim tanks first."

"What if he scans your tank?"

"Then you'll have to shoot him," I said with a grin.

"That's the only part of this plan I like," he said truculently.

* * * *

When the scrubberbot finished cleaning the tank's interior, Izin attached a tiny sensor to its underside which changed color to match the tank's dirty white paint job.

"They'll never see it," I said with approval.

"I can see it," Izin declared.

"Yeah, but they don't have your bug eyes," Jase said.

"I do not have bug eyes!" Izin snapped indignantly.

Jase and I exchanged amused looks, then we pushed a metal container holding my gear into the tank. I sealed my pressure suit, which Jase and Izin double checked, then climbed into the nitrogen-filled tank. My p-suit had consumables for thirty hours, long enough for the trip to the prison, and the optical sensor gave me a visual feed from outside the tank.

"Reception is good," I reported, settling down to watch our cargobots move the hydrazine tanks out of the hold. My tank was last, placed at the end of the line formed alongside the ship.

"Heads up, Skipper," Jase's voice sounded in my

helmet a short time later. "They're coming."

I turned the optical beneath my tank toward the black skimmer. It led a convoy of two light armored vehicles followed by twenty-two flatbed transporters. When it reached the ship, Basu Manjhi climbed out, escorted by his two overdressed knuckle draggers. He eyeballed the tanks, quickly counting them as he approached the ship. Jase waited at the top of the ramp while Izin watched from the bridge in case the ship's k-cannons were required to bring negotiations to a sudden and bloody conclusion.

"Where's Kade?" Manjhi asked from the bottom of the ramp.

"On the bridge."

"Doesn't he want to get paid?"

Jase held up my vault key. "Sure he does. He's just cautious." Jase glanced meaningfully up at the k-cannon mounted high on the hull.

Manjhi followed his gaze, saw it was aimed at the hydrazine tanks and instantly understood we'd put the tanks out where we could destroy them without damaging the ship.

He nodded appreciatively. "I see why Glebb hired you."

"We won't be ending up like the other crew," Jase assured him.

"I assume you won't incinerate us all if my men scan the tanks?"

"Scan away."

Manjhi motioned to his two bodyguards who produced hand scanners and went to the middle of the line. They headed off in opposite directions, recording the stims in each tank as they worked their way out from the center. The guard approaching my end of the line was faster than his companion. He finished the tank immediately ahead of mine and started toward me.

Jase had his arms crossed with one shoulder against

the hatch frame and his eyes riveted to the guard approaching my tank. He tensed, ready to start shooting, but the other bodyguard called from the front of the line.

"It's all here, Mr. Manjhi."

"Satisfied?" Jase asked.

"Perfectly," he replied, summoning his men with a wave of the hand.

Jase ambled down the ramp to the diminutive drug lord and proffered my vault key. "We'll take payment for both cargoes."

"Both?" Manjhi said surprised.

"We'll hold the credits for the other crew, in case they get released."

"You know that won't happen."

Jase smiled happily. "More for us."

Manjhi shrugged indifferently, produced a pocket terminal and made the payment. Jase nodded with satisfaction and pocketed the vault key.

"We've got it, Skipper," he said into his communicator, backing up the ramp, never taking his eyes off the stim dealer. "Don't blow yourself up on the way out."

Manjhi scowled and nodded to the lead armored vehicle. The soldier in the suppressor turret touched a control, then twenty-two robotic arms lifted the hydrazine tanks off the ground together. My tank swayed through the air, almost knocking me off my feet, then it landed with a shudder and a series of clicks sounded as the flatbed's magclamps engaged.

"All locked, sir," the soldier reported.

Basu Manjhi and his bodyguards climbed into their black skimmer and drove off across the dusty landing ground followed by the first armored vehicle. The twenty-two flatbeds fell in behind them, then the second armored vehicle brought up the rear, immediately behind me. The driver and his gunner were clearly visible on my head-up display, although the sensor was too small and well hidden to catch their eyes.

Even over rough ground, the ride was smooth, showing the transporters were designed to cushion their explosive cargo. We followed the road toward Khandwa, then just as the city came into sight, the convoy turned onto the graded road heading north. Running alongside the road through ten-meter high relay towers was the blindingly bright transmission beam from the e-plant, feeding power to Kota's equatorial cities.

Knowing it would be hours before we reached Kota Prison, I lay on the tank floor and tried to get some sleep, preparing myself for the long night to come.

* * * *

The convoy stopped for lunch at the biome engineering camp we'd flown over the night before. Basu Manjhi, his bodyguards and the soldiers, all climbed stiffly out of their vehicles and went into a dusty white prefab with dirty windows, bench seats and clean metal tables. They collected precooked food from a counter and sat down to eat, watched suspiciously by a handful of forestry workers on shift change.

The camp was almost halfway between Khandwa City and Kota Prison and judging by the familiarity Manjhi and his men showed, it was a place they'd visited many times before. They neglected to post guards near the vehicles, confident the remote location was safe, although several soldiers sat where they could keep watch through the windows. While Manjhi's men ate hearty meals, I sucked protein-rich fluid from a straw inside my p-suit, washed down with stale water from the suit's recycling system.

Sometime later, two heavy forestry trucks drove into camp from a dirt track on the east side. Four men in hard hats, dirty coats and heavy boots climbed out. Three headed to the canteen while the fourth tinkered with one of the trucks for a while before looking over the rear armored vehicle. He showed particular interest in its top-mounted suppressor turret, then started toward the canteen, giving my gas tank a cursory look. Suddenly, he stopped, his mechanic's eye caught by something out of place at the bottom of the tank. He stared straight at me and I knew, he'd spotted Izin's sensor. His confused expression said he didn't know what it was, then he stepped up to the tank and leaned in for a closer look.

"Get away from there!" a soldier barked from the cafeteria entrance.

The mechanic straightened in surprise and turned toward the canteen as the men inside filed out.

"I was just–"

"I won't tell you again!" the soldier yelled, drawing his sidearm.

The mechanic raised his hands. "All right, all right..." he said, all thought of the sensor gone. Mumbling irritably under his breath, he gave the soldiers a wide berth and joined his companions inside.

The soldiers boarded their vehicles, then Basu Manjhi's black skimmer led the convoy back onto the road for the second leg of the journey to Kota Prison. Before the camp had passed out of sight, a HUD indicator inside my helmet began blinking a warning that toxic particulates were interacting with my p-suit's pressure seals. Trace elements of hydrazine had escaped the scrubberbot's best efforts and were now eating their way into my p-suit.

Fearing lying on the tank floor would only make it worse, I sat uncomfortably on my gear container and watched the endless Siberian forest slide by. All through the afternoon, the seal warning flashed, slowly changing from white to yellow to orange.

By nightfall, I could smell a faint whiff of ammonia and still the tiny sensor beneath the tank showed only empty road ahead, flanked by the darkening boreal forest and the brilliant light of the transmission beam.

* * * *

My p-suit's seal indicator was flashing red by the time a tiny glow appeared on the horizon, blooming into an island of light rising beyond the dark trees ahead. Soon, the forest on one side of the road gave way to a broad clearing with a cluster of buildings at its center. Kota Prison was ringed by two, glowing purple laser fences and swept by search beams that ranged from the prisoner huts, across no man's land to the forest's edge. Beyond the prison was the long white building, a landing ground, and smaller accommodation blocks that looked more like a campus than a concentration camp.

When the convoy reached the prison, it turned onto a dirt road and stopped in front of high metal gates. Floodlights illuminated the vehicles and twin autoturrets targeted the skimmer as Basu Manjhi got out and spoke to a comm panel beside the gates. After a brief discussion, he returned to the limo and the outer gate rumbled open, letting the skimmer and the first armored vehicle through. It closed behind them, then the inner gate opened and they drove into the compound and waited for the rest of the convoy to cycle through, two at a time.

Once inside, the convoy followed a road along the inner fence past wooden prisoner huts, each with a single door at one end and small windows set high along the walls. Curious faces peered from several windows as the convoy passed while a solitary guard checked hut doors and windows, ensuring no prisoners were out after curfew. Two more guards in heavy coats walked the inner perimeter fence with weapons slung from their shoulders and hands in pockets against the cold.

We drove around behind a single-story camp

headquarters to an unlit parking area flanked by the giant storage tank. The white building beyond the storage tank was clean and well lit and its opaque windows glowed with light. The pristine structure stretched on past the prison to a landing ground surrounded by towers equipped with sensor domes, autocannons and search beams. With Trask's Sixth Brigade to the north and a ring of surface batteries in the surrounding forest, the white building and its private spaceport was easily the most heavily defended place on the entire planet.

"What's going on Lena?" I said suspiciously, convinced this was Operation Windfall's true objective, not the rundown warehouses at Kota Spaceport.

The flatbed transports parked side by side against the inner perimeter fence as two Sep army officers came across from the white building to speak briefly with Basu Manjhi. I feared they were going to begin siphoning the hydrazine now, but the officers headed back to the white building and the stim dealer returned to his limo. The skimmer and its armored escort drove off in a cloud of dust, back to the main gate and along the road north to the army base.

Spurred on by the blinking indicator in my HUD, I rotated the tank sensor to confirm there were no guards close by, then opened the maintenance hatch and lowered my gear container onto the flatbed. The HUD indicator turned critical as a p-suit seal ruptured and the stink of ammonia assaulted my nostrils. Desperately, I dropped onto the flatbed, dragged the container to the ground and crawled under the transport.

My eyes were watering from the ammonic stench as I opened the gear container and quickly peeled off my contaminated p-suit. Carefully avoiding its outer surface, I crawled away–gasping for fresh air–and checked my hands for signs of neurotoxic poisoning. When I saw they were clean, I breathed a sigh of relief, then the crunch of heavy boots on dirt sounded nearby.

I ducked behind a large wheel as a beam light played over the flatbed and the crunching footsteps ambled toward me. Light caught my p-suit's gloves and there was a grunt of surprise, then a guard knelt down to peer under the transport. He focused his beam on my discarded p-suit and crawled under the transport for a closer look. Suddenly, he sensed my presence and turned toward me, shining the light in my face.

I launched myself at him, pinning him to the ground. He tried to throw me off, but I hung on, punching him in the side, then his body shuddered unexpectedly. I saw his face was pressed against my contaminated p-suit and threw my weight forward, driving his head down hard against it. He spasmed from toxic shock, frantically trying to break free, choking and frothing at the mouth, unable to call out. Slowly, the fight went out of him and his body went limp.

When he didn't move again, I rolled off him. His face was covered in a flaming red rash, one eye was leaking blood and he was no longer breathing. I stared at him in horror, knowing if I hadn't gotten out of the tank in time, that would have been me.

Regaining my senses, I switched off the guard's beam light and hid his body behind one of the transport's big wheels, then watched the camp for any sign I'd been spotted. When no-one appeared, I retrieved my equipment and the chameleon suit from the gear container, being careful not to touch its contaminated exterior.

The heavy chameleon suit had circular oculars for my eyes and was coated in millions of microscopic, receptor-emitter nodules that captured incoming light on one side and retransmitted it on the other. It was a technology suited to the night when there was less light and the chance of nodule reflections was greatly reduced, although the illusion of invisibility quickly broke down with movement.

I pocketed my equipment, pulled on the suit and scrambled out from under the flatbed. When the suit powered up, I vanished into the darkness and went to the middle of the convoy where I placed a target designator beneath a hydrazine tank. Satisfied the local stim lord would soon be out of business, I crept back along the line of transporters toward the camp headquarters.

It was locked up for the night, although the exterior was well lit and watched by a pair of three hundred and sixty-degree opticals at opposite corners of the building. Crouching in the darkness between the flatbed transports, I pulled the chameleon suit's faceplate open and drew my P-50, setting the magnetic accelerator to subsonic so the projectile wouldn't emit a sonic boom. With the gun rigged for minimum noise, I put a heavy eight-millimeter slug into the slender housing above the optical. There was a bang as it hit, then I pocketed my gun and resealed the faceplate as a guard ran toward the building. He aimed his beam light at the optical, but couldn't see the entry hole in the housing, then spoke into his communicator.

"It must have shorted out," he said in Hindrasi and walked off toward the prisoner huts.

When he was out of sight, I headed for the HQ building, moving slowly to preserve my invisibility in the bright light. The front door was secured by a low-grade civilian combination lock which my EIS decryptor unpicked in a heartbeat. The door slid open and I stepped into a dark reception area with a wooden table equipped with a simple comm set and a floor plan on the wall behind it. My bionetics translated the floor plan's Hindrasi text at a glance, then I hurried down an unlit corridor to Perimeter Control.

I slipped on my knuckle stunner, keeping my hand inside the suit access slit, and stepped inside. A soldier sat lounging back in a chair with his feet on a central console reading a data pane, paying no attention to the four wall screens cycling with images of the camp. When he heard the door open, he looked up, staring at me in the darkness.

"Hello?" he called as I crept away from the proximity sensor.

When the door slid shut, he shrugged uncertainly and returned his attention to the naked women pictured on his reader. I let him relax, stepped up behind him and pushed my knuckle stunner into the back of his neck. He tensed and was out like a light as his spinal cord took the full jolt, then I lowered him to the floor and studied the console.

The camp's security system impressively integrated laser fences, sensor towers, search beams, and autoturrets, no doubt putting to good use what Domar Trask had learned in Babakin Crater supermax on Mars before his escape. The whole system was locked for the night and required the Camp Commandant's DNA scan and a physical key to disarm, putting it beyond the reach of my EIS decryptor.

With no way to access the system, I hid an orbital targeter under the console and hurried down the corridor to Prisoner Records. It was a small room with a high-density data core, several holopanes, and an operator console. My EIS decryptor cracked the system's simple fractal lock in moments, then I retrieved hut numbers for Marie, her crew and the Hadleys.

I was about to leave when a thought struck me. I ran a search for 'hydrosequestium', but rather than find information regarding the strange black rock, a near-empty prisoner file appeared. To my surprise, it was for Dr. Margaux Baston, the woman Lena had sent me to kill. She'd become a prisoner five weeks ago, although there was no indication what crime she'd committed, only a terse statement:

Transferred from HS Lab by order of General Trask.

I guessed her doctorate wasn't in medicine and her crime was falling out with Trask. I memorized her hut number and hurried back to reception. As I arrived, the front door slid open and a beam of light shone in through the darkness. It caught my shoulder, which reflected a nodule flash back at the doorway, then I darted sideways into the shadows. I cursed myself for not locking the front door, guessing its proximity sensor had opened when the man outside had passed in front of it.

"Who's there?" a man called in Hindrasi, peering into the darkness. He wore coveralls and carried a toolbox, and panned his light over where he'd seen the flash. If he'd known anything of chameleon suits, he'd have sounded the alarm, but instead, he stepped inside. "Raunak, is that you?"

He walked past me–close enough to touch–then I crept behind him and slipped outside. I moved out of the light and waited for the technician to emerge. When he did, he tried lowering the optical I'd blasted, but it was jammed at roof height. He gave it a frustrated look and strode off toward the main gate and I headed toward the prisoner huts.

The dark silhouette of a guard appeared, strolling between the buildings, but he didn't look my way. When he passed out of sight, I followed the hut numbers to Marie's barracks. It had a simple timer lock on a door that I could have easily kicked in, but I wasn't there to break her out, not yet.

I crept around to the side, opened my faceplate and pulled myself up to the window using the metal bars for support. I rapped lightly on the pane, triggering a burst of startled female whispers, then a plump face appeared in the window. Her eyes widened in surprise when she saw my disembodied face peering in at her through the bars.

"Open the window," I mouthed silently.

She slid the small pane sideways and whispered,

"Who are you?"

"I want to talk to Marie Dulon."

She called softly over her shoulder. "Marie. There's a man outside. He wants to talk to you."

She climbed down, then Marie's face appeared.

"Sirius?" she whispered alarmed. "What are you doing here?"

"I came to turn your bed down and put a chocolate on your pillow," I said lightly.

"Are you crazy?" She looked fearfully past me for guards. "They have eyes everywhere."

"That's why I dressed for the occasion," I said, looking down at my invisible body.

"They might not be able to see you in that thing, but if we set one foot outside those fences, we're dead."

"Leave that to me. You know where the others are?"

"Yes, their huts are close. The Hadleys too."

"Good. We have a few hours yet. Just be ready."

"For what?"

"You'll know when it starts. By the way, do you know Margaux Baston in hut thirty-eight?"

"I've met her, but she's not here anymore." Marie nodded at the white building. "They took her back over there this morning."

"What are they doing over there?"

"She wouldn't say, only that she refused to work for them. That's why they put her in here with us."

"Why'd they take her back?"

"I don't know.

A young woman's face appeared beside Marie's. "I'm a cleaner on the work detail," she whispered. "There's an underground mine over there and a lot of machines making something. Whatever it is, there's a problem only Margaux can fix."

The young woman stepped down, then Marie said, "Sirius, they made me fly the Mendi up here and familiarize a pilot with her controls. Not a very good pilot."

The *Mendiant* still hadn't launched, although her cargo doors were now sealed. Once the fleet arrived, Trask would order his ships to launch, to avoid them being destroyed on the ground. That didn't give me long.

"If I'm not back in time, get out of here," I said. "Go south. Jase and Izin are down there with the Lining. They'll find you."

"Where are you going?"

"To get the Mendi back." I feigned exasperation. "I can't afford to buy you *another* ship."

"Sirius, we don't need two ships," she said, implying for the first time that we could fly together.

"I'll remember you said that." I kissed her through the bars and dropped to the ground. "Don't wait for me."

"Be careful," she whispered anxiously.

"What can happen? I'm invisible," I said with a grin and resealed the chameleon suit.

Leaving her bewildered face peering after me through the window, I headed back between the prisoner huts to the gas storage tank. Just beyond the tank was a gate in the laser fence and a path from the prison to the white building covered by an autoturret outside the fence. Its cannon was angled down, ensuring it couldn't accidentally hit the overhead gas pipe running from the storage tank to the white building. Perched atop the pipe, inside the autoturret's blind spot, was a narrow walkway enclosed by a cage reached by narrow ladders at each end.

It was a difficult climb in a heavy chameleon suit, but the ladder allowed me to place a targeter above the walkway where it couldn't be seen from the ground. My EIS decryptor then made short work of the walkway's security lock and I climbed inside, locking the gate behind me.

Partly hidden by the cage, I followed the walkway

over the laser fence, then just as I neared the autoturret, a roar of engines sounded from the landing ground. Brilliant yellow-orange light lit up the camp as an old Procyon IV freighter, half the size of the *Mendi*, climbed on sputtering thrusters into the night sky. She was barely spaceworthy but somehow managed to clear the trees, drawing the attention of every guard in camp.

I crouched down, fearing the harsh light would overload my chameleon suit, then the ship's main engines lit up, turning the old grain hauler into the brightest star in the night sky. For a moment, my invisibility wavered, but all eyes were on the ship as she boosted for space, not my ghostly silhouette on the walkway.

When the glare of the ship's engines faded, I continued across to another gate. It was unlocked, so I stepped through and climbed the ladder to the roof. There were no guards up there, only an elevator, a communications array in the center of the roof and a tower at the western end of the building receiving the transmission beam from the e-plant.

The communications array was powerful enough to handle spaceport traffic, except it was directional and aimed at the orbital relay station. I hid my last targeter on it, hoping a direct hit would cut the ground commander's ability to redeploy his seeker mines, giving Talis a chance to clear a path through the minefield.

Confident the building would soon be rubble, I went to the roof's landing ground side for a closer look at Trask's flotilla of confiscated ships. They were all parked in bays alongside the building, far enough from the launch apron to escape engine backwash and close enough to get out fast if they needed to boost in a hurry. The *Mendi* was there, all sealed up and ready to launch, while the other three ships still had their hull doors open and their cargo holds empty.

The ships were guarded by a handful of Sep soldiers

whose eyes were on the forest, fearing saboteurs and spies more than infiltrators. Between the ships and the building was a row of large gray cubes sitting on cargobots straining under the weight. Wondering what the cubes were, I went back to the elevator and took it down to ground level.

It opened into a darkened cargo dock. Four load masters in overalls sat around a small table near the back wall gambling for drink money, paying no attention to the elevator. I ignored them and slipped past a tow vehicle to where I could study the ships from the shadows. With the exception of the *Mendi*, they were all in a parlous state. One was an old Indian Republic troop transport with a flaking thermal coat and a heat-stressed hull. The other two were elderly freighters, one with fractured main engine mounts, the other with thrusters so corroded they risked exploding every time they fired. The only signs of recent maintenance were new bubble emitters added to the hulls without any attempt to match paintwork. They were clearly intended for long voyages where spare parts and friendly ports were in short supply.

No wonder Trask had grabbed the *Mendi*. She was fitted with Earth Navy's best and had the legs for a long haul. Compared to her companions, she must have seemed like a gift from heaven. She was big enough to take twelve of the gray cubes and from the way her landing struts were sagging, I guessed they'd given her a full load. She had to be over her maximum launch mass, although her navy certified engines would get her into space.

The same could not be said of her sisters.

"Where are you ladies going?" I wondered softly to myself.

After ensuring none of the soldiers were looking my way, I crept out to the row of gray cubes. They were encased in a hard, synthetic material, possibly an insulator polymerized from Trask's hydrazine. There were no access panels, no way to unload the contents, so they weren't transport containers. At one corner was a short-range comm link and timer assembly. The guards couldn't see me behind the cube, so I placed my EIS decryptor against the panel, but to my surprise, it fell into an infinite loop. That made the cubes worth destroying, but I was all out of target designators.

Voices sounded from the loading dock, so I quickly pocketed the decryptor and slipped into the narrow space between two cubes. Footsteps approached, then General Trask and three civilians appeared, escorted by two soldiers. Two of the civilians were men. One was swarthy with dark rings under his eyes and gray flecked hair. The other was short and stocky while the female was a middle-aged woman my DNA sniffer identified as Margaux Baston.

"Check the readings again," she snapped.

The two men glanced at Trask, who nodded, then they grudgingly moved alongside the cubes downloading data. They transmitted the information to her data pane, which she scrolled through with growing annoyance, frowning and shaking her head.

"Well?" the general demanded.

"They're all decaying," she replied with an accent similar to Marie's. "I warned you. HS90 is inherently unstable."

"It could be a flaw in the enrichment process," the swarthy scientist suggested.

"Or some weird quantum effect," the other added.

"Or maybe the cryo unit's too cold? Or not cold enough. Or maybe it just doesn't work!" she snapped, berating them both.

"The cryo settings are correct," the swarthy scientist insisted. "They're all steady at minus two hundred, exactly what the–" He caught himself, glanced warily at the nearby guards and added more carefully, "–what they told us it should be."

"It's not the purity," Shorty said wearily. "We tested every batch, thoroughly."

"Then you tested it wrong," Dr. Baston declared.

"It's our instruments," he added. "They just aren't sophisticated enough for this kind of work."

"They told us they were," Trask said.

"It's a miracle we got to ninety-nine percent," Shorty said, "even with their help. The enrichment process requires picofarad scale control. That's orders of magnitude beyond anything we've ever attempted."

The general scowled. "It's their technology. It works."

"It's their physics and blueprints," Dr. Baston said, "but our equipment. We should reprocess the material and conduct a proper test."

"That'll take weeks," Trask growled. "And the first ship is already on the way."

"You shouldn't have launched until we were ready," Baston snapped.

"I had no choice. It's the slowest ship in the fleet."

"Its HS90 will have decayed before it reaches its target," Baston declared.

"She's lying, General," Swarthy said. "I've gone over her calculations. The devices will work even at this decay rate, if we launch now."

"You don't know what you're talking about!" she said contemptuously.

"She's trying to delay us, General, to give the HS90 time to decay."

Trask turned to Dr. Baston. "You've got one hour to prove they won't work. If you can't convince Nasim, we launch with or without your agreement." He glanced at the two soldiers escorting her. "Don't let her out of your sight," he ordered and went back into the building.

"I'll go over the enrichment logs again, in case we missed something," Shorty said and followed after

Trask.

"Shall we?" Dr. Nasim asked coldly, motioning for her to lead the way.

Dr. Baston glared at Nasim. "You're a fool," she said and strode off through the loading dock so fast, he and the two guards had to rush to keep up.

I gave them a short head start, then hurried to stay close enough to pass through security doors before they closed, breaking invisibility several times. They led me through a factory full of robotic fabricators that would have been at home in Earth's most advanced precision engineering works, then we passed through a door into a long corridor. One side was all window, overlooking a deep vertical shaft with a cylindrical ore conveyor at its center. The conveyor was supported by metal gantries anchored to the excavation wall that wound all the way down to a tiny pool of light deep below ground level. Opposite the window was a wall of screens showing subterranean views of mining engineers supervising robotic diggers eating away at the remains of a dirty black asteroid.

I had to run to reach the door at the end of the corridor before it closed, becoming momentarily visible, then I stepped into a large meeting area surrounded by office doors marked with glowing nameplates. Dr. Baston was already on the far side, standing by a door with her name on it.

She turned to the soldiers. "You don't have to follow me inside."

"General's orders," the corporal replied implacably.

She scowled, tapped the DNA scanner and led them into her office. I darted across to the door, just managing to stop it closing with an invisible boot, and slipped inside.

The office was dark, lit only by large data panes glowing on her desk and a spherical cloud of light floating in the center of the room. It was a mathematician's interface used to interact with simulation processors, the kind reserved for Earth's leading theoretical research centers. Somehow, the Consortium had procured one for its resident genius on Kota.

Dr. Baston placed her hands in the light cloud. A mass of mathematical symbols appeared which she used to build equations with the speed and grace of a ballerina, while Dr. Nasim furrowed his brow, unable to keep up.

The two soldiers stood idly by as I slipped behind them and drew my gun. One soldier glimpsed my P-50 appear out of thin air and scrambled to get his rifle up, but I fired four shots in quick succession, dropping both soldiers before either could shoot. Dr. Nasim turned as the two guards went down, saw my disembodied P-50 and grabbed for the second soldier's weapon.

"Don't do it!" I yelled, but he scooped the assault rifle off the floor, forcing me to put one into his head, sending him slumping over the second soldier's body.

Dr. Baston withdrew her hands from the luminous interface, glanced at the three corpses on the floor in surprise, sighed wearily and faced my gun without fear.

"I knew they couldn't keep this place a secret," she said calmly. She straightened her shoulders, expecting me to end her life. It was what Lena had sent me to do. "I'm ready."

Certain Dr. Baston was no willing enemy, I switched the chameleon suit off and opened the faceplate. "You could defect."

"You'd let me live, knowing what I know?"

"I know they're forcing you to work for them. You could join us."

"And do what?" she sneered, shaking her head. "If you want what I know, you're no better than them."

"What's in the gray containers?"

She looked surprised. "You don't know?"

"I'm guessing it's got something to do with an asteroid that hit this planet three billion years ago."

She nodded thoughtfully. "They're HS90 hydrospheric annihilation devices."

"For the dummies," I said, indicating I had no idea what she was talking about.

"Have you ever heard of hydrosequestium?"

"It's a shiny black rock, kind of heavy."

"When heated to very high temperatures, it has one extraordinary property, an insatiable appetite for hydrogen. Do you know what happens when hydrogen atoms are extracted from an Earth-like atmosphere?"

"No water?" I guessed.

"No planetary hydrosphere."

"Wait. Those things are planet killers?"

"The planet remains, but the hydrogen atoms within the atmosphere are extracted and trapped–sequestered–in rock."

"That's why Kota's so dry? It was the asteroid."

She nodded. "It separated the planet's hydrogen from its oxygen, destroying its water. That's why there are no oceans, no rivers, no snow at the poles."

"We're made of water."

"Human beings are approximately ten percent hydrogen. For us, for all carbon-based life, water is the most precious substance in the universe." She glanced at the two dead soldiers at her feet. "The military call them dry bombs, not technically correct, but…"

"Close enough."

"We enriched the natural element, created an isotope called HS90. When it's heated to a plasma, HS90's affinity for hydrogen is amplified millions of times over."

Izin had said the black rock had a strange exothermic property. He was right, even if he couldn't identify what it was.

"So HS90 turns planets into deserts?" I said.

"Into frozen, sterile wastelands. Water vapor is Earth's most abundant greenhouse gas. Without it, the planet would freeze. All our planets would. They'd be uninhabitable." She sighed sadly. "This was once a fertile world. The fossil record confirms it. When I first came here, I dreamed of freeing the hydrogen sequestered by the asteroid, of watering this entire planet, creating a new Earth."

"But Trask came and forced you to build his dry bombs instead."

"I didn't know what they were at the time. When I realized what he was planning, it was too late." She shook her head. "Twenty years…and this is my achievement, destroyer of worlds."

"Do they work?"

"Yes. They use novarium to start an accelerated quantum overflow that heats the HS90 core. Eventually it becomes too hot for the container's magnetic confinement field and the plasma is released."

Novarium was in every e-plant, in every starship, and on every colony world. All they had to do was shave a cold core and they could power as many dry bombs as they could produce.

"Is there no defense?"

"From a cloud so hot it vaporizes everything it touches?" She shook her head. "All they have to do is accelerate a ship toward a planet and detonate the bomb. Once the ship is destroyed, the plasma cloud drifts into the planet's atmosphere, reacts with its hydrogen and creates a global firestorm."

"How could you not know, if you designed the bomb?"

"Trask had the bomb design when he got here. I didn't see it until much later. My expertise is in the material itself. I oversaw the enrichment process."

"If you didn't design the bomb, who did?"

She gave me a sour look. "The Matarons. It was

part of a deal made with a race I'd never heard of before. Insectoids. Not from Orion."

"The Xil?"

"Yes, that's them. The Consortium agreed to help the Xil disgrace the Tau Cetins in the eyes of the Galactic Forum if they helped the Separatists defeat Earth. The Matarons were in on it. They were all working for the Spawn, all wanted the Tau Cetins out of the way. The dry bomb was the Consortium's payment. It was years in the planning. They built this facility, digging in secret and funding my research without ever telling me what was really happening."

"What are the target-worlds?"

"Only Trask knows."

"Is Earth a target?"

"I don't know, but they have a ship big enough to attack Earth."

"The Mendi!" It would take her almost a year to get there, but once she was in space, there would be no stopping her.

For the first time since leaving Hades City, I understood the mission, knew why Lena and Earth Navy were throwing everything they had at Kota and why Earth Council had lifted its ban on orbital bombardments. Operation Windfall wasn't about looting enemy supply bases, it was a strike against a snakehead super weapon that Separatist fanatics were about to unleash on loyalist worlds throughout the Core Systems. If successful, mankind's richest and most populous worlds would be turned into lifeless, frozen wastelands.

"Where's Trask now?"

"In his office, at the other end of the building. This level."

"Are there other facilities like this one?"

"No. Kota is the only source of hydrosequestium in all of Mapped Space."

"What about the Mataron tech?"

"It's all here."

"Show me."

"It would be meaningless to you."

"Show me anyway."

She went to her desk and touched the data pane which filled with equations and technical drawings. "That's all of it."

I put my hand on the glowing pane and issued a command: *Initiate bionetic interface and data download.*

Bionetic filaments in my hand linked with the screen and began pulling data from the lab's information core. The screen started scrolling rapidly through pages of mathematics and hundreds of schematics, far faster than any human could have read it.

"What are you doing?" Dr. Baston demanded, stepping toward me with rising anger. "Stop that! At once!"

I pointed my P-50 at her, keeping my attention on the screen. Her face flushed with anger as she realized I was recording everything.

"Are there copies?"

"No, it's all siloed here," she said sullenly. "I thought you came here to stop us, not steal it for yourself."

Keeping my hand on the data pane, I issued another command: *Load Pestilence Four, clean and burn.*

The data pane went blank as a highly compressed AI from my bionetic memory loaded into the lab's system, then a message appeared on the screen requesting level nine clearance.

"Have you got that?" I asked, breaking contact with the screen and stepping back from the desk. Dr. Baston didn't answer, ready to die rather than help me. "Yes, I took a copy, to study it, to find a way to stop it." I lowered my gun. "If you want to make sure this weapon is never used, enter your code."

She hesitated, deciding if she could trust me, then

thrust one hand into the light cloud and moved her fingers, quickly selecting a series of fractal patterns. When she finished, the data pane unlocked and went blank.

"You need to get out of here, now," I said.

"Are we going to be attacked?"

I nodded. "Tonight. Get as far away as you can. Keep your head down and in a couple of days surrender yourself. Ask for Lena Voss. She'll look after you."

"Hmm...I'm sure she will," Dr. Baston said dubiously. "Before you came, only two people understood this technology. One of them is dead." She glanced meaningfully at Dr. Nasim's body. "And he relied on me most of the time. Now I'm the only one left."

"Help us find a way to stop it."

"You can't. That's why there'll always be people like Trask forcing scientists like me to build these weapons."

I wanted to tell her we were the good guys, that we'd never allow these weapons to be built again, but I had a terrible feeling she was right. Lena was mega-psi. If she wanted to, she could take control of Dr. Baston's mind and force her to build planet killers for Earth.

If she wanted to.

Dr. Baston read my face. "You know I'm right." She sighed as if a great weight lifted from her shoulders. "I have some calculations I'd like to finish. It'll take a few hours. Will that be long enough?"

"Yeah, it will."

Dr. Baston looked relieved at the prospect of death. "I'll be getting back to work now. You can show yourself out."

She turned her back to me and slid her hands into the cloud of light that was her sanctuary. Her fingers flowed through equations, moving and arranging them as if she was composing a symphony that only she could hear.

I raised my gun, aimed at the back of her head, knowing I should make sure she never helped the Seps again, then thought of the target designator on the comms tower above. It was close enough that when the strike came, she wouldn't feel a thing.

The distant rumble of an explosion reverberated through the building from the north. It wasn't the rolling thunder of an orbital blast, but the sharp, hypersonic roar of an N-grenade detonating over the brigade camp. A moment later, another more distant blast sounded, this time from the west as Dietz leveled the e-plant's perimeter defenses.

Trask now had more to worry about than a recalcitrant scientist, so I holstered my gun and left Dr. Baston amid her swirling equations of light. Outside in the corridor, I reactivated the chameleon suit and went in search of a traitor plotting genocide.

* * * *

A Sep soldier in dress uniform with a polished Vel Penetrator stood at ease outside General Trask's ground floor office. He was eyes front and statue still, giving me an easy approach. I clamped my hand over his mouth and drove my knuckle stunner into his neck, holding it there until he passed out, then I pocketed the stunner and held his palm against the wall-mounted DNA scanner.

The door slid open, letting me into a spacious, sparsely decorated office. Against the far wall was a utilitarian desk equipped with a ruggedized data pane and a military comm set. To the left of the desk was a full-sized holowall, to the right, a north-facing window with a view through the trees of the army camp. Uncontrolled fires burned furiously between thermotents and wooden walled barracks as sporadic tracer fire flashed through the trees.

Trask stood at a small pedestal console in front of the holowall wearing a soft cap, green and gray fatigues, and camo boots. He was about my height with a heavier build and the kind of swagger common to the worst type of Orie mercenary. In the safety of his office, he'd left his JAG-40 special forces gun in its chest harness on the table beside his utility belt, giving me a chance to take him alive.

The holowall displayed the inner Chambal System with Kota at its center, the corona of the system's star to the right and two barren inner worlds to the left. A cluster of red contact markers floated high above the two inner worlds while halfway between them and Kota were two markers with glowing white labels:

ENS Solar Constitution (Battleship)
ENS Nanjing (Assault Cruiser)

Every few seconds, narrow flashing triangles emerged from the two ships and joined a growing line of triangles heading for Kota. They were heavy stand-off drones on their way to obliterate the planet's surface defenses, if they could find them.

An image box appeared on screen between Kota and Chambal's corona showing the face of a young lieutenant in a control room filled with screens.

"We have twenty-three contacts, sir," she said, "more appearing all the time."

"What class? What size?" Trask demanded.

"They're diffracting our scans. We've only got accurate readings on the two nearest ships."

"I need to know how many warships, how many transports." His jaw tightened. "What are their drones targeting?"

"We don't know, sir. They're not target locked."

"They're riding tracers?"

"It looks that way," she said, confirming Navin

Dhar and his relatives had done their job.

"Alert all commands. Have them conduct searches immediately."

"Yes, sir," she said, then he switched channels.

A bearded sergeant wearing coveralls appeared. "General," he said, straightening to attention.

"They'll be going after the ships," Trask said. "Tell Nasim to launch the Mendiant and start loading the other ships immediately."

"Sir, Dr. Nasim isn't answering."

"What? Go find him. I want our ships gone before their drones get here."

"What about the stabilization tests?"

"It's too late for that. We've got to go now."

"Yes sir," the crew chief replied, then a brilliant flash lit up the forest.

Trask looked back through the window, shielding his eyes as he studied the N-grenade blast, trying to figure out what it was. When the blast faded he turned back to the pedestal and selected another channel, then I started creeping toward him, intending to take him from behind with my knuckle stunner.

A soldier clad in body armor inside a large thermotent command post appeared in the image box. The tent flaps behind him were open revealing fires burning and soldiers running in confusion through the brigade camp.

"What are those explosions?" Trask demanded.

"They're too big for ground effect, sir. Must be orbital."

"Can't be!" Trask snapped. "Their drones are still outside the minefield." A huge orange flash flared behind the soldier, casting harsh light through the open tent flaps. "What the hell was that?"

The soldier ran to the entrance and looked out, assessing the situation, then came back to report. "It was ammo dump four, sir. Looks like a direct hit."

Trask grunted angrily, saw soldiers outside the thermotent firing into the dark. "What are those idiots shooting at?"

"Snipers."

"That's impossible! It'll be hours before they land."

"We've got three dead already, sir. Confirmed."

Trask hesitated. "Hmph. Where's Stina Kron?"

"Prepping an assault on the e-plant. Sentries reported enemy ground troops before we lost contact with them."

"Ground troops? What strength?"

"They didn't say."

"Well find out, goddamnit!"

"Yes, sir."

I circled around behind Trask, knowing all it would take to decapitate the planet's military leadership was one eight-mil round to the back of his head, but I needed to know where that Procyon IV freighter had gone, what world it had been sent to destroy.

He tapped the console again and an officer facing a semicircular holoscreen that wrapped around him appeared. "Tactical," he said, then saw Trask's face. "General?"

"Why haven't you opened fire?"

"We've got positive locks on two capital ships, sir, but they've stopped ten thousand kilometers short of our envelope."

"Hmm. Can you hit their drones?"

"Yes sir, but we're maintaining concealment. Standing orders, hold fire until their ships are in range."

"I'm rescinding those orders. Open fire on the drones."

"Their ships will see us, sir."

"They already have, Colonel. Their drones aren't scanning, they're following tracers, right to you."

The officer nodded. "Understood." He touched his own console. "All batteries, this is Surface Control.

Switch to counter bombardment mode. Target incoming drones. Open fire. Fire at will."

The surface battery commander's face disappeared from the screen, then Trask turned to the window and watched energy pulses arc up into the sky toward Earth Navy's incoming drones. I froze as Trask looked right past me, then his console beeped. He turned back and accepted an incoming transmission.

A tall soldier in battle armor, kneeling among trees, appeared in the holowall image box. Fires burned in the distance and tracer flicked through the forest, all going one way. The soldier pushed her helmet's black visor up revealing a woman's face with a scar across her cheek and piercing midnight blue eyes. Unlike many Sep officers, Stina Kron was a hardened professional with over sixty orbital jumps under her belt and a record any URA drop leader would have envied.

"General. You wanted me?" she asked crisply.

"Stina! Yes. The e-plant's a diversion. Must be local resistance. Their transports are still out beyond Cham Four."

"How many ships?"

Trask shook his head. "Can't tell yet, they're still jumping in. Looks like Talis brought his whole damn fleet–and some. They won't start dropping troops until tomorrow at the earliest."

There was a massive novarium blast off to her left. Debris flew through the trees, blasting Kron with gale-force winds. She hunkered down, shielding the comm set with her body, then when the shockwave faded, her face came back into frame.

"What was that?" Trask asked.

She shook her head uncertainly. "Some kind of new weapon. Definitely not local militia."

"Yeah." Trask nodded agreement. "I need you down here defending the facility until the bomb ships are away. Send Rogov to retake the e-plant."

"Rogov's dead, sir. I'll send Alvarez."

"And tell Captain Harrak to prep the cutter."

"Evac, sir?" she asked surprised.

"Talis knows what we've got, otherwise he wouldn't be throwing everything at us. When we go, it'll be you, me and the science team. I'll bring the bomb specs with me."

"We've got six thousand troops here, sir," she said, wanting to make a fight of it.

"I know, but Talis has a fleet that'll obliterate them from orbit."

She nodded grimly. "Yes, sir."

"And Stina, make sure he doesn't get those prisoners."

"Yes, General," she said without enthusiasm, then the image box vanished.

Trask studied the twin lines of incoming triangles on the holowall, noting the first drones were entering the minefield, then another N-grenade burst over the camp to the west. The flash flooded the office with light, casting my shadow onto the holowall. Trask's eyes went straight to my ghostly silhouette. He knew instantly what it meant and lunged for his gun on the table.

I darted across to a wall and froze, vanishing from sight as he pulled the gun from its harness and sprayed where I'd been standing with heavy caliber slugs. The raking fire peppered the wall to my right and shattered the windows, letting cool air and the distant crackle of gunfire spill into the room. Knowing he'd missed, he backed toward the holowall, keeping his gun level at chest height.

"Lights, maximum illumination," he yelled, attacking the chameleon suit's weakness.

The ceiling's glow bars, initially set low for the holowall, brightened sharply, trapping me in light. Knowing any movement risked breaking invisibility, I reached slowly into the chameleon suit for my gun. I couldn't risk shooting through the nodules. They'd deflect my shot and might shatter, showering me in splinters. I had to be patient, knowing Trask couldn't wait me out, not with Talis and his entire fleet bearing down on him.

When Trask realized I wasn't moving he put a single shot into a tiny ceiling sensor, blinding the building's security system so it couldn't overrule him, and yelled, "Manual alarm! Chemical fire."

A warbling siren began wailing as white gas sprayed down from tiny ceiling holes. Trask was trying to coat my chameleon suit in fire suppressant, disrupting its invisibility. His eyes scanned left and right as the gas sank into the room, threatening my suit, but also diffusing the light, giving me a chance.

I started edging toward the broken windows, hoping the inrushing cold air would push the gas away from my suit. As the white mist descended, filling the upper third of the room, I doubled over, staying below it. When I was halfway to the window, another N-grenade detonated outside, outlining me in light.

Trask saw my silhouette and fired as I dived away, drawing my P-50. One of his heavy rounds winged my suit, triggering an alert that flashed before my eyes, warning my back was now visible. When I hit the floor, I shot low, grazing his leg but missing bone, then Trask limped around the table, firing through the thickening white cloud. I rolled away, ripping more of the suit and filling my oculars with static, forcing me to tear open the faceplate to see.

"Kade!" he exclaimed in surprise when he saw my face.

I put one into his gun and it flashed and shorted out. His jaw tightened angrily as he looked down the barrel of my P-50, then he dropped his weapon and spread his hands in surrender.

"Hello General," I said, getting to my feet and

peeling off my crippled chameleon suit, keeping him covered the whole time. "The war not going as you expected?"

"I should have killed you on Acheron Station."

I smiled. "You should have killed me on Krailo-Nis." He frowned, not recalling our first brief encounter, then I approached his desk, never taking my eyes off him. The data pane was active but locked. "Open it." He didn't move. "Die here or in Babakin supermax. Your choice."

He stiffened, surprised I knew he'd escaped from the toughest maximum-security prison in Mapped Space, then he limped to the table as I backed away, careful not to let him get close. He might have been unarmed and wounded, but he was still a trained killer who could snap my neck in a heartbeat if he got half a chance.

He placed his hand on the data pane's DNA scanner. "Vocal authorization Domar Trask," he said, then the data pane unlocked

"Now the target list."

Understanding flashed across his face as he realized I knew all about his planet-killing super weapon. "You're wasting your time, Kade. Once those ships bubble, it's over."

"Then you've got nothing to lose," I said, picking a spot between his eyes.

He scowled and summoned a list of fifty Core System worlds, each with a thirty digit alphanumeric code beside them.

I glanced at the target list, thought, *Create image imprint*, then my threading took a copy.

"You don't have enough ships to hit all of those planets," I said.

"More are coming."

"Where's the ship you launched headed?"

Trask shrugged. "Only it knows."

"Wrong answer." I extended my arm to shoot.

He gave me a bored look. "The system randomly selects targets based on payload size. Even I don't know where it went."

"How could you be sure the Mendi would go to Earth?"

"The payload guaranteed it."

"Because Earth has so much water." With a full load of bombs aboard the *Mendi*, the targeting system would choose no other world.

He nodded. "It's launching as we speak."

"No, Nasim's dead."

Trask's smugness wavered as he realized the *Mendiant* was still on the ground. "You'll never get out of here alive, Kade," he growled, then the building exploded around us as the targeter I'd left on the roof did its job.

Windows and walls shattered and the lights went out as Trask and I were hurled apart. I landed hard, striking my head. My gun skidded off into the darkness as part of the ceiling collapsed and the holowall went blank but remained standing. The rumble of the building collapsing and the boom of chemical explosions from the factory filled the air, then a huge cloud engulfed me.

I blinked, trying to focus, glimpsing the star-filled night sky through swirling dust. Glowing orange trails arced above us as navy drones dived on their targets through streams of energy pulses rising to meet them. An incoming navy drone landed nearby and exploded, shaking the ground, then another was caught in the sky by intersecting pulse streams and burst into a fireball. Higher up, tiny points of light marked where seeker mines, now acting autonomously, intercepted drones diving for the atmosphere.

I watched the opening moves of the bombardment in fascination, then Trask grunted noisily to my right, bringing me to my senses. He pushed rubble off his body as I groped blindly into the dark for my gun, unable to recall in which direction it had gone.

Enhance infrared red, I thought, ramping up the bionetic filaments in my eyes.

Trask appeared as a red blur getting slowly to his feet. He looked around, couldn't see me, and stumbled away over the rubble. When he reached the wall, he pushed a fallen beam aside with the brute strength of an Osynian ox, clearing a way out, then clambered through what was left of the doorway.

Now alone, I looked for my gun, spotting the faint heat signature of its power pack beneath fallen masonry. I started crawling toward it when scraping footsteps sounded from the ruined doorway. Trask appeared holding the guard's Vel Penetrator and fired a sweeping blast, trying to flush me out.

"What's the matter, Kade, the war not going as you expected?" he sneered, peering into the dust and darkness.

Keeping my head down, I crawled toward my gun as the scraping of Trask's boots limping after me grew louder. He raked the rubble with several bursts, showering me in splinters, then when I didn't show myself, he hobbled forward again looking for a kill shot.

I pulled out my knuckle stunner and set it to full power, then as he stepped into the open, I flung it at him with ultra-reflexed precision. He didn't see it tumble through the darkness, but he felt a jolt as it glanced off his arm. More surprised than hurt, he fired at the knuckle stunner as it clattered to the ground while I lunged for my gun. Seeing his mistake, he turned toward me and sprayed the air with heavy slugs. They whizzed close to my face as I rolled away and put a single round between his eyes. His face went blank, then he dropped the big Vel and fell back.

I got to my feet, cleared my infrared booster and saw Trask's dead eyes staring blankly up at the streaking lights and explosions filling the night sky. Knowing

Stina Kron and her reinforcements weren't far away, I holstered my gun and scrambled through the ruins.

Once outside, the full extent of the damage was evident. The transmission beam from the e-plant was gone, all the lights were out and the center of the building had collapsed in upon itself. Margaux Baston was certainly dead, the mine shaft was buried and the precision engineering works was on fire. The eastern end of the building was still standing, shielding the ships on the landing ground from the blast, although the guards had abandoned their posts and were running for the trees, looking up in terror at the orange comets falling on them from space.

To the northwest, tracer flashed through the forest as Separatists hunted the super soldier who'd attacked their base. In the encampment, soldiers sprayed massive fires with extinguishers while, silhouetted by the burning ammo dumps, a skirmish line of soldiers came south through the trees. It had to be Stina Kron's force, arriving too late to save Trask or his bomb-making facility, but in time to stop the prisoners from escaping.

A hypersonic drone landed with a huge white flash to the east, uprooting trees and hurling them into the air as a pillar of flame blasted skyward from a direct hit on a surface battery. Higher in the atmosphere, a continuous procession of drones dived toward the ground. It wasn't the massed alpha strike I'd imagined and the opposing pulse streams crisscrossing the sky were far greater in number than predicted. At a glance, I knew Kota's defenses would take much longer to reduce than planned, leaving Dietz's team cut off for days rather than hours.

To avoid Stina Kron's force, now emerging from the trees, I ran around the western end of the building and headed for the prison. Deprived of power, the laser fences, search beams, and autoturrets were all down. The prisoner huts were mired in darkness, lit only by the glare of distant explosions and the flash of surface batteries. Some guards milled around the main gate uncertainly, watching the lights in the sky, while others deserted for the safety of the forest.

Ignoring the wavering guards, I ran through the deactivated fences toward Marie's hut, hoping she'd had the sense to head south as soon as the perimeter went down. I shot out the lock of one hut door, kicked it open and yelled at the surprised faces peering out at me from the dark interior.

"You're free! Get out!" I ran to the next hut and did the same. "Run! Hide in the forest."

Prisoners in other huts forced open their doors and came outside. Some saw their chance and headed for the safety of the trees while others, too confused or weak to escape, milled around in groups watching the sky uncertainly.

"What's happening?" a woman wrapped in a thin blanket asked.

"The navy's coming," I shouted. "Get out! Stay away from the bunkers."

I ran on to Marie's hut. She was outside with her crew and the Hadleys staring up at the lights in the sky. It had been over a year since I'd seen Emma and her father. Both were thinner than I remembered and her father was missing the ugly metal prosthetic arm he'd been so proud of.

"They took it," Quentin Hadley explained, following my eyes. "I clubbed a guard with it."

"We'll get you a new one," I promised.

"Is Jase here?" Emma asked. She was short, blonde and, like her father, had thick bones and strong muscles from growing up on a heavy gravity world.

"He's waiting for you south of here. Let's go."

They started for the fence line, but Marie hesitated, looking toward the landing ground.

"You couldn't save the Mendi?" she asked,

glancing at the top of the *Mendiant's* hull rising above the building's eastern wall.

"No, we have to leave her here," I said, then a brilliant white comet hurtled down out of the sky, coming straight for us.

Terrified screams filled the air as prisoners huddled together in horror, then the navy drone plunged into the row of flatbed transports and detonated. A wave of explosions rippled through the closely packed hydrazine tanks, turning the parking area into a firestorm. Moments later, a second drone struck the big storage tank, sending a gigantic fireball roiling into the night sky. The shockwave tore the roofs off nearby huts, shattered windows and hurled perimeter fence poles and light towers at the forest.

Marie stared wide-eyed at the wall of flame. "What was that?"

"Basu Manjhi's stim business going up in flames," I said with satisfaction.

"No, Sirius. What *was* that?" she demanded, sensing the hidden truth.

The moment I saw her face, I realized my mistake. Gloating at the destruction of Basu Manjhi's stim supply, relying on the drone attack to knock out the perimeter defenses, even my certainty the guards would be too busy to stop us escaping, they all revealed I knew too much. I hesitated, searching for a cover story, for anything that would deflect her attention, for any excuse she might believe, but nothing made sense.

"They're drones."

"I know that. Whose?"

The sounds of war suddenly disappeared. The explosions, the sonic booms, the frightened screams vanished into silence.

"You won't like it." She stared at me, waiting, then I gave it to her straight. "Earth Navy."

"They're here?" she said puzzled, looking at the

burning fires. "You *knew* they were coming?"

I nodded. "I knew."

"You work for them?" she asked with revulsion.

I considered telling her they'd paid me well, that I was a mercenary, that it was only about the money, but she wouldn't have believed it. And I was done lying to her.

"It's why we're here, now, on Kota," I said. "I'm Earth Intelligence Service, Marie. Deep-cover."

"EIS?" she whispered, stepping back from me in horror. "You? Since when?"

"All along."

Her face paled with shock. "You promised me. You said you weren't on anyone's side."

"I couldn't tell you, Marie. You're a Separatist sympathizer."

"Does Jase know? Does Izin?"

I shook my head. "No. They're part of my cover."

"You've been lying to them, to *me*, all this time?" It was more than an accusation, it was a shattering of her dreams. Her eyes filled with tears. "I thought you loved me."

"I do," I said, stepping toward her, reaching for her arm.

"Get away from me!" She cried, swatting at my hands.

"We have to go, Marie. Now."

"I'm not going anywhere with you, ever again!" she pushed me back and ran toward the camp headquarters sobbing, tears running down her cheeks.

"Marie! Not that way," I shouted, knowing she was running toward the target designator I'd planted there.

I started after her, then a shot struck the hut wall beside me. I turned toward the source, a line of Sep regulars crossing the fence perimeter. They were shooting over the heads of the prisoners, waving them back. One soldier was motioning at me.

I ignored him and ran to the end of the hut searching for Marie. She was heading past the camp HQ, ahead of Ugo, Omari, and Eddie who were trying to catch her.

A burst of automatic fire flashed in front of me, so close I felt a blast of air on my face. Another burst struck the wall, forcing me back. Marie ran behind the building with Ugo and the others close behind. I started after them, then a navy drone hurtled down out of the sky and slammed into the camp HQ, blowing its walls out and turning the wooden structure into an inferno.

"No!" I yelled as an unbroken sea of flame consumed the eastern end of the camp.

In a panic, I charged toward the burning building, then gunfire kicked up the ground at my feet. I stopped, saw four soldiers ordering me back. In a blind fury, I drew my gun and shot them all, then stared at their bodies in horror as I realized what I'd done, my rage ebbing away.

I started toward the fire again, dreading what I'd discover, then sensed movement above me and looked up. A dark mass was blotting out the stars, diving silently toward me. I was puzzled by the lack of a glowing contrail, by its rapid increase in size, then the plunger struck the ground between me and the camp HQ, unleashing a kinetic blast that hurled me back.

I landed hard and lay stunned as a dust cloud billowed over me, then I coughed weakly and got to my feet, my head spinning. The dust cleared around the plunger hole as a four-legged spotter leaped out and began swaying back and forth, scanning the area. I blinked, trying to focus, unable to hold my gun steady as I fired several times, missing with every shot. The spotter darted sideways and stopped, then I took a deep breath, focused on my aim and drilled it.

"Skipper? Where are you?" Jase's voice sounded in my ear.

I grabbed the communicator off my belt and started circling around the plunger hole. "I'm here."

"There's a spawnship above us."

"I know," I said, searching the flames beyond the plunger hole for any sign of Marie.

"Where are you?"

"At the camp."

"Did you find Emma?"

"Yeah, she's on her way," I replied, then a wave of relief washed over me as I saw Marie. She was beyond the flames, running toward the *Mendi*, followed by her crew.

"What about Marie?" Jase asked.

Marie opened the *Mendi's* forward airlock, motioned her crew aboard, then climbed in after them. When she turned to seal the outer door, she saw me watching. For a moment, she stood wiping tears from her cheeks, then without even a wave of goodbye, she closed the hatch.

"Skipper?" Jase persisted.

"She's not coming."

A pair of bipedal flankers leaped out of the plunger hole, then two Sep regulars, not knowing what they were, opened fire and were immediately killed. Other Sep soldiers, seeing their comrades fall, started shooting from further away, drawing the flanker's attention. Knowing the camp would soon be crawling with autacs, I pocketed my communicator and ran toward the forest.

Halfway to the treeline, a four-legged spotter landed in front of me. I shot it twice without slowing, then ran on past the shadowy forms of prisoners heading for the forest. They walked and hobbled, moving singly and in pairs, some helping the weak, most simply fleeing for their lives.

When I reached the forest's edge, a brilliant blue light bloomed from the camp, casting harsh shadows through the trees. It was the *Mendi* lifting off. She turned away to the north, barely clearing the landing ground before Marie powered her twin main engines. The ship's bow lifted sharply, recklessly blasting the ground with her backwash, then she soared into the dark night sky, rising on a long blue contrail, boosting hard for space.

Below the *Mendi*, the whine of magnetic accelerators rolled out from Kota Prison as more Sep regulars joined the fight against Intruder autacs. Their ordinary kinetic rounds sparked harmlessly against autac shields while the Intruder energy weapons mowed down entire squads ill-equipped for such a fight. They died, unaware their leaders were de facto allies of the forces now slaughtering them and the war they waged against Earth was no more than an insignificant sideshow in an interstellar war fought between ancient galactic superpowers.

As the irony of the situation struck me, a long dark craft flew in low over the treetops and raked Kota Prison with energy blasts. Huts and humans were obliterated in the maelstrom as more Sep soldiers, not realizing the danger, rushed to their deaths, buying time for a handful of prisoners and one EIS agent to get clear.

I holstered my gun and ran into the forest, wondering how we'd ever escape Kota now that the Spawn had arrived.

* * * *

"I'm heading back," Jase said. He'd driven the buggy away from the *Silver Lining* so if the spawnship detected his signal, it wouldn't find the ship.

"I'm close," I said, pocketing my communicator.

I was well south of the ring of surface batteries the navy drones had been pounding since the bombardment began. The ground fire snaking across the sky had thinned, even if Kota's defenses were far from beaten. To the northwest, the giant e-plant dome was still visible above the treetops, although it was no longer floodlit. The occasional blast of N-grenades confirmed Dietz was still hanging on, while the stark white flashes of Intruder energy weapons were now visible all across the Sixth Brigade's encampment.

To the Separatists, it must have appeared as if autac forces were part of a coordinated attack, even though the One Spawn had no interest in Kota. They wanted Arleen and the memory crystal and were occupying any spaceport that might provide an avenue of escape. If Jase hadn't moved the *Silver Lining* to the forest and if Izin hadn't darkened the ship, Arleen would now be their prisoner.

At the crest of a low hill, I spotted a dark Intruder craft gliding silently above the treetops, sweeping the forest with search beams. I hurried down a gentle slope, crunching cones under my boots, knowing my body heat would be starkly visible to their sensors.

When I neared the bottom of the hill, a skinny bipedal form leaped over me. It landed close, glowing with a contour shield and equipped with dissimilar devices for hands. I fired immediately, without slowing. The flanker made no attempt to evade, expecting my shot to bounce off its shield, but the snakehead killer round punched through its thin energy barrier into its torso. Sparks burst from its chest as it was knocked over, then it rolled to its metal feet and sprinted away at incredible speed, blurring as it circled me.

"Oh ho," I muttered, certain it was reporting an encounter with a human armed with static force projectiles. I aimed after it, firing twice, but it was too fast. Dietz's super soldiers might be able to score hits with their predictive psionic abilities, but I was just wasting ammo.

I ran south as metallic feet rapidly crunched pine cones behind me and to my left, signaling a second flanker had joined the hunt. The damaged autac turned sharply and charged at me through the trees. I waited until it was almost on top of me, then blasted it on full auto, blowing its rhombus-shaped head off as its companion stopped behind me.

I spun around as the second flanker fired a crackling sphere of ball lightning into my chest, knocking me onto my back, paralyzed from head to toe. My threading pumped adrenalin through my body, to no effect, then the flanker's shield went down and it began scanning me with its non-stunner arm.

A spawnwarrior in an armored fighting suit landed nearby with a thud and stepped toward me, then the autac's unshielded torso exploded, struck in the back by a detonating sniper round. The flanker's legs fell across my chest as the spawnwarrior turned and raked the forest with a panning burst of energy pulses from a shoulder-mounted weapon. Tree trunks exploded in flames and toppled to the ground as if a scythe cut through the forest, but Izin–who had to be hiding out there–didn't show himself.

The spawnwarrior's energy weapon fell silent, leaving fires burning in a wide arc. He stood studying the forest, but seeing no movement, he came toward me, glanced at my paralyzed body and reached out toward my P-50. A thin blue magnetic beam shot from his hand, sucked my gun off the ground and clamped it to his metallic hand. He examined the weapon briefly, quickly figured out how to eject the magazine, then dropped the gun and scanned the static force ammo with a sensor in his other hand.

Before he finished, a slender form came leaping through the trees toward us, jumping from branch to branch. The spawnwarrior, sensing the approach, turned toward the shadowy form. Before he could fire, Arleen leaped through the air and landed in front of him. She was unarmed, wore ill-fitting chest armor drawn from Dietz's spares, and no shoes. Her arms and legs–once delicate and soft–now rippled with hard, lean muscle.

"Itsa kir sesh!" the spawnwarrior ordered.

Arleen spread her arms as if surrendering, but the cold intensity in her eyes indicated that was not her intention.

"Ka sesh!" the spawnwarrior yelled in a confused, wavering voice.

Arleen started walking calmly toward him, then he opened fire. Energy pulses flashed all around her, every shot missing, while her eyes remained intensely focused upon him. When she neared the spawnwarrior, his weapon stopped pulsing while he stood frozen like a metal statue before her. A seam on the left side of his battle suit opened from the neck to the hip and the chest clamshelled open. Soft yellow light spilled out onto the forest floor and a small gloved hand fell limply out of the armored suit.

Arleen reached inside and pulled the spawnwarrior out with one hand. He wore skin-tight brown coveralls and appeared to be sound asleep. She dropped him like a rag doll and reached into his fighting suit, then the yellow interior light winked out and it fell back like scrap metal.

Arleen turned to me. "Can you walk?" she asked in a deeper, harsher voice than I'd heard her use.

"No…" I croaked, barely able to move my lips.

She lifted me off the ground and slung me over her shoulder like I was a feather.

"Gun," I whispered, then she scooped up my P-50 and locked it into my holster. "What…you do…to him?"

"Mind sleep," she said, then she sprinted through the burning forest with dizzying speed.

"Empath…trick?" I asked, my head swimming as she wove gracefully between the trees.

"Arleen was an empath. I am Arlon, a guardian, and male," *he* explained, vaulting over a deep gully and landing on the far side without breaking stride.

"You changed?" I said, noting it wasn't just his muscles that had changed. His skin was paler than before and drawn tightly across his bones, giving his features a gaunt, angular quality.

"To survive." He leaped onto a fallen tree, sprang onto a branch and back to the ground. "I could not defend myself as Arleen. I can as Arlon."

"How?"

"Uvo are elective hermaphrodites," he said, coming to a sudden stop.

Izin emerged from behind a tree holding his long-barreled sniper rifle. "Is the spawnwarrior dead?" he asked.

"He sleeps," Arlon replied. "I deactivated his armor. It will take them time to find him."

"You should have killed him."

"I cannot. All life is precious, even the life of a spawnwarrior."

"I will do it."

Arlon stepped in front of Izin, barring the way. "They will send autacs to discover why his armor stopped communicating."

"He'll tell them we're here."

"He will sleep for days."

"Leave…him," I said to Izin, who reluctantly shouldered his sniper rifle, then led us through the forest to the *Silver Lining*.

She was wedged between trees on a dirt track, surrounding by millions of square kilometers of Siberian forest. The cargo ramp was down and her lights were out. With her thermal skin masking her internal heat signature, her particle dampened e-plant barely ticking over and her active sensors off, she was virtually invisible to orbital sensors, at least until dawn.

"Did the Hadleys…make it?" I asked, stretching my jaw, tapping Arlon to put me down. He lowered me to the ramp where my knees almost gave way.

"Yes Captain," Izin replied. "They're aboard."

"OK, let's get out of here."

Izin hurried off to begin the power-up sequence, then Arlon walked back down the ramp.

"I will remain here," he said. "I'm the one they want. I will tell them you left me behind because you were afraid. It will give you time to escape."

"They're after the memory crystal, not you."

"The One Spawn trust no one, Captain Kade, not even each other. They would never expect me to give you the memory crystal. They will believe I hid it on this world because that is what they would have done. It will take them time to extract the truth from me. By then, you will be far away."

I sighed wearily and sat heavily on the ramp. Arlon gave me a puzzled look, then I drew my P-50, blew dirt off it and fed in a new magazine.

"What are you doing?"

"If you stay, we stay." When the magazine locked, I checked the power level. "Hmm, this thing needs a recharge."

"But…you have a chance to escape."

"It's only an escape if we all go." I looked up from my gun and waited for him to decide.

Arlon studied me with growing understanding. "You humans are a sentimental and obstinate species."

I smiled. "We sure are, especially where our friends are concerned."

"I am beginning to understand why the Tau Cetins trust you, Captain Kade," he said then walked up the ramp and helped me to my feet.

We went up to the command deck where Jase was watching a sky scan constructed from passive sensors only. Sitting on the spare couch beside him was Emma Hadley while her father lounged back at an unused science station with his feet on the console.

"Nice ship you got, Kade," Quentin Hadley said.

"Hope she's fast."

"Nope, but she's quiet," I said, sliding onto my couch and studying the bridge screen. "Where's the spawnship?"

"Other side of the planet," Jase replied.

"They'll surface scan the sunlit side, following the day-night terminator," Arlon explained as he took the spare couch to my left.

"Kota won't give us much cover," I said, thinking our e-plant neutrinos would go straight through the planet to the spawnship.

"There are other ships out there, Skipper," Jase warned, pointing to a cluster of markers in a corner of the screen. "It's Earth Navy."

"The spawnship didn't destroy them?" I asked, surprised.

"Not yet. There are two ships standing off, blasting the planet. The rest are mid-system."

"Your ships are no threat to them," Arlon said. "If they don't interfere, the Spawn may ignore them."

Talis must have seen the spawnship by now. If he had any sense, he'd bubble away and leave Kota to the Spawn, but he didn't know the dry bomb facility had already been destroyed. That meant he was coming, no matter what the cost.

"They will interfere," I said, "and they'll all be destroyed."

"Only if the spawnship is here when they arrive," Arlon said meaningfully. "This planet has no strategic value for the Spawn. Once they realize who we are, they will come after us."

He was right. The spawnship wanted us, not Kota or Talis. I activated the intercom. "Izin, how long?"

"Spinning up now, Captain," he replied from engineering.

I glanced at my console, saw available power begin to rise and wondered how long it would be before the spawnship detected our emissions. I tapped my fingers impatiently on the console, eager to get moving.

"Captain," Emma Hadley said. "I never sent any letter. I don't know who did, but I want to thank you for getting us out of there."

"Don't thank me yet. With that thing up there, we may not even reach orbit."

Quentin Hadley grunted agreement. "We'd rather take our chances with you, Kade, than be stuck in that prison."

"I don't care who wrote the letter," Jase said, giving me a knowing look, "I'm just glad they did."

I realized he thought I'd written it, that one of my contacts had tipped me off about the Hadleys. I hid my surprise, letting him believe what he wanted to. "I wish Marie felt the same way."

"Where's she going to meet us?" Jase asked.

"She's not."

I didn't know where she was headed, but she had enough dry bombs on board to wreak havoc throughout the Core Systems. Once Lena and Talis found out, the *Mendi* would be shoot on sight to every ship in the navy. I just hoped Marie had sense enough to blow the dry bombs into space, not hand them over to her Sep friends.

When the power indicator had risen enough for lift-off, I said, "We're going."

I fed power to the thrusters, lifting the *Silver Lining* vertically through the trees. Branches scraped our hull as our down blast lashed the forest, then as we cleared the treetops, Kota Prison and the e-plant came into view, surrounded by Intruder and human weapon flashes.

"Give me a direct beam on Dietz," I said to Jase.

He locked a comm-beam on the e-plant and nodded. "He can hear you."

"Silver Lining to Dietz. We're leaving. You want a ride?" Giving him and his team a chance to escape would burn valuable minutes, but I at least owed them that.

"We ain't going nowhere," Dietz replied in a relaxed tone, "but I'd appreciate a goodbye gift."

Jase gave me a puzzled look. "Gift?"

I nodded with understanding. "Where do you want it?"

"Fifty meters northeast of the dome."

"That's too close."

"So is the enemy."

"Oh, a *gift!*" Jase said.

I fed the targeting coordinates to a drone, turned the *Silver Lining's* bow toward the e-planet and fired.

"Heads down, Dietz, here it comes."

A bright light shot from the bow, skimmed the treetops at high-g lighting up the forest, then nosed down close to the big dome and exploded in a brilliant orange flash. The blast rolled against the dome, searing one side black and turning the nearby forest into a burning, treeless wasteland.

"Right down their throats, Kade," Dietz said. "Not bad. Next time we meet, I'm buying."

"Good luck," I said, nosing up to forty-five degrees and opening up our main engines.

"You'll need it more than us," he replied as we lit up the night sky.

"Actives on," Jase said, sending pulses blasting from our sensors.

With full scanning and neutrinos radiating from our e-plant, we were flaring like an Issarion pinwheel, visible to every eye. If the spawnship hadn't known a human ship was making a run for it before, it did now.

"Something's coming up after us," Jase said, activating the shield and throwing a rear optical feed into a bridge screen image box.

A vaguely triangular craft with 'wing' mounted engines and a pair of oversized, underbelly cannons was climbing after us. We were nose to the sky, forcing it to do the same to bring its cannons to bear. When it fired, I pulled the bow back sharply as energy pulses flashed under our hull, tickling our shield.

"It's going for our engines!" Jase said.

"They're trying to force us down."

"It's an airblaster," Arlon said, "a ground support unit. It cannot follow us into space."

"With weapons like that, it doesn't need to," Jase said

I locked a drone onto it, selected evasive maneuvering and fired.

"Your weapons will be ineffective against it," Arlon said.

"I just want to slow it down."

The drone performed a tight turn and dived at the airblaster, jinking unpredictably, sacrificing straight-line speed for lateral movement. The flying autac's intelligence prioritized self-preservation over shooting us down. It fired at the drone, which corkscrewed out of the way, than as it closed the distance, I hit the self destruct. The drone exploded and the airblaster automatically banked sharply, avoiding a cloud of drone wreckage and the shockwave.

Jase nodded appreciatively. "They're not so smart."

Arlon gave me a surprised look. "You tricked it into evading."

"I figured it'd save itself before scanning the explosion."

"Intruder machine intelligence would not anticipate you destroying your own weapon."

"They will now," I said as the darkness of space appeared before us.

The airblaster fired again, this time from further away, giving me time to roll clear as we shot out into space. Now in vacuum, we pulled rapidly away from the planet, while the airblaster leveled off at the edge of Kota's atmosphere.

"It can't keep up," Jase said.

It dived back into the atmosphere to rejoin the surface battle, then red contact markers appeared across the bridge screen as our sensors detected a mass of seeker mines ahead.

"Why aren't the orbitals jamming us?" I asked.

Jase studied his scans and shook his head. "They're gone, all of them."

"The spawnship would have interpreted any jamming, no matter how primitive, as an attack," Arlon said.

"I see wreckage," Jase confirmed.

"Cannons to defensive auto fire," I announced, letting our two kinetic cannons shoot at anything heading our way.

"We got sensor waves on the hull," Jase warned. "It's the mines. They've seen us."

"What about the Mendi?" I asked, wondering if they'd got Marie.

Jase studied his sensor screen. "I don't see her."

Trask must have programmed the minefield to ignore the bomb ships, letting the *Mendi* get away clean. I was relieved Marie was safe but feared what the Consortium would do when they realized what she was carrying.

I focused on the wall of seeker mines blocking our escape, searching for a way through, but they were everywhere. When we neared the minefield's inner periphery, both kinetic cannons opened fire, detonating two dark ovoids ahead of us. The flashes highlighted other mines further out, hiding in the darkness.

"Two down, ten thousand to go," Jase said lightly.

"Let's see how smart they are," I said, and launched a drone to fly ahead of us.

It flew into the minefield slightly faster than our ship, broadcasting its position and false sensor returns, but the seeker mines didn't take the bait. Instead, their engines glowed to life and they turned toward us.

"They're backtracking the decoy," Jase said as points of light winked on in the darkness ahead.

"Not my best idea."

"Dive back into the atmosphere," Arlon said.

I scowled. "Uvo ships might be able to turn on a whim, but we've got four thousand tonnes of inertia to deal with, and that airblaster is still back there."

"One's gone terminal," Jase warned as the nearest seeker mine prepared to launch its statically charged warhead into our e-plant.

A k-cannon sprayed it with high-density ballistic rounds, then as the drone exploded, our other cannon fired at another mine further out. In seconds, the k-cannons were firing bursts in all directions, picking up seekers by their targeting pulses and homing trajectories. Each destroyed mine awoke its neighbors, drawing more of them onto us in an ever-widening sphere of hostility.

"They're swarming!" Jase declared.

Our k-cannons fired continuously as seekers closed in from all sides. Exploding mines filled the screen and mine fragments struck our shield as we plowed deeper into the minefield. Our navy certified rapid-fire guns did their best, but there were too many seekers coming from too many directions.

"What's that?" Emma asked, pointing to the bottom corner of the bridge screen.

It was an unidentified contact marker, passing above Kota's atmosphere at tremendous velocity, heading straight for us.

"It's too small for the spawnship," Jase said.

"It's an interdictor," Arlon said.

"It'll get here in time to see us blow up," Quentin Hadley declared bitterly.

Our k-cannons ran hot, depleting their ammunition as seeker mines from further out came hurtling toward us, some getting close enough to arm their penetrators before being destroyed.

"Number two's down to twenty percent," Jase called as the starboard k-cannon's ammo counter ran down so fast it blurred.

"No time to reload," I said as a seeker fired its penetrator, then one of our cannons blasted the spear-shaped warhead as it reached our shield.

"That was close!" Emma exclaimed, then the interdictor streaked up beside us, instantly matching our course and speed.

It was shaped like an elongated trapezoid, black and thickly armored with a powerful shield and weapons of a type I'd never seen before.

"It's beaming at us," Jase said, then our k-cannons fell silent, our shield vanished and our engines died.

"I guess they don't want to take us alive after all," I said when I realized we were defenseless against the swarming mines racing toward us.

Thin white beams flashed from the interdictor, hundreds of times a second, obliterating every seeker mine within thousands of kilometers. In the blink of an eye, they were gone.

"It got them all!" Hadley declared incredulously.

The interdictor moved ahead of us, using its hull to shield us from a storm of mine fragments spinning through space.

"Why doesn't it destroy us?" Emma asked.

"They want us alive," I said. "Izin, can we bubble?"

"No Captain. We're still deep inside Kota's gravity well."

"Here comes another one," Jase said as a second ultra-fast contact marker raced toward us from the far side of Kota. "Oh ho." He stared at the mass indicator on his console. "That's no interdictor."

The spawnship appeared above us, blocking out the stars. Its hull was covered in slab armor, pockmarked with enormous docking bays and bristling with weapons, large and small. A circular port irised open above us and a black metal disk glided down onto our hull. A metallic clang reverberated through the ship as it made contact, then its outer edge glowed and we began sliding beneath the gigantic spawnship toward a tiny square of light several kilometers away.

"Captain," Izin said, "I no longer control the energy core."

"They don't want us blowing ourselves up when they take us inside," I said.

The *Silver Lining's* lateral movement stopped suddenly, then we were pulled sharply up against the spawnship's hull. One massive sheet of black armor filled the bridge screen, then Izin's voice sounded from the intercom.

"Captain, did you bubble the ship?"

"I'm not even steering," I said, nodding to Jase, who switched the feed to an underside optical. The spawnship's black hull was replaced by the dull gray blur of an immense superluminal field.

"They're piggybacking us," Hadley said surprised.

"Taking us somewhere in a hurry," I said, certain wherever it was, we weren't going to like it.

* * * *

Izin summoned me to engineering soon after the spawnship bubbled. When Jase and I arrived, he was watching sensor data scrolling across six screens simultaneously.

"I've been analyzing why the spawnship activated its superluminal drive so close to the planet," he said.

"Their bubbles are stronger than ours," I said. "Gravity wells don't affect them as much."

"Even so, Captain, they were moving us to a docking port, but had an unexpected change of plan. This was captured by a bow optical just before we bubbled." On one of his screens he replayed imagery of space up to the formation of the spawnship's superluminal field. "Did you see it?"

"See what?" I said, exchanging puzzled looks with Jase.

Izin wound the optical log back to the moment before we jumped and pointed at a faint sliver of light at the bottom of the screen. "That."

Jase squinted. "Looks like random photons."

Izin rolled the log back and forth, showing the sliver appear and disappear. "Spectral analysis indicates it is a solid object." He expanded the image until the single thread of light became a long pixilated blur. "Do you recognize the profile, Captain?"

"It could be Tau Cetin."

"Leaving it a bit late, aren't they," Jase said. "We could be halfway across the galaxy by now."

Izin rotated the image and superimposed a familiar Tau Cetin ship profile over it. "There is an eighty-three percent probability it is a sentinel."

Sentinels were Tau Cetin scout ships, as big as Earth Navy battleships, formidable in their own right, but no match for a spawnship.

"Where there are sentinels, arbiters aren't far behind," I said hopefully. "How much did it see?"

"It was twenty million kilometers out. That would put it in-system with the spawnship for almost sixty-seven seconds."

The spawnship bubbled the moment it detected the sentinel, but by then, light containing our last minute in the Chambal System was already on its way to the sentinel's position. After the spawnship jumped, the Tau Cetin ship would have received that light, giving them a delayed view of what had happened.

"They saw the spawnship grab us," I said.

"If their fleet's at Ansara," Jase declared excitedly, "it could get to Kota easy."

"They won't leave Ansara undefended."

"That's true, Captain," Izin agreed, "and yet, the spawnship jumped, fearing attack."

"It's just one spawnship, alone in the heart of Orion where the Tau Cetins are at their strongest."

It's why they were so twitchy and how desperate Vidah'ra was to hide her failure from her sisters, although I couldn't tell Izin and Jase that.

An indicator flashed on one of Izin's screens, then he announced, "The spawnship has unbubbled."

We hurried up to the bridge where the big screen was filled with two brilliant, hollow disks of light orbiting each other.

"It's a black hole binary," I said as I climbed onto my acceleration couch.

The two black holes orbited each other so closely their accretion disks touched. It was a colossal tug of war, such a rare cosmological event that none existed in human Mapped Space. Suddenly, the image stretched diagonally, warping both accretion disks off the corners of the screen.

Quentin Hadley furrowed his brow in confusion. "What is that?"

"A supergravity wave," Arlon replied. "That's why we're here."

Once the great ripple in spacetime had passed through us, the warping image shrank back to a relatively undistorted perspective. A moment later, the brilliant accretion disks swam across the screen–turning seventy degrees–as the spawnship changed heading, then the blur of the Intruder superluminal field filled the bridge screen again.

"They're hiding their tracks," I said, turned to Arlon for confirmation. "Aren't they? It's like the Lhekan black hole."

"The supergravity waves will disrupt the spawnship's spatial wake. The Tau Cetins will be unable to follow us beyond this point."

"Battle tactics," I said, the kind used by galactic superpowers fighting on a battlefield that spanned the galaxy. "This is why the Tau Cetins kept Lhekan slide space a secret, in case they needed somewhere to hide, somewhere local."

"Yes, Captain," he replied.

The spawnship had brought us thousands of light years from human Mapped Space simply to evade their enemy. The Matriarch Vidah'ra had regained the initiative, and there was nothing we could do but wait and see what she did with it.

* * * *

The spawnship unbubbled in deep space far from any star system. Our autonav fixed our location, finding we were halfway to the Scutum-Centaurus Arm thousands of light years from Sol, then the spawnship made a sharp turn and jumped again. Once more cut off from the galaxy, I instructed the autonav to plot our trajectory based on the spawnship's new axis.

"Where?" Jase asked anxiously.

"Back into Orion," I replied with relief.

While I kept watch on the bridge, Jase and Emma had dinner together in the galley. When they returned, she wore one of his spare fraggers on her hip, showing they weren't going to simply surrender to the One Spawn when they came for us. Quentin Hadley reached the same conclusion and disappeared for a while. When he returned, he carried Izin's shrapgun, a nasty hand cannon capable of filling a corridor with a hailstorm of razorshot.

"Gift from the little guy," he said as he returned to his acceleration couch. "He's real friendly, once you get to know him."

Izin was anything but friendly, but he knew once

the One Spawn got their hands on him, they'd make a slave out of him and a traitor to all he'd ever known.

I leaned toward Arlon and whispered, "The armory's back there, in case you change your mind,"

"I will not," he said simply, unmoved by the prospect of being reduced to a laboratory experiment.

When the spawnship's superluminal field vanished again, a tiny yellow pinpoint appeared on the bridge screen, small and distant, yet brighter than any other star. The autonav analyzed the heavens and plotted our position, then we realized we weren't alone. Sensor readings flooded in revealing hundreds of Intruder behemoths lurking in the darkness. It was the entire Spawn Fleet, spread out in a vast spherical formation with the tiny yellow sun at its center.

"It's their whole goddamned fleet!" Hadley declared in astonishment.

"Is that Sol?" Jase asked.

"No," I replied, studying the spectral analysis. "It's a G8, smaller than the Sun."

"G8?" Jase said, trying to recall which of our worlds orbited such a star, then the autonav completed its calculations.

"It's Tau Ceti," I said darkly.

"Where's the Tau Cetin fleet?" Emma asked.

"It's in the wrong place," I said grimly. "It's guarding Ansara, nine hundred light years away."

After all the maneuvering, the planning, the spying, the One Spawn had tricked the Tau Cetins. Their ships were protecting the wrong system and their homeworld was now open to attack from the largest Spawn Fleet ever assembled.

Worse still, Earth lay defenseless less than twelve light years away.

Chapter Seven: Serris Orn

Ornithian Origin World
Tau Ceti System
Inner Cetus
11.9 light years from Sol
2 billion inhabitants
Outer Defense Zone Thula

The sphere of spawnships surrounding Tau Ceti shrank toward the distant blue-green world of Serris Orn, birthplace of the Ornithian race. The great ships disgorged immense black clouds of interdictors that streamed toward tens of thousands of giant hexagonal prisms orbiting Tau Ceti. Trailing behind the main fleet was a thin outer layer of spawnships that played no part in the battle, but shadowed the main fleet as it tightened its grip on Serris Orn.

The planet had been carefully preserved in all its pristine, arboreal beauty for Ornithian habitation while the largely automated prism-shaped orbitals provided the industrial and technological base of the ancient

Ornithoid Consociation. After millions of years of interstellar civilization, Serris Orn was the only natural celestial object remaining within two light years of its star. Every other planet and all the moons, asteroids and comets within Tau Ceti's gravitational influence had long ago been consumed for their resources.

"There's some kind of spatial disturbance between those outer spawnships," Jase said.

I turned to Arlon. "Any ideas?"

"The Spawn have not used this strategy before," he replied uncertainly.

Billions of kilometers inside the siege sphere, the interdictor swarms reached the first orbitals and began circling. Some orbitals were singular prisms, others were composed of multiple hexagons mated together, all with central, tunnel-like holes several kilometers wide for docking ships.

The interdictors poured withering barrages of white pulses into the orbital's spherical shields, turning them into glowing, purple orbs. Brilliant blue beams flashed out from the great prisms and raked through the autac swarm, destroying everything they touched. In an instant, the orbitals revealed themselves transformed from unarmed civilian structures to mighty battle stations armed with the most powerful Ornithian shields and weapons, yet the interdictor numbers were vast.

A handful of long, sleek Tau Cetin arbiters supported by smaller sentinels raced out from Serris Orn to help the giant prisms. They added their own blue energy beams to the orbital's fire, then clouds of interdictors hurled themselves at the super-fast Ornithian warships like angry insects. The annihilation shields surrounding the mirror-hulled dreadnoughts and their escorts glowed brilliantly as they sliced through the autac masses, cutting them to pieces, then they burst through into clear space. The arbiters turned and plunged back into the autac cloud, while the sentinel squadron continued on toward the spawnships.

"Here they come!" Jase said excitedly.

When the sentinels approached the inner siege sphere, the Spawn Fleet opened fire. The Ornithian ships didn't engage, but evaded the Spawn's white beams with weaving, spiraling maneuvers. They raced through without firing a shot and headed for the outer sphere while the inner spawnships maintained their positions, refusing to follow.

The Ornithian ships streaked out to us in seconds, avoided the outer spawnship's fire and dived into the gaps between them. When the first two sentinels entered the spatial disturbance, their engines lost power and they began to drift. Unable to evade, the spawnships concentrated their beams on them, turning the Ornithian shields into brilliant violet spheres of light. The shields flickered and collapsed with surprising speed, then both ships exploded like supernovas. The other sentinels, seeing the danger, immediately veered away at high speed.

"What's wrong with their ships?" I said.

"The Spawn have found a way to disable their engines," Arlon replied, shocked.

The remaining Tau Cetin ships wove through white beams, launching glowing points of light into the gaps between the spawnships, making no attempt to attack the Intruder behemoths.

"Why aren't they fighting?" Quentin Hadley asked.

"They're not weapons, they're message carriers," Arlon explained. "The Tau Cetins are calling for help."

One by one, the points of light entered the spatial disturbance and winked out then, unable to break through, the surviving sentinels raced back into the inner system.

"They're retreating," Jase said disappointed.

"They're trapped," I said.

"Show me one of their outer ships," Arlon said.

Jase focused an optical on the nearest spawnship. It was similar in size to the vessel holding us captive, except its hull was smoother and long dark spines extended horizontally from both sides.

Arlon studied it carefully. "It's less well armed than a spawnship, and those spines are new."

"They've got spineships now?" Jase asked.

"They're radiating positive pressure waves through spacetime," Izin said as he came onto the bridge. "Overlay our curvature readings and you'll see them."

Jase fed the sensor feed used for detecting gravity wells onto the screen, then ghostly ripples appeared radiating from the long black needles protruding from the spineship's sides.

"That wouldn't stop the Tau Cetins bubbling out," Jase said, unconvinced.

"The geometry is a side effect." Izin replied, turning to Arlon. "Could that positive force dampen dark energy's negative pressure?"

Arlon looked surprised. "It could." Understanding flashed across the Uvo's face. "The Spawn are neutralizing dark energy, creating a zone of null space."

"Tau Cetin ships use a dark energy siphon for power," I said.

"That's why their ships can't get through," Arlon said. "There's no energy to siphon."

"The waves are radiating across a narrow plane," Izin added. "The effect is negligible outside that plane."

"Yes," Arlon agreed, studying the screen, "but they've angled their ships to enclose the entire system. There's no way out."

The Spawn Fleet's dispositions now made sense. The outer spineships had established a thin sphere of null space around the Tau Ceti System, ensuring no Tau Cetin ship could enter or leave, while the inner sphere launched fleets of interdictors to attack the prism orbitals.

The sentinels rejoined the arbiters and together they retreated from the interdictor swarm, many with their shields turning purple. They dived back through the layers of hexagonal battle stations to Serris Orn while the interdictors resumed their attack on the outer orbitals. A brilliant nova bloomed deep in the Tau Ceti System as thefirst great station exploded and the peeling open of Tau Ceti's defenses began in earnest.

While the battle between Intruder and Ornithian machine intelligences raged, the Spawn Fleet watched from a safe distance. They bided their time, blocking breakout attempts, while millions of interdictors bludgeoned the battle stations to death, one layer at a time, drawing ever closer to the Ornithian homeworld. Damaged interdictors soon trickled out to the spawnships for repair while replacements flowed in, keeping the autac swarm at full strength.

The Serris Orn Squadron did not reappear while orbitals exploded with disheartening regularity. Once destroyed, the great prisms broke apart, filling space with drifting wreckage the size of mountains. After each victory, the interdictor cloud flowed to its next victim, beginning a new fight with the same inevitable, cataclysmic result.

Orbitals in quiet sectors moved to fill the gaps left by those destroyed, causing the layered battle stations to withdraw inwards as their numbers dwindled. It was a fluid defense, presenting the autac swarm with a constantly changing battlefield, yet the orbitals faced overwhelming odds and their strategy was doomed to fail.

The view of the battle suddenly slewed off the screen as the spawnship holding us captive turned toward a Tau Cetin ship that had just arrived from interstellar space. It had lost its bubble and was now trapped, powerless in the thin veil of null space surrounding the Tau Ceti System. Our captor and three spineships fired immediately, instantly destroying the Ornithian cargo ship. The armored spineships, though formidable in their own right, revealed themselves to be considerably weaker than the far more heavily armed spawnships reinforcing their position.

"Nothing in, nothing out," Jase said, then the screen swam again, only this time the spawnship wasn't moving–we were. The enormous black hull slid above us as we were carried toward the rectangular hangar we'd been heading for back in the Chambal System.

"I thought they'd forgotten us," Hadley said.

"No chance of that," I said grimly.

"They'll want to question us," Arlon whispered to me, referring to the memory crystal.

The bridge screen went blank. "They're blinding us," Jase said. "I'll stow the masts."

"No, leave them out, fully swept," I said. "They might stop jamming us once we're inside."

Jase shrugged and angled the central masts back along the hull while leaving the bow and stern masts fully extended.

"Guess I'm going to find out if this really is as nasty as you said," Hadley declared to Izin, hefting the shrapgun.

"They've got control of the stern door," Jase announced

"We'll shoot them as they come aboard," I said and hurried to my stateroom to collect the last of my snakehead killers.

* * * *

We spread out on the lower cargo deck behind storage containers and cargobots. Jase and Emma were together with their fraggers, Quentin Hadley had Izin's street sweeper while Izin had opted for his long-barreled sniper rifle.

"You sleep the warriors," I said to Arlon, who was unarmed, as usual. "Everyone else, focus on the autacs."

None of their guns could penetrate autac contour shields, only my snakehead killer ammo could do that, but everyone firing at once might disguise our only effective weapon long enough for me to do some damage before they overwhelmed us.

"We've stopped moving, Captain," Izin announced, reading from a portable data pane.

I aimed my P-50 at the stern cargo door as dull thuds sounded on the hull, then the stern door's servos hummed and it began to open.

"Here they come," Jase said, aiming at the stern door.

It cracked open a finger's width and stopped.

We waited in silence, then Hadley said, "What are they playing at?"

I glanced at Izin. "They still got the door?"

"Yes, Captain, they have complete control," he replied, then a gray cloud seeped through the narrow slit between the cargo door and the hull.

"They're gassing us," Jase said.

The cloud floated toward us, holding its form and density, not wafting off into corners of the hull. It seemed to know where we were and came straight for us.

"That's not gas," I said suspiciously and fired a single shot into it. When my snakehead killer round hit, it disappeared in a sparkling ring of light.

"It's nanotechnology," Izin said.

We backed away as the nano-mist reached the containers and cargobots we'd used for cover. It glowed briefly, evaporating them on contact, then divided into ghostly strands that reached for our weapons and forced us back against the bulkhead.

At point-blank range, Jase sprayed the nano-mist with his twin fraggers, then we all opened fire. The gray cloud shimmered with rings of light as wraith-like fingers wrapped around Jase's beloved guns and dissolved them before our eyes.

"What the hell...?" he muttered in astonishment.

Another demonic tongue enveloped my hand and my P-50 vanished, giving me only a brief tingling sensation. The cloud's slender sinews consumed our other weapons effortlessly, confirming we never had a chance. The One Spawn were millions of years ahead of us and weren't ever going to fight on our terms, not after Dietz and his grunts had shown them what we could do.

When all our weapons were gone, the nano cloud withdrew back across the cargo hold and out through the slit opening. Servos hummed and the cargo door-ramp lowered, revealing six Intruder males and a squad of flanker autacs. The males wore dark, one-piece uniforms emblazoned with a dark red crescent moon crossed by a thunderbolt below their necks.

Behind them was Vidah'ra, the matriarch I'd seen on Niedarim, wearing the same dark red bodysuit, silver decorations, and headpiece. She was unarmed although the males all wore metallic waistbands equipped with hand weapons and other devices.

The autacs rushed forward and surrounded us. One flanker fired a ball lightning stun field at Arlon, ensuring he couldn't use his Uvo mind sleep ability. He fell unconscious onto the deck, then the matriarch walked up the ramp followed by her escort. She was a head taller than the males and strode forward with an air of complete authority.

Vidah'ra stopped close enough for me to reach her in one leap, but the flanker autacs kept their weapons on us at all times, ensuring I'd never reach her alive. She ignored us humans, glanced curiously at Izin, then studied Arlon.

"The Uvo has metamorphosed," she said in the One Spawn tongue, translated by my threading. "A pity. The females are of far more interest to us."

"We could force him to change back," one of her lieutenants suggested.

"I doubt that. The males are extremely resistant. Find out where he hid the Buratu memory crystal, but do not harm him. My sisters may have use of him."

"Yes, Matriarch."

"And search this ship. He may have hidden it aboard."

"I will have the autacs search every compartment, Matriarch."

Vidah'ra turned her attention to Izin, who showed none of the sycophantic deference oozing from her male attendants. "You are a survivor descendant, are you not?"

Izin removed the triangular vocalizer covering his mouth to reply. "I am not your descendant. I am a free citizen of Earth."

"Are you indeed?" she said, intrigued by his defiance.

"Clanless mudspawn," one of her lieutenants sneered, motioning to a flanker which stepped forward and held its weapon to Izin's head.

"No!" Vidah'ra snapped, preventing Izin's execution. She stepped close to him, then my sniffer flashed a message into my mind.

ALIEN ECTOHORMONES DETECTED.

The Intruder Matriarch was dosing Izin in pheromones, imprinting him. He stiffened as the ectohormones hit him, then his small shoulders relaxed and his head bowed toward her.

"What is your name?" she asked.

"Izin Nilva Kren."

"What clan?"

"I have no clan, Matriarch."

"No crèche? No spawning season?"

"No, Matriarch, that is not our way."

"What of the other Earth males?"

"Some are imprinted, but only for mating purposes to preserve our numbers."

"How many clanless males are there on Earth?"

"Millions."

"So many," she said intrigued, sensing an opportunity to increase her power. "You are now Izin Nilva Kren of the Siraksha Clan Majestic."

"Thank you, Great Queen."

"You shall share your knowledge of Earth with me and me alone."

"As you command."

"I find your speech strangely toned. It displeases me."

"My apologies, Matriarch. We have been apart from the Mother Spawn for over two thousand years."

"You will learn the proper inflections at once. My attendants will teach you."

"As you wish, Matriarch."

I'd seen a Spawn female take control of him once before, knew how helpless the males of his species were once they were imprinted by the domineering females. Whatever Izin had been, whatever friendship we'd once had was now gone. He was her slave and would gladly sacrifice his life–or ours–for her.

Vidah'ra glanced at her human prisoners curiously. "These lessers serve you?"

"No Matriarch, they were my shipmates."

Were! It rang like an alarm in my ears. In Izin's mind, we were already the past.

"Are they useful to you?"

"Sometimes."

She considered his reply. "You may keep them for now. They may be of service during the next stage."

"Thank you, Matriarch."

"Come with me, Izin Nilva Kren. Tell me of my sisters on Earth." She started back across the cargo hold with Izin following meekly behind. "Are they as helpless as I have heard?" she asked, already plotting their extermination so she could replace them and add Earth's males to her retinue.

"They have no weapons, Matriarch."

"So, it is true," she said. "Perhaps Izin Nilva Kren, I will make you ruler of this Earth where you spawned."

"It would be my great honor to rule the humans of Earth in your name, Mighty Queen," he said, completely in her power.

I watched him scurry after the Matriarch Vidah'ra, wondering if I'd ever see him again, then the autacs fired their stun weapons at us and the nightmares began.

* * * *

I surfaced, gasping for air amid an infinite blue sea, then a strong hand pushed my head down and held me under. My arms flailed and my feet kicked furiously as I sank into a bottomless ocean pierced by sunbeams that faded into the dark depths below. There were no sea creatures in this aquatic hell, only me, a tiny boat and my tormentor.

I exhaled bubbles as my lungs burned and my lifelong fear of drowning overwhelmed me, then the strong hand pulled me back up. A familiar face similar to my own, but different, looked down at me, laughing. His eyes were shaped like mine, but instead of green, they were cold and blue, and rather than my bent nose, his was straight. He was seventeen and stronger than I remembered, but his laugh had a relentless taunting quality that reminded me of all the times he'd used his size and strength against me.

"Where'd you hide it, Sirius?" he demanded.

There was no land in sight, only a cloudless azure sky and a hot orange sun I didn't recognize. My brother held me at bay with one hand, stopping me from reaching the safety of the little boat. He slapped my face hard and forced me down again before I could answer.

I tried pushing his hand away, but my blows were powerless against his strength. Even underwater, I heard his tormenting laughter delighting in my pathological terror. He drove my face down, forcing me to look into the limitless depths below, menacing me with its sheer size and emptiness. I coughed involuntarily and swallowed water, then on the verge of drowning, he dragged me back to the surface.

"The old man said I can do this all day, Sirius."

I knew he was lying. Our father had been a strict disciplinarian, but he wouldn't tolerate torture, not for a second, yet it made no difference. My fear of the water, my inability to swim and the sense that I was on the brink of drowning filled me with all-consuming panic.

"Where is it, Sirius? Where's the memory crystal?"

"The what?" I gasped.

"You know what," he declared and pushed me back under.

I saw his face through the water above, laughing pitilessly. It seemed so real, a nightmare come true, even though I knew it was all an illusion. Canopus had been a tough older brother, relentlessly competitive, but never a sadist.

I thrashed wildly about, exhausting myself, desperately fighting to survive, yet unable to break free. When my heart was pounding so hard I felt it was about to burst, he dragged me back to the surface again.

"Did you help Arlon Torel hide it?" he demanded. "We searched your ship, Sirius. We couldn't find it."

"Let me up!" I screamed in my teenage self's voice.

"Arlon Torel couldn't hide it without your help. You know where it is, don't you?"

"I don't! I swear!"

"Don't lie to me, Sirius. You know I hate it when you lie. You're a liar Sirius, liar, liar, liar!"

Somewhere in my fear crazed mind, I realized they

hadn't broken Arlon. He was holding out, forcing them to break me, hoping I could give them what he would not. They'd found the thing I feared most–drowning–and were using it against me.

"Tell me where the memory crystal is, Sirius, and I'll pull you into the boat."

"I don't know…" I spluttered, swallowing water.

"Wrong answer little brother," Canopus said coldly.

He pushed me under again, forcing me down deeper than before, far deeper than his arms could possibly reach. I sank into the deep blue depths, realizing his hands were no longer holding me, but it made no difference. The hull of the little boat shrank as I was sucked down into the darkness, vainly clawing at the water.

My lungs burned, then spasmed uncontrollably. Air exploded from my mouth and water flooded in, choking me as I sank into the depths, taking an eternity to die. When the blackness of the deep ocean finally overwhelmed me, my body stilled and the final horror of my lonely, choking death filled my mind.

I closed my eyes, thankful it was over, then a strong hand pulled me back to the surface, and my brother looked down at me with that same laughing face.

"Where'd you hide it, Sirius?" he demanded as it began again. This time the fear was amplified by the memory of my last drowning death, added to the cumulative memories of all the deaths that had preceded it, too many to count.

And so it went, on and on, each time worse than before.

* * * *

"We searched your ship, Sirius," Canopus said as I floundered in the water. "We couldn't find–"

The ocean and my teenage brother vanished.

I sensed my eyes were closed, my body numb and unresponsive. Metallic strips pressed against the sides of my head as alien voices spoke in an incomprehensible language, then a message flashed into my mind.

BIONETIC SYSTEM RESTART INITIATED.

A list of activating functions passed before my eyes as my threading threw off the crippling hold of the Intruder interrogation system. In moments, my listener came to life and translated the One Spawn's high pitched speech forms.

"…Uvo do not fear death, Matriarch. They believe it is a form of freedom, not an end of existence."

"Nonsense," Vidah'ra snapped. "You haven't found his weakness."

"The inducer projected more than a thousand scenarios into his mind with no effect."

Feeling returned to my eyelids, but I kept them closed, hiding my return to consciousness.

"He must know they are psycho-simulations."

"The Uvo believes they are real, Matriarch, but he observes them with the detachment of a spectator, not the feeling of a participant. With such an attitude, it is impossible to induce fear. That is why we cannot break him."

"He must fear something," Vidah'ra said.

"I could apply physical trauma to the simulation."

"No, he must not be harmed. He may yet prove useful in designing implants to replicate Uvo abilities."

"Matriarch, those abilities are myths. There is no physiological evidence to support their existence."

"The Uvo are one of the oldest races in this galaxy, far older than us or the Tau Cetins. We do not believe their powers are mythical."

"As you command, Matriarch. The Uvo will not be harmed."

"What about the humans?"

"They know nothing," the male replied as the click

of footsteps approached.

"Even this one?" She asked in front of me.

"He is hiding something, but his primitive hominid brain is unexpectedly resistant."

"He is the one who aided the Ornithians on Centralis?"

"Yes, Matriarch."

"Izin," she said, "why did he help them?"

"They gave him no choice, Matriarch," Izin replied, his voice sounding for the first time.

"They are not as different from us as they claim," Vidah'ra said, taking satisfaction from the thought that Tau Cetins manipulated lesser species as readily as did her own kind. "How close to death is he?"

"He is at his species' physical limit," the first male responded. "If we increase the intensity, he will die."

There was a pause as she considered the assessment. "Increase the intensity, slowly."

"Matriarch, we promised him to the Matarons."

"The Matarons will do as they are told," she said dismissively. "They can have his body once it is no longer of use to us."

"And the remaining prisoners?"

"Great Queen," Izin interjected respectfully, "they have knowledge of many worlds within the Orion Arm."

"So do the Matarons," she replied indifferently.

"Do you trust the Matarons?"

"No, they are an inherently treacherous species."

"Humans, on the other hand, can be manipulated," Izin said.

She paused in thought. "Very well. Keep those you deem of use. Eliminate the rest."

"As you command, Matriarch," Izin replied, then the click of her footsteps faded as she walked away.

"How long did you live with these creatures?" the first male asked.

I opened my eyes a fraction, finding I was floating

in a slender alcove. The opposite wall was lined with similar alcoves, all empty. There were no control panels in the room, only Izin and four males. He wore a dark jumpsuit uniform emblazoned with Vidah'ra's clan majestic crest and a metallic belt with a small Intruder weapon attached. Circular white patches that could have been adhesive bandages dotted his head.

The male that had reported the progress of the questioning stopped and listened to something only he heard, then he turned and stared straight at me.

"Who switched off that human's inducer?"

The other three males turned to me in surprise, then Izin drew his Intruder energy weapon and shot them in the back, killing them all. The inducer nodes disengaged from my head and the field supporting me vanished. I dropped to my knees, surprised how weak my legs were.

Izin hurried to my side, pulling on his vocalizer. "Breathe Captain. The inducer after-effects will clear quickly."

"How long was I in that thing?" I asked hoarsely.

"Three days."

"What!" It had seemed like only minutes. "Has Serris Orn fallen?"

"Not yet, but more than half of their orbitals have been destroyed. The Tau Cetin homeworld will be within bombardment range in a matter of hours."

"No sign of the TC fleet?"

"No, Captain. Serris Orn is completely cut off." He took my arm. "Can you walk?"

I looked into his large, bulbous blue-green eyes uncertainly. "How'd you break her imprint?"

"I did not," he replied simply. "I was never imprinted, at least…not by her."

"I don't understand. I saw her do it."

"I am imprinted to the Matriarch we encountered in the Duranis-B System more than a year ago."

"But she's dead."

"Yes, but…she is still *my* beloved."

I stared at him, trying to grasp the One Spawn's strange biochemical relationship. "You love her, even though she enslaved you?"

"Love is an inadequate term for it, Captain. I am possessed by her. Not a day passes when I do not dream of her," he replied, revealing the great sadness he'd been hiding from me all this time.

"I'm sorry, Izin."

"Do not be, Captain. Her imprint made me immune to Vidah'ra, to all of them."

"You played along."

"We could not fight our way out. Fortunately, loyalty within the One Spawn is to the Matriarch, not the race," he said, helping me out of the alcove. "If Vidah'ra had known I belonged to another, she could have overwritten my beloved's imprint, but it would have taken her much longer and she is in a hurry."

Beside my alcove were others holding Jase, Arlon, the Hadleys and Marie and her crew. They were all sleeping peacefully, deeply entranced in their own nightmares.

I stumbled to Marie's alcove, looking up at her sleeping face. "What's she doing here?"

"The Siraktar, this spawnship, captured the Mendiant soon after she launched," Izin said. "They could not let her leave in case she carried the Uvo and the memory crystal."

"You know about that?" I asked, turning to him in surprise.

"As one of Vidah'ra's attendant males, I was briefed on her mission."

"You know what's on it?"

"Yes, Captain, the Spawn Fleet's strategic plan for the conquest of Orion and the destruction of the Ornithian Civilization. Vidah'ra pursued a Buratu agent to Niedarim. She conquered the Lhekan homeworld because they gave him shelter. In her mind, the Lhekans broke the Xil Neutrality Pact. By the time she caught the Buratu operative, he had passed the memory crystal to Arleen Torel, whom you helped escape from Niedarim."

"Have they changed their plans yet?" I asked, fearing the opportunity was lost.

"No, Captain. The Siraksha Clan Majestic will only admit their failure once they know all chance of correcting their mistake has gone. When they discovered the Uvo was aboard our ship, they believed it was only a matter of time before they recovered the memory crystal."

"Hmph. Risky."

"To the One Spawn, the Silver Lining is primitive and slow, and they spent centuries preparing for this attack. Gaining agreement from the Majestic Clans was a difficult task, as was building a vast fleet and constructing secret bases throughout the galaxy. Changing such a complex plan is extraordinarily difficult, especially considering the distrust the Majestic Clans hold for each other. They are akin to independent fiefdoms, more suspicious of each other than they are of the Tau Cetins."

"Hell of a way to run a galactic war."

"Do you know where the memory crystal is, Captain?" Izin asked.

My spine tingled with suspicion. I studied Izin's amphibian face, unable to tell if it was really him I was talking to or an Intruder slave trying to deceive me. "No," I lied. "Arlon wouldn't tell me where he hid it."

"That was wise," Izin said, turning to the Uvo guardian. "He is far more resistant than any human, even you Captain."

I watched Izin closely but saw no deception. "How do we get out of here?"

"The Silver Lining is close."

"So is an army of Spawn."

"When Vidah'ra told me to choose which of you I could keep, she gave me prisoner transfer authority." He pointed to the tiny white patches over his skin. "And I have been implanted with their technology, to better serve the Matriarch."

I winced, eyeing the white surgical seals. "Do they hurt?"

"No, Captain. My ancestors were genetically engineered to receive Intruder technology. All tamphs inherited those changes from birth, although Earth lacks the technology to utilize them."

"So you're what now…Cyborg-Izin?"

"There are two million Spawn on this ship, Captain. I can communicate instantly with all of them and with every subsystem, including with Vidah'ra herself. That is how I knew you were close to breaking and how I disabled the inducer before it killed you."

"Thanks for that by the way," I said, recalling my aquatic nightmare with a shudder.

"If you are my prisoner, anyone who challenges me will see I have Vidah'ra's authority." Izin approached a panel which slid open revealing rows of oval-shaped devices. He handed one to me. "You must wear this prisoner restraint."

I looked the device over uncomfortably, hoping it really was Izin I was talking to. "Can you order this spawnship to self destruct?"

"Only Vidah'ra can do that, but I do have access to many lesser commands."

"Such as?"

"Hangar door control, diagnostics, maintenance, combat systems."

"You can disrupt their weapons?"

"Not for long."

"But long enough to escape?"

"No, however, the Siraktar salvaged three Tau Cetin message carriers for study by Intruder scientists."

"Did they?" I said intrigued.

"They are stored in the same hangar as the Silver Lining."

"So you can operate TC tech now?"

"Not me, Captain," he replied, turning to Arlon floating peacefully in his inducer alcove. "Him. All we have to do is get the message carrier through the null space barrier."

"Oh, is that all?" I said lightly. "With all those spawnships shooting at us?"

"We don't need to escape, Captain. The Spawn Fleet is moving toward Serris Orn. The spineships are following them in. We only need to hide until they move out of range, leaving us outside the barrier."

"Hide where? We're in space. It's empty."

"Not anymore, Captain," he said slowly. "The battle is going very badly for the Tau Cetins."

It took me a moment to realize what he meant. "The orbitals?"

"Yes, Captain. Their wreckage is everywhere and the Siraktar is near the outer edge of null space. We won't have to wait long."

"OK, we hide," I agreed, turning to Marie. "Now get her out of there. Get them all out."

The inducer alcove lights blinked off, the head nodes detached and they all dropped to their feet. Some knelt, others stumbled out in a daze. I caught Marie who looked up at me in surprise, then pushed me away.

"What are you doing here?" she demanded, her eyes flaring with anger.

"Same as you. They caught us boosting out."

"Plug me back into that thing," she demanded, preferring One Spawn mind torture to my company.

"You've got one ticket out of here. I'm it. Your choice."

She glowered at me, then saw Ugo on his knees, his face pale and sweating. She pushed past me and hurried to his side. "Ugo," she cried, grabbing his shoulders.

He gave her a reassuring nod as Omari Jang and Eddie Nubaker emerged from their inducer alcoves, disoriented and exhausted. Jase stood holding his head with both hands, eyes squeezed shut.

I stepped over to him. "You OK?"

He breathed deeply and nodded.

"What was your nightmare?"

"Don't ask," he said, trying to forget.

Izin began handing out oval-shaped prisoner restraints. "Put these on."

The others eyed him and the devices with suspicion, refusing to comply.

"Do as he says," I ordered. "It's the only way we'll get to the ship."

"Like this," Izin said, placing one of the devices over Jase's temple. On contact, it glowed and Jase relaxed with a blank look.

I waved my hand in front of his unseeing eyes. "What happened?"

"His personal will is suppressed. It will convince anyone we meet that you are my prisoners."

Arlon looked at the restraints in Izin's hand. "They won't work on me."

"I know." Izin tapped his weapon. "That's what this is for."

"I'm not wearing that," Ugo wheezed obstinately. He was having trouble standing, taking longer to recover from the inducer than the rest of us.

"You are if you want to come with us," I said. "It's the only way."

Marie nodded encouragement to her barrel-chested first officer, then she motioned for Izin to put one on her. "Make sure you take mine off before his," she said, nodding at me.

"As you wish," Izin replied and attached the device to her temple. She relaxed, glassy-eyed, then he placed them on the others.

"No more nightmares," I said guardedly.

"Only compliance, Captain, which in your case will be an improvement."

"Nice," I said, then to avoid my threading disrupting the restraint, I thought, *Bionetics, shut down and bunker.*

My biotech switched off and Izin attached the device. Suddenly I was sleepwalking, fully conscious without a care in the universe, yet completely aware of my surroundings. I felt a compulsion to form into two columns with the others, then Izin aimed his weapon at Arlon. Without knowing why, I started walking.

Under Izin's thought guidance, we marched into a broad corridor where male Spawn crew dressed in variously colored jumpsuits hurried about their business. They paid us no attention, as if alien prisoners marching through the ship was commonplace.

I was vaguely aware of passing through a maze of corridors, heard the faint hum of machinery and the high pitched chatter of Spawn. There were no ship-wide announcements as on human ships because they were delivered to the crew via their implants. Mixed among the diminutive, bulging-eyed amphibians were a handful of other races I'd never seen before, all from species long ago conquered by the One Spawn. The conquered aliens seemed free to move about as they wished, but their freedom was illusory. Subjugated 'lesser races' were always fitted with implants that kept them under constant observation and ensured they could refuse no order.

Soon we entered a gigantic hanger, larger than a colonial spaceport and higher than the tallest skytower on Earth. Thousands of autac interdictors were docked in a multi-story latticework cradle on the far side while hundreds of heavy strike craft sat on shelf-like landing pads stacked above us. The hangar bustled with activity as an army of machines repaired damaged interdictors and prepared the strike craft for the coming assault on Serris Orn.

At one end of the hangar was an enormous rectangular portal directly open to space and equipped with the largest pressure field I'd ever seen. Spherical craft towed interdictors to and from a launch point in front of the portal, minimizing the risk of accidents in the congested hangar. At the other end of the hangar was a line of black-hulled Intruder ships, all hard edges and long sloping slab armor, each bigger than an Earth battleship. Wedged between them like small toys was the *Silver Lining* and the *Mendiant*. Both were parked stern to the rear bulkhead and, while the *Mendiant's* hatches were buttoned up, the *Silver Lining's* rear cargo door was down, showing the Spawn had not yet given up searching for the memory crystal.

Izin marched us along the hangar wall, partially hidden from sight by deck level strike craft. They'd played no part in the battle so far, but the preparations surrounding them now suggested the One Spawn were intending to occupy Serris Orn, rather than destroy it.

A few Spawn engineers glanced at us as we passed, but made no attempt to stop us, then we walked up the stern ramp into the *Silver Lining*. Izin shepherded us through the transverse bulkhead into the forward half of the cargo deck, then deactivated the restraints with a thought.

Jase blinked as his mind cleared. "That was easy."

"For you," Izin said dryly. "I received a hundred and seventy-four security challenges. Fortunately, a matriarch's authority is absolute." He turned to me. "No one reported us, Captain, but it is only a matter of time before the dead inducer technicians are found."

"How close are the message carriers?" I asked.

"They're in interdictor cradles not far from here."

"OK, let's go," I said, expecting him to sleepwalk

me over there.

"No, Captain. A human approaching Tau Cetin technology would draw too much attention. I will go alone. You must all stay here, out of sight. I have reported you are now in confinement cells. They will not be searching for you."

"Should we prep the ship?" Jase asked.

"Do nothing until I return," Izin said.

"What about the Mendi?" Marie asked.

"One human ship moving through the hangar will be suspicious," Izin replied. "Two will trigger a security alert."

"We've got to leave her here," I said.

"So you're grounding me," she said, barely able to stand the sight of me.

"Just saving your life."

Izin went off to collect the message carrier, then Jase tapped his empty holsters. "I'm going up to the armory. Anyone else?"

"But…your weapons are ineffective," Arlon said.

"Yeah, but I feel naked without them," he said, then we all went up to the command deck to arm ourselves.

I grabbed my K7 rifle and turned to Jase. "I've got to take care of something."

He gave me a surprised look. "You're going outside?"

"If I'm not back by the time Izin gets here, don't wait for me," I said, then headed for the crew elevator.

"Izin told us to stay here," Marie said, following me.

"It's important." I stepped onto the elevator and selected the lower cargo deck.

Marie jumped on as it began to descend. "Something for your EIS masters?"

"I'd like to tell you, but that would be consorting with the enemy."

When we reached the lower cargo deck, I ran to the

ramp and peeked outside. There were no Spawn engineers in sight and the Intruder strike ships beside us hid the *Lining's* stern from distant eyes. I was about to step onto the ramp when a pair of six armed ordnance units appeared from behind the *Mendi* carrying dark blue ovoid-shaped weapons. I pulled back behind the door frame to hide, feeling Marie's gaze upon me.

"It's a spawnship," she whispered angrily. "Where could you possibly go?"

"To my other ship."

"Why?"

"I'm sentimental. I want to say goodbye."

"You'll get yourself killed."

"At least you won't owe me anything."

I stole a look outside, saw the ordnance units move out of sight, then Marie caught my arm.

"How exactly are you getting aboard *my* ship?" she demanded.

I hesitated. "You changed the entry code?"

"It was the first thing I did."

"We don't have time for this, Marie. I need to get aboard the Mendi, if not for you, then for your crew."

She balked. "You can't scuttle her. You heard Izin, they'll detect a power-up. Besides, you need this." She held up her hand, indicating her DNA was required.

I sighed. "Have it your way."

We hurried down the ramp and ran under the *Silver Lining's* port engines to the *Mendiant's* number six landing strut. Marie entered the code, palmed the DNA reader and the airlock swung open.

We climbed inside without a word between us and cycled through into the *Mendi's* dark interior. The cargo hold was filled with stale air and the massive gray shadows of Trask's planet-killing super weapons. A few tiny emergency lights provided the merest light, while our footsteps echoed hollowly in the kind of silence only a complete shutdown could produce.

"She's dead," Marie whispered sadly. "We'll have to use the crawlway ladders."

"Don't need them."

"Aren't we going to the bridge?"

"No." I pointed at the nearest dry bomb towering above us, so high it almost touched the cargo hold's overhead.

"What are they?" she asked. "They caught us before I could open one."

A soft humming came from the other side of the cargo hold as a glimmer of light illuminated the overhead. I motioned Marie to silence, raised my K7 and watched the light crawl across the overhead toward us. The humming came closer, then light spilled across the deck as a slender sentrybot floated into view. I immediately raked it top to bottom, sending it clattering onto the deck in a shower of sparks.

"You think it reported us?" Marie asked.

"We'll know soon enough," I replied, approaching the nearest gray cube's control panel.

Recall image imprint zero one, I thought, then the list of target-worlds and arming codes I'd seen in General Trask's office appeared in my mind. I entered the first key, which was promptly rejected.

"What are you doing?" Marie whispered.

"Arming it," I said and entered the second key, which also failed.

"They're weapons?" she asked, surprised.

"Planet killers."

"What?"

"That's why Trask impounded the Mendi," I said, typing in another incorrect code and moving to the next on the list. "You've got enough of these things on board to destroy all life on Earth. That's where they were sending her. Your Sep friends were going to murder twenty billion people."

"That can't be," she gasped.

I entered another code that failed. "The snakeheads gave them the tech, in exchange for betraying the Tau Cetins."

"I...had no idea," she whispered, her face white with horror.

"That's why I lied to you, why I'm against them." I turned to her with a searching look. "Why are you for them?"

She opened her mouth, but could find no answer.

"I would have told you everything, one day," I said sincerely. "I've wanted too...for a long time."

Her eyes filled with sadness and confusion as her anger drained away. "You should have trusted me, Sirius."

"I couldn't, not with so much at stake."

I entered another code, then a green glowing message appeared on the screen:

DETONATION SYSTEM ACTIVATED.

The control panels on every dry bomb in the *Mendi's* hold illuminated with the same message as the code chained through them all. I estimated how long it would take to get the *Silver Lining* into space and set the timer.

Initiate thirty-minute visual countdown, I thought, then a timer appeared in my mind, counting down to zero.

"You think this will work?" she asked.

"Once the spawnship realizes we're making a run for it, we're dead, unless we blow it to Spawn-hell first."

"Is that even possible?"

"These things can destroy a planet. Why not a spawnship?" I stepped back from the control panel. "Let's go."

We hurried back through the airlock and ran to the *Silver Lining*. Izin was waiting inside the cargo hold with

Arlon, who was examining a mirror-like spear five meters long cradled on a multi-armed Intruder ordnance carrier.

"It was unwise to leave the ship, Captain," Izin said with annoyance.

"No one saw us," I assured him and closed the cargo door.

"You destroyed a caretaker unit."

"Oh? You saw that?"

"I am fully networked into the ship, Captain. I had to send a fake malfunction report to conceal your carelessness, but they will not be deceived for long."

I turned to Arlon. "Can you make it work?" I asked, indicating the mirrored spear.

"Yes, but we'll have to launch it through the cargo door."

I studied the Intruder ordnance carrier, a multi-armed bot floating on a repulsor field. "Where's its brain?"

Izin pointed to a small dark sphere located at one end. "Its logic unit is—"

I put a burst into the black sphere, shattering it, then the bot crashed onto the deck with a metallic thud.

"That was unnecessary, Captain," Izin said. "I had control of it."

"Yeah, until they lock you out and order it to smash a hole through the hull." I slung the rifle over my shoulder. "How are we getting out of here?"

"I will disable the hangar's artificial gravity. Internal sensors will be offline for several seconds, enough for a short thruster burn using emergency power."

"And we drift out? That's your plan?"

"If we try to reach the space portal under power, they will destroy us."

"How do I steer?"

"You don't."

"One burn won't get us there."

"If you must use thrusters, Captain, I will disrupt the hangar sensors, but that will draw their attention."

"When do I get main power?"

"When we reach the space portal. I will trigger a spawnship wide sensor recalibration to give us time to get clear."

"If you still have access," Marie said.

"Correct."

Marie and I exchanged dubious looks, then we went up to the command deck while Izin returned to engineering and Arlon remained behind to tinker with the Tau Cetin message carrier. We stopped at the medbay where Ugo was being attended to by Eddie and Omari. He was having trouble recovering from his Spawn torture session and was flat on his back, stimmed and sweating.

"He'll be OK," Omari assured Marie, then we continued on to the bridge.

Jase and the Hadleys were watching the big screen apprehensively. The hangar was a flurry of activity as Spawn engineers supervised interdictor repairs, spawnbots armed strike craft and spherical tugs moved interdictors to and from their cradles.

"It's twenty-two hundred meters to the space door," Jase said skeptically as I slid onto my couch.

"They won't even know we're here." I ordered the autonav to plot a short burn with aft thrusters then activated the intercom. "Ready up here, Izin."

"Standby," he replied. "Initiating artificial gravity overload...now."

The moment I became weightless, I released the autonav and our aft thrusters fired for three seconds, pushing us off the deck at a shallow angle. We drifted forward as Spawn engineers and robotic workers floated free of the deck throughout the hangar. Some caught the interdictor lattice or landing pad supports while others flailed helplessly into the air. The locks holding interdictors and strike craft deactivated, allowing them to drift free as localized inertial dampening failed. The cumbersome strike craft nudged each other into slow tumbling trajectories, disguising the *Silver Lining's* movement, then a thud drummed through the ship as something hit us.

Jase checked his console. "That was a bot."

"No damage," I said as the autonav warned the impact had changed our trajectory slightly and suggested course corrections. Unable to risk using thrusters, I let her wallow off course, then a multi-armed ordnance unit holding an Intruder ovoid weapon narrowly missed colliding with our forward sensor mast. Another clang reverberated through the ship, this time from the stern, adding a slight roll to our drift.

"Two degrees off-angle and widening," Jase said.

Several more spawnbots nudged us, then I leaned toward the intercom. "Izin, I'm going to need to correct."

"Very well, Captain."

"Say when," I said, deciding to adjust manually.

"Thruster burn in five seconds. Four, Three, Two, One."

I tickled our thrusters, not enough to draw attention, just to edge our bow toward the space portal. We were moving slightly faster than any ship in the hangar but much slower than fast-moving spawnbots that had shot into the air when the gravity had failed. They careened off hulls, bounced against bulkheads and each other and occasionally rammed us. One struck a container in the interdictor latticework, triggering a small explosion. The ensuing fire engulfed an interdictor that exploded, setting more of its kind alight. Secondary explosions sent flaming debris spinning across the hangar, creating a timely distraction.

A sharp crack sounded from the *Silver Lining's* underside as a piece of flaming wreckage hit us at speed, tilting our stern up as a Spawn engineer drifted toward us. He executed an impressive zero-g somersault, caught the end of our bow sensor mast by his fingertips and pulled himself in.

"Izin," I said, "their engineers are plugged into the spawnship, aren't they, like you? Because one of them just hitched a ride."

"If you maneuver, Captain, he will report it," Izin replied.

We watched the engineer crawl hand over hand along the mast toward the bow. His face filled the bridge screen as he climbed over an optical, then Jase reset to another feed. When he reached the base of the sensor mast, he placed his boots on the hull and held tight.

"What's that damn fool doing?" Quentin Hadley demanded.

"He's going to jump," Marie said.

The bow continued to drop away from the space portal as we slewed to port, increasing the need for another correction.

"Come on," Jase muttered impatiently, urging the engineer to get clear.

"What's he waiting for?" Emma asked.

"The right angle," I said as two blunt-nosed Intruder craft slid together. The two hulls ground against each other, crumpling both, then one tumbled leisurely away while the other rolled toward us.

"Captain," Izin's voice sounded, "Spawnship security is investigating the gravity system failure. They suspect sabotage."

"I'm no pilot," Hadley said, transfixed by the massive black ship about to smash us like an egg, "but that thing's *big!*"

"Izin," I said anxiously, "I need to steer."

"The engineer will report us," he replied.

"No, he won't. I'll tell you when." I watched the Intruder strike craft slide toward us with my fingers hovering over thruster control, then when it was about to hit, I yelled, "Now Izin!"

Without waiting for his confirmation, I rolled the *Silver Lining* along its axis letting our bow scrape the strike craft's hull, shearing off the forward sensor mast and crushing the engineer between the two ships. The bridge screen flickered momentarily as an alternate optical took over the feed, revealing a bloody smear on our bow and the engineer's body splayed across the strike craft's hull.

"Ouch," Jase winced as Emma Hadley looked away in horror.

"Damn! Never seen that before," Quentin Hadley said. "Kade, you know more ways to kill a man than anyone I ever knew."

"Izin, did they see us?" I asked as the dry bomb timer counting down inside my head indicated the *Mendi* was only minutes from destruction.

"No, Captain, but I will be unable to disrupt their sensors again."

We were now on an agonizingly slow slide toward the burning latticework. It stretched from the deck to the overhead and ran almost the full length of the hangar. Spawnbots and engineers clung to it, desperately pulling themselves away from the fire. We were moving too slowly for the empty cradles to puncture the hull, but it wouldn't take much for us to become hopelessly entangled in the lattice.

"I need to make another correction," I said to the intercom.

"Wait, Captain," Izin replied. "Subsystem monitors have detected improper use of command authorizations."

Jase eyed the skeletal structure apprehensively, gauging the distance to the space door. "Let's run for it."

The angle to the space door was narrowing and the *Mendi* countdown in my mind's eye told me we were almost out of time. Worse, if they restored gravity now, we'd crash onto the deck like an upside-down turtle.

"How long before the Mendiant explodes?" Marie asked.

"The Mendi's going to blow?" Jase said surprised.

"Yeah, and we don't want to be here when she does," I said.

"So what are we waiting for?" Hadley asked.

I nodded agreement. "Izin, we're done sneaking around. Give me main engine power, now."

I fired the bow thrusters, turning the ship toward the space portal, then fed full power to the aft thrusters, blasting engineers and bots off the interdictor cradles astern of us.

"Hangar sensors are scanning us, Captain," Izin warned.

My eyes flicked from the bridge screen to the available energy indicator on my console. We still didn't have enough power for main engine start, leaving us a sitting duck on thrusters alone and the portal still hundreds of meters away.

"Push it, Izin, I need those engines," I said as lights around the space portal began flashing orange.

"They're trying to close the space doors," Izin said. "I'm blocking them."

I retracted our landing struts as we moved away from the interdictor lattice, then the moment we had enough power for a two engine start, I fired one and six. The *Silver Lining* lurched forward, blasting the engineers and bots on the lattice astern of us and ramming a spawnbot, sending it spinning toward the deck as we picked up speed.

"How big an explosion?" Jase asked, feeding a view of the *Mendiant* into an image box on the bridge screen.

I shrugged. "I don't know. Big!"

"Should I raise the shield?"

"Engines first," I said, feeding power to two more engines.

The *Silver Lining* kicked forward again, accelerating faster than before. I rolled her to port, sliding past a drifting strike craft as big as an Earth Navy frigate, scraping its hull and filling the bridge with a painful grinding sound, then my *Mendi* counter hit zero.

"Brace for shockwave!" I declared.

Everyone grabbed their couches, held their breathes and watched the *Mendiant's* image on the bridge screen, but nothing happened. She just sat there, wedged between a battleship sized Intruder ship and the empty space left by the *Silver Lining*.

"They must have got to it!" Jase said bitterly.

"Or the Sep super weapon isn't so super," I said.

"Sirius!" Marie yelled anxiously as an interdictor drifted in front of us. It was too big to ram and too late for the shield.

"Switching to weapons," I said, targeting it with a drone.

"It's too close," Jase warned, fearing with our shield down, the blast would destroy us.

I quickly set the warhead parameters and fired. A brilliant point of light flashed from the bow, instantly going hypersonic as I rolled the ship hard away, then the drone slammed into the interdictor's side and shattered into a thousand pieces.

"It was a dud?" Emma said surprised.

"There are no duds," Marie said, turning to me. "You deactivated the warhead."

"I threw a rock," I said as the drone's kinetic impact nudged the interdictor to port and our thrusters pushed us to starboard. We narrowly avoided each other, then I slewed the stern around, brought our last two engines online and steered for the portal.

"Captain, the Command Nexus has regained portal control," Izin said, then the bulkhead surrounding the portal began contracting toward a central point. The was no door, only a quantum restructuring of the spawnship's armored hull.

"We're not going to make it," Quentin Hadley said.

I got the *Silver Lining* back on course for the portal, sending our brilliant blue ion trail streaming back through the hangar toward the rear bulkhead. Just below our ion stream, the *Mendi* was changing color from dull silver to luminous red.

Marie furrowed her brow. "That's too hot for an ion burn."

"It's not us," I said. It was novarium heat, cooking the *Mendi* from the inside out. In moments, her hull turned white-hot. "I'll be damned. They actually got it to work."

Marie stared at the radiant *Mendiant* in horror, calculating the billions she could have killed. "You were right," she whispered, glancing at me, then our optical filters cranked down the brightness to shield our eyes.

"It's melting," Hadley said incredulously.

"There's twenty-four thousand tons of super-hot plasma in there, and it wants out," I said.

The *Mendi* hadn't exploded on schedule because the dry bombs needed time to heat their HS90 cores to millions of degrees Celsius. That heat had overloaded the containment fields inside the insulation cubes and was now eating through the ship's hull. Her outer skin dissolved and she vanished in a brilliant white flash, unleashing a cloud of orange plasma as hot as the interior of a star. It expanded rapidly, consuming the surrounding bulkheads, flooding into the spawnship and surging toward us like a tidal wave.

The *Silver Lining* plunged through the shrinking space portal, shearing our ventral sensor mast off as we shot out into space. The lower quarter of the bridge screen flashed with static from the lost sensor, creating a permanent blind spot, then I swung the ship hard over seventy degrees toward the spawnship's outer hull.

A plume of orange plasma streamed through the

shrinking space portal behind us and jetted into space. The portal continued closing, choking off the radiant jet stream, trapping the plasma cloud inside the spawnship's thick, armored hull as an orange sliver of light streamed off into space.

"We made it!" Marie exclaimed in disbelief.

"We're not clear yet," I said, leveling off and skimming the spawnship's massive hull.

Part of the bridge screen looking toward Serris Orn flashed with white pulses and blue beams as the interdictor swarm and a diminishing number of Ornithian orbitals appeared in the distance, locked in a fierce battle of annihilation. The flash of energy weapons was punctuated by the twinkle of interdictor explosions and the less frequent, but much larger spheroidal detonations of dying orbitals. After each cataclysmic explosion, the defeated battle station broke into huge sections that drifted apart, rippling with fires and eruptive explosions.

Enveloping the titanic struggle was the Spawn Fleet, arrayed in two nested spheres, slowly strangling Serris Orn and its crumbling defenses. They now occupied what only days before had been Tau Ceti's outer layer of defenses. It was a vast expanse awash with shattered Ornithian superstructures and wrecked interdictors, although not a single spawnship had been lost.

"Izin, can they hit us?" I asked.

"I've scrambled their targeting systems, Captain," he replied, "but they know one of their own is working against them."

I banked the *Silver Lining* away from the *Siraktar* and headed for a dark mass four thousand kilometers away. The spawnship opened fire immediately, but its immense white beams shot erratically into space, unable to get a lock. Some beams passed uncomfortably close, but near misses counted for nothing.

"Do not evade, Captain, do not shoot back or raise the shield," Izin said. "The Siraktar is tracking ten trillion targets, one of them is us. They don't know which one."

"Good odds," Jase said optimistically.

"They can still kill us if they get lucky," I said. "Izin, can we bubble?"

"One moment," he replied as we pulled away from the *Siraktar's* hull. "Our space-time distorters won't hold charge, Captain, and the e-plant is bleeding energy. I don't know how."

"It's the null space effect," Arlon said. "You must wait for it to pass."

"At least we still have engines," Jase said. "That's more than the TCs had."

"I guess dark energy siphons aren't all they're cracked up to be," I said, thankful for once that our primitive novarium reactor didn't drain the universe's infinite supply of energy.

The dark mass ahead grew in size, blotting out the stars. It had four smooth sides and one ragged edge where a third of the hexagonal orbital had torn away. It showed no lights, although it glowed in several places from cooling blast damage and was surrounded by debris sucked from its interior by explosive decompression.

"Why wasn't the spawnship destroyed?" Marie asked, watching the crippled monster blindly shooting at phantoms.

"It's a thousand times bigger than the plasma cloud," I replied, realizing size was on the spawnship's side. Deadly as dry bombs were to planets, they weren't designed to attack armored, compartmentalized super dreadnoughts.

"The Siraktar is damaged, Captain," Izin said over the intercom, "but it is far from defeated."

"Beware the wounded beast," Hadley warned.

The slowly tumbling orbital grew to fill the bridge

screen as misaimed energy blasts flashed from the spawnship in all directions, obliterating phantoms. It was time to roll ship, to decelerate down to the wrecked orbital, but with Izin's decoys all accelerating, such a maneuver would be certain death. Instead of slowing, I stayed on a collision course with the derelict, hoping the *Siraktar's* gunners would assume that meant we were a phantom image.

"The Command Nexus has severed my link," Izin announced. "It won't take long for them to clear their sensors."

"Understood," I replied as we entered the outer edges of the orbital's debris field. Its surface was scarred by thousands of black blast burns and pockmarked with ragged holes, testament to the tremendous punishment it had received before its destruction.

"Are we ramming that thing?" Marie asked apprehensively.

"That's the idea," I said as the *Siraktar's* beams flashed wildly through space all around us, obliterating ghost images aiming to pass by the orbital.

"Impact in twenty seconds," Jase said.

The spawnship's weapons suddenly ceased firing, leaving us alone in space.

"Why'd they stop shooting?" Emma asked apprehensively.

"They're resetting their targeting system I guess," Jase said.

"One shot ought to do it," Quentin Hadley said pessimistically as we plummeted toward the burned-out hulk now filling the bridge screen like a wall in space.

"Sirius!" Marie gasped, seeing we were too close to avoid an impact.

"Time's up," I said and fired the thrusters, changing our angle of approach.

The massive structure slowly rotated before us, revealing the mouth of a dark tunnel through its center, then we dived into the axial spaceport as the spawnship opened fire. Beam blasts struck the tunnel wall while the *Silver Lining* thrust sideways out of sight of the spawnship and a growing circle of stars appeared ahead.

We hurtled past docking ports and towers, some containing the wrecks of Ornithian ships destroyed before they could retreat to the safety of the inner system. There were crashed interdictors too–some still burning–shot down by the orbital's defenses before its final defeat.

I yawed the *Silver Lining* enough to counteract the orbital's rotation, narrowly avoiding crashing into the tunnel's inner wall, then we shot out of the axial tunnel into open space. I fired the thrusters, completing the bow over stern maneuver, and decelerated in the shadow of the Ornithian orbital. Above us, the *Siraktar's* energy blasts pounded the orbital's upper side and flashed around its outer edges, keeping us hemmed in.

"You're using it like a shield," Hadley observed.

"When only the strongest armor in the universe will do," I said as the *Silver Lining* came to a stop and began crawling back to the derelict battle station, now silhouetted by the flash of the *Siraktar's* bombardment.

"Izin, drop to sensor mode. Leave me enough power for thrusters," I said, then he powered down the e-plant to its lowest level and Jase silenced our active sensors.

"Maybe they'll think they hit us," Marie said as our sensor profile faded away in the shadow of millions of tons of Ornithian armor.

"Don't count on it," I said.

"Why don't they come after us?" Emma asked.

"They will," I assured her, "once they get that plasma fire under control."

I throttled back, creeping up on the once mighty battle station as it turned its severed side toward us, revealing torn decks and exposed compartments. When the broken side drifted past us, I spotted a canyon sized tear in the orbital's hull.

"That'll do," I said, matching rotation and steering into the hull breach.

The *Silver Lining* glided into a cavernous chamber filled with drifting debris like a tiny insect entering a giant's dark lair. Once inside, I eased the ship in behind the orbital's armored hull, pushed up against the inner wall and maglocked our landing struts to it.

"Izin, go dark, zero emissions."

"Yes, Captain," he replied.

I turned Jase. "Retract the dorsal mast."

Jase tried and shook his head. "It's stuck. We bent it clearing the spawnship."

"In that case, I need to suit up."

Marie looked alarmed. "You're going outside?"

"Have to." I leaned toward the intercom. "Arlon, have you got that TC carrier pigeon working yet?'

"The message carrier is ready, but we're still in null space."

I glanced at the screen, saw the carnage the interdictor swarms were wreaking closer to Serris Orn and shook my head. "Not for long," I said, slipping off my couch. "Don't launch without me. I have a present for you."

Jase's eyes widened in surprise. "You've got the crystal?"

"It's in the dorsal gamma wave receptor, the one we lost going into New Deal. I figured they'd catch us and search inside the ship, so I hid it in plain sight, outside the hull."

"Huh," Quentin Hadley said, recalling his torture session. "Good thing I didn't know that or I'd have told them for sure."

"Me too," Marie added softly.

"How'd you do it?" Emma asked. "Hold out I mean?"

"Just stubborn I guess."

I forced the memory of the drowning nightmare from my mind and hurried down to the airlock. It was only a matter of time before the spawnship came looking for us and I didn't want to be outside in nothing but a p-suit when it got here.

* * * *

Arlon held my transparent helmet while I suited up. "You don't have to do this, Captain Kade. The message carrier will summon the Tau Cetins."

"If that spawnship finds us before they get here, they won't get the crystal."

"You expect to die?"

"I intend to survive, but if the worst happens, I don't want it to be for nothing," I said, reaching for my helmet. "When can we launch?"

"Soon. The null space effect is weakening."

"The Spawn must be getting close to Serris Orn," I said, knowing we didn't have much time.

Arlon locked down my helmet, then I took a laser cutter from the toolbox and cycled through the airlock. Once outside, I used a thruster pack to glide up over the bow. The tear in the orbital's side was hundreds of meters away, framing a sliver of stars in ragged metal. Stark white flashes from beam blasts pounding the orbital's hull illuminated debris floating in the chamber's vast interior. Furniture, handheld devices, eating utensils and children's toys drifted alongside giant trees and dirty grey icebergs. Reaching out from the interior wall were houses with their windows blown out and a handful of towering frozen trees that had resisted being uprooted by explosive decompression. Amidst it all, adrift in the darkness, were bloated Ornithian corpses–adults and children–all coated in dust-like ice crystals.

Ignoring what had become an Ornithian tomb, I glided to the *Silver Lining's* dorsal sensor mast on the topside hull. It was bent back beyond its swept aspect and several of its sensors were smashed or missing, but fortunately, the box-like gamma-ray receptor was still intact.

Anchoring myself to the mast, I sliced into the receptor housing with the laser cutter. When I was halfway across the first panel, I sensed movement behind me and spun around to see a Tau Cetin floating only meters away, watching me curiously. He appeared normal in every way, except we were in vacuum and he wasn't wearing a pressure suit. He was dressed all in white and wore two glowing wristbands that he used to move effortlessly about. His eyes dropped to my torch, which I quickly deactivated, then he floated to the receptor housing and looked inside. After a moment, he motioned a question to me, confirming I wanted it opened.

I nodded, then he speared his small fingers through the metal housing and peeled the cover back. When he withdrew his hand, the flesh covering his fingers had torn away exposing a shiny metal skeleton beneath.

"Flexion-carbon," I muttered, wondering if this Ornithian-form android was the orbital's only survivor. He floated back, giving me room, never taking his eyes off me.

"Thanks," I said, even though he couldn't hear me through vacuum.

I reached into the gamma-ray housing, found the memory crystal right where I'd left it, wedged between two photon receptors. I removed it, being careful not to snag my pressure suit, then he drifted in for a closer look.

"You know what this is, don't you?" I said, wary of his interest. "Wish I had the time to explain, but we're about to have company."

I went to slide the memory crystal into a suit pocket when the TC android caught my wrist. For a moment I thought I was in trouble, then he pointed into the darkness and slowly moved his hand to the right.

"They're over there?" I asked, realizing he was warning me the spawnship was coming.

Seeing I understood, he released my wrist. Rather than pocket the memory crystal, I held it up in front of his eyes, pointing to where the Intruders were and dragging my hand across my neck. It was a human gesture, but he got the message, then his wristbands glowed and he shot away into the darkness.

"I'd hide too if I'd been through what you have," I said, watching the light of his wristbands weave through the debris at high speed and vanish into a distant passage.

Eager to get back inside, I pocketed the memory crystal and returned to the airlock. Arlon was waiting for me on the other side.

"Any trouble?" he asked.

"Nope, but I'm reliably informed we're about to have company."

"By who?"

"A friendly birdbot in a white suit."

Arlon gave me a curious look, then we hurried across the lower cargo hold to the message carrier. It was still sitting on the loader I'd lobotomized, only now a small oval hole had appeared in its mirrored hull a third of the way from its nose. A holographic cone of stars projected up into the air from the hole, pierced by a single glowing line of light.

"You got it open," I said impressed.

"It is not difficult when you know how," he replied, offering no hint as to the workings of Tau Cetin technology. "I have instructed the astrogation system to go to Elsiyon, a major Tau Cetin world nine thousand light years from here."

"Ansara's closer."

"Ansara may be under attack," he said warily.

"The Tau Cetin fleet's there. That's why Ansara is the one place the Spawn won't be attacking."

"Very well." He slid his finger into the hologram and touched a star, then the course line reset. "It is done."

"Now this," I said, handing him the memory crystal.

Arlon passed his hand through the astrographics hologram, causing a translucent cylinder to slide out of the carrier's side containing a spherical ruby.

"Nice rock," I said.

"It is Serris Orn's technical analysis of the Spawn Fleet's tactics."

"You read it?"

"The carrier has full transcription capabilities. I added my report to theirs."

"Your report?"

"I warned them about the null space effect the Spawn are using. The range of Tau Cetin weapons is markedly greater than the effect."

"So they can destroy the spineships if they don't get too close?"

"Yes. I have given them the necessary field equations, enough for them to defend themselves."

"You know the equations?" He gave me a blank look and I nodded with understanding. "Of course you do," I said, studying him suspiciously. "Isn't that sharing Spawn secrets? Something the Uvo never do."

He hesitated, considering the moral dilemma. "Hmm...I will not tell the Sibylline Sisterhood, Captain Kade, if you do not."

I smiled. "Deal."

He pressed the memory crystal against the end of the translucent cylinder, then it sank into what appeared to be solid metal beside the ruby. When he removed his hand, the star map hologram vanished and the cylinder retracted, restoring the carrier's perfectly mirrored hull. "Its star drive will activate automatically once the null space effect is gone, but we must move it out to where it can see the stars."

"Will the spawnship detect it?"

"Yes, when it powers up."

"And we'll have company," I said, then went to get a fresh air tank and a weapon while he suited up.

* * * *

I plugged a cable into Arlon's p-suit, hard-wiring our comms together to avoid transmissions giving away our position. Our only weapons were his sleep trick and my K7 rifle, even though it couldn't fire snakehead killer ammo. I nodded at the optical sensor above the cargo door, signaling to Jase, who depressurized the hold and lowered the door-ramp.

I ordered the hull crawler waiting nearby to grab the message carrier and follow us down the cargo ramp. It strained under the weight until it was outside in zero gravity, then it moved forward cautiously, keeping three of its spider legs magnetically locked to the orbital wall at all times.

It followed us as we mag-walked toward the hull tear while flashes from the spawnship bombardment illuminated debris and dead Ornithians above us. Just before we reached the hull breach, a brilliant white beam blasted into the chamber so close, it triggered our helmet's glare filters, turning them opaque.

"Wait here," I said, then unplugged the comms cable tying us together and mag-walked to the hull breach for a look.

Floating several clicks out was the crippled *Siraktar*, gliding slowly through space. Thin glowing streams of orange plasma ran from open ports amidships, back along her hull like radiant waterfalls before dispersing into space astern. Her fore and aft weapons pounded the orbital's battered hull, then another brilliant white beam flashed into the chamber. With thermal warnings blinking on my p-suit's head-up display, I hurried back to Arlon and reattached the comms cable.

"The Siraktar's venting plasma," I said. "Looks like she'll make it."

"Spawnships are difficult to destroy."

"At least they don't know where we are, not yet anyway."

We hid in the darkness as the *Siraktar* circled the orbital, keeping up a constant bombardment, hoping we'd run.

"Not long now," Arlon said. "Instruct your machine to release the message carrier."

I stepped back to the hullbot, had it loosen its grip, then we floated the Tau Cetin mirrored spear free. There was now nothing to do but wait for the null space effect to fade away as the spineships moved closer to Serris Orn.

"So, how come you know so much about TC tech?" I asked.

"Physical science is finite," Arlon replied. "There is only so much to know."

"And you've learned it all, but the Uvo aren't a great power."

"It depends on your definition of greatness."

"What's yours?"

"The opposite of yours." When he saw my confusion, he added, "Human thinking is materialistic."

"Yours would be too if you were stuck at the bottom of the galactic heap with us."

"That is merely your perception because humans are trapped in illusion. We see reality."

"Oh yeah? What's it look like?"

Arlon made a sound that may have been Uvo laughter. "Exactly."

I turned to him, puzzled. "What?"

"You assume appearance is reality. That is how you

define who you are, by the way you look, the pigmentation of your skin, the biology of your bi-gender species. Such definitions of self begin at birth and end at death–a very ephemeral perspective. Intelligent life is so much more than that."

"So you never look in the mirror?"

"Why would we? Our sense of Self transcends form-based characteristics. True identity precedes physical birth, exists during appearance and lasts eternally after form existence ends."

"So the Uvo are immortal?"

"All Life is, yours included. You just don't know it yet. Our identity is defined by our eternal consciousness. Its qualities are expressed through what you call the heart. What is true for us, is true for all intelligent life in the universe. It is what unites us all, makes us One."

"You think Uvo and humans are the same?"

"In every way that counts. It is that same inner Unity which makes the Galactic Forum possible. The founding members saw through the illusion of appearance. Even though their physical characteristics were vastly different, they understood they were truly One. It is why they succeeded."

"And why we fail."

"You see diversity of form where we see Unity of Spirit. Your imagined differences separate you into smaller and smaller groups that inevitably turn upon each other. That, my friend, is separativeness. We see ourselves, our livingness, in all beings. That is Unity."

"That's why you won't kill the One Spawn."

"They are us, even if they are trapped deep in illusion. It is a pity. They could have been so much more."

The *Siraktar* came past again, blasting the wall we hid behind, then as the spawnship moved away, the focus of its bombardment shifted to another part of the orbital.

"So did the Uvo help found the Galactic Forum?" I asked.

"Life on my homeworld had barely begun when the Forum was created. We appeared later."

"So where'd the founding races go?"

"When all knowledge in this universe is acquired, some lose interest in this plane of existence and cease to appear. Others seek to explore the multiverse, although they are few in number."

"So it exists?"

"None have ever returned to say and the Uvo have not ventured that far."

"What about visitors from other universes?"

"We have never encountered them."

"But you believe they exist?"

"The Uvo believe in infinite possibilities, all of which are explored, each governed by different physical laws. That is why exploring the multiverse is so difficult. Only the principle of Life itself is consistent between universes."

"Different physics? So our science wouldn't work?"

"Not as it does here."

"Our bubble won't even work in null space," I said, realizing how such a small change had crippled us and the Tau Cetins.

"We theorize that universal constants vary for every universe, and then there is the problem of crossing the Immutable Void to reach those other universes. The challenges are almost insurmountable, even for us."

The message carrier's mirrored hull glowed softly, driving back the darkness around us.

"We're up!" I said. "How long before the Siraktar detects it?"

"Any time now. We should move out to where it can see the stars."

We took up positions either side of the message carrier and heaved it forward together, sending it gliding along the orbital's inner wall. We mag-walked behind it, stopping at the hull breach as it drifted away. When it was well out, it turned toward interstellar space, getting its bearings and glowing with increasing brightness.

"Go!" I urged impatiently. "What's it waiting for?"

Every second it delayed gave the spawnship a chance to find and destroy it. After what seemed an eternity, a slender cocoon of light formed around the message carrier and it streaked away toward the stars, then a brilliant white beam flashed through the space it had occupied a moment before.

I squinted against the beam's radiance. "Can they track it?"

"Yes, but it's much faster than a spawnship. They won't catch it."

The spawnship glided into view, blotting out the stars. Its open hatches amidships framed the plasma inferno raging inside as rivulets of orange fire trickled back along its hull. The glow of the plasma cast an eerie orange radiance into the orbital's interior, then the *Siraktar* fired into the orbital, forcing us back into the shadows.

White energy blasts vaporized the debris and blew holes through the housing deck, shattering Ornithian homes and frozen trees like matchsticks. A hatch opened below the *Siraktar's* bow and two lines of flanker autacs and battle armor-clad spawnwarriors streamed toward us. They all carried two-handed weapons and were surrounded by the soft glow of contour shields.

"Oh ho," I said, retrieving the K7 from the top of my backpack, knowing there wasn't time to mag-walk back to the *Silver Lining*.

The flankers fanned out into an expanding spiral, ensuring a miss on one did not score a hit on another. Their spacing was perfect and precise, showing a robotic mastery of zero-g combat. They were followed by the spawnwarriors who were far fewer in number and carried heavier weapons. When they were halfway to us, several autacs fired small conical objects into the habitation chamber. The objects flew past us and stopped, then strobed the darkness, lighting up the *Silver Lining* with every flash.

"They're targeting us," I said and fired a burst from my K7 at a conical strober, but it darted sideways, easily evading my shot.

"They want us alive, to tell them where we sent the message carrier," Arlon said as the Intruder assault force wheeled toward us like a single machine, then a voice sounded inside my helmet.

"RELEASE YOUR WEAPON!"

I replied with a long burst at the lead autac, but the hard tips flashed harmlessly against its shield. Knowing our weapons couldn't harm them, the assault force held its fire and continued toward us.

"Can you reach the warriors from here?" I asked, lowering my gun.

"Yes," he replied, fixing his gaze upon the nearest spawnwarrior.

The battle armor clad Spawn leader drifted out of line, turned and shot the lead autac in the back. The flanker's torso exploded, then the spawnwarrior switched his aim to another autac as three spawnwarriors behind him and five autacs blasted him without hesitation, shredding his battle armor.

"You can control them," I said surprised.

"With difficulty."

"The warriors are the leaders. Get them to kill each other."

"I can only use their weapons against the autacs," he said, even now refusing to take a life.

"OK, shoot the bots," I said, urging him to hurry.

"SURRENDER OR BE DESTROYED."

Arlon focused on another spawnwarrior, who destroyed the flanker in front of him and was immediately killed by those following.

"They still end up dead," I said.

"Yes, but not by my hand."

It was a fine distinction, but a kill was a kill.

"Get another one," I said, then a thin blue beam flashed from the orbital's dark interior and hit the lead flanker's torso, cutting it in half.

In an instant, the entire Intruder assault force wheeled toward the habitation chamber's interior, no longer interested in us. Deep within its dark interior, a single point of light blinked on, then another and another and a thousand. Tiny points of light were everywhere, speeding through drifting debris like fireflies at midnight. Blue Ornithian energy beams blasted autac and spawnwarriors alike, slicing through their shields and cutting them to pieces.

The spawnwarriors fell back as the flankers moved forward, firing at the tiny lights racing toward them, then white-clothed birdbots wearing glowing wristbands and holding handheld energy weapons burst out of the darkness. The birdbots flew into the Intruder assault force, circling and shooting at high speed. They had no armor, no shields and no regard for their own survival and many were destroyed, but they kept coming and they were fast, overwhelming the autacs with their numbers.

Flanker arms and legs spun in all directions as their torsos exploded. Others shorted out and tumbled away while the spawnwarriors fell back toward the *Siraktar*, firing as they retreated. Their contour shields sparkled with static as the birdbots went after them, burning holes through their armor and sending blood spurting in droplet streams into space.

Powerful hands grabbed my backpack, wrenching me away from the orbital wall. Suddenly, I was flying backward, towed by two birdbots toward the *Silver Lining*. Two more were dragging Arlon back, so close that our comm cable hadn't parted.

The flankers retreated after the spawnwarriors, then the *Siraktar* opened fire, blasting the white-clothed birdbots with her heavy weapons. Many were vaporized as they raced back into the orbital, taking cover behind its thick hull and shooting back between spawnship salvos while Arlon and I were carried into the *Silver Lining's* hold.

Our rescuers lowered us to the deck, then three of the four flew back out to join the battle. Jase immediately closed the cargo door from the bridge, cutting us off from the flash of energy weapons and flooding the hold with air. When the deck had repressurized, we released our helmets and turned to the fourth birdbot. The shredded flesh on one of its hands told me it was the same Ornithian android who'd helped me recover the memory crystal.

"Where did you send the message carrier to, Captain Kade?" it asked in perfect Unionspeak.

"You know me?"

"The Consociation has a detailed profile of your activities."

"How about that?" I said with a grin, glancing at Arlon. "I'm famous."

"We have over three billion aliens on record," the birdbot corrected.

"Oh," I said deflated. "I sent it to Ansara, and thanks for the rescue. Your soldiers showed up just in time."

"We have no soldiers. The synthetics fighting the One Spawn are service units assigned to this orbital. I am Vanix-Four-Seven, a level two administration unit. We synthesized these hand weapons as a defensive measure when the One Spawn attacked." He indicated the small, vaguely pistol-shaped device attached to his belt.

"Can this orbital still fight?"

"No. Our heavy weapons and the energy siphon

have been destroyed. Some critical systems remain operational, powered by a crippled pathfinder."

"Pathfinder?" I asked, throwing a questioning look at Arlon.

"A long-range survey ship," he explained.

"Right," I said turning back to Vanix-Four-Seven. "Has it got any weapons, something we can use against the spawnship?"

"No, it is unarmed."

"What about your pistols?"

"Collimators are effective against One Spawn ground units, but are incapable of penetrating a spawnship's armor and shields."

"How many you got?"

"One for each of us, twenty-three thousand, four hundred and fifty-two."

"Twenty-three *thousand*! That's an army."

"We are service units equipped with minimal self-defense response patterns. We are not an army."

"The hell you're not. You guys kicked ass out there."

"We suffered heavy losses."

"You realize that spawnship's crippled?"

"We are aware it is discharging a type of anti-covalent plasma not used by the One Spawn. Was that your doing, Captain Kade?"

"Yeah, but there wasn't enough of it."

"It is surprising you were able to inflict such damage on a spawnship."

"I got lucky."

"Your profile indicates you are often lucky."

"Oh yeah? What else does it say?"

"The Ornithian Consociation considers you a friend."

"Well, one friend to another," I said, taking his skin shredded hand and lifting it up in front of his face, "there are twenty-three thousand of you guys, all made of flexion-carbon, the hardest substance in the universe–"

"The hardest substance known to the Tau Cetins," Arlon corrected.

"–and you've got blasters, lots of them."

"I told you, Captain Kade, our collimators are useless against a spawnship."

I gave him an exasperated look. "How did you guys ever get to be top dog?"

"What is a top dog?"

I released his shredded hand, ignoring the question. "You don't have to fight the spawnship. Its shields are down. Its hatches are open. All you've got to do is go over there and get in their faces."

The birdbot stared at me in silence, freezing momentarily as if deep in thought, then it said, "The service units of Orbital Nirala Sorin have considered your plan, Captain Kade. We concur."

"So what are you waiting for?"

"The spawnship is too far from the orbital for us to attack. Once we reveal ourselves, it will move away and destroy us from range. It must be brought closer."

"Closer?" I said deflated.

"Our tactical analysis indicates the spawnship wishes to capture you and your vessel."

"Yeah, they do."

"You could draw them–"

"I got it the first time." I stepped to the intercom. "Izin, light her up. We're moving." I turned to Vanix-Four-Seven. "These orbitals make stuff, don't they?"

"Yes. Orbital Nirala Sorin is an Elsoria Class component fabricator."

"Ah-huh. Can you make anything useful, like a bomb big enough to blow-up a spawnship?"

Vanix-Four-Seven froze again, descending into another discussion with the rest of the wrecked orbital's white shirts. "I have inventoried our remaining resources. We have the capacity to construct thirty-one galidium ionization amplifiers."

I gave him a blank look. "Pretend I don't know what you're talking about."

"They will increase the temperature of the plasma inside the spawnship by sixty thousand ketarons."

"Sounds like a lot," I said, having no idea what a ketaron was.

"It is," Arlon assured me.

I gave Vanix-Four-Seven an approving look. "OK. We'll give the spawnship something to chase. You get your army ready."

"With your permission, I will remain here to provide a link with the service units."

"Fine by me."

"Thank you, Commander Kade."

"Commander?" I said, wondering why I'd been demoted.

"As this is your plan, the service units of Orbital Nirala Sorin have placed themselves under your command."

"They what?" I said astonished.

"The decision was unanimous."

"Huh," I said thoughtfully, wondering what Lena would think of me leading an army of white-shirted Tau Cetin birdbots against an Intruder Clan Majestic spawnship. "Do you have a schematic of this place?"

"I will upload the required information into your navigation system," Vanix-Four-Seven replied.

I peeled off my p-suit, leaving it where it fell. "Let's go reel in a whale."

"A whale, Commander?" the birdbot asked.

"That's human for spawnship," I replied, then led Arlon and the birdbot to the bridge.

* * * *

The *Silver Lining's* power came surging back, then we pushed off from the orbital's inner wall and turned toward the birdbots clinging to the ragged edges of the hull breach. They were leaning out between the *Siraktar's* salvos, shooting at the autacs spiraling in space and ducking back behind cover before the spawnship could blast them with her heavy weapons.

"Give me targets," I said as we drifted forward.

"They'll see us," Jase warned.

I smiled. "They sure will."

The spawnship knew from our e-plant neutrinos we were moving, and now that the message carrier and its secrets were long gone, Vidah'ra had to be itching for revenge. All I had to do was show her a clean pair of heels and hope she took the bait.

Jase activated our targeting scanners as we glided along the wall, then a forward optical glimpsed the bleeding spawnship through the hull breach.

"This ain't a good idea, Kade," Hadley said.

"Just salting the wound," I replied, keeping the orbital's hull between us and the spawnship while autac flankers moved in and out of view, exchanging fire with the birdbots.

"Sirius, the orbital's hull can't take much more," Marie warned, watching it bend and crack with each spawnship blast.

"We won't be here long." I promised

When my console showed green vectors, I fired drones from both bow launchers and applied full reverse thrust. Our two drones swung in tight curves over the heads of the birdbots, shot out into open space and detonated amid the autac's spiral formation. Flanker shields caught in the twin explosions shimmered and collapsed, then the birdbots poured a withering fire into them.

The *Siraktar* replied with its heavy weapons, blasting the orbital's armored hull as we backed off. A section of the inner wall collapsed in front of us, sending armored slabs rolling across our bow, then I rotated the *Silver Lining* hard away and boosted toward the orbital's dark interior.

"Destroying those autacs was a futile gesture," Arlon said.

"They're one of the most powerful civilizations in the galaxy–and we're the weakest–and I just kicked dirt in their face, again." I grinned. "Now they really want to kill us."

Arlon studied me, perplexed. "You are a most antagonistic individual, Captain Kade, but you are correct. No Matriarch will tolerate such impudence, especially from a lesser species."

"And we're about as 'lesser' as they get," Jase said proudly.

I turned to Vanix-Four-Seven. "One angry spawnship coming up. Where do you want it?"

"Our service units are deploying along lateral ninety-four, near the axial starport."

I glanced at the complex schematic on Arlon's console impatiently. "Just point."

"We are here," Vanix-Four-Seven said, indicating a large chamber. "We need the spawnship…there." His robotic finger indicated our destination, then he traced a path through a maze of passages. "Follow these air transport corridors."

"Looks easy enough." I glanced at Jase. "Open a channel. Open them all." When he'd done as I asked, I announced, "This is the Earth ship Silver Lining. We have the complete Spawn Fleet plans for the conquest of Orion. First Tau Cetin ship to reach us can have them all." I motioned for Jase to close comms.

"But we don't have the memory crystal," Arlon said.

"They don't know that," I said, angling the bow toward the first dark passage Vanix-Four-Seven had indicated. Behind us, the spawnship blasted the orbital's hull with increased intensity, confirming Vidah'ra had got my message. "Shield up."

"The galidium ionization amplifiers have been fabricated, Commander," Vanix-Four-Seven announced. "They are being transported now."

"How many birdbots are you using?"

Vanix-Four-Seven hesitated. "Commander?"

"Service units."

"All of them. Self-preservation motivators have been deactivated."

The *Silver Lining* plunged into a transport corridor, bouncing debris off her hull. The glow of our engines cast harsh shadows through the passage, then we emerged into a spherical chamber with tunnels branching off in five directions.

"That one," Vanix-Four-Seven said, pointing to a dark circular opening to port. Ignoring his advice, I nosed up into a vertical shaft leading to a circle of stars. "Commander, this is the wrong way."

"Not if you want that spawnship."

We shot out into open space and rolled hard over until we were skimming the orbital's battle-scarred surface. Even though the spawnship was out of sight, hidden below the orbital's hull, she knew exactly where we were. Our e-plant's neutrino signature was blazing like a bright light on a dark night, drawing her to us. The *Siraktar's* weapons' flashes stopped abruptly, then she rose beyond the orbital's horizon like a monster rising from the deep, her bow angled up.

I immediately dived the *Silver Lining* into a ragged hole in the station's hull as brilliant white beams flashed across our stern. Blindly, we plunged into a dark shaft, then in an astonishing burst of speed, the spawnship's massive hull appeared above the orbital, blotting out the stars. I banked sharply into a passage as energy blasts flashed down, blistering our stern. Unable to pull up in time, the *Silver Lining* pancaked onto the deck, trailing sparks from her belly and assaulting our ears with the groan of grinding metal.

Before I could get her nose up, we flew out into an enormous industrial chamber crammed with machinery. Horizontal and vertical gantries equipped with robotic cranes and field conveyors crisscrossed before us, forcing me to roll and weave to avoid a collision. We plowed through drifting debris like a speeding cannonball, sending shudders and hammer blows reverberating through the ship, then an auxiliary sensor mast struck a gantry and sheared off.

"You don't have to hit every single thing out there, Skipper," Jase complained through gritted teeth.

"He did miss one," Marie said wryly, "a small one."

"Small ones don't count," I said.

The orbital's hull above us was littered with holes and gliding just beyond them was the *Siraktar*, bleeding thin streams of hot orange plasma. I banked the ship left and right to avoid passing beneath the holes as the spawnship fired down through them. Beam blasts flashed past us on one side, then the other, as the orbital's hull restricted the spawnship's aim.

Three interdictors dived down through different holes and swooped toward us, colliding with drifting debris and banking to avoid the towers and horizontal conveyors. As they came racing up behind us, I banked the *Lining* into a circular opening too small for them to follow, forcing them to pull away in different directions. We flew on through a short passage and emerged into a long cylindrical chamber dotted with dark circular transit tunnels.

"Which way?" I asked.

"That one, Commander," Vanix-Four-Seven replied, pointing at the bridge screen, not the schematic on Arlon's console.

I swung the *Silver Lining* toward the passage

entrance as an interdictor dropped down through a tear in the orbital's hull wall. A second interdictor shot out of a side passage and, a moment later, the third blasted open a bulkhead and came flying through. They closed on us fast as we flew into the passage, slewing back and forth as our engine housings on both sides scraped the passage walls.

The first interdictor followed us in, its nose cannon glowing as it charged to fire, then we flew through a circular exit and a massive pressure door irised shut behind us. The interdictor slammed into it at full speed, battering a circular bulge in the door.

"Got your doors working I see," I said with relief.

"Take that access deck," Vanix-Four-Seven said, pointing at a horizontal slit several hundred meters across.

I put the *Silver Lining* into a steep climbing turn, leveling off just in time to fly into a broad, recreational plaza that explosive decompression had turned into a ghost town. Furniture and Ornithian bodies drifted through the shadows, some bouncing off our hull, others being swept away by our engines as we maneuvered.

The two remaining interdictors followed us in, racing to catch us. I banked the ship between windowed structures, giant screens and tall statues, using them for cover as the large Intruder ships used their shields like battering rams, crashing through everything in their path.

When they had nearly caught us, we flew out into a cavernous chamber high above a vast frozen forest rising from an ocean of darkness. Above us, enormous windows spanned the ceiling, all shattered by the bombardment and framing the *Siraktar's* sprawling hull as it drifted forward trailing rivulets of orange plasma.

The two interdictors burst out of the plaza deck side by side, spraying debris before them, while the spawnship held its fire, giving them room to finish us off. With nowhere to run, I activated our kinetic cannons. They fired back along our topside hull, but the interdictor shields soaked up our barrage with barely a ripple, then our cannons fell silent as their ammunition ran out.

"It was worth a try," Jase said as both interdictors raced up behind us, matched velocities and prepared to fire.

Emma Hadley gasped as she realized what was about to happen, then Marie reached across and put her hand on my arm.

"You nearly did it," she whispered.

We exchanged a silent look, then tens of thousands of thin blue beams flashed down from the darkness between the shattered windows and up from the frozen forest below. They caught the interdictors in a devastating collimator crossfire that instantly overwhelmed their shields and cut their hulls to pieces.

The beams vanished and in the darkness surrounding the wrecked windows, a myriad of tiny lights winked on as wrist thrusters activated and thousands of birdbots swarmed through the windows toward the spawnship. They fired at tiny hull blisters–too small to be weapons–as they raced across the void to the *Siraktar's* open ports, while below us, thousands more lights climbed out of the dead forest. Suddenly, white-clothed birdbots were everywhere, surging past us, towing slender cylindrical devices toward the spawnship.

"Go get them!" Jase yelled.

Birdbots streamed in their thousands through the spawnship's open hatches into the searing inferno within. Their white clothes and synthetic skin were instantly vaporized, stripping them back to shiny metal skeletons, not slowing them in the least.

"Flexion-carbon, hardest substance in the universe," I declared triumphantly.

"Known to the Tau Cetins," Arlon corrected.

"Not in my book."

"We have achieved complete surprise, Commander," Vanix-Four-Seven said. "The heat from your plasma weapon has damaged the spawnship's ports. They cannot close them."

The roiling orange plasma storm inside the *Siraktar* flashed as birdbots and autacs fought each other in an hellish environment only they could endure. Each time birdbots towing a galidium device tried to enter an open port, white energy blasts erupted from the plasma cloud, destroying them before they could deliver their weapons. Realizing the futility of a frontal assault, the remaining galidium teams anchored themselves to the spawnship's outer hull and waited while machine intelligences from both sides slugged it out inside.

The *Siraktar* continued firing down through the windows with all its weapons, shooting at the birdbots, not us. They destroyed some, but most now clung to the spawnship's hull inside the firing arcs of her weapons.

"They have analyzed our plan of attack and have deployed forces to counter it," Vanix-Four-Seven said.

"What can we do?" I asked.

"Fire your anti-ship weapons into the ports."

"But your guys are in there."

"Yes, but the plasma cloud has overloaded the autac shields. They are vulnerable and we are expendable."

"No shields," Jase grinned. "I like those odds."

Marie gave me an encouraging nod, then I asked, "Where do you want them?"

"Detonate your weapons at the edge of the coronal gases, before the heat destroys them," Vanix-Four-Seven replied.

Jase scanned for open ports while I armed our remaining drones and pulled the *Silver Lining's* bow up sharply. We climbed out of the darkness toward the broken windows and the immense spawnship floating beyond them. The *Siraktar* was barely moving, her open ports flashing with weapons' fire while the galidium teams clung desperately to her hull. The spawnship's big beams blasted down all around us, obliterating the frozen forest below, but easily missing us.

"What's wrong with their weapons?" Hadley asked.

"They can't see us," I said, realizing the small hull blisters the birdbots had destroyed were the *Siraktar's* eyes.

"That is correct, Captain Kade," Vanix-Four-Seven said. "We have destroyed the sensors on this part of the spawnship's hull."

We climbed unchallenged through a shattered window, then I put the *Silver Lining* hard over and narrowly avoided crashing onto the *Siraktar's* armored hull. We skimmed her hull so close, the rivers of plasma scorched our underside black and her defenses–unable to depress low enough to hit us–sprayed white energy pulses above us. Ahead in the distance, a thin line of stars stretched between two great metallic plains formed by the spawnship and the orbital, now so close they almost touched.

Clustered around her open ports were thousands of birdbots with their precious galidium weapons, waiting their chance to go down into a multi-million-degree firestorm where Ornithian and Spawn machines fought face to face. I began firing alternate launchers, weaving between the *Siraktar's* defensive beams and her open ports. First one drone, then another, leaped from the *Silver Lining's* bow like radiant stars, arcing away to the left and right before diving down into the open ports and detonating.

Shockwaves rolled into the blistering plasma storm, destroying birdbots and autacs alike, sending fiery geysers spurting up behind us from the open ports. When the blast waves faded, the birdbots waiting outside poured through the open hatches with their galidium weapons, this time finding no autacs to stop them.

The drone counters on my console ran down as our

magazines emptied and behind us, pillars of orange reached from the *Siraktar* to the orbital, binding them together in fire. The *Silver Lining* rocked from one side to the other until our launchers ran dry and the last birdbots vanished into the inferno.

"You've done it, Commander!" Vanix-Four-Seven declared. "We've broken through. The service units are taking the devices into the heart of the spawnship for detonation."

"How far do we need to be to survive the blast?" I asked, eyeing the sliver of space we were trapped in between the *Siraktar* and the orbital.

"Five hundred million light seconds."

It might as well have been a light year.

"We can't bubble, not here," Jase said desperately.

A cave-like darkness in the orbital's surface appeared ahead, approaching fast. I killed engine power and rolled the stern under the bow, aiming our engines at the spawnship. The move started us drifting down toward the *Siraktar's* hull as we hurtled sideways, unpowered.

"Sirius!" Marie said, eyes wide as she thought we were going to hit, stern first.

"Brace for high-g!" I yelled as we reached the circle of darkness and I fired the main engines at maximum thrust.

Crushing g-forces slammed us down into our acceleration couches as our engines overpowered the ship's inertial field, sending the *Silver Lining* blasting away from the *Siraktar* into the orbital's cylindrical spaceport. The orbital was so close, it blocked the spawnship's weapons as we dived into the axial tunnel, fighting lateral drift. Under high-g, we quickly straightened up and raced between the starport's structures, using them to shield our stern from the spawnship's erratic weapons' fire. Cranes and docking platforms exploded all around us and beams flashed overhead, but with her sensors disabled by the birdbots, the spawnship couldn't get a lock.

"Seventy percent of our service units have been destroyed, Commander," Vanix-Four-Seven reported, unaffected by the high-g, "however, eleven galinium devices have survived. Detonation sequences have been initiated."

"Just a few more seconds…" I wheezed, barely able to breathe as we shot out into open space.

I banked under the orbital as a brilliant light bloomed behind us. In the darkness of space, thousands of pieces of debris drifting around the orbital were caught in a harsh white glare and were instantly vaporized by a relativistic blast. A column of white light flashed from the axial starport as the massive orbital suddenly surged toward us–millions of tons hurled through space like a pebble.

I kept our engines at full power, trying to outrun it as wrecked Ornithian ships and docking towers from the spaceport swept past us. The massive orbital got so close, our ion trail spread across its surface, then the light pouring through the axial spaceport and around the orbital's outer edges faded and I throttled back.

"That was too damn close," Hadley said, sweating.

"Close isn't dead," Jase said with relief, taking Emma's hand.

Marie relaxed and nodded she was OK.

"I think it's safe enough for a look," I said, steering the *Silver Lining* beyond the orbital's outer edge.

I decelerated, letting the Tau Cetin orbital drift past, bringing its blast facing side into view. It was covered by a molten lake with oddly shaped lumps and shrouded by a steaming cloud of super-heated metallic gas that was slowly cooling into droplets. Beyond it was the remains of the *Siraktar*. Her midsection had vaporized and her huge bow and stern sections were drifting apart. They were shrouded in brilliant red and orange gas and wracked by explosions that broke her into smaller pieces and vented long gaseous plumes into space. Surrounding it all–us included–was a great circle of light, rolling away through space at tremendous speed. It was the orange-white, relativistic shockwave the orbital had shielded us from, the energy release that had cut the mighty *Siraktar* in half.

Jase nodded belligerently. "You wanted some. You got some."

"Congratulations, Commander," Vanix-Four-Seven said. "That is the first spawnship destroyed in this war."

I turned to Vanix. "How many of you survived?"

"Elsoria Class orbital Nirala Sorin has one survivor."

"Only one?"

He looked at me, feeling nothing. "We destroyed a spawnship, Commander. No survivors would have been a victory."

Arlon stared at the bridge screen in silence.

"They gave us no choice," I said.

"I never thought they would."

I fixed my attention on the screen. Tau Ceti was now a tiny yellow orb in the distance. Between it and us, thousands of blue and white flashes and a myriad of interdictor explosions confirmed Serris Orn's last remaining orbitals were close to defeat.

"They don't have long left," I murmured, realizing it had all been for nothing.

"We should get out of here, Sirius" Marie said soberly.

"Yeah." I plugged in a course away from Tau Ceti and released the autonav, but nothing happened. "We still can't bubble."

"The shield's down too," Jase added.

"We're on emergency power, Captain," Izin announced over the intercom.

I glanced at my console, saw our energy levels were

way down. "What happened?"

"The particle release from the Siraktar disrupted the e-plant's confinement field," Izin replied. "That stabilizer you installed in Hades City automatically shut down our e-plant to prevent a core breach."

It was the Tau Cetin modification. It had been designed to save us from disaster, and it had done exactly that, although they'd never mentioned it could pull the plug on us in less than a nanosecond.

"Izin, kill the stabilizer."

"I'm locked out, Captain. All I'm seeing is a slowly decreasing particle count."

"We must wait for spacetime's energy levels to equalize, Captain," Arlon said.

"How long will that take?" I asked, then three spawnships appeared before us. I sighed. "Never mind."

The three giant leviathans hung in space, scanning the wreckage, reconstructing the disaster, then they focused upon our tiny, defenseless ship.

"I don't suppose they're here to surrender," Marie said wryly.

"You know," Quentin Hadley said philosophically, "I'm glad I didn't stay on Kota. I wouldn't have missed this for anything–even a new arm!" He held up his stump and grinned.

We stared at it, and exchanged amused looks, then Izin stepped onto the bridge. He saw us smiling as the spawnships glided toward us, preparing to finish us off, and turned to me in surprise.

"Captain?"

We all saw his confusion and laughed, much to his consternation, then a contact marker glowed as a streak of light came racing toward us from interstellar space.

"Something's coming in," Jase said with sudden seriousness, "real fast!"

"Now what?" I said wearily.

A gleaming, mirror-hulled arbiter appeared behind

us, glowing brilliant white inside its annihilation shield. The three spawnships turned toward it–forgetting us–and focused all their attention on the solitary Ornithian dreadnought. It didn't move, didn't try to run, it just sat there watching its enemies approach, then another beam of light flashed in and a second arbiter appeared alongside the first.

And a third.

"What the hell?" Jase said surprised.

Suddenly, hundreds of streaks of light filled the sky, forming a wall of Tau Cetin arbiters tens of thousands of kilometers across. They floated behind us in perfect battle order, mirrored hulls shining, shields glowing brightly. White beams flashed from the fleet, instantly overwhelming the three spawnships with massed firepower. The Intruder dreadnoughts exploded together, never having got a shot away.

"Oh ho," Marie said as three immense blast waves raced toward us.

The first arbiter raced forward and extended its shield around the *Silver Lining* moments before the blast waves hit. The Ornithian annihilation shield shimmered as the three energy waves rolled over us, quickly recovering once they had passed, then a familiar dappled Ornithian face appeared on the bridge screen.

"Captain Kade," he said formally. He wasn't actually speaking as Tau Cetins couldn't make human sounds. The words were produced by a small silver disk on his collar that read and vocalized his thoughts for transmission.

"Fleet Commander Siyarn," I said, "It's good to see you again."

"I got your message. Thank you. We will take it from here."

His image vanished, then the Tau Cetin Grand Fleet streaked past us as one toward their unsuspecting enemy. We watched in silence as they destroyed the spineships at long range, punched through the outer sphere and fell upon the Spawn Fleet they'd been chasing for months. Nova-like explosions bloomed as white and blue beams filled the blackness of space with a light show not seen anywhere in the galaxy for two and a half thousand years.

Formations of super fast arbiters raced back and forth across the system, firing in concentrated waves at the heavily armored spawnships and devastating their swarms of interdictors with massed precision. The Serris Orn squadron came out to meet them, reinforcing the Ornithian ships assembled from Tau Cetin worlds across the galaxy.

Some arbiters were destroyed, but many more spawnships were obliterated, outnumbered and outgunned for the first time in the war. The Spawn Fleet abandoned its spherical structure and retreated to a point above the star to concentrate its firepower, but the Tau Cetin arbiters were too fast and too numerous for the beleaguered Intruder dreadnoughts.

After three hours, the Intruder Inter-Command Nexus–the Spawn Fleet's combined intelligence–decided the battle was lost. An instant later, the surviving behemoths from the Minacious Cluster retreated to interstellar space. Intent on their total destruction, the Ornithian Grand Fleet followed, knowing their chances of cornering the fleeing spawnships were slim.

They left the Tau Ceti System littered with wrecked orbitals, derelict spawnships and burning arbiters, but the beautiful blue-green world of Serris Orn, the birth world of the Ornithian race, remained serene and untouched. The Tau Cetin gamble to concentrate their fleet had paid off, even if they had been tricked into guarding the wrong system. In the end, they'd caught the Spawn Fleet on better than equal terms and made them pay.

Eleven point nine light years away, the inhabitants of another blue-green world even more beautiful than

Serris Orn would soon breathe a sigh of relief when they discovered their mighty ally had saved Orion. In their rejoicing, they would be unaware of the role played by a tamph, an Uvo elective hermaphrodite and a ragtag group of humans from the edge of Mapped Space.

Chapter Eight: Ray Station Sol

Ornithian Consociation Outpost
Former Civilization Monitoring Base
Sol System Oort Cloud
0.91 Earth Normal Gravity (Artificial)
57.8 light days from Sol
160 Tau Cetins, 2,100 Humans

A silver-gray Earth Navy battlecruiser floated above the Ornithian starport's landing deck two kilometers from my tower window. The lights on the warship's sensor masts illuminated the hull showing its weapons, small and large, were angled forward in the traditional dress ship aspect, not that Tau Cetins were impressed by such displays.

Beyond the metal landing deck was a barren, crater-strewn plain that reached through deep shadows to a curved, oddly near horizon. The dark, moonless dwarf planet had no name, although the Ornithians called the base a ray station because cosmic rays were stronger here than the solar wind. Under galactic law, that meant it wasn't human territory even though it orbited the Sun, which was still visible to the naked eye.

The Tau Cetins had used the base to monitor the evolution of intelligent life on Earth for over five hundred thousand years, only revealing its presence to mankind after interstellar contact. The outpost had become a place where Human and Tau Cetin leaders met in private and, more recently, where super-fast TC courier ships carried Earth dispatches and senior personnel to and from our far-flung colonies.

There were now many more humans here than Ornithians, a sign of the relative importance each placed on the relationship. The Tau Cetins still owned and ran the base while Earth filled it with diplomats and military and intelligence specialists. Significantly, no Earth leader had ever asked the Tau Cetins to vacate the base as the Council saw its remote presence as a safeguard rather than an intrusion.

The starport was on the hemisphere permanently facing away from the Sun, ensuring no Earth telescope in pre-interstellar days ever saw it. It was extraordinary for a tiny world, not gravitationally locked to another celestial object, to maintain such an aspect, proof the Tau Cetins themselves had changed its rotation to suit their purposes.

The planet's gravity was barely six percent of Earth Normal although the base itself was set to Serris Orn Standard. When the battlecruiser entered the station's gravity field, its thrusters fired, catching it before it fell, then the warship settled onto one of the berths reserved for human ships.

Several kilometers away, a pair of Tau Cetin sentinels sat with their bows docked to one of the tower complexes used by Ornithian ships. Between them and the Earth Navy ship was the tiny *Silver Lining*. Her hull was scarred, her sensor masts bent at odd angles or sheared off, and wispy clouds of Tau Cetin nanobots floated around her repairing the damage as if by magic. It was the kind of treatment the battlecruiser's bridge crew could not help but notice as the Tau Cetins rarely, if ever, repaired human ships.

The door buzzer sounded, drawing my attention away from the picture window. "Pause recording," I said, suspending the mission report I was dictating for Lena. "Enter."

The door slid open and Arlon Torel stepped in, dressed in a white, long-sleeved robe with a dark blue belt. "I have come to say goodbye, Captain Kade. The Tau Cetins have assigned a ship to take me home."

"That's generous of them," I said, stepping toward him.

"Our peoples have a long shared history and I did assist their Buratu agent," he said, giving my quarters and the landing deck outside a cursory look.

"And you helped save their homeworld. Don't let them forget that."

"They won't, and I will not forget your help."

"I didn't have much choice."

"On the contrary, you could have left me on Niedarim or Jel Kara or Kota, or you could have surrendered the memory crystal to Vidah'ra to save yourself, but you chose none of those alternatives."

I shrugged. "I don't like being pushed around."

"You forget, I was Arleen. I know there is more to you than you pretend."

"Good thing you're leaving. So, what will you do now? Change back?"

"It will be many years before I can elect again. Not that it matters. I am the same Self I always was, irrespective of the form I use."

"I see that."

"When I return, the Sibylline will want to share my knowledge of the One Spawn, and perhaps, of the human who defeated them. She may decide it is time we establish contact with your people."

"Are you going to teach us wisdom now?"

"We do not choose impossible goals, Captain Kade, but I'm sure there are ways we can work together. In any event, the best teacher is always one's Self."

"If you're prepared to teach us how to build spawnship killing super weapons, I'm sure we can work something out."

"Weapons will not solve the problem of the One Spawn. To do that, one must first understand the true enemy, the enemy of all intelligent life in the universe. It is an enemy that must be defeated by every species, on every world, in every age."

I gave him a puzzled look. "We're not talking about the Spawn now, are we?"

"Separativeness, Captain Kade, that is the greatest evil in all the cosmos. To destroy it, one must see beyond the illusion that lies before your eyes: the illusion of form. Such apparent differences have no meaning."

"The One Spawn are no illusion."

"They are trapped in the illusion. They do not know the Unity of Life binding us all together as One. They seek to divide what is truly One. That is the essence of separativeness."

"The way the civil war divides mankind."

"Yes. You call your human adversaries Separatists, a rather apt name I think. Separativeness has the power to destroy mankind as quickly as shatter galactic civilization itself, if you let it."

"Will you feel the same way if the Spawn get to your homeworld."

"They have to find it first."

I blinked in surprise. "Surely they already know where it is."

"They think they do, but that too is an illusion. Our true home is beyond their reach."

"How is that possible?"

He leaned toward me, studying me with a searching look. "Continue on as you are, my friend, and one day, you may get there." Arlon Torel extended his hand in the human fashion and we shook hands. "Goodbye, Captain Kade."

He went off to catch his Tau Cetin ride home while I returned to the window, gathering my thoughts for the conclusion of my report. On the landing deck below, a transparent pressure tube had extended to the battlecruiser's hull and dignitaries from Earth were now visible, walking toward the docking tower.

"Resume recording," I said, then a lightgram containing my report appeared in front of my eyes. "Based on the Silver Lining's sensor logs, over two hundred spawnships were destroyed during the Battle of Serris Orn. Fifty-nine arbiters were also destroyed. We detected an additional ninety-two energy releases on the far side of the Tau Cetin System we could not identify. The Tau Cetins will not verify ship losses for either side, however, they confirm Intruder forces repulsed included seventeen Clan Majestic Striking Forces and four Clan Imperial Battle Corps. The Tau Cetins report losing contact with the Spawn Fleet at V404 Cygni, a black hole / K star binary, seven thousand, eight hundred light years from Sol. The present location of the surviving spawnships is unknown. The Silver Lining's sensor logs and our scans of the Clan Majestic flagship Siraktar accompany this report."

The door buzzer sounded again.

"Pause recording." I went back to the door, expecting Arlon had forgotten something. "Enter."

When the door slid open, Marie stood there holding a small suitcase. We hadn't spoken since the Tau Cetins had transported the *Silver Lining* here in one of their gigantic conveyors several days ago. She'd been distant after the battle and had locked herself away in an empty cabin, which I took to mean she was just waiting for a chance to get off the ship and away from me.

"Marie," I said surprised, glancing at her suitcase.

"I um…just wanted to say goodbye," she said with uncharacteristic awkwardness.

"Where are you going?"

"Earth. France. I have relatives there I've never seen. I've spoken to them. They want me to visit and I may never be this close again."

"Everyone should see Earth, at least once," I said, thinking this might be the last time I ever saw her. We fell into an uncomfortable silence as she struggled to say what was really on her mind. "Do you want to come in?"

"No, my shuttle's leaving soon." She took a deep breath. "I…didn't know anything about those bombs or what they were going to do with them, the people they were going to kill." Her eyes clouded with tears.

"I know that."

She choked back tears. "I understand now why you're against the Separatists, what they're capable of. I know you could never support people like that."

I didn't tell her Earth Navy had captured Kota and now controlled mankind's only supply of HS90, along with the ruins of the weapons lab.

"Marie, I wanted to tell you everything, a long time ago, but…"

She nodded. "You couldn't. I know that now. That's why I'm going to Earth, to find out for myself which side I'm really on. Maybe I already know."

"Will I see you again?"

"I hope so." She gave me a regretful look. "I always thought if I ever saw Earth, it would be with you."

"Me too."

She sighed sadly, then noticed the suit the Tau Cetins had synthesized for me. "I've never seen you in a suit before."

"They're making me wear it."

"I heard there was a big meeting with people from Earth."

"The whole Council's going to be there."

"You look...good." She smiled, imagining me presenting to Earth Council. "My shuttle leaves in twenty minutes." She leaned forward and kissed me on the cheek. "I'm proud of you," she whispered and hurried away. I watched her walk to the accelerator, then returned to the window, deep in thought.

"Edit report."

The lightgram appeared again. "Delete all references to HS90 dry bomb technical specifications." I watched the offending paragraphs disappear and quickly checked the report made sense. "Close report. Mark as final. Transmit to Lena Voss."

A report sent indicator appeared in the lightgram. I watched it blink, wondering what to do with the technical readout still stored in my bionetic memory. It was all there, every last planet-killing detail, and all I had to do was hand it over to Lena. I tried convincing myself that would put the technology in the hands of the good guys, making it no longer my problem.

With Earth Council members now inside the tower complex, I hurried out into the low ceilinged corridor. Jase's room was next door. When I buzzed, Emma Hadley answered the door, securing a robe over her naked body. Her hair was tousled and her cheeks flushed, which was no surprise considering she hadn't left Jase's room since we arrived.

Emma gave my suit an approving look. "Someone's out to impress," she said, then called to the bedroom, "It's only Sirius." She stepped back to let me in. "Want a drink?"

"Can't. I've been summoned."

"Are they giving you a medal?"

"I doubt it." Lena had been forced by her Earth superiors to present me, but formal decorations were something else entirely.

"I want a medal," Jase said as he came out of the bedroom dressed only in shorts and holding a slender glass half-filled with golden liquid. "And a pair of Bisarlan pearl-handled fraggers."

Emma put her arm around his waist. "If you want a medal, you're going have to earn it." She took the drink from his hand, sipped it and carried it into the bedroom.

The living room behind Jase was strewn with clothes, empty glasses, and plates of Earth's finest delicacies. "Looks like you got your reward already."

He grinned, glancing at the bedroom door, then leaned toward me and whispered. "You wouldn't believe how strong she is." He exhaled, exaggerating exhaustion. "Hardfall gravity. I can't keep up."

I nodded knowingly. "I heard you screaming."

"You did?" he asked uncomfortably.

"These Tau Cetin walls aren't as soundproof as they look." I let him wallow in embarrassment, then grinned, letting him know I was kidding.

He punched me lightly in the shoulder, then looked into the corridor. "No Marie?"

"She's leaving." I sighed and quickly changed subject. "The Tau Cetins said the Silver Lining will be ready for inspection this afternoon, if you need a break."

"Hmm..." He glanced toward the bedroom door. "Maybe tomorrow."

"No hurry."

He looked me up and down, assessing the fine clothes the Tau Cetins had synthesized for me. "So this is it, huh?"

"I couldn't get out of it."

"The TCs might have smoked a bunch of spawnships, but we got the first one. That's something they'll never live down." He ran his fingers along my jacket lapel with growing interest. "What's this made of?"

"It's Tau Cetin, so it's probably indestructible."

"You almost look respectable. Don't let those Earth Council heavies offer you a job."

"Not a chance."

I left him to the muscular delights of Emma Hadley and took the accelerator up to the tower's top floor where Lena was waiting alone by a window high above the landing deck. The Tau Cetins had transported her and Admiral Talis here from Kota, just for the Earth Council briefing.

"I wasn't sure you'd make it," Lena said as I joined her by the window.

"And miss hearing a bunch of bureaucrats droning on for hours about nothing? How could I pass that up?"

"It won't be that bad," she said encouragingly. "By the way, the Tau Cetins showed us what you did to that spawnship." She smiled. "You should have seen Talis' face. He must have watched it a hundred times."

"I got lucky," I said nonchalantly. "He watched it a hundred times? Really?"

"He'll never admit it, but he respects you."

"Maybe I should ask for a bigger ship."

"Be careful what you wish for. He might just give you one, and a commission."

"In the navy? Me?" I shook my head. "No thanks."

Sergeant Dietz in full dress uniform, accompanied by Izin, got off the accelerator and strode toward the conference hall. They nodded to me but didn't come over.

Lena followed my gaze. "Looks like your tamph made a friend."

"Well, he did save Dietz's life, although I'm surprised you're letting Izin attend."

"Wasn't my choice. Dietz insisted," she said with a hint of annoyance. "He wants to train with them, thinks psionics and tamphs would make a good team. Maybe he's right."

"Homicidal humans and psychopathic tamphs," I said with a chuckle, "what could possibly go wrong?"

"Dietz told your tamph you didn't know he was Union Regular Army, to protect your cover." She watched them walk toward the conference hall thoughtfully. "He and his team did well, better than anyone expected."

"I was sorry to hear about Ibanez. He was a good man." He'd single-handedly tied up six thousand Sep soldiers for over an hour while Dietz and the others took the e-plant before the engineers could sabotage it.

"It wasn't the Seps that got him. The naval autopsy said he was killed by an Intruder weapon."

"Ah," I said somberly. "Is Dietz speaking?"

"He's here to answer questions about Spawn ground forces."

"Does Earth Council know what he is?"

"No."

"You'll have to change that. We'll need more of his kind."

"I have to convince them to change the law first." She watched Dietz and Izin enter the conference room, then turned back to the view of the landing deck. "I'm surprised you got the Hadleys out. That was an unnecessary risk."

"I had my reasons."

"It's always the same reason with you, Sirius," Lena said, leaving me in no doubt she knew all about Marie.

"Trask is dead."

She nodded approvingly. "Yes, the army found his body. That almost makes it worthwhile, although I'd rather you hadn't marked the research facility. We wanted it intact."

"You should have told me." She should have told me a lot of things.

"Mission parameters only, Sirius. You know the drill." She frowned. "We almost captured one of their bomb ships."

"Where?"

"The Tarnavi System. A frigate intercepted it as it maneuvered to hit Denedus. The crew scuttled the ship before we could get aboard."

"What happened to the HS90?"

"It detonated early. The cloud missed the planet by eight thousand kilometers. It's spiraling in toward Tarnavi now. We've got a science ship tracking it, but it's too hot to sample."

"Was that the only bomb ship?"

"There was one other, a small cutter carrying a prototype weapon. It escaped Kota after the spawnship went after you. The Tau Cetins caught it halfway to Anoris." She gave me a weary look.

"No chance they'll hand it over?"

"Not to us."

"A pity," I said, hiding my relief. "You say it was a cutter? Anyone on board we know?"

"They didn't say."

"Trask had a cutter, for him and Stina Kron."

"We haven't found her," Lena said, then sighed with regret. "We were so close."

A chill ran down my spine as I realized how badly she'd wanted to capture the Separatist super weapon, how close she still was. She was mega-psi, could freeze me in place and force me to hand over the dry bomb technology with a thought–if she knew it was stored in my bionic memory.

Hoping she didn't sense my fear, I framed a command in my mind, one I'd been wrestling with for days:

ERASE HS90 WEAPON SPECIFICATION.

In a heartbeat, the entire technical readout for the Separatist genocide weapon vanished from my bionetic memory. If Lena and her shadowy associates on Earth wanted to build a dry bomb, they'd have to invent it themselves. That would be no easy task, considering the science was far ahead of our own.

Lena turned to me, puzzled, sensing something strange. "Are you all right?"

"I had something on my mind, but it's gone now."

A large group of civilians and senior Earth military officers arrived, fresh off the battlecruiser from Earth. The four Collective Presidents were all there, along with several other junior members of Earth Council. They were led by Admiral Talis in his full dress black uniform, replete with gold trim and service medals. As a Tau Cetin ushered them through, Talis gave me a curt nod which, coming from him, was a sign of approval, a medal and a bear hug all rolled into one.

I gave him a disrespectful, but good-natured wink. Rather than show displeasure, the hint of a smile appeared on the admiral's lips.

"What do you know," Lena said amused, "that cold-hearted bastard really does like you."

"What's not to like," I said, wishing I was anywhere but there. "So what are they going to tell us?" I assumed she'd probed the minds of every Tau Cetin she'd come in contact with since Serris Orn and already knew everything that was to be discussed.

"That Orion is saved, for now, and warn that the One Spawn have enormous forces in the Minacious Cluster, enough to reinforce their fleet here."

"It's not over," I said, wondering if it ever would be.

"The Tau Cetins won, but their industrial power took a beating. Every Ornithian habitation system in the galaxy is building new orbitals for Tau Ceti, and more ships."

"I assume they'll leave that part out."

She nodded. "They'll mention the memory crystal. It gave them the locations of Intruder bases, rendezvous points, and tactical and strategic objectives throughout

Orion. Earth was a secondary target. Apparently, the Spawn think it's close enough to Tau Ceti to be a useful base and weak enough to be conquered with minimal forces."

"They would."

"The Tau Cetin Fleet is having a field day, blasting Intruder bases from one end of Orion to the other. It's a blood bath. What we don't know is whether the One Spawn will keep fighting, and where. If they decide to fall back and hold the Cygnus Rim, we may not see them again in our lifetime."

"Don't bet on it."

A Tau Cetin motioned for us to enter, signaling the Earth Council briefing was about to begin. Somewhere inside the circular theater, Grand Fleet Commander Siyarn was preparing to speak to the leaders of his nearest and weakest ally, commending them for their help. My help. It was a great moment for Earth and a diplomatic courtesy for the Tau Cetins.

"Let's go," Lena said, eager not to miss a word of Siyarn's speech.

I didn't move but fixed my gaze on the landing deck far below.

"Sirius?" Lena said with a puzzled look.

"They don't need me in there."

"You've earned it and they'll have questions."

"It's all in my report," I said, my mind made up. "Besides…there's somewhere else I'd rather be."

"Sirius, the leaders of all four Earth Collectives, the independent minors, and our most senior admirals and generals are all here. They want to meet you, shake the hand of the man who destroyed a spawnship and saved Orion."

"Tell them…I had a better offer."

She gave me an incredulous look. "You are out of your mind."

"They could try talking to Izin." I grinned and

hurried across to the accelerator.

"Starport," I said, and was carried by the magic of Tau Cetin technology through the tower complex to a long, well-lit hall with floor to ceiling windows looking out across the floodlit landing deck. The accelerator deposited me on my feet, then I ran past empty docking bays to the Earth bubble jumper exit lounge. A handful of passengers with their luggage stood waiting for the doors to open while off to one side, Marie stood alone looking out through the window, wiping tears from her eyes.

I stopped behind her, wondering what to say, then she saw my reflection in the window and turned to me with a bewildered look.

We stared at each other in silence for several seconds, then I asked, "Can you keep a secret?"

She shook her head. "Not like you."

"You'll have to learn. I'll teach you."

"Are you recruiting me now?"

I shook my head. "My controller would never allow it, but I won't ever lie to you again, Marie. I promise."

"Oh, so now I have to keep *your* secrets?" she said with a watery smile.

"Every dirty little one of them." I stepped forward and took her in my arms. "But don't worry, I'll make a liar out of you yet," I said gently and kissed her for a long time.

For more information on the
Mapped Space Universe
visit the author's webpage at:

www.StephenRenneberg.com

If you enjoyed this book, please post a recommendation and rating on the site where you purchased your copy.

Printed in Great Britain
by Amazon